The Secretkeepers

The Secretkeepers

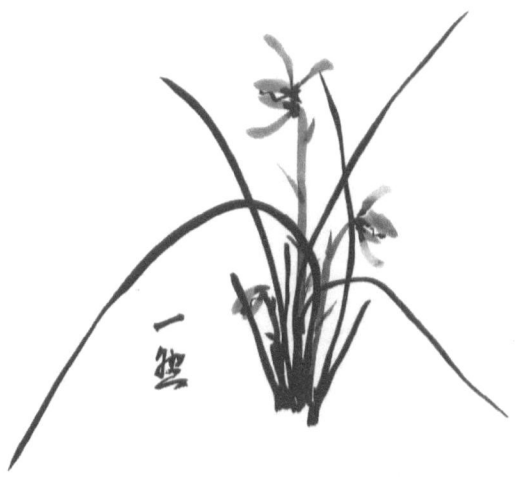

Michael Taromina

OVER
THE EDGE
BOOKS

los angeles

ISBN: 978-1-944082-01-7 (print)

ISBN: 978-1-944082-02-4 (electronic)

Printed in the United States of America

www.overtheedgebooks.com

For my wife, Jessica, and our three children—
Michael, Jake, and Trey—for giving me everything I value
in this world and allowing me to write a story that was
not about vampires, superheroes, or dinosaurs.
Next time, I promise.

CHAPTER ONE

1988

Outside Gemco Jewelry Store
Canal Street, New York City
November 30, 10:17PM

The passenger made a final check of his watch. As usual, he and the driver wore long, black leather overcoats and matching gloves. "Uniforms of the bad intentioned," they joked earlier. They wore their hair longer than usual, their faces shadowed by beards. Within an hour, their clean-cut, clean-shaven looks would return. But for now, in the dark corners of the New York night, the two men were precisely the way they wanted to be—unidentifiable. Within an hour, their vehicle would also look different, surgically broken down into many parts at a junkyard across the river in Queens.

After a nod by the driver, they both exited the black car. Their mission had begun.

The two assailants slalomed through bustling Chinatown. They were masters at blending with the crowds, which, perhaps more than anything else, had allowed them to pull off moments like this several times before. Mists of breath escaped their nostrils, dissipating quickly into the chilly night air. Frigid temperatures had no effect on them. They were cold-blooded creatures.

As they simultaneously slipped tight nylon masks over their heads, they entered through the glass front door of the building. No looks were exchanged, no words were spoken. As planned, each of them took three synchronized steps sideways in opposite directions. Their eyes, like radar, locked onto their target. In front of them, behind an illuminated counter of jewelry, the salesman did not bother to look up. He didn't have to—he already felt their deadly intention. As a decorated soldier of war, he had a sixth sense when it came to danger. Although over fifteen years and forty-plus pounds removed from his days as a sleek jungle warrior, his battle instincts hadn't dulled. He was expecting one final battle; he knew his visitors were not fellow soldiers. *Soldiers would not have come through the front door,* he thought to himself. But he saw that they were, indeed, professionals. They had drawn their guns, submachine guns. "Fistfuls of fury," they had nicknamed them.

This soldier felt his final seconds ticking by with a pulsing heartbeat in his chest. His senses of sight and sound intensified. A warrior's end, when it is inevitable and violent, closes in this way. He made no attempt to flick the alarm. *Why bother?* He knew his assassins would be long gone within minutes. Instead, he reached for the gun secured at the small of his back—a Colt .45 caliber pistol—an old-timer's weapon of choice. "One squeeze of stopping power," he bragged in the old days. He had worn it every day for the past fifteen years. Recent circumstances had made him itchier to reach for it—itchy like the old days.

He knew he had no chance to survive. He had been in their boots too many times to think otherwise. His objective now was to draw blood, to aim low so the wound would not be fatal. A hit in the leg would draw blood, but not kill. Blood was all that he wanted this time; blood leaves the best trail of evidence. He needed to make sure somehow, someday, one of his killers would be caught—alive—so this story would finally come out. Once he was dead, that would be his only chance. Not a chance for justice but a chance for truth. It was far too late for justice. But not too late for truth.

As he drew his pistol and fired once, two streams of bullets roared from each side of the room and cut him down in a violent crossfire. His trusted weapon fell out of his hand as the bullets completely pierced his upper body. Blood drained onto the glass containers of soft-glimmering jewels. Chunks of his flesh dropped to the floor. His once-handsome face would soon be unrecognizable even to his children.

It had been a long time since he felt the sharp, hot burn of bullets. But this time would be different. This time, retired Major John Russo, decorated Vietnam War veteran and recipient of two Purple Hearts, would not live to tell about his final battle. His dying body slammed the wall behind him and then fell forward. Before his face hit the jewelry counter below him, he felt a warm, strange feeling of thankfulness, a rare sentiment in a cold man. He thanked God—whose existence he had never before acknowledged—that his son had left the store a few minutes earlier.

One of the executioners drew his handgun and shot the fallen war hero once in the temple, spraying his brains out the other side of his head and onto the wall. "Insurance," he liked to call it. A single handful of bloodied necklaces were scooped from the shattered counter. All of this took less than three minutes; the mission was complete, the "burglars" were gone.

Back inside their black car, the passenger took off his nylon mask and checked his watch. "Did he get you?" he asked his partner.

The driver started the car, pressed the gas pedal, and dropped it into gear. "Naaah," he stated calmly over the spinning tires. "How 'bout you?"

"Nope."

CHAPTER TWO

1992

United Nations Main Ballroom
New York City
August 9, 8:18PM

Dominic Russo temporarily distracted the ladies in the room as he passed by them one by one. He pretended to be unaffected by their affectionate stares as he politely cut his way through the crowd and leaned over the L-shaped mahogany bar. Sunday night drinking was not a part of his typical routine, but that Sunday evening Dominic was drinking like everyone else. Such gala events made even the devotedly sober dive for the bottle. It seemed to be the universal way to deal with the dense crowds and the manufactured personalities of the night.

Dominic was alone, but at twenty-five years old, one of the youngest in the packed room, he was not at all uncomfortable. He was never uncomfortable in social settings; he chose to arrive alone at events like this. It was more than just a routine. It was his philosophy. *Why bring fish to the ocean?* summarized his reasoning. He looked over the vast and bountiful ocean he would soon be fishing, with all its exotic and diverse offerings.

While waiting for the busy bartender to make his way to him, Dominic scanned the dense ballroom crowd with supreme confidence. His fit body was dressed in a perfectly tailored handsome navy blue suit, touched off perfectly with a tightly knotted red tie. A wave of dark hair, set at one length and pushed back altogether, crested his sculpted complexion. To most onlookers, his classic

Mediterranean face roused either envy or desire. And in most cases both.

Apart from the bitter memories sparked now and again from similar reflections in the mirror, Dominic Russo had to admit that it was fortunate he had inherited his divine looks from his old man. They shared the same dark brown expressive eyes, the same olive-tinted skin and chiseled cheeks. He even had the same rigid body and naturally strong hands. He knew that physical inheritance from father to son is beyond his control. Those not as favorably awarded from their heredity would perhaps call it a blessing. The more jealous ones might call it unfair. Those older and similarly physically appealing during their lives might sum it up, in retrospect, as an invitation to danger.

With his inherited good looks and independently cultivated charm, Dominic had confidence that one of the ladies passing in the crowd would likely not remain a stranger through the night. He thought about her for a moment, whoever she might soon be. She'll probably be older, maybe even much older. There's a chance she'll be twice his age as much older women were better suited for him. They don't play games. Will she be married? The possibility was always there.

During these kinds of occasions he preferred them that way…even fewer games. Most likely she'll be from another country—perhaps one he'd never heard of. She'll probably speak very little English, with a heavy accent. The ideal combination for romance. She'll definitely be well-dressed in a long, well-fitting gown, wearing high heels for sure. But even more important than that, she'll smell good. Not a strong perfume that can be detected from miles away but a subtle natural aroma that enhances the desire from up close. That, above all else for him, was mandatory.

Given his track record, Dominic's romantic aspirations for later in the evening were less cocky than commonplace. Somewhere in this crowd his overnight guest was socializing her way towards him. It was still too early to actually meet her…but it was a perfect time to choose her.

Though he was considerably younger than the other fellow invitees, this caused no discomfort for Dominic Russo. He indeed looked his twenty-five years, but his young mind was far ahead of its years. Rarely is such a long road of experience crammed into a quarter century, but in Dominic's case this was true. Daringly, he had forced himself upon the world. And continued to do so.

His daring had sprouted four years earlier. To him, it seemed like only yesterday—it would always seem like yesterday to him. He heard the phone ringing that night. It must have rung a dozen times; still no one picked it up. If he could go back in time, he wouldn't have either. He would have stayed in the shower and never picked up that damn phone. Maybe, just maybe, if someone else answered, the news would have been different. Maybe it would have rung forever.

But Dominic jumped out of the shower that night and, still dripping wet, grabbed the phone. From the short pause of a voice on the other end, he immediately sensed something wasn't right. When the voice did speak, Dominic knew for sure something terrible had happened. The stranger was friendly and sympathetic—the worst kind of stranger. He introduced himself as a doctor and then said "how sorry he was" and "how difficult it was to say this." Dominic was voiceless. His body, still warm from the shower, immediately froze. The kind and apologetic doctor went on to explain "there was nothing they could have done," his beloved mother had been pronounced "dead on arrival." She was a victim, he would soon learn, of a highway hit-and-run.

Less than six months later, the doorbell rang. Dominic had just arrived home. He knew the men at the door; they were detectives from the local precinct. Dominic was happy to see them. He hoped they came by to tell him in person that they had finally caught the hit-and-run perpetrator who killed his mother. But the expressions on the detectives' faces told a different story. They had come for another reason. An unexpected, yet familiar reason. This time it was about a heist at the jewelry store. Again, Dominic froze in anger. He had just left there! The detectives said his brave father had tried to thwart the robbery, but he ended up the victim of unimaginable violence.

Impossible. Two parents…two deadly bolts of lightning.

The aftermath of these two tragedies left Dominic at an unplanned crossroads in his young life. Given the tragic series of events, not to mention his strained relationship with his father, no one expected Dominic to do what he did next—take over his father's business. He ignored everyone's advice, dropped out of law school, and re-opened the small jewelry store his father had named Gemco. The person most disappointed with his decision was his only sibling, Marie. She hated the store, just like she hated everything to do with their father. She desperately pleaded with her younger brother to sell the Gemco inventory and finish law school. What frustrated her even more was that Dominic turned down a sizable offer to sell Gemco after the funeral…an offer that could have paid for Dominic's entire legal education.

But he had other ideas—new, daring ideas, now that John Russo was gone. These ideas shined much brighter than Gemco's jewels and sailed high above the blanket of security Marie had hoped to securely wrap around her younger brother. Men with such bold ideas could never be satisfied in a career representing others, no matter how much they paid him.

Marie Russo had her own ideas, too. Ideas that existed long before John Russo went so violently to his grave. And ones that remained undaunted thereafter. But after failing to persuade her brother to stay in school, Marie packed her bags and continued on her own path in life—a path far away and far different from her brother's.

Fortunately, Dominic was not a fool to his ambition. Before he reopened Gemco's doors, he prepared himself properly for the unforgiving world that he knew lay ahead. First, he set out to acquire what gem dealers call "the expert eye." This skilled eye was not something he could have inherited from his old man. John Russo indeed had one, but he, like everyone else, had to earn this title over time through practice, patience, and experience.

In his typical intense fashion, Dominic immersed himself in geological and technical books. He taught himself everything he could learn about jewels— how they were cut, engraved, faceted, and polished. He held and examined thousands of precious stones and jewelry pieces at museums, auction houses, and jewelry stores. He mastered the use of microscopes, ultraviolet lamps, scales, and other equipment of the trade.

Dominic's obsessive pursuit of this expertise did not begin from total ignorance. He had worked at Gemco for the previous couple of years to help pay for law school, usually only on the days his father was not there. He gained a general familiarity with these kinds of rocks that people paid to know about and wanted to own. But the responsibilities and risks of Gemco as a business were quite different now. Simply stated, they were all his.

Most important, after several months of intensive self-training, Dominic was so well-educated in the science of precious stones and metals that he was able to become a gem dealer with this coveted "expert eye." With that, the technical preparation was complete. What remained to find out was whether he had the street smarts to survive the unforgiving gem business in the New York City.

John Russo had never allowed his son to become involved in that side of the business. Even when they were getting along, John never explained the rules of the streets to his son; Dominic only had experience in selling jewelry to store customers. After all, he was as chiseled and gorgeous as a diamond. He was not, however, accustomed to buying precious stones from friendly villains. Unfortunately, there were no how-to books written on the business of the streets. And his good looks offered no advantage among thieves. The only way to learn how to negotiate and make money in the streets was to do it. For Dominic, that time had finally come. The roll-up door was raised, the newly installed alarm was encoded, and the fresh bulbs lining the new glass cabinets in the store were flicked on. At the tender age of twenty-three, Dominic Russo re-opened Gemco and threw himself, prematurely many had felt, into the jungle of buying and selling polished earth rocks.

As expected, the wolves immediately circled at the door.

Dominic called these dealers, wholesalers, and precious stone importers his cunning colleagues—"wolves in sheep's clothing." To him, they were no more than a collection of well-mannered crooks wearing tailored suits and ties often asking you how your family is doing—the type of robbers who never kick down the door and stick you up but rather sit across the table from you and try to trick you into paying for something you're not getting. It could be one synthetic diamond in a lot of twenty real gems or one gold-plated setting in a group of solid gold ones. There were no set protocols really, except one. If a wolf was caught cheating, the pilferer would simply claim to have been fooled himself. That way everything remained innocent, inoffensive, and devoid of shame. More important, during the very next visit, another smiling scam could be attempted.

Thanks to his expert eye, Dominic was able to determine the genuine value of the precious stones that he examined. This, combined with his natural street-negotiating skills, enabled the young newcomer to indoctrinate himself quickly into the fiercely competitive New York City jungle of gemstones. Soon he gained a reputation among the rest of the wolf pack—*the new, young proprietor of Gemco was not a man who could be fooled.*

Pulling a dollar out from his pants, Dominic finally corralled the bartender and pitched his order for a glass of red wine.

"Where's your tip glass?" Dominic asked him. The tuxedoed bartender smirked while he drilled a corkscrew into a fresh bottle of inexpensive wine. "Not allowed," he replied.

"Really?"

"UN policy," said the bartender, lifting the cork from the bottle's neck. "Between me and you," he continued over the air-pressured pop, "I ain't losin' much with this crowd."

Dominic smirked. "I know what you mean." If not for his sister, he would still be at the store down on Canal Street trying to peddle engagement rings to passersby, knowing that the late night shopper, usually male, is always the easiest sell. Typically he is under intense pressure to buy something. Maybe his anniversary is tomorrow and he needs earrings; or perhaps he had forgotten his wife's birthday; or, best of all, his girlfriend's engagement ultimatum is about to expire.

Tonight however, Dominic would forego any opportunities to sell precious stones and show his support for his sister's charitable work—especially since she told him in her last letter that he had no choice. *You better be there*, she wrote in bold lettering, *because a very special announcement will be made that night*. It wasn't too bad, really, the occasional fundraiser or reception that his sister made him attend. Sure they were boring, but they were ideal places to meet short-term companions.

For the moment, Dominic kept his position at the bar. The first drink would be going down quickly, and he didn't want to lose his valuable spot. At the other end of the ballroom, the announcements were set to begin. Dominic had a feeling of déjà vu. His mind flashed back to the last time he attended a reception at the UN. He smiled at the recollection. The Ambassador from Thailand was the guest speaker that night and his speech seemed to go on forever. Throughout the speech, Dominic was "working"—trading whispers back and forth with a beautiful foreign lady. He forgot her name. He recalled she was doctoral student at Columbia. *Or was it NYU?* He remembered clearly her stunning looks. Dark skin, high cheeks, cat-like eyes, and legs that stretched all the way to her neck. For a while, their conversation sailed smoothly. Grins and giggles were mutually exchanged. Foreplay, in essence, was well under way, at least until Dominic made a comment about the exhausting length of the Ambassador's speech. Upon hearing Dominic's statement, the young woman shot back, "That's my father!"

Rare was a moment when Dominic was rendered wordless, especially when it came to courting beautiful women. But at that moment the promising romance train abruptly screeched off the tracks. When she moved her pretty face in closely to his ear, Dominic braced himself for impact Dominic of her slap or splash of her drink. To his surprise, she whispered, "You're lucky…you only have to listen to him tonight."

With that, the train was back up on the tracks…continuing successfully on a downhill course to its inevitable final destination…the bed in her Upper East Side apartment.

Tonight the guest speaker was from a different country. Dominic watched him carefully as he ascended the stairs onto the soundstage. His elderly arms and legs moved in slow animated fashion as he made his way over to the podium. Flashes from the press cameras ricocheted off the straight line of gold medals pinned to his snow-white suit. It was a poetic sight, watching proud vestiges blink like stars during an obviously proud moment for a proud man. He was smiling, and you could tell by its fresh design across his cheeks that he was not a man who did so often. The packed ballroom was brimming with fanfare, arrogance, and a bit of heartburn from the catered food. Using no more than a raised arm and robotic scan of the audience, he was able to command the undivided attention of the five hundred-plus invitees. The few lingering whispers in the ballroom died out altogether once he tapped the face of the microphone. Dinner was over. Schmoozing would have to wait. Ambassador-General Huong, the celebrated representative from the Socialist Republic of Vietnam, was set to begin the long-awaited announcements. Clearing his throat, the Ambassador spoke slowly and deliberately into the microphone in order to minimize his thick accent:

"Goooood evening friends. Welcome to this wonderful reception. On behalf of the Permanent Mission of Vietnam to the United Nations, I would like to thank everyone from the international community for joining us at our annual fundraiser this evening. It is wonderful to see you all here. Your contributions will help save lives in my country and I thank you for your continued support."

Pausing, as if he were recalling lines, the former warrior and recent diplomat added: "Every five years, the International Special Projects Division of the United Nations donates money, supplies, and aid to a charity whose work and efforts promote peace, prosperity and livelihood in the world. Today, the committee unveiled its selections, and I am pleased to announce that the AFP, the Army for Peace, shall once again receive a donation. It is the single largest grant in UN history…ten million US dollars."

The crowd erupted in applause as Ambassador Huong stepped down nodding in delight. Dominic turned back to the bar and ordered another glass of red wine. He was surprised and pleased by the news. He knew his sister was thrilled about it, and that made him happy. Suddenly, a deep voice whispered in his ear over the loud applause: "Mr. Krauze would like to see you."

Dominic leaned back slightly, but did not turn around. There was no need to look at the messenger's face. The directness of the message gave him a good enough idea of what the messenger looked like. "Where's he at?" he coolly asked out of the side of his mouth.

"Outside on the terrace."

"I'll be right over."

With that, Dominic leaned back over the bar and called out to the bartender. "You got any kosher wine?"

"Sure."

"Good. Gimme two glasses."

"You got it."

Carrying a glass of red wine in each hand, Dominic took his time making his way over to the other side of the ballroom. Politely he cut his way through the heart of the well-dressed, ethnically diverse crowd, inhaling over a dozen different colognes in passing, and wondering the entire time whether to feel honored or worried. Shay Krauze had summoned him in the middle of a gala event. But Shay Krauze was very rarely seen in public. Some people, he concluded, would be running to meet with him…others would be running for the door.

In front of the glass doors to the terrace, Dominic was forced to stop walking. He encountered a human barrier. A virtual mountain of a man, totally detached in both dress and body language from the rest of the smiling guests. The messenger, Dominic presumed, had switched roles. He now stood upright with his hands behind his back displaying the face of a perpetually angry man, his expression intending to ward off any curiosity. Obvious, too, was his struggle to project his barrel chest out further than his colossal stomach. Not far off to his side stood another equally unfriendly-looking boundary of flesh. The struggle of his upper body was the same as his partner's. Both had pitch black skin and clean shaved heads. Covering their bloated frames were identical black turtlenecks and sharkskin colored suits. The two massive men were interchangeable physically and, as employees of Shay Krauze, equally expendable. Dominic grinned to himself. *The UN was truly a diverse ocean tonight. It even had two of its whales disguised in sharkskin.*

Upon spotting Dominic, the two men shifted mechanically to the side and opened the glass door to the outdoor terrace. Neither said a word, but Dominic could feel the weight of their piercing glares as he passed between their burly bodies. With caution, he stepped outside the air-conditioned ballroom onto the large empty terrace, where the fast current of the East River below generated a refreshing breeze in the otherwise still night. In the darkness of the far corner of the terrace, Dominic saw the unmistakable silhouette.

Shay was alone, leaning on the chest-high ledge with his back to Dominic, admiring the city he controlled from the shadows. In the background, the multi-colored lights of upper Manhattan's skyline lit up the sky, an imposing urban backdrop for an imposing man. "Mr. Krauze?" Dominic called meekly to the shadow. Shay waved his young guest over without turning his head.

As Dominic approached, his sweaty toes crimped from nervousness in his shoes. He wished he had more time to think about the reasons behind this pending encounter. He prided himself on preparation, especially when it came to matters as compelling as a one-on-one meeting with the most feared Hasidic Jew in New York City. But there was nothing he could do about it now except to do his best to look cool and unaffected in stride. Gazing into the windows that lined the adjacent ballroom, Dominic couldn't prevent a disturbing thought from entering his head. *There must be over five hundred people inside the grand ballroom,* he fretted, *but only two of us are out here on the terrace.* As Shay's dark image came into focus through the shadows, Dominic pushed one final gulp down his dry mouth before the encounter.

"Ahhhhhhhhhh, Dominic!" Shay bellowed. His voice, like his body, was operatic.

"I brought you a drink," Dominic responded. "It's kosher."

"Salud!" Shay toasted in Italian. The two men raised their glasses and sipped.

A first impression, Shay Krauze's unsightly appearance indicated that not a single mirror hung in his humble home. After all, those devoted to Hasidism find no value in outward appearances. A photo portrait of him would cast identical images taken with black and white or colored film; he had no pigment. His long coat and top hat were black, his button-down shirt white, and the rest of his observable physical features exuded different shades of gray. His bulging eyes dug deep into his face. Captured inside them were his colorless, lifeless eyeballs. To make matters worse, the thick round lenses of his silver wire eyeglasses magnified the frightening stature of his attacking eyeballs twofold.

Shay's face offered not one visually pleasing sight to focus on during a conversation. His snub nose offered the unwanted opportunity to see the forest of nose hairs blooming inside his nostrils. The rest of his facial features were unavailable for direct viewing, hidden entirely behind a heavily thatched beard. Beginning only inches below his eyes, thousands of foot-long light gray whiskers sprouted out of his cheeks and continued like ivy down the rest of his face, completely covering his lips, jaw, and neck. Dangling in front of his ears were, of course, the two thick corkscrew curls, trademarks of those believing to be God's chosen people.

His never-shaven, plain-clothes appearance was the same as all Hasidic men, which, at least for the others, symbolized their total devotion to God. For Shay Krauze, it symbolized a dichotomy, particularly to those who knew the whispered rumors about him to be true. His whole life was a contrast of means—a hypocrisy, in religious terms.

On the surface he was a holy disciple of Hasidim, whose followers were direct descendants of an 18th century religious revival movement in Eastern Europe. In close-knit communities, the Hasidic Jews lived together in strict adherence to the ancient word of God. They rejected modernization and physicality, believing that each day on earth called for devoted prayer, sacrifice, and communion with God. Man, they believed, is on earth solely to praise God, procreate with his wife, and prepare for the coming of the Messiah. But the other side of Shay Krauze was far removed from his devoted fellow worshippers. Far removed from his hours of evening prayers and medieval chants. The other side of Shay Krauze was his real side—all about business… and it was far scarier than his face.

Dominic noticed that in the flattering shadows of the night sky, Shay's face served notice of his split personality, as it appeared to be perpetually frozen into a continuous metamorphosis from human to werewolf, or perhaps the other way around. Either way, it unpleasantly reminded Dominic that a vicious killer was not far off from surfacing.

Gulping his first sip of wine, Shay asked, "So tell me Dominic, when are you getting married?" His effortless voice smoothly hummed his words. The last words of each of his sentences were accented, allowing his every statement to flow upward in a rising melody.

"Married?" Dominic replied incredulously. "Well—that probably won't happen for a while."

Shay shook his head slowly. His voice purred in thought. "I don't understand your people sometimes. They never seem to learn. They base their most important life decisions on such unreliable reasoning…like love."

Dominic was curious to hear the elder Hasid elaborate his thoughts, especially considering he was married to the same woman for almost fifty years. "So you find that it is better to have marriages arranged?"

"Of coooourse," Shay crooned. "At first, it may seem nice to have love between two people. But you must beware…if you make love the foundation of a partnership you are also unknowingly placing a lot of pressure upon it. Later on, if the love disappears or even shrinks a little, the foundation you built your entire partnership on cracks and the partnership then breaks down." After another sip of wine, Shay continued, "Now—if you enter into the partnership without love, you can raise your family with no worries. There is absolutely no pressure, no break down, no divorce. You see?"

Dominic grinned, taking a moment to digest Shay's unusual theory on relationships. He appreciated the old man's strictly logical approach. And he had to admit to himself that a business-orientated rationale of marriage was difficult to put down in an age of more than likely divorce. But there was one glaring problem with Shay's reasoning.

"What about happiness?" Dominic pointed out. "Doesn't that have to be at least part of the equation?"

"Ahhhhhh," Shay hymned in response. "Therein lies the problem, Dominic. Your people continue to search for happiness in places it can't be found."

"I see," Dominic responded, cracking a smile.

"I only tell you these things because you're a friend of mine, you know? You must promise me that you will keep them in confidence and not spread the secrets…or else you'll put us both out of business." At that, Shay chuckled in choppy, monotone layers. "Divorce happens to be one of the reasons why we both decided to go into the diamond business, is it not?"

Dominic chuckled along, but his amusement was more the result of Shay's understatement than his joke. For he and Shay were far from being considered fellow associates in the diamond business. More accurately put, Shay *was* the diamond business, hence, he *permitted* Dominic to deal gems by doing business with him.

The Hasidic's rumored ascent to power in the streets of New York City was unlike any of its kind in the criminal underworld. Unlike Italian underworld figures, Shay did not allow anyone to get close to him nor would he ordain a ruling structure. He had no underbosses, capos, or consigliores; they only appeased egos and increased risks. He consolidated *all* power and *all* control in himself. After him, everyone was equal, and, more importantly, each person's role was kept very limited.

As a matter of his own design, Shay was a mystery to even his men—who themselves were more like sub-contractors of a large corporation rather than criminal soldiers. His "company" was a network of well-compensated, highly specialized mercenaries that dealt with the boss, if at all, only in their limited capacity. Hit men, for example, did not also engage in smuggling. Their role was murder. Murder was what they did. Murder was all they did. No one was ever given more information than needed to fulfill their job; and no one was ever given information about someone else's job. This was indeed a criminal monarchy.

For his dirty work, Shay was an equal opportunity employer except when it came to one ethnicity—his own. He refused to let Jews, much less Hasids, carry out his underworld business affairs. His revolutionary policy of discriminating against his own people and associating with other criminal factions seemed suicidal at first, but over time Shay's methods proved to be ingenious. Hasids, in the perception of the outside public looking in, were mysterious holy men who kept among themselves to worship God most of the day and night.

To Shay, the religious image of Hasidim was perfect cover. Consequently, he divided up the streets of New York City like an apple pie. For downtown matters, he employed Chinese gangs as muscle. Uptown, African-Americans were hired for exterminations. He also split up the surrounding boroughs. Hispanics were mostly utilized for issues in Queens; the Albanians took care of business in the Bronx; and in Brooklyn, it was the Russians who carried out his wishes. With this arrangement, any trail of evidence would point to other directions—namely, the rivalries within criminal factions of other races and nationalities. Surely nothing would suggest to an investigator that behind these seemingly unconnected crimes was the business of a single Hasidic Jew from Brooklyn.

Shay had the best men in the business carrying out his orders—not because they were his friends, family, religion, or race—but because he paid the best. Unlike La Cosa Nostra, trust and loyalty were never mixed with business. His pioneering tactics insulated him from investigation and prosecution while the rest of traditional organized crime was being wiped out by its very own rats. So much for trust and loyalty.

Shay Krauze was the sole master of the grandest, most sophisticated, and impenetrable criminal enterprise in the country. And no one really knew it. Perhaps due also to his criminally unorthodox style, no one else in the underworld dared to mount a challenge to Shay Krauze's throne…at least not yet.

Gently, Shay perched his glass of wine on the ledge. He reached out and rested his fat paw on Dominic's shoulder. "So how's business going at the store?"

The inquiry really was just small talk because Shay was well aware of how business was going at Gemco. He was well aware of how business was going for every gem dealer in the city. He was, after all, supplying most of them with their jewels. "All right," Dominic answered, "always could be better."

"Well, I hear you're buying a lot of stones from us…You must be making *some* money."

"Yes, well, you know…some is not *enough*."

Shay grinned at Dominic's response. He was visibly impressed with the young entrepreneur's outlook on business. "That's exactly what separates you from your old man…God rest his soul." After a sigh, Shay continued, "You know we did business together for many years. He was a good man, an honorable man, and he was always satisfied with *enough*."

Dominic thought about the irony of a "good man" being such a bad father as Shay continued, "Did you know that for years I tried to get him to work for me, but he never would? Every time I would ask him, he would say the same thing, 'Thanks, but no thanks.' I was offering him twice the money, half the aggravation, but he didn't care. He still refused. He preferred to stay in that store of his. Because to him that store was always enough. But you seem to me to be far different from your father…"

You have no idea, Shay, Dominic thought.

"I see in you a hungry man. And hunger is good. Hunger is necessary for survival. But as you know in this business, hunger is not always sufficient. You must have more than that. You need intelligence. And this, too, is something I see you have earned for yourself…" With that Shay paused, and slightly raised one of his gray eyebrows. Although Dominic could not actually see Shay's lips behind his thick beard, the movement of hairs indicated a smile had come upon his face.

Dominic's mouth and eyebrows remained fixed where they were. To his surprise, he was able to remain firm and unrevealing in silence and expression. He didn't nod, say "thank you" or anything at all in response to Shay's flattery. The "hungry, intelligent young businessman" was intent to not succumb to a seduction of words from the most powerful and mysterious man in the city. He first wanted to hear exactly what Shay was getting at before unmasking a response.

Shay kept his intriguing smile intact and stared at Dominic for a few extended moments. Dominic stared back, trying his best to keep his face unaffected. It was a standoff, really. Not a harsh standoff, it was a polite one, but a poker-like standoff nonetheless. Dominic then noticed the hairs covering Shay's lips eventually shift back to their usual position. The other eyebrow on Shay's face slowly rose up to the same level as its counterpart. The pious-looking businessman continued his sermon using a godly voice, "But hunger and intelligence are still not enough in our business."

Dominic remained outwardly unfazed, but inside was another matter altogether. Shay was finally getting to the point. By now, Shay's welcoming smile had faded completely from his hairy chin. Perhaps he was sensing Dominic's resoluteness. After sipping his wine, he asked curiously, "I hear you're heading over to Vietnam to visit Marie?"

Dominic was uncomfortable hearing his sister's name spoken by a man who ordered murders. He was not surprised by his information, though, for he knew Shay was a man who found out all he wanted to know. Clenching his wine glass, Dominic responded, "Uhhh, yes…that's right. I leave tomorrow, as a matter of fact."

"That's great," Shay purred. "The world is fortunate to have people like your sister in it. Can you believe the size of the grant the Army for Peace has received? Ten million dollars, if I heard correctly."

"That's right. They said it was the largest grant in the history of the UN."

"Did Marie have anything to do with that?"

Dominic smiled at the thought. "Naaah. She's a social worker for them. Fundraising is not her forte."

"Still. I must imagine that she is very pleased by that grant."

"Yeah, she's happy."

"You know, I hear they are about to open up the market over there. I guess the US Government has finally come to its senses and wants to get rid of that trade embargo."

Dominic had heard the same rumor from Marie. The United States' fifteen-year trade embargo against Vietnam was in all likelihood going to be lifted before the upcoming presidential election. However, hearing this from the mouth of Shay, a man with obviously deep political connections, was as good as getting a confirmation from the President himself. "Yeah, that seems to be a possibility," Dominic responded.

"They sent that senator from Florida there," said Shay, "you know, the veteran…what's his name?…*Haynes*…Senator Haynes. He's supposed to be looking into the whole POW issue. If all goes well, and he finds that Hanoi is cooperating with everything, then he'll recommend to Congress to lift the ban. And I hear that Congress will do whatever he recommends."

"And that should open up a floodgate of business opportunities," Dominic pointed out.

"That's right," Shay said, again enjoying a sip of his wine. "I think it's about time anyway. What has it been now? Over twenty years since the war?"

"Just about."

"Yeah, well—enough is enough already. Embargoes are bad for business. Look at Cuba—it's ninety miles away from the coast of Florida and we, as Americans, are not allowed to go there. That's nonsensical. If the politicians were wise they would reverse their policies and encourage everyone to go there.

Do you know what the secret to defeating communism is?"

Dominic did not venture a guess. Instead, he shook his head no.

"Tourism," Shay answered prophetically. "Tourism brings with it all the excesses of the world...American blue jeans, Italian colognes, French food, and Japanese electronics. Once a man gets a chance to see, hear, taste, touch, and smell the best products from around the world, well, then you got him."

Dominic's mind wondered silently, *if that was true, then how come Hasidic Jews manage to resist the excesses of capitalism all around you?* But he held back from voicing his curiosity.

Shay pointed into the grand ballroom and continued speaking, "Look at the collection of people in there. Some of them, as you know, call themselves 'communists,' right? And as a young and ambitious businessman, you may think is a bad word for business. But in reality it's really nothing more than a disguise. Business is business, Dominic. And someday you will learn like me that nothing can stop a supply when there is a demand. That goes for every business in the world...from drugs to gems. In fact, in some instances communism is better for business."

Shay sipped his wine while Dominic glanced around the lively ballroom. "Some of the men you see in there, Dominic, are from countries that consider Jewish people bitter enemies, but do you think that prevents us from conducting business? Of course not. That sort of thing is only foolish politics. Beneath all of it, in dark alleyways and behind the shadows, every one of those politicians in there is united by a common denominator—they're all out for themselves. Show me a diplomat in New York City, my friend, and I'll show you a profiteer."

Dominic grinned with intrigue. His head was swirling in an attempt to figure out what Shay was leading up to. But experiencing the buildup was priceless. He was getting an invaluable education from an enigmatic man—the same man who sat atop the criminal business food chain. Wisely, he remained passive with Shay, continuing to keep his answers brief until the point of the meeting was revealed. "I believe it," Dominic stated.

"Of course you believe it," Shay declared. "You trust that these things I know all about." Dominic nodded in agreement with Shay's statement. After a slight pause, Shay continued in a more solemn tone: "This brings us to the reason why I requested time with you this evening, Dominic. I think you and I should look into buying some gemstones while you are in Vietnam. Supposedly—and I am sure you are well aware of this—they have more stocks of rubies in the ground than anywhere else in the world."

At last, Dominic thought to himself, the purpose of the conversation was revealed. Shay was correct in his assumption. Dominic, like any informed gem dealer, was well aware of the untapped potential for gems in Vietnam. In fact, though he missed his sister and respected her work, the lure of treasured jewels was indeed the primary purpose behind his upcoming trip to Vietnam. He was scheduled to leave from Kennedy Airport tomorrow morning, the itinerary already etched in his mind. In all, two full days of travel and over twenty hours in the air. Quite a long journey but well worth it if he could make some inquiries and establish connections for buying stones there.

Dominic wanted, more than anything else, to become an importer of stones. That way he could break his reliance on middlemen like those who worked for Shay Krauze and finally start making some big money. Nevertheless, in the conversation at hand, Dominic proceeded with caution so as to not disclose his ambitions. Coyly, he reminded Shay: "The last time we spoke you advised me to stay away from the gem business and be a lawyer."

Shay's facial hairs parted, indicating a smirk. He was charmed by Dominic's composure. He knew for sure that Dominic was nervous, but impressed that he was able to maintain a quick wit. "Ahhh, yes," Shay acknowledged. "But that was years back. And the reason why I advised you in that manner was because your father was killed at the store. I knew how difficult it would be for you to go to that same store every day and constantly be reminded of that awful tragedy. And if my recollection serves me well, you were a promising student of law at the time. That is why I offered to buy Gemco from you. So that you could continue on in school."

Dominic tested Shay further. "But now things are different?"

"Things are very different now," Shay announced with a nod of his head. "From what I hear you have become quite an expert with stones. And I must commend you. You chose a difficult path. Everyone, including myself, thought that this business would swallow you up, but you have thus far proved us wrong. Tonight I see before me a wise businessman, one who knows his trade and how to deal with the people in it. He is a long way off from the naïve law student I last spoke with."

Again, Dominic did not respond to Shay's flattery. They were talking business, and Dominic was mindful to not be softened by calculated praise.

"But," Shay continued, "To move up you will need more than your hunger and intelligence…you need money and influence behind you." Shay paused purposely and took a sip of wine. "The type of industry Vietnam offers you, Dominic, is completely different from the jewelry business. That industry is about buying rough stones. At their source. The question is whether you are willing to take the proper steps to be successful with it."

Dominic sipped his wine to buy time to think. On one hand, like everything else in his life, he wanted to pursue his Vietnam business venture alone. He despised the thought of partners—business or personal ones. When he took over Gemco, he did so alone. He could have taken in partners at that time, but he didn't. He was proud of that and that was the way he wanted to keep things. Furthermore, dealing intimately with a man like Shay Krauze was a very risky proposition. And one that he may not be able to break away from once he started

On the other hand, Shay was right. If there was a viable chance to secure distribution of Vietnamese rubies, Dominic did not have the clout or finances to secure the deal alone. His sister may be a highly respected social worker for the AFP, but all she could do is perhaps provide him with some trustworthy introductions. After that, the bottom line in making the deal would be exactly what Shay had said: cash and clout. Shay Krauze offered both in a big way. Representing such a man in Vietnam would bring Dominic immediate credibility and respect.

Dominic realized it was pointless to deliberate further. It was settled. Alliances would have to be formed. And in this case, unholy ones.

"Who's gonna cut the stones?" he asked, implying his acceptance.

"We will worry about that when the time comes. Who knows, perhaps you will see that they can cut the stones there."

"Do you think they will be skilled enough?"

"Not likely, but that's no matter to me. We can cut in Bangkok. Or Taiwan if need be. Remember, in the beginning we first must ship the stones to another country anyway due to the embargo. What you need to do is find out if we can buy stones from there at the right price. I am certain that if they have the capability to supply us, you are capable of negotiating us a desirable price. The stones they have are rumored to be some of the best in the world. We won't know if this is true until we see them. Now, I cannot advise you about what it's like over there when it comes to business. I'm sure it can be dangerous. But they may also be inexperienced, and if that's the case, our opportunities will be much greater."

Dominic sipped his wine and nodded his head in agreement. He did not respond to the mention of danger. He knew Shay was testing his resolve. And both men knew that inexperience in the gem business is like a license to rob.

The most important point of all, however—*splitting the money*—still had not been mentioned. They were now at this point in the discussion, the most important point, and Dominic did not want to be the first to bring it up. Instead, he wanted to hear what Shay had in mind—to find out how generous he was willing to be. But Shay was in no rush to show his hand on the matter. Instead, he sipped his drink and pretended to turn his attention toward the view of the New York skyline. After a minute elapsed, he realized Dominic's negotiating ploy, but he took the initiative. "You will be the broker," Shay stated blankly. "You will negotiate the deal for me and take a cut."

Again Dominic kept silent, trying to get Shay to elaborate further. Shay obliged. "My people tell me you know stones as good as anyone. So whatever you can put together for me, I'll take. And you get to make money without having to put up anything. Nothing is better than that."

Dominic realized that Shay was attempting to outsmart him by persuading him to agree to a deal without knowing exactly what his piece of the action would be. It was indeed shrewd business strategy, but Dominic knew from experience that there can be no worse mistake made in the business of the streets. If he didn't set his cut now, Shay would have the power to assign it unilaterally later, at a time when Dominic would have no leverage. Dominic calmly stroked his soft hair back with his hand as his mind raced. *Five percent? Ten percent? The difference could be hundreds of thousands! What is too much? More importantly, how much is too little?* Suddenly, as numbers flashed in his mind, the answer came upon him. A bold, confident feeling calmed his frantic thoughts. He felt willing to ignore the traditional rules of the street and leave the question of his cut of the action open. He would play right into Shay's hands. For now. The young entrepreneur had come up with a daring plan.

"Sounds good to me," Dominic professed raising his glass one last time.

Visibly pleased by the ambiguity, Shay downed the last gulp of wine, reached into the inside pocket of his suit coat, and pulled out a small piece of paper. "Go see a General Kien in Hanoi," he stated. "He's the head of the Vietnamese Secret Police. It's their KGB. Here's the address." Dominic took the piece of paper. Shay continued, "Tell him you are my consultant and that I may be interested in buying some product. My mobile phone number is also on the paper. It is untraceable. Call me in privacy as soon as you see the product. Don't negotiate pricing until you speak to me. And don't forget to bring a camera. I want pictures of the product."

Dominic put the piece of paper in his pocket. The deal was done.

"Good luck," Shay wished his new associate.

"Why don't you come with me?" Dominic said jokingly.

"Me? At my age? I don't even like leaving Brooklyn to come into

Manhattan."

Dominic shook hands with Shay. When he turned and began to walk away, Shay asked, "By the way, how's Marie doing? Is she still saving the world?"

Dominic turned around but kept walking. "Always," he said while opening the glass door to the ballroom. "One kid at a time."

"Please give her my regards. And ask her if she needs anything."

"Will do!" Dominic turned to him and waved goodbye. He then stepped into the ballroom between Shay's human pillars and headed straight for the men's room. Already he was second-guessing his decision and needed to splash cold water on his sweat-moistened face.

Once inside the restroom, Dominic wet his heated palms and splashed his cheeks. There were no more paper towels, so he dried his hands by pushing back his hair a few times. Glaring into the mirror he began to shake his head in disgust. *I hope you know what you're doin'*, he admonished his reflection, *'cause you just sold yourself to the most dangerous man in New York…without setting a damn price!* An incoming patron opened the bathroom door and interrupted Dominic's thoughts. Nonchalantly, Dominic checked his watch, straightened his tie, and walked back out into the ballroom.

Throughout the ballroom, the liquor had settled into the crowd's bloodstream. The volume of conversations was noticeably louder. The level of flirtations had amplified. Dominic considered indulging himself, but only for a second. His mind was too preoccupied to stick around and fish, even in this fish tank. On his way towards the exit, he gazed back across the ballroom through the bustling crowd out the glass window to the terrace where he had stood with Shay. There, in the faint dark distance, he saw a man in a white suit talking with Shay. It was Ambassador-General Huong.

For once Dominic was heading home from the UN the same way he had arrived, alone. But with a "partner" unlike any other in his lifetime.

CHAPTER THREE

1972

The White House Basement Lounge

Washington, DC

May 17, 10:05PM

Once their traditional bet was made, the two presidential advisors walked up to the closed door. The first knock was a gentle one. "Mr. President?" David Lewis whispered in formal voice. No response. Peter McCabe pushed his ear against the door and rolled his eyes. His knock was a little harder.

"One second!" an irritated voice from inside eventually blurted out.

Both Lewis and McCabe looked at each other and smirked. They were used to exercising patience at this late hour. It gave added suspense to their customary wagers. After two minutes passed, the door finally opened and out walked Amanda, the voluptuous twenty-five-year-old White House secretary, whose panoramic bust and flirtatiousness sparked adulterous thoughts in most men besides the President. As always, she was smiling, not at all embarrassed about the obviousness of the circumstances. Her fresh splash of perfume filled the air as she passed them, politely bidding, "Have a good evening, gentlemen." Both men returned a smile. McCabe's, of course, was the more genuine of the two; he had won the bet. He would have to wait to be paid by Lewis until after the meeting.

"*Vietnam...Vietnam...Vietnam...it can ruin anything,*" President William Keane stated out loud to himself without bothering to look up at his entering visitors. He was busy gazing into the china cabinet mirror, re-styling his straight brown hair off to the side. At forty-three, he was both the youngest and handsomest President in recent history. As a little known second-term Republican Senator from Kentucky, his looks and oratory skills propelled him into the national spotlight during the 1968 primaries, and won him the presidency in a very close race against the seventy-five-year-old Democratic incumbent. The polls indicated that the difference in the election was Keane's overwhelming and unprecedented popularity among women voters. Outside his presence, his advisors would joke about how he had "earned" their support one encounter at a time.

Three years later, President Keane's suave personality and radiant smile had not yet enabled him to fulfill his pre-election promise to bring the troops home from Vietnam. The country was divided. The President's political support was dwindling. And the election—later that year—at one time considered in the bank, was now in jeopardy.

The two men who entered the dimly lit living room were the President's closest advisors and his brain trust on foreign affairs. The press deemed the powerful trio "The Three Musketeers" because of their notorious late night meetings. The political cartoonists had a field day with the caricatures. Tonight, however, would be the first time in over two months that they met together. As usual, it was unofficial.

Peter McCabe was the director of the Central Intelligence Agency as well the President's longtime friend and closest confidant. Their shared trust and loyalty were historically uncommon given the often strained co-existence between the respective offices. Physically, McCabe was a tall and wiry man who often let too much time elapse before trimming his stringy, black and white mane. He was only three years older than the President but not nearly as attractive or gifted in the public's eye. In the early 1950s, McCabe spent two years in Vietnam as a CIA advisor during the French-Indochina War. After the French withdrawal, he covertly engineered a number of "strategic" political assassinations in North Vietnam as well as a few more obvious coups within the government of South Vietnam. In 1967 he was appointed director of the CIA, an unusual achievement for an internal agent. A year later, rumors in the press surfaced regarding his "underhanded role" in President Keane's narrow victory in the 1968 election. Nothing was ever substantiated and the story was quickly dropped in the press. With future political aspirations, and as heir apparent to President Keane, he, too, was consumed—probably the most consumed—with securing an acceptable resolution to the conflict in Vietnam.

David Lewis was Secretary of State and at sixty-one years old, the eldest statesman of the three. He was a short, grayed, and obviously well fed rotund man with wide features, including his black-framed glasses. Standing alongside the tall slender McCabe, their physiques could easily be mistaken for the number ten. Lewis first gained national prominence twenty years earlier as an admiral during the Korean War and one of the masterminds of the famous Inchon landing. He was more of a Harvard-type intellectual than a gritty military man. A staunch anti-Communist with firsthand foreign affairs experience spanning three previous administrations, Lewis was a virtual living encyclopedia of knowledge and experience in Cold War diplomacy. For the past two years, he had conducted ongoing secret negotiations with representatives from North Vietnam. It appeared that he was finally on the verge of a breakthrough for peace—or better stated, a politically acceptable end to the war. But before a deal could be struck, the business of the night would need to be addressed.

Inside the living room, no handshakes or greetings were exchanged. The irritated President sat on the sofa, crossed his legs, and opened the secret meeting by asking his Secretary of State: "What do you got for me, David?"

Lewis made himself comfortable on the sofa across from the President. He began: "You need to make a decision about the situation."

"In Cambodia," President Keane clarified.

Lewis went on: "As long as we keep up the bombing, the North will have no choice but to accept our new compromise proposal when I meet with them again in six weeks. However, before we can commit ourselves, it is imperative that we decide what to do with those men."

As usual, the President's first reaction was to turn to McCabe. "Pete—you told me that if we left them out there it was only a matter of time?!"

McCabe was sitting on the sofa chair. He was much too tall to look comfortable crossing his legs. "It's *still* only a matter of time," he said back to the President, "but we have to be prepared in the event that the Vietnamese or Cambodians don't show. Either way, we cannot set free something that can come back to hurt us later on."

"I agree with Peter," Lewis cut in, "and if I have to adjust these proposals, I don't think we will get an agreement."

"Of course not!" snapped the President. "Those pricks got me by the balls and they're squeezing 'em tighter and tighter every day! They know that their support is growing in South Vietnam and mine is shrinking by the minute here!" Neither advisor offered a response. They had discussed such matters a thousand times before and had all agreed that the situation in Vietnam was desperate. With no hopes of a definitive military victory, an unstable political base in the South, and increasing protests and divisiveness in the United States, the young President's political future was on the line. He needed a peace accord before the primary convention.

Visibly annoyed, the President got up and walked across the room away from his advisors. He was mumbling to himself. The two men remained seated and silent, awaiting their commander-in-chief's decision. "Who can we use?" the President asked in low voice without turning around.

"I got someone in mind," McCabe quickly responded.

"One of your men?" inquired the President.

"No. I'd rather not," said McCabe.

"Well, are you sure we can get him?"

"Positive."

The Secretary of State softly clapped his hands, got up from his chair and announced: "Well, now that I know where we stand—then the proposal remains as is. I'll let you two iron out the details regarding the camp. Unless I hear otherwise, I'll assume it's a non-issue. I have a plane to catch."

With the President's attention focused on the pouring of two glasses of cognac, Lewis reached into his pocket and handed McCabe a twenty dollar bill during their farewell handshake, satisfaction of their earlier wager. "Have good evening, gentlemen," he said and left the room.

The President walked back over to McCabe and handed him a drink. "You sure you got the right man for this one, Pete?" he asked.

"Absolutely."

"Who is he?"

"Mazer."

"The Colonel?"

"Yeah, that's his neck of the woods and he's one of the best there is. I've known him a long time. He's perfect. I'll leave tonight."

The President's tone of voiced changed. "You know there is no room for error on this one. I don't have to tell you that if this thing gets out we'll all go down in flames."

McCabe nodded. He knew it better than anyone. He also knew that he, more than anyone, could ill-afford to let any cats out of the bag. "I know it," he replied. "That is why we need Mazer."

There was a brief, uneasy silence between the two friends. They each had a good sense for the other's thought process. And they each knew that one last thing needed to be discussed or at least stated. The President took a step closer to his trusted advisor and stated in a lower, more compelling tone: "I don't want to owe any favors to anyone on this one, Pete…and more importantly, neither should you."

McCabe raised his quarter-filled glass of cognac and toasted: "No debts."

The two men of destiny clinked glasses and downed their drinks.

CHAPTER FOUR

1992

Thirty miles east of Hanoi
Vietnam
August 11, 5:35PM

The tropical sun burned strong. Not a cloud had mercifully hazed its path. And by the late afternoon, it still had not grown weary from baking the brilliant green landscape of northern Vietnam. At the receiving end of the sun's pounding rays were bountiful and endless tracts of segregated rice paddies meticulously tilled by peasant women and children wearing sun-barring conical hats—some of the world's poorest people harvesting the richest, most fertile land on earth. Each thin long blade of grass in the endless patchwork of rice fields patiently awaited the individual attention it was bound to receive. Tireless hands of women and children would eventually pluck each blade and pin it back down into the glistening mirrors of moisture supplied by the myriad of irrigated waterways. On display outside of Dominic's back seat window were some of the most labor-intensive and brilliant farming techniques in the history of civilization.

Dominic felt ashamed sitting in a chauffeured, air-conditioned, black Mercedes, but he had no choice in the matter. Marie was unable to meet him at the airport so Colonel Mazer, ever the gracious host, sent his personal car. Dominic reflectively gazed out the closed window into the blistering heat while the back seat vent winded cool air into his face. He couldn't help from noticing his faint reflection in the foreground staring back at him off the window. He tried looking through the reflection defiantly, but that also failed. His reflection refused to be slighted. Like a haunting ghost cast over the sights of poverty passing by, Dominic's conscience was making its presence known, reminding him that, unlike his sister, he had come to this foreign land for money. He fought to discount the uncomfortable message claiming attention in his head. *How foolish*, he scolded himself, *allowing your thoughts to stray from their path.* Sympathy. Guilt. Those pesky feelings would simply have to stop. He had no time for it. *There was business to be done!*

Within an hour, the black Mercedes entered Hanoi, the capitol city of Vietnam. Another fifteen minutes later the car pulled into a long tree-lined driveway and stopped at a gated entrance. Dominic was amused by the irony on display out of the front windshield. Two heavily-armed soldiers were standing guard at the gate of AFP's charity headquarters. After a brief exchange in Vietnamese with the driver, one of the guards slid open the heavy iron gate. As the car rolled onto AFP property, each of the guards offered a warm smile and welcoming wave to Dominic. He returned them a smile and a nod. *It was a good sign*, he thought to himself, *when men holding rifles appear happy to see you.*

Inside the gate, the car slowly continued down a tree-lined road that became an unpaved trail. The climate outside the car changed dramatically. The bright, late afternoon sun disappeared, shaded out completely by the tall peach, plum, and tamarind trees that lined the pathway. The breath of the dense surrounding foliage cooled the humid, summer air. A few yards into the shade, the driver switched off the air conditioner and rolled down the car windows. Instantly, the distinctive smell of Hanoi's thick musty air filled the car.

A few bumpy minutes later, the trail opened into a large circular expanse where the sun was again glaring. They entered the open circle and parked. A water fountain, set in the middle of a perfectly manicured garden, splashed its contents down into a small container. Red, blue, and yellow flowers, arranged and planted in grouped colors, were in full bloom around the spouting fountain. Two Vietnamese women wearing conical hats were on their hands and knees weeding any unplanted growths from the patch. Consumed in their work, the busy gardeners didn't bother to look up when Dominic and the driver slammed the car doors shut. Behind the cascading fountain waters stood a grandiose two-story, bright yellow colonial mansion. Behind the mansion, in the far distant background, a dazzling aqua-blue lake glistened in the descending afternoon sun. The pictures Marie had sent Dominic failed to capture the lush magnificence before him. Only a painter's brush, he realized, might possibly record the beauty of such a scene. To Dominic, AFP's grounds seemed more like Disneyland than a charity headquarters. And viewing it after traveling thirty miles through indigent villages only added to its visual wonder.

The two white doors to the front of the mansion opened and the man responsible for it all came out to greet his guests. He was doing exactly what Dominic expected—gnawing his trademark cigar. Colonel Mazer's close-cropped hair and healthy build made it hard to imagine that he had been retired from the service for almost twenty years. He was wearing a white, crisp shirt, straight blue slacks, and brown sandals. Except for maybe a few extra pounds clinging to his midsection and a powder dusting of gray throughout his light brown hair and mustache, the Colonel's overall appearance had not changed in the two years since Dominic had last seen him. But to Dominic, two years wasn't long enough.

"Welcome to the Socialist Republic of Vietnaaaam!" the Colonel announced to his new arrival. "How was the trip?"

"Long!" Dominic yelled back smiling and waving his hand.

"Don't I know it!" the Colonel said, stepping down the stairs. Dominic's eyes zeroed in on his host's descent. Seeing the Colonel's cowboy-like swagger took his thoughts back in time. Right before planting his feet on the ground, the Colonel kicked out his legs to the side, slightly yet distinctively, just like Dominic's father used to. It had been a long time since Dominic had seen that familiar strut. The resemblance was uncanny. Both men seemed to walk with a chip on their shoulder. It was like someone had challenged them to a duel and at any moment they were going to spin around and draw. Marie called it a "military thing." She was probably right. The two veterans did spend many years together, much of the time fighting side-by-side and cheating death. Dominic had to tip his chin down to hide his smirk. Coming down the stairs of the mansion exaggerated the already exaggerated stride.

"That's why I never go back to the States," the Colonel said as he got closer to Dominic. "Too damn far. By the time I get off the plane after twenty-plus hours in the air I feel like I should be on the damn moon!" The two men shook hands firmly and embraced loosely.

"Where's Marie?" Dominic asked.

"She told me to apologize. She got tied up at one of the hospitals. We've launched a big vaccination campaign and we never have enough supplies. She should be back in a couple of hours."

Dominic knew his sister would be very busy during his visit. She was, after all, always busy. It was the nature of her field. And her own nature. And with plenty of his own work to do, Dominic realized that he and his sister might not get to spend as much time together as he would have liked. He took a moment to think it about that. With this being the case, he clearly preferred staying in a hotel, away from the Colonel, rather than at the AFP compound. "Thank you for the car and the invitation to stay here, Colonel," Dominic said sincerely, "but I know you're very busy and I don't want to disrupt anything here, so I'll just get a room in a nearby hotel."

"Absolutely not!" the Colonel ordered. "You're family. Did Marie tell you? Senator Haynes will also be staying here for a couple of days as our guest."

Dominic shook his head and raised his eyebrows to give the impression like he was honored. "No, she didn't say…"

"I just got off the phone with him. He should be here in a few hours. I'm putting him at the other end of the compound. Between me and you, it's not as nice as where you're staying, but that's too bad. Besides, he has an entourage of security with him. I don't want to be bothered with all their political commotion. You'll have your own guesthouse. Number twelve. It's only a five-minute walk down that trail. C'mon, I'll walk you down there."

Dominic was not pleased with the plans. Any of them. Despite being a renowned international humanitarian, the Colonel was a dreadfully uncomfortable man to be alone with, especially for the son of John Russo. The Colonel's walk was not the only thing that reminded him of his father; their personalities were also similar. They both projected their disciplinary attitude in unnecessary circumstances. They shared an intoxicated sense of authority that made them sound abrasive and intrusive, even when they were being nice. Being so similar, Dominic wondered how the Colonel and his father ever got along.

"What about the bags?" Dominic asked in hopes that it might change the Colonel's mind about escorting him.

Turning to the driver, the Colonel spoke some orders in Vietnamese. "He'll take care of 'em," he told Dominic, tossing his weathered cigar in a trashcan.

Dominic reluctantly followed the Colonel's lead down the trail to the guesthouses. "So how are things going in good ol' New Yawk?" the Colonel asked without turning around.

"Not too bad," Dominic answered briefly.

"Not too baaad?" the Colonel abruptly repeated. "Well, if that's the case, why don't you stay here with your sister and give us a hand?"

Dominic grimaced at the Colonel's back, pausing for a moment before answering. "Thanks, but no thanks Colonel. Maybe someday. Right now I'm too busy at the store."

"Sitting behind the counter of a store is no life! Here I am offering you travel and adventure…not to mention the opportunity to save lives."

"Sounds exciting," Dominic cut in, "but like I said, I have business to attend to."

The Colonel didn't push it. "Perhaps Marie can change your mind."

I wouldn't bet on it, Dominic answered in his head.

Thankfully, the Colonel changed the small talk, by adding, "Did she tell you about the big reception tonight at the Metropole?"

"Yes she did…oh! And that reminds me—congratulations on the big award from the UN. The largest ever. Very impressive."

By now Dominic had caught up to the Colonel and the two men were walking next to one another. "Thank you. Did you go to the announcement?"

"I was there."

"Marie said you would be there. So how was it?"

"Well, very interesting…"

"You know," the Colonel cut in, "I hate those pompous events."

"Yeah, I know what you mean."

"A bunch of goddamn millionaires dropping change in a bucket. Did you know that for every dollar spent on charitable causes in the world, over ten thousand is spent on military defense?"

"No, I didn't."

The two men stopped walking as the trail reached the lake. The vast aquatic scene before them demanded observation from all who passed. Ahead, almost eight miles of calm waters glistened in the sunlight.

"It's beautiful to look at, ain't it?" the Colonel stated.

"Sure is," Dominic acknowledged.

"Hanoi is known for its many beautiful rivers and lakes. In fact, 'Ha-Noi' means 'within the rivers.' "

"Oh yeah?"

"This is called West Lake. It's one of the largest lakes in the region. And it's also believed to be one of the most magical. Legend holds that many years ago, a large quantity of bronze was a given to a Buddhist monk who had rendered a great service to the emperor of China. The monk made a huge bell out of the bronze and placed it out there. The sound of the ringing bell could be heard all the way to China, where one day a golden buffalo calf mistook the bell for its mother's call. The young calf came all the way here to Vietnam and trampled on the site in a frenzy, searching for her mother and turning the ground out there into a lake."

The Colonel brushed his fingers through his mustache and continued: "Now they say that all of life's craziness and stresses can be taken away by the spirit of that calf out there. The lake supposedly brings peace and sanctity to everyone around it."

Dominic, being more a realist then a spiritualist, asked, "Does it bring you peace and sanctity?"

"Absolutely! Why do you think I built the compound on its shore?"

Both men smiled. "See my boat over there?" the Colonel said pointing to the left. "It's no yacht, but I enjoy taking her out on the water. Maybe if we get a chance we'll take her for a whirl."

"Sounds good to me," said Dominic. Had Dominic voiced his honest thoughts, he would have told the Colonel that he'd rather schedule a root canal done without painkillers than spend more time with him.

"The Vietnamese are very spiritual about their lakes," the Colonel continued. "They all know that the water, as well as the land, has protected them…and has saved many of their lives during battles."

"Really?" Dominic inquired.

"For sure. During the ancient tribal conflicts, the Vietnamese consolidated around Hanoi because all the lakes and rivers would flood during a typhoon season, and that made it impossible for invading Oriental tribes to conquer this area."

"It drowned their enemies out…very clever."

"You will see that the Vietnamese are very clever people indeed…and very resourceful. They used the same knowledge of the land as a great advantage during the war against the French, then us. And that was five hundred years later!"

To his surprise, Dominic was actually beginning to enjoy the conversation with the Colonel. And learning about Vietnamese customs was valuable to him; knowledge of local history and culture bodes well for business. "It must have made your job difficult trying to fight on unfamiliar terrain?" he questioned.

"You're damn right!" exclaimed the Colonel. "It gave your Dad and me fits!"

With one slip of the tongue, the flow of conversation hit a brick wall. A pause ensued. Although both men knew that their talking would inevitably lead to this—a mention of Dominic's father—it was obvious from their expressions that neither man expected it to come so soon and so naturally. As for the Colonel, there was really no way to consciously avoid the topic of Major John Russo once the conversation turned nostalgic. And now that it was out in the open, he did not, as Dominic expected, shy away from their touchy topic, though the tone of his proud voice sobered. "Your father and me were here in the jungle trying to win that damn war all by ourselves," he stated while still looking out upon the lake.

Dominic was relieved to hear that the Colonel didn't change the subject. And now that his father was mentioned, he was already feeling a little more comfortable. Not comfortable enough for eye contact, however. "I heard that you two were a great team," he responded also looking around the scenery.

"The best," the Colonel boasted, still avoiding eye contact. "Your Dad and me…we led the missions everyone else was afraid of."

Although Dominic did not want to push the conversation too far, there was no denying his interest. His father never told him his war stories nor did he explain why he and the Colonel never spoke after the war. "It must have been something 'cause he never really talked about it."

The Colonel looked at Dominic as if he knew exactly how he felt. Reaching inside his pocket, he said, "Yeah, well…that's because this place at that time could really change a man." He pulled out a folded metal cigar case. Without asking, he offered Dominic one by holding it open. Dominic said no thanks with a shake of his head. "We are all creatures of our environment, ya hear?" the Colonel continued, selecting a cigar for himself. "Put us in a mansion and eventually we'll behave like rich folk. Put us in the ghetto and eventually we'll act like poor folk. Put us in the jungle and soon we'll act like animals. That's the way of the world, kid." His face then disappeared in a cloud of smoke as the flame from his lighter ignited the fresh stogie.

"Put us in a charity and eventually we'll have compassion again?" Dominic chimed. Despite its hypothetical flavor, it was a very personal question. At first, the Colonel didn't respond to Dominic's pointed words. He continued to puff flames out of the tip of his cigar. The awkward pause had Dominic thinking perhaps he should not have been so curious or so comfortable. After a couple more puffs, the Colonel allowed the flame to die out. The lit tip stilled into a slow, deep red burn. The cloud of smoke dissipated. The Colonel's face came back into focus. And his expression suggested deep thought, not discomfort.

"I guess that's right, son," the Colonel finally answered. He then plucked the cigar from his mouth and drew a deep, rare, smoke-free breath, adding: "When you've been to hell, believe me, you'll do anything to get into heaven."

"What about those who can't tell the difference anymore?" Dominic asked.

The Colonel knew Dominic was referring to the late Major John Russo, a man who in totally different ways had deeply affected both of their lives. He also sensed that the conversation was becoming philosophical so he quickly puffed on his cigar. "Well," he said wistfully, "when you spend a lot of time in hell, it becomes hard to see anything clearly anymore."

Dominic looked away with a blank stare, recalling some of the many clashes with his father. It seemed as though the war and all its hell raged inside his old man to his very last day. To Dominic, John Russo was more of a drill sergeant than a father—mean, authoritative and void of compassion. Dominic could still hear the echoes of barking criticism in his head, as though it was happening all over again: *You don't know what it's like to struggle for anything! You're spoiled!* When he drank, it would be worse. *Your college is no good! Your attitude is no good! Your friends are no good!* Nothing he ever did was ever good enough.

During the nights when he was very young, Dominic would often wish for a brother. A brother, he felt, would divert at least some of the overbearing critical attention away from him. If given the choice, he would have selected either a drug addict or criminal as an ideal candidate for his brother. Then perhaps his father would have been more appreciative of him.

Marie unfortunately was no help because, in Dad's view, "she is a girl...and girls don't have to support a family." Besides, Marie never cared enough about her father's "foolish opinions" to let them affect her life. She had never felt any inclination to prove anything to her father. Dominic always admired his sister for that. Her life, the antithesis of John Russo's, was so caring and trusting of the world, not loathsome and defensive.

Dominic peered at the Colonel. Here was a man, he said to himself, who went through hell as his father had, but was nevertheless able to triumph the pain and anguish of the war and move on to happier days. Dominic shook his head in frustration. He was disappointed with himself, for he, too, was trapped by his past. Trapped by a burning desire to still prove something to his father. Three years removed from his death, the ghost of John Russo was still haunting his son.

The Colonel responded almost intuitively to Dominic's personal thoughts. "Look—although we didn't talk after the war, I knew your Dad perhaps better than anyone. He was a complicated man, but believe me he was a true warrior. In fact, he was the best I ever saw, but he was also...how do I say it? A disturbed warrior." Again, he puffed. "You see, it's hard to understand, son. They made us fight half a war here and that was very hard to digest. We didn't win here in Vietnam 'cause we weren't allowed to. Hell, it pisses me off to this very day whenever I think about it. We were betrayed by the system, the government, the bureaucrats, the press, you name it. But the problem was that your Dad...

he took all of it personally. By the end, the whole purpose behind the war was so screwed up that nobody even knew what it was. Meanwhile, people like your Dad and me, we were the ones who were here! We were the ones fightin'! It was our asses that were on the line. Your Dad had a family back home, for crissakes, yet he fought on!" After taking a moment to cool down, the Colonel shook his head and added, "He just couldn't stomach the politics."

Dominic was absorbed by the Colonel's words, feeling as though he was finally getting a firsthand look into his father's closed mind. He seized the opportunity for insight. "If you let the system bother you forever, then you can't just blame the system anymore, can you?"

The Colonel knew that Dominic was questioning his old man, really. "Well, part of that was my fault, son. You see, when you fight together for so many years you become beyond friends, beyond even brothers…you become each other's guardian angel. Hell, we must have saved each other's lives half a dozen times. So because we were so close I would tell your Dad about all the inside politics goin' on, you know, how Washington was holding us back and all. Technically, I was his commanding officer and didn't have to share any political bullshit with him. But I did. And to this day I regret it. Because it backfired on me."

"How so?"

"After a while, right before the end of everything, he turned on me. He felt that I was part of the system and therefore I was part of the problem. I only told him stuff so that he would understand it's all bullshit, but instead of helping him, it made him angrier. Unfortunately, he never spoke to me again after the war. In fact, the next time I saw him was at his funeral and that really broke me up because I realized that if I had never let him in to all the behind the scenes bullshit then maybe he wouldn't have become the way he was."

"So how did you deal with it?" Dominic asked as if his father was somehow listening.

"It was different for me," the Colonel responded without hesitation. "Your old man was right. I was part of the damn system. So at least I got to tell all the bureaucrats and so-called experts that they were full of shit."

"That was consolation enough?"

"It definitely helped. But more important, I accepted the way things were."

"The system?"

"Yes, but I knew it was all really just a bunch of bullshit. When you're in the military, there's nothing you hate more than goddamn politicians and bureaucrats telling you what to do. Ideally, they should only be allowed to determine if we go to war, not how we should fight it. But this was America, and America is all about politics. The difference between your father and me was that I knew that from the get-go. I accepted it. After all, that was the how the game was played. And if you couldn't accept the rules, then you shouldn't be playing. Your father wanted to change the rules. And then when this didn't happen, he couldn't bear it. Why do you think he never made Colonel?"

"Because he refused to accept the system," Dominic said in a disappointed voice.

A few moments of silence passed while both men reflected. In a way, Dominic was glad to have had the discussion for it revealed more about Major John Russo in a few minutes than his father ever did in over twenty years. But he was also disappointed because it further confirmed that his father had let his time as Major John Russo ruin the rest of his life.

The Colonel sensed his statement was a catalyst for thought in his young guest. "Listen, true warriors are not necessarily good fathers or easy people to deal with for that matter. Believe me, I know."

"So do I."

"But there is a lot you can learn from your father's life."

Dominic was curious to hear the Colonel explain what he meant. "Really?"

"Absolutely. Hell, I can see you already have. And you should consider yourself lucky."

"How so?"

"You've learned that your father was his own worst enemy, haven't you? And from what I hear, it seems you are determined not to be the same way in your life. Many people are their own worst enemies because, let's face it, we all have things in life that we can't control—things that make us frustrated and angry. But if we can't change them, then we have to learn to simply accept them and move on. Hell, if we don't accept things we can't control or change, like the past, then we will be miserable forever. Life is too short for misery, kid. You know that as much as anyone."

Dominic nodded. He thought back to his mother's accident. It devastated him to think about how she died. The worst part to stomach was that the killer who hit her was never found. That bastard was still out there somewhere.

As for his father, sure, he died relatively young and tragically also. But his life was much different. His whole life was a tragedy in Dominic's view. A self-perpetuated tragedy inflicted upon himself, his wife, his children.

From the look in Dominic's eyes, the Colonel realized they had talked enough about the past. The two men began to walk again. After a few more minutes, they came to a small white bungalow set among the trees. "Do you know Mother Theresa stayed in this same guesthouse, number twelve, during her visit with us last year?" he asked.

"Is that right?"

"That's right. She was with us for three days."

A one-sided smile moved across Dominic's face.

"So this will make two famous guests in that one little house," the Colonel spoke lightheartedly.

Dominic turned to the Colonel and faked a frown. "Two?" he said playing along, "Who's the other?"

"The other would be you! From what I have heard you are going to be a pretty famous businessman. Isn't that why you're here?"

"We'll see."

The Colonel grinned. "You'd better," he insisted. "I expect a sizable donation from your first million. None of that dropping change in the bucket crap like they do at the UN!"

"You got it."

CHAPTER FIVE

1972

The silver-haired secretary interrupted the meeting by knocking on the door. It was the last thing she wanted to do, but she had no choice. "Colonel Mazer, sir," she stated firmly, "there's a phone call for you."

"I told you no messages!" an irritated voice barked back.

"Ummm...I'm sorry sir," she voiced nervously. "I told him you were not to be disturbed but the gentlemen absolutely insists that he speak with you."

Inside the smoky rectangular room, Colonel Mazer mumbled his frustration under his breath, slammed his pen down, and arose from his chair. "This will only be a minute, gentlemen," he announced to the twelve men of similar stripes sitting around the conference table. "No need to break."

The remaining decorated strategists resumed their discussion while Mazer stomped into a back office and picked up the telephone. "What is it!" he snapped into the receiver.

"It's McCabe," the voice on the other side stated. "We need to talk."

The harsh Colonel's anger was instantly humbled. "When are you comin' in?" he replied cordially

"I'm here," McCabe said. "At the airstrip. Meet me on the south runway. I'll wait for you here. And one more thing..."

"Don't worry," Mazer injected, "I'll drive myself." The Colonel hung up the phone and walked back into the conference room where the rest of the team of advisors was busy plotting offensive strategies against the Vietcong, the communist arm of South Vietnam. "Everything okay, Colonel?" one of his peers asked.

"Yeah," Mazer replied. "They say one of my men down at the hospital is not gonna make it. He wants to see me." The Colonel grabbed his olive baseball cap and mirrored sunglasses off the conference table. "I'll be right back," he stated hurrying out of the room. "Carry on without me."

In the hallway, the Colonel chuckled at his suggestion. *Carry on without me?* It's not like he would be missing anything, really. They had been brainstorming for hours, and, as usual, they hadn't accomplished a thing. Mazer smirked while descending the stairs. *Those idiots couldn't all agree on what year it was by the time I get back.*

The impatient young Colonel exited the building and stopped for a moment to ponder his choices. After scaling the parking lot a couple of times, he decided to take a military police jeep over to the airstrip instead of his car. "Not today, Private," he said to the saluting driver who offered to escort him. The driver knew better than to offer to accompany Mazer as a passenger. He was too young to die, he reminded himself.

The Colonel hopped into the jeep, fired it up, and pressing his booted foot all the way down on the gas pedal, dropped it into gear. A stream of smoke was left behind in the parking lot as the spinning tires struggled to gain a grip of the road.

The madcap manner in which Colonel Mazer drove matched his reputation of a man not afraid to die. If the gas pedal was stuck to the floor and the brakes failed, Colonel Mazer's attitude behind the wheel wouldn't change a bit. The jeep's fat tires screamed around every turn without slowing down. Stop signs and traffic signals were completely ignored. The right of way was seized by force.

Amazingly, Mazer was able to light up a cigar without having to slow down. During the madcap ride, the Colonel's tight face frowned with concentration, his thoughts speeding as fast as his borrowed vehicle in anticipation of his pending encounter. He knew Peter McCabe was not scheduled to be there nor was he staying—therefore he must have come to the Philippines just to speak with him. This conclusion managed to lift an eyebrow on his serious face.

The Colonel completed the twenty-minute drive in a quick ten minutes and raced toward the guarded airport entrance. The young soldier stationed at the gate squinted at the oncoming jeep. He wasn't new to the job therefore he wasn't alarmed. He didn't raise his hands nor draw his gun at the speeding vehicle, as proper security protocol would suggest. There was only one man in the world so recklessly crazy…and he was on the same side. At the last second, the guard managed to confirm his expectation with a fleeting glimpse. "Afternoon, Colonel," he said sarcastically as the jeep blew by him.

Mazer grumbled to himself while he made his final turn onto the south runway, "That bastard already knows I don't come cheap."

————————

By 1972, Colonel Mazer was already a legendary warrior. Back in early 1968 he launched a number of acclaimed counteroffensives and search-and-destroy missions within the Ca Mau Peninsula on the southern tip of Vietnam, helping to drive back the massive enemy "Tet Offensive." From there he went on to engineer and lead a number of secret incursions into Cambodia, whose swift and sudden strikes ceaselessly disrupted North Vietnamese supply routes.

Other men in uniform regarded Mazer as a "trench colonel," and rightfully so. His men revered him. He directed them more by aggressive example than by dialogue—commanding respect from his actions, not just demanding it from his words. He was young, tough, and no-nonsense. The select units he led battled for him with unmatched fervor. They were a personification of his iron-will and fearless tenacity. His platoons had some of the highest enemy kill ratios of the entire war. Colonel Mazer was arguably Uncle Sam's finest young leader. Unquestionably, he was his toughest.

Clifford Mazer did not become Colonel Mazer solely because he was a courageous combatant. No one ascended the United States Army power ladder by mere gallantry alone. He was also a well-schooled politician, a trait he inherited from his deceased father, Josef Mazer. Born in Germany just before the turn of the century, Josef Mazer served as a combat soldier of high merit for the German army during World War I. By 1930, he had defected from the Nazi army and became a naturalized US citizen as well as a founding father for the US intelligence community. Later, under the auspices of the Office of Strategic Services (OSS), the precursor to the Central Intelligence Agency (CIA), Josef Mazer organized an elite group to penetrate the Nazis. His covert squadron was sent into Nazi-occupied Norway where they spent the next five years conducting unconventional warfare, intelligence gathering, and sabotage missions against the Nazis.

During his time in Norway, Josef met and fell in love with Clifford's mother, Helen. She worked as a spy for the Norwegian underground, an anti-occupation resistance faction. In 1942, two weeks following their secret wedding, Helen Mazer was arrested for "insurrection" and sent to a small Nazi prison camp where she gave birth to Clifford. Despite Josef's best efforts, he was able to save only his young son from the clutches of certain death. His twenty-five-year-old, beautiful, brave new bride was killed in an alleged "altercation" with an SS Officer. She died a martyr. A new mother. A war hero.

Devastated beyond repair, Josef Mazer returned to the United States with his new son and settled in a small town in rural North Dakota. Young Clifford was Josef's Mazer's life. He never remarried and had no other relatives. From his son's earliest days in military school, Josef bred Clifford to be a man of distinguished valor. "It's your destiny," he would say, "as the son of the bravest woman in history." Not a week went by where Josef did not tell Clifford a story about his mother's heroics.

Through his father's influence and connections, Clifford was afforded the opportunity to attend West Point, where he graduated at the top of his class. His schooling, though, did not stop there. Josef made sure to teach his handsome son the things in life he couldn't learn in a classroom or on the battlefield—the invaluable art of self-promotion. The future colonel learned from his father how to foster and nurture key relationships in both the military and intelligence communities. The training worked. For Clifford Mazer went on to become a wanted man in both.

In 1967, having already spent two years of distinguished service in Vietnam and one month removed from his father's mysterious death, the twenty-five-year-old soon-to-be-colonel turned down a post as a special operatives agent within the Indochina division of the CIA—choosing instead to return to Vietnam and complete what he considered "unfinished business." The gentleman who was the head of the Indochina division of the CIA at that time had vigorously tried to recruit the upstart Mazer for a post within his division. Although he was unsuccessful in his quest to enlist Mazer, he himself went on to become the director of the CIA later that year. He was also the same gentleman presently awaiting Colonel Mazer's arrival at the airstrip for an impromptu meeting.

———

The beige airstrip of the south runway was a mile-long stretch of pavement that sat next to the ice-blue angry waters of the South China Sea, whose circuitous swirls of wind whipped unrestrained across the open expanse. Heading down the windswept runway, Mazer could see the fuel emissions from the small jet blurring much of the air around his destination. The fuzziness of the jet and limousine images in the nearing distance symbolized his mixed emotions along the way. He was not particularly fond of McCabe. He was arrogant, very bureaucratic, or, in Mazer's more specific words, full of shit. Such was not an unusual opinion of a career military man, since they are not widely known for their fondness of the demeanors carried by government agents. On the other hand, Mazer knew by word of mouth that Peter McCabe had always seemed to demonstrate respect and admiration for his colonelship, which was, of course, consolation to Mazer's inflated ego.

The Colonel parked his jeep and hopped out, immediately pulling his military baseball cap down to his eyebrows to protect it from the thievery of the gusting wind. The fit commander stood statuesquely with his hands on his hips, tight-lipped, gnawing his cigar like a fat piece of bubble gum, a pillar of stoutness in the whistling wind. Save for his looks, Colonel Clifford Mazer had the presence of a much older man. In military years, which measure age by battles, he was indeed a senior citizen.

The door to the black limousine opened and Peter McCabe, wearing a black suit and sunglasses, stepped out alone. He struggled for a moment to gain control of his flapping suit coat as it, along with his hair, blew ungovernably in the ocean gusts. After buttoning his suit coat, McCabe began to approach Mazer, walking upright, evidencing his six foot, three inch frame. *His ugly face looks much better hidden behind those mirrored sunglasses*, Mazer amused himself. The two men had met on a number of group briefings over the course of the past few years, but they were about to meet alone for the first time since Mazer snubbed McCabe's job offer.

"How we doing, Colonel?" McCabe asked, pushing back his wayward hairline.

"That depends on what you're referring to," Mazer replied. "Do you mean me personally or this counterinsurgency they have us working on?"

McCabe grinned. "I guess I mean both."

"Well, hell, I'm doin' all right. This so-called operation they have me working on is a different story. I keep telling those know-nothin' bureaucrats that we should turn our attention to the North Vietnamese. All they seem to be worried about is the damn Vietcong. I've tried to explain to them that we've been fighting this thing the wrong way from day one. If we eliminate the VC in the South, then we still got the North to contend with. But if we defeat the North, the war is over. The 'Cong is only as strong as the will of the North. It's that simple. But nobody else seems to get that but me."

"That's Washington for you Colonel, backasswards," said McCabe.

The two men turned together and walked slowly toward the edge of the runway, where the crashing waves were hitting the mammoth ocean rocks and the setting sun painted a kaleidoscopic horizon sky. But the spectacle Mother Nature bestowed before them failed in all of its breathtaking beauty to distract either man's attention.

"Well, Cliff, the reason why I wanted to see you," McCabe said, coiling his hands tightly around his mouth to light up a cigarette, "is because the President needs someone he can trust for this one."

The Colonel nodded slightly and began to chew his stogie with a little more vigor. The whip of the wind and crash of the ocean demanded a loud volume of conversation.

"What we need to do," McCabe continued, "is dispatch a team for an undercover intelligence mission inside Cambodia."

"You mean more 'Ho Chi Minh Trailbusters'?" Mazer injected sarcastically, quickly adding, "There are plenty of your agency boys qualified to sniff around that area, ain't there?"

McCabe shook his head. He expected Mazer to test his own value. "Not this time, Cliff," he responded. "This has nothing to do with scouting the Ho Chi Minh Trail. And none of the Agency's boys will be used on this one. This team will be made up of six men, all of your choice. The only requirement I have is that most of them are low-level rank. No high profiles. You'll be helicoptered in about twenty-five miles southeast of Parrot's Beak. You will proceed under the radio command of Agent Phillips stationed in Saigon who will be receiving direct orders from me."

"What about our units and bases around the area?" the Colonel queried.

"They will be completely unaware of your presence," McCabe answered. "The only other thing I can really tell you at this time is that this mission, if successful, will finally put an end to this whole fuckin' Vietnam fiasco."

The Colonel paused for a few seconds, reflecting on the tacit weight of McCabe's last statement. The goal of the mission was immaterial, really. The proud Colonel knew that his familiarity with the area and unequaled success with small platoon offensives made him the best, if not the only candidate, to head the President's covert mission.

But Peter McCabe would not get an answer that easy though because Colonel Mazer was not only a masterful politician, he was a also calculated opportunist. He knew that President Keane was probably on hold on the portable phone in the jet, patiently awaiting McCabe to relay the Colonel's answer. He also knew by the immediacy of the meeting that President Keane did not want him to think very long about his decision.

In reality, the President was right. Unlike six years ago, Mazer did not need to think very long about McCabe's latest offer. But before he would commit his services, he needed to settle one very important issue. Peering into the mirrors of McCabe's sunglasses, Mazer asked his own reflection point blank: "And how's the President planning to reward an unknown hero for his unofficial mission?"

"Well, you know, Colonel," McCabe responded cautiously, "I'm personally hoping that you'll decide to stay on permanently with us at the Agency. You know we can use you." After a quick drag of his butt he added, "But the President has indicated that there will be a chair with your name on it on the Joint Chiefs after the election."

McCabe's response provided Mazer with all he wanted to know. The validity of the political promise was of no concern to him. Surprisingly, he did not require any further clarification or confirmation from the President as McCabe had thought he would. As far as Colonel Mazer was concerned, this time—for the first time—a promise just had to be spoken, and not necessarily intended to be kept.

"Where will I train my team?" the Colonel said, implying his acceptance of the proposed task.

"Here on the Isles," McCabe said flicking his cigarette into the open sea, "but over on Palawan. I'll be back in three weeks. That should give you ample time to recruit. Remember, all we ask is that you don't use any superstars. And as for your fellow advisors back at headquarters…tell them that you are finally taking some R&R."

McCabe turned away without a goodbye or handshake, just a nod. He had his man. He walked briskly to the jet while Mazer stared blankly into the white-capped ocean. Once McCabe was back inside the plane, the pilot immediately turned it around, and with a loud rush, the sleek jet raced down the runway and took off into the swirling wind.

Inside the soaring iron eagle, McCabe picked up the portable phone from his seat. "He's ours," he said into the receiver. "Yes. On our terms."

Mazer looked up at the shrinking jet knowing exactly what was being said inside it. He smiled and puffed his stogie in the setting sun. He, too, had his man. *On his terms.*

CHAPTER SIX

1992

Metropole Hotel Nightclub
Hanoi, Vietnam
August 11, 9:33PM

The music and mood on the dance floor was fast-paced, yet she seemed to move in slow-motion. She was dancing in a group, but as far as Dominic was concerned she was the only person out there. Her thin body was loosely fitted with a light-blue, high-cut dress that tortured all admirers by being one step behind her twirling figure. The varying dance floor lights randomly colored her bleached white skin—incessantly radiant in shades of blue, red, and green. Her angelic aura remained aglow even during the intermittent flashes of darkness in the smoke-filled nightclub. Being the only blonde hair, blue-eyed woman in all of Hanoi, perhaps all of Vietnam, her beauty was already legendary long before Dominic was introduced.

"Julie," Marie declared to her fixated brother, returning to the seat next to him. "Julie Perry." Although older than her brother by almost two years, Marie's delicately petite face and figure, and long, reddish-brown hair gave her the appearance of a still-growing girl. As often is the case for those who devote their efforts to others, care for her own looks was not a time-consuming effort.

A few moments passed before Dominic realized Marie had said something to him. "What?" he asked.

"Her name is Julie," Marie said, rolling her eyes.

Dominic frowned feebly with confusion. "Who?"

Marie inhaled her cigarette and ignored her brother's temporary cluelessness. "She works for AFP. She's French-Canadian. Originally from Montreal, but she's bounced around a lot. Went to college in Paris. Worked in London. Let's see, what else? Hmmm…oh yeah! She's also my roommate." With that she smiled and turned away.

"Roommate, eh?" Dominic said sharply. "How come you never…"

"Relax," she interrupted, "She's been with AFP only a few weeks."

"Is she…"

"No," Marie answered, again reading her younger brother's mind with psychic precision. "She's single."

Dominic tried to fight it, but he had to break out a grin. As usual, Marie couldn't resist injecting her personal take on the situation. "But I wouldn't get too excited ol' bro' of mine."

"And why's that?" he questioned innocently enough.

"Well, not to stick a pin in your over-inflated ego, but she is, as you can see, in very high demand in these parts."

Dominic was not one to worry about competition when it came to women. He sipped his Singha beer and took a long look at Julie's rhythmic elegance. Three guys, like bees swarming sweet honeycomb, were dancing around her, seemingly battling for her exclusive attention. Scattered throughout the bar, a few dozen or so less bold ones were likewise in awe of the hypnotic back-and-forth bounce of Julie's firm lower body. Occasionally the keen observers were rewarded with a split second of perfect timing—when Julie would raise her arms behind her head while under a direct shine of a dance floor spotlight, revealing the entire outline of her figure underneath her dress.

"That's not a problem," Dominic finally answered confidently to his sister.

"Oh yeah?"

"Yeah. I'm not worried at all. I got a secret weapon."

"And what's that?"

Dominic pointed at Marie. "You mean *who's* that?"

"What's that supposed to mean?"

"Well, every night before you go to bed you can tell her how wonderful I am."

Marie shook her head back and forth. "Oh no. Absolutely not! You're on your own. I am not lying for you. You have to do that all by yourself." Despite their absence of regular company, Marie still maintained a stabbing sense of humor when it came to her brother.

"Oh, I'm not asking you to lie," Dominic countered. "I want you to tell her the truth about me. Don't you think I'm wonderful?" He spread his arms anticipating a compliment.

"Sure, you're wonderful," she replied bluntly, "but that's only as a brother. As a boyfriend, you're downright rotten!"

The two siblings smirked at each other and enjoyed their drinks.

Despite her petite frame, Marie Russo was as immovable as a skyscraper. At an early age she was already refusing to accept her father's parenting. He would yell and she would rebel, typically by running away down the block to a girlfriend's house for a few days. Eventually her mother would coax her to come back home, but it was only a matter of time before a new battle would erupt. By the time she graduated high school, Marie was battling back against her father, verbally, as well as in other ways. Dominic still swears his sister dated derelict older men throughout high school solely because it, in his words, "pissed off Dad."

One time Dominic felt compelled to physically throw one of his sister's dates out of the house—"before," he explained to her, "Dad comes home and gives the guy a much worse beating."

"Who do you think you are?" Marie yelled at him. "I will not allow you or anyone else to control my life!"

After the incident, she refused to speak to her brother for weeks. Dominic later responded casually to his sister's silent treatment by telling her, "You don't like that dirt bag anyway. You only like the fact that Dad hates him."

By the time Marie enrolled to study social work at New York University, she had shut her father out of her life completely. When her mother died tragically in the car accident, father and daughter had a brief reconciliation. But just like old times, the ceasefire was fragile and short-lived. And by less than a year later, at the time of his tragic death, Marie and her father were once again not on speaking terms.

After college, Marie became a "soldier for peace". She accepted an invitation from Colonel Mazer to join his AFP charity at her father's funeral service. At the time Dominic believed his sister's decision to join up with the Colonel was another way of her rebelling against Dad. Colonel Mazer was, after all, a name that was not to be used growing up in the Russo home. Why? No one was ever told.

While placing his drink back on the table, Dominic told his sister that he had a long conversation with the Colonel earlier in the day.

"Good, I'm glad," she answered. "He's really not that bad when you get to know him. You just got to know when to avoid his moods."

"Actually, he was better than I expected him to be. You know sometimes he reminds me of Dad."

"That walk of his!" Marie quipped.

"Yeah," Dominic smiled. "You know it's funny. We ended up talking a lot about Dad."

"Really?" Marie's expression was somewhere in between amazement and bewilderment.

"That's right. At first he was brought up by accident…but after his name was out in the open, well then, we just kept goin'. Do you two ever talk about him?"

"Naaah. There's nothing to discuss."

"He gave me an explanation on why Dad got all fucked up from the war."

"Fucked up?" Marie interjected, her tone unnaturally resentful. "Boy is that an understatement. The man's whole life was a war. And everyone was the enemy…including himself." After an uncharacteristic big gulp of her gin and tonic she continued, "Ya know…the most tragic part of it all was that Dad should have been happy with his life. Sure, he was wounded mentally and physically from the war, but it was not like he was confined to a wheelchair or anything. Besides, he's the one who chose to be a soldier for all those years. No one made him stay on that long. And when he finally did come home, he made a good living with the store. Also, he had a good family. If anyone should have been miserable it should have been me, you, and Mom for having to always put up with Major John Russo."

Dominic took a long slug from his bottle. Marie looked at her brother and with a hopeful smile told him: "Let's just hope you can file for divorce in the afterlife. Mom put up with enough of his shit during her life."

"Cheers," Dominic toasted. His hope was certainly the same.

With that, Dominic placed his finished bottle down, excused himself, and headed toward the men's room on the other side of the club. While making his way through the crowd, he scanned the dance floor in search of Julie. He knew Marie was watching him, so tried his best to be discreet.

Turning his head towards the dance floor, Dominic could not locate Julie there. She was gone. Casually he glanced over at the bar; she wasn't there either. Turning his head forward, Dominic was taking aback. There she was, only a few steps up ahead in his path. Their eyes met for a split second before they both quickly looked in another direction. For Dominic, it was too late to change his path, so he slowed down and made the best of it.

He could not have planned it better. The cooperative squeeze of the crowd abolished the risk of rudeness and enabled him to pass behind her very closely, seemingly by mere chance. Dominic seized this incidental opportunity of fate by reaching out and feeling the delicate smoothness of her skin as he maneuvered behind her. Politely, he murmured "Excuse me" in her ear during his leisurely pass while gently touching her elbow. He made sure to inhale deeply as his nose slid past the back of her neck. His eyes stayed shut for a little more than an eye blink while he savored her captured sweet aroma. He didn't exhale. He held in the apprehended air of her fragrance until he arrived at the men's room.

Once inside the bathroom, he released his breath gradually and was again weakened by her sweetened bouquet. Turning on the sink, Dominic gazed into the mirror. Be it physical or mental, every look in the mirror triggers a self-evaluation of sorts. In Dominic's case, this look triggered both. Sweat had surfaced on his brow from the combination of the crowd and his nervousness. Before reaching under the faucet, he raised the hand he had touched her with and ingested a final faint dose of her presence before washing it away.

Dominic was far from shy. Women had come too easily for him to be bashful. But now, for the first time in his memory, he found himself intimidated by a woman's beauty. He also found himself embarrassed by his insecure behavior. Staring blankly into the cloudy mirror over the sink, he rehearsed lines in his head. How should he introduce himself? What question should he ask her? What witty remark can he say in passing? He splashed water on his face. *Stop it*, he told himself. *Get yourself together, dammit.* After all, practicing lines was ridiculous. Julie was too beautiful for rehearsed preparation. Men must act unnaturally around her every day of her life. He drew upon his own experience, which reminded him that women who are that attractive and enchanting can usually see right through a man's intentions. They have the uncanny ability to smell a premeditated pick up a mile away.

In the back of his head, Dominic's subconscious alarm clock suddenly rang, reminding him that it was time to leave. Remaining where he was any longer would, he feared, allow Julie to make unflattering assumptions about his bathroom behavior. Impressions, at least for now, meant everything. So all must be perfect. Or at least appear that way. After pushing back his thick hair, he exited back into the boisterousness of the club, as if nothing but quick business had gone on in there.

Making his way back through the crowd, Dominic could not locate her again. This time his eyes scanned slowly; he was hoping to only capture her image in the corner of his eye. A direct look would certainly reveal the obviousness of his interest—an unfavorable consequence given the inevitability of their introduction. Arriving back at the table, he froze like a deer facing oncoming headlights. The introduction would be sooner rather than later.

There she was, sitting with her legs crossed in his former chair. She was talking with Marie, but all Dominic noticed was that her wonderful thin dress was unable to reach over her knee. She sat as alluringly as she danced, he thought to himself. Marie gladly interrupted her brother's awe. "Hey Dom? I want you to meet a friend."

Julie looked up smiling at him. Thankfully Dominic's natural charm didn't fail him. It kicked in on cue and subdued his nervousness. With a handsome smile, he approached from around the other end of the table, extended his hand and declared with a tender, natural, unplanned look in his expressive eyes, "Hello. Nice to meet you. I'm Dominic Russo."

"Hi, Dominic," she said, offering her hand. "I'm Julie Perry." Her pleasant voice was as appetizing to his ears as her face was to his eyes.

Dominic took the offering of Julie's delicate fingers gently into his palm, bowing his head ever slightly in homage. His symbolic act was so subtle that any onlooker, including the most suspicious ones, like his observant sister, would be unable to pick it up. A handshake can speak a thousand words. In that case, this simple handshake becomes a valued opportunity for a man to silently yet unequivocally proclaim his reverence to a very special person.

Julie, on the other hand, was fully aware of the gesture. Equally inconspicuous, she declared her appreciation by simply resting her hand in Dominic's palm for a brief, yet undeniable, extra moment. In that very instant, her requited message was clear. As they let go of each other's hands, they each grinned, having profoundly communicated without speaking.

"Hey Dom," Marie asked, "Did you meet Senator Haynes yet?"

"Not yet," he said, sitting down.

Marie was tempted to stay and torture her younger brother, but she was merciful. "I'm gonna go see if I can find the Senator. Anyone want to come?"

"No thank you, Marie," said Julie.

"Maybe later," said Dominic.

Winking so that only he could see, Marie got up and left her thankful brother. She had known all along that Dominic and Julie would be attracted to one another. It was inevitable. They were both confident, independent, and great-looking. And besides, they had both already asked her everything about the other.

"You're not interested in meeting a Senator from your own country?" Julie asked, her question having a hint of sarcasm to it.

"Not particularly," Dominic responded and confidently added, "But if you would rather that I leave, I most certainly will…"

"Oh no," she had to say. "Please stay here as long as you like."

"Thank you," he said, smirking, having won a small flirtatious victory.

"So how do you like Hanoi?" she asked.

Dominic nodded his head a few times. "It's an experience."

"Actually this party is quite deceiving. Usually Hanoi is a very boring place at night. Your sister was the one who convinced the Colonel to have this celebration."

"That doesn't surprise me," he answered and then asked, "Do you like it here?"

"I love it. The Colonel and the rest of the people at AFP are wonderful. They are like a family. I've only been here a month, but it has been a very rewarding experience. The work we do for children is so amazing. I'm glad I came."

"That's great. It's always nice to see someone who really enjoys what they are doing."

"I agree. And so what is it that you do back in New York?"

Dominic used the question as an invitation to slide his chair closer. This way, they would not have to speak so loudly. And more importantly, Dominic could take in her scent.

Strategically speaking, being closer also came with a share of risks. Dominic was now forced to control the roam of his eyes, which had already been a difficult struggle. His eyes desperately fought to betray his gentlemanly nature and stare down at those naked inviting thighs peeking out from her dress. Being right next to her, breathing in her fragrant aroma, made it all the more difficult to restrain the powerful instincts of his vision.

It was clear by her return of body language that Julie welcomed Dominic's gesture. She, too, shifted her chair a little closer to his and crossed her legs in the other direction. Dominic took a quick, seemingly unintended glance down, her thin dress was still falling well short of her knee. Her dress seemed to be cooperating perfectly, almost too perfectly, like it had been paid off in advance by all the men in the room.

Dominic took in an extra-long breath and again sampled her fragrance. The temptation was torturous. "I own a small jewelry store," he finally answered while breathing out.

"Oh really," said Julie. "Your girlfriend must be delighted." Her abrupt statement was really a question.

Dominic stared directly into her eyes. They were truly captivating, like crystal-blue marbles. "That's exactly why I don't have one," he declared with a smirk. "I need to be very wary of a woman's intentions."

Julie smiled and squinted her eyes slightly. Such a statement was easy to make so far from home. Whether she was ready to believe him was another story.

Dominic was quick to respond to her doubtful expression. "Let me put it this way," he admitted, "there's no one in particular."

Julie smiled without the squint this time. She knew she had gotten a little more honesty.

"And so is it Mrs. Perry or Miss Perry?" Dominic asked. His usual confidence and comfort level was settling in smoothly. Besides, being fortunately armed with striking looks himself, he had the luxury of not having to procrastinate his objectives.

"Neither," she rebutted. "Ms. Perry." Apparently, she had a similar philosophy regarding procrastination.

"I see," Dominic nodded. "So is there anyone…"

"No one in particular," she interrupted.

With the end of her statement, the first slow song of the night began to play on the dance floor. Dominic didn't hesitate. He stood up over her, bowed his head, and held out his arm in the same manner a servant ushers a queen. "Would you mind showing me how they dance here in Hanoi, Ms. Perry?"

"Sure," she said smiling and placing her hand in Dominic's.

Once on the dance floor, they embraced in royal fashion at first. Not too close. Not too far. Their body language, though—the most honest, involuntary communicator of all—soon took over, engaging them further in intimate wordless conversation. With each simultaneous step, they inched a bit closer together. In one hand, Dominic held the shapely curve of Julie's back, in the other, her soft fingers. They smiled at each other, jointly amused at their undeniable instincts. Their physical magnetism and their spiritual chemistry definitely meshed.

Their voices grew softer as they drew nearer to each other's ears. Soon their bodies were pressing up against each other's, swaying rhythmically as one. They talked, laughed, and shut out the rest of the world for three songs. Three memorably slow songs.

With every step, exchanged glance, and shared laugh their attraction swelled, culminating later that night in guesthouse twelve where it took nearly three hours to exhaust their volcanic passion. The process started out slowly.

Just the way Dominic wanted. He knew patience, if it could be exercised properly, would only intensify the moment. A moment he wanted to savor forever.

Julie's milk-white body was a festival to his eager senses. And he made sure to devote plenty of time to ingesting her through each one. He first watched her slowly slip off her heels…step out of her fallen dress…and lay down next to him on the bed. Gently, he then slid both his hands down and back up her face…shoulders…waist…and legs. Her thin body squirmed with desire from the touches of his gliding fingers.

Julie was also very patient with the moment. She surrendered her body completely to Dominic, allowing him to control the pace and push her passion to its brink. Her slithering body was his to indulge. All of it. Without the restraint or caution natural to first time encounters. His ears tuned in to the sounds of her gentle purring. While above her reclining body, he stared into her closed eyes. She was so enchanting…so innocently and perfectly beautiful.

Dominic teased the tempting moment further by kissing her sweet soft lips. Then delicately he made his way downward, tasting the salty skin covering her now pulsating body. Deeply he inhaled each one of her natural fragrances. Her scents of passion put him over the edge. He could no longer fight his erupting desire.

When he could no longer hold back, he wrapped his strong arms around her and pulled their bodies together. She immediately wrapped her legs around him and pulled him in. Attached, they whispered continuously into each other's ear. Never before had Dominic surrendered so much emotion to a woman. He couldn't stop a single word from exposing his deepest thoughts. Fervently, he pushed into her and told her how she had him…how he was not letting her go…ever!

Julie responded with overwhelming and uninhibited desire. Her thin back arched, again and again, as she pulled him in. With each powerful lunge she gripped his waist tighter. Together, in a tidal wave of emotion, they repeatedly pushed each other to the height of ecstasy. Like it was the first time for both of them. Like it was the last time for both of them.

CHAPTER SEVEN

1972

Kampot, Cambodia
August 29, Daybreak

The dark shadows shrouding the beach's landscape start to soften when Mother Nature is well rested and eager to begin her return to color. The true essence of her beauty is found not in the destination of her transitions, but the journey she takes to get there. At this hour, she likes to slowly pale the blues of the ocean, greens of the surrounding foliage, and yellows of the soft sand gradually out of darkness into various shades of gray. To simply turn on all the lights at once would spoil the gentle splendor of one of her most glorious moments.

Without a sound, she next introduces the first rays from the rising morning sun, travelling low and parallel along the awakening landscape. The waves of the Gulf of Thailand swell up to capture these twinkling rays. With x-ray precision, the unique fingerprints of each curling wave are illuminated by the diagonal beams of sunlight upon the crashing surf. Slowly and surely, as the altitude and intensity of the sun rises, she allows her light to paint its way across the rough deep-blue ocean. Inch by inch, the uprising rays of the sun sparkle the surface of the vast waters, showering color and luster upon the muted images in its path. Within an hour's time, sunlight finally reaches all the way across the distant visual horizon. Full color is again restored. And once again, a new day of war and misery in Southeast Asia begins magnificently.

This dawn, in all its peaceful glory, arrived on the fifth day after Colonel Mazer's Operation Inferno unit was dropped in at Kampot, Cambodia, thirty-six miles from the Vietnam border. The Inferno unit's two youngest members, Greene and JD, were lying low like predators in the elephant grass at the edge of the beach. Their assignment was to scout the waters of the Gulf of Thailand for merchant vessels that were believed to be supplying Vietcong strongholds located near the Inferno unit's position. However, if they saw a suspicious vessel, the crouching, vigilant lions were not to attack nor even alert the rest of their deadly pride. Their orders were to only mark it down in their logs. A tough task for two agile and ferocious cats.

Greene, his freckled, white skin hidden behind a cake of camo cream, lowered his binoculars and took a drink of water from his canteen. "Ain't she beautiful?" he said to his partner close by.

"Who's she?" JD responded, still peering through his binoculars.

"Right out there…the ocean, man! She's most gorgeous during sunrise!"

JD dropped his binoculars and shook his head slowly at his partner. His brown skin was hidden behind streaks of green and black camo cream. "You're in trouble, man. You are definitely in big trouble…"

"Why's that?"

"We've been here less than a week," JD explained, "and you're looking at ocean water like it's your damn girlfriend or somethin'. That ain't no good, man."

"Naaaahh!" Greene replied smiling. "You just can't appreciate nature like I can!"

JD unscrewed the cap to his canteen. "I can see that shit every day back home in LA!" After taking a gulp, he proudly declared, "And there's plenty of bikinis to appreciate with it!"

"Yeah…well, I never saw the ocean until I joined up."

"Get the fuck outta here!"

"I'm serious, man. There ain't no ocean in damn Cincinnati, Ohio!"

"How 'bout lakes and shit?"

"We got some rivers and all, but nothin' like this. Man, this is like fuckin' paradise if you think about it. Clear blue ocean, deserted beach, palm trees…"

JD smiled. "All we need are two ladies!"

"Yeah," Greene smirked, "and another for you!"

The two soldiers, both eighteen, shared another one of their many laughs together. Apart from geography, their backgrounds were identical—poor, inner-city, and tough—the exact profile Colonel Mazer wanted on his Inferno team. Being the two youngest members on the Inferno team, they bonded from the initial days of training back in the Philippines, where they met for the first time. By now they were the closest of friends. And friendships forged in battle are the strongest bonds in the world.

They were also both fathers, though never husbands. Greene had a four-year-old daughter, JD, a two-year-old son. They talked about their kids, but most consistently they talked about girls. Their favorite pastime was to brag to each other about how many girls they'd already been with and how many will be added to list once they were, in their words, "back in da' States...back on da' prowl." In that way, they were no different from their fellow fighting peers. All soldiers of war are self-proclaimed legendary lovers. Just ask them.

JD and Greene stood out from their peers in other ways though. Both had experienced heavy bloodshed in their first tour of duty. Their reports cited them for their outstanding combat skills and remarkable composure under treacherous, even hopeless circumstances. Naturally they each jumped at the opportunity to serve the renowned Colonel Mazer when he contacted them. "Hungry, disciplined, humble," Mazer later described them to McCabe, "with killer instincts that raged like teenage hormones."

Although JD and Greene were the most inexperienced combat soldiers on the Inferno team, McCabe was nevertheless pleased by the choice. And shortly into the Inferno's team training, it was clear to everyone that Colonel Mazer had accurately diagnosed the skills and resolve of the two youngest kittens in his elite litter of killers.

Back at the unit's encampment, five hundred yards northwest of Greene and JD's morning post on the beach, Colonel Mazer had just finished his radio call with CIA Senior Operative Agent Steve Phillips in Saigon, the team's only outside contact. Together with Major John Russo, Phillips was the only man in the unit he had known prior to the Operation Inferno mission. The rest of the team, Hilliard, Doc, and Mendez, were all handpicked by Mazer from reports of their outstanding skill sets.

Russo was busy cleaning grains of sand from his Avtomat Kalashnikov, Model 1947—a weapon more commonly recognized under as an AK-47 assault rifle. True to his unique character, Russo was the only Inferno soldier who chose to arm himself with the weapon used by the enemy. He had his reasons, though, and they were certainly difficult to dispute.

Originally the AK-47 was developed and manufactured by the Soviets after the Second World War. The one in Russo's hands, as well as those in the hands of the rest of the communist forces in Southeast Asia, were—like everything else a decade later would be—made in China. Though heavier and slower-firing, the AK-47 was more robust, more reliable, and more accurate than its American counterpart, the M-16.

Russo used to carry an M-16 in the jungle but not anymore. A year and a half earlier during the heat of a fierce fire fight, his M-16 jammed. While he scrambled to clean the barrel, he was hit in the thigh by two enemy bullets. From that point on, the Major chose to carry into combat the same gun that had wounded him. At that time, very few veteran gunslingers would argue against the AK's unofficial title, "the best small firearm produced in the world."

The rest of the Inferno soldiers carried the US forces standard issue M-16, except for its leader. Colonel Mazer chose to prowl bearing an altogether different weapon. It was a gun that fired only a single shot, but such a connotation was misleading because that single shot could, in the Colonel's blunt words, "end the party." The US Army weapon designers called it the M-79 grenade launcher. To its infantry carriers, it was simply known as "the Blooper." Under any name, it was a one-of-a-kind killer, for at that time, no counterpart existed in any armed force on earth.

Visually, it resembled a sawn-off shotgun. In the expert hands of the leader of Operation Inferno, the Blooper, with a maximum range of 300 meters, could launch a finned grenade into a bullseye 175 meters away. Upon impact, anyone within a five-meter radius would be killed from the blast. End of party.

Mazer turned his head and asked his Major, "What time they due back?"

Russo stopped dusting his gun and checked his watch. "Twenty minutes… why? Do you want me to call them in?"

Mazer's eyes looked away from Russo's face before he responded. "No," he stated. "That should be fine."

"What's up?" Russo questioned.

"We're moving out."

"Where to?"

"Northwest," Mazer said nonchalantly.

"Where?" Russo again pried.

"Toward Parrots Beak."

The Colonel knew his Major wouldn't like the orders. After several years together in Vietnam, they knew exactly how each other thought, which, apart from combat strategy, was almost never alike. In recent times, Major John Russo had grown increasingly brash and confrontational with his Colonel. Mazer accurately described him as an incapable politician who would often talk first and think second.

By choice, Russo was also Colonel Mazer's right hand man. He had helped the Colonel engineer and direct each one of his famed offensives and counteroffensives dating back to 1968. And the deserving Major never objected to the fact that legend, as well as superiors, gave all the credit and glory of success to the Colonel. Even so, the tumultuous relationship between the two veteran soldiers was more accurately described as a partnership, rather than a friendship. A true shotgun marriage if there ever was one. Together on the battlefield, outnumbered and outgunned, they routinely overcame the enemy. Yet together in a bar, the same two men could not get along long enough to finish one beer.

When he first thought it over, Colonel Mazer almost declined to ask his longtime teammate to join him on the Operation Inferno mission. *It's not worth the bullshit*, he tried to persuade himself. It was, however, only a fleeting debate, for he had no choice but to recruit his longtime partner. Despite his unpolished attitude, Russo was a truly masterful battle strategist as well as a dauntless soldier. Operation Inferno, the most important mission of the entire war, called for the best—and Major John Russo was by far the finest warrior the young Colonel had ever known.

Born and raised in Brooklyn, the only child of Italian immigrants, John Russo had an unguarded character. In the early 1940s, before he was born, his newlywed parents, Giuseppe and Sylvia Russo, had lost their modest home outside Palermo, Sicily, in one of Mussolini's violent purges against anyone rumored to be "anti-Fascist." Although a renowned bricklayer by trade, Giuseppe Russo was left with no job to support his family, no money to pay for the bricks to rebuild his home, and therefore, no choice.

In the summer of 1943, when General Patton and the Allies landed upon the soil of Sicily, Giuseppe and Sylvia Russo left. With husband carrying two bags of clothes and wife carrying their unborn child, the young couple spent borrowed money on a one-way ticket across the Atlantic Ocean. They were headed to a place where Giuseppe was told by friends "a million bricks a day were being laid."

Once in America, Giuseppe Russo's luck soon changed, as he was able to support his wife and young son with his gifted, callous-ridden hands. He found work in his trade, and, eventually, during the height of the post-war construction boom, he managed to become a well-salaried union laborer. Unfortunately, the hard work caught up to Giuseppe two weeks before his thirty-third birthday. Early that morning, while working on a building's foundation in lower Manhattan, Giuseppe fell face first into his mortar mix. A massive heart attack had tragically cut his life short. His widowed wife was twenty-eight. His son, only five.

At a very early age, the writing on the blackboard was clear: school was not for the rambunctious John Russo. It seemed like every week he was involved in another fight. Most of the time it was with fellow students, but sometimes he would even lose his cool with his teachers. Of course, if what young John said was true, then none of it was ever his fault. Ultimately however, Sylvia Russo's undying dreams of a highly educated son were put to their final grave when John punched the principal of his high school and earned himself an indefinite expulsion.

Three jobs in three months also convinced Sylvia that her angry young son did not have the discipline for work. After she threw him out of the house for the umpteenth time, John Russo, young, confused, and pissed off at the world, finally turned to another relative—his open-armed uncle. Uncle Sam.

To the surprise of everyone who knew him, most notably his mother, disgruntled citizen John Russo's transformation into Private John Russo was successful. He didn't, as everyone predicted he would, challenge the army's system. At least at first. He easily adjusted to a life of strict routines and adapted immediately to discipline. Most shockingly, he accepted the constant overriding authority in his new life. John Russo, the soldier-to-be, was indeed a new man. His former unyielding character was gone, or at least put aside for the moment. There were no outbursts or personal rebellions against authority. Defiance, it seemed, was a part of his immature past. For now, it was replaced by order, discipline, and patriotism.

Putting on training fatigues and leather boots did not change the fact that deep inside John Russo was still an angry young man. What the military—the warring US military—provided him with was the perfect outlet for his anger. A few rules did not bother him much. He managed to channel all his rage into his training. He committed himself to the challenges before him and fiercely dedicated himself, for the first time in his young life, to accomplishment. Before long, Russo was running further and faster than the rest of his outfit. He was also working harder and yelling louder than the others during drills. His unparalleled dedication paid off. Both physically and mentally he quickly blossomed into a skilled soldier. He had found his calling.

Within two and a half months the verdict was in. The reports were exceptional. Superior officers raved about him, calling him "a quick learner"; "exceptionally skilled with light-infantry weapons"; "an expert in hand-to-hand combat"; and "a natural strategist." The experienced men who trained John Russo were all in agreement. The young private from Brooklyn, New York, was born to fight. "If we had more like him," one of his training officers professed, "the war would have been over by now."

On the jungle battlefields of Vietnam, the young new soldier did not disappoint the hype. His performances quickly surpassed the highest expectations pinned on him and he moved meritoriously through the ranks. His courage, skill, and ingenuity were not only vital, but often heroic, to the missions that he was assigned. The combatant he had trained so hard to become was complete. And he was one tough son of a bitch.

For years, Russo relished the rush of being a soldier of war. He loved the camaraderie, charge of a battle, chess game of strategy, struggle of survival, euphoria of victory. Soldier of war was his made-to-order personality, and he was proud of it.

But the steel pot helmet covering his shaved head did more than protect him against bullets and shell fragments flying through the bush. It was also a cover up. John Russo's newly molded persona as a soldier of war was, in part, a denial. A distraction. A way of not having to deal with the more complicated side of him, John Russo, the man. The formula behind his two separate personalities was inverted. The more he spent time as a soldier of war, the less he needed to be a man. So the soldier roared ahead.

The soldier had "Charlie" to deal with—a fanatical, fearless adversary. Charlie was brutal, unrelenting, and most important, an external enemy. Russo was often dropped into Charlie's backyard. And he had to be totally committed to the cause to not leave in a body bag. To defeat Charlie on his home turf, the soldier must think every thought, dominate every feeling, and act each action. If you strayed from that mind-set in the jungles of Vietnam, you were dead.

As for consciences, they were a civilian concern. Soldiers of war had enough physical weight to carry on their backs. Remorse? Regret? No way. Safer to wear fluorescent uniforms in the Southeast Asian jungle than to ponder such dangerous sentiments. There's no room for hesitation in war. Not a moment can be wasted for reflection. When dealing with Charlie, there's no time to second guess or ask why. No time for ideals. In other words, no time for the inner man.

But a man can only deny his doubts for so many years. Sooner or later his mind, protected underneath the metal helmet, will embark on a mission of its own, whether the soldier wants it or not. And the goals of that internal mission are often at odds with the goals of the combat soldier. That mental mission pursues a separate identity, surfaces a different personality, seeks a different perspective. The process can be counter to all his training and perilous to a fighting cause. A battle erupts internally when a soldier focuses on his own thoughts and feelings. If it is not contained, eventually the process culminates with the soldier seeking to justify his actions—a fatal journey in the midst of a horrific, prolonged war.

To John Russo, the mission going on inside his head was the real enemy. Perhaps the only enemy in the world that scared him. As the years wore on and the casualties piled up, the cause behind the war blurred. It seemed like each new day brought with it another destroyed village. Or a decimated family. Or a dead child. With every dead friend and foe, the loyal soldier—who John Russo had worked so hard to create—was wearing off. The cover up was melting in the sweltering Southeast Asian heat. Someone else inside him wanted to take over. Exactly what this personality was all about, he didn't know. He didn't want to find out either. Not while in Vietnam. Not ever for that matter. Yet despite his best efforts, the soldier of war found it more and more difficult to ignore the thoughts and questions battling inside his head.

In desperation he belligerently fought back, attempting to force his inner self back into hibernation by totally consuming himself with more of Charlie. He fought more battles, took more chances along the way. It wasn't working though. His thoughts...his conscience...his search for an identity kept surfacing. Finally, the soldier he created he was unable to repress John Russo alone. He needed help. So he enlisted more responsibilities to his life. This allowed him to create more personas, more ways to repress. He got married. Now he was a supporting husband. He had a couple of kids. Now he was a father whose kids needed him. More mouths to feed, less time to think. His country needed him. His fellow soldiers needed him. John Russo had done all he could to eliminate any time for reflection in his life.

But the enemy inside still haunted him.

After a reflective pause, the olive-skinned, dark-haired, ruggedly handsome Major finally responded to his Colonel. "Parrot's Beak?" he said in disturbed tone.

The Colonel continued his nonchalance. He didn't want to get into it. "That's right."

"Is Phillips fuckin' crazy!" Russo barked. Then, not referring to the temperature, he added, "He knows how hot it is up there!"

The Colonel didn't look up, nor respond. Instead he began to calmly gather and pack his gear. Obviously, he didn't like the idea of invisibly trekking through some of the most hostile territory in Southeast Asia either, but those were the instructions. And there was no room for debate. He was to radio Phillips in exactly three days when the team reached its coordinates, fifty miles northwest of their present position, and not a minute earlier.

Russo pushed the debate. "Can we just stop and think about this for a minute? There is absolutely no strategic advantage—no goddamn reason at all—for us to reposition ourselves to the northwest. You know better than I do that we are opening ourselves up. Not only for detection, but for a fuckin' engagement with the VC or anyone else out wandering around up there." Russo then leaned his powerful assault rifle up against a large rock and spread his arms apart. "Then what is the CIA gonna say…huh?…it wasn't us because we don't fuckin' exist. It was fuckin' aliens or something shooting at the Vietcong. You know the VC is gonna have some fuckin' renegade reporter from the States with them just waitin' for a scoop like this. What are we suppose to do then…kill him too?"

The Colonel had his back turned to his Major. He answered calmly, seemingly inattentive, "We do whatever is necessary to accomplish the goals."

Russo took a few steps closer to his long time boss. "Goals?" he implored. "What fuckin' goals…? So far, all I see are unknown, undetermined goals. And all they are giving us is piecemeal bullshit! If we keep operating like this, their hidden goals are sure to get us all killed!"

Unresponsive, the Colonel continued packing, avoiding eye contact with his Major. After a few moments of silence, Russo pressed, "You've got to get some more information from them…something…anything. Dammit, we can't just head north without knowing what we might find along the way. I don't care how invisible we are…I don't care how well-trained we are…we got no friends up there."

Fed up with the conversation, Mazer turned around and looked directly into Russo's eyes. "Now you listen, dammit! You knew as well as me that this is not some bullshit intelligence gathering mission. These are seven of the best-trained soldiers in the whole fuckin' military for crissakes! Why do you think we're here…to take a few fuckin' snapshots for National Geographic?" The angered Colonel hesitated for a moment realizing his voice was getting too loud. The last thing either of the two men wanted was for the other members of the unit to hear their two leaders arguing about orders. Bringing his voice down to a harsh whisper, the Colonel continued, "You know as well as I do that information is more dangerous than anything, John. If I tell these boys where Charlie is then they'll be times when they'll relax and let their guard down—and that will certainly get us killed. So I do not want them to know where Charlie is. Just like I do not want you to know where Charlie is. And just like I don't want me to know where Charlie is."

Russo stared back at Mazer in a manner no other man dared. His eyes intensely scanned the Colonel's face, evidencing his frustration. He wanted to argue further, but he knew it was pointless and even detrimental to the team.

"Look," Mazer continued calmly, "I know you want something more to go by…but like I said in training, we got to operate this thing on pure instinct. This is a well-oiled and fully primed machine we put together here, John. These boys are ready for anything. Let's not underestimate them now."

Russo's eyes softened, but he still wanted to make some points. "This team may be the best," he responded, "but we're all alone out here. We both know that this team is not capable of sustaining a test of attrition, especially if things heat up like you know they're gonna. We only got enough ammo to last one or two dog fights, and that's it. And we got no air cover. We got no ground support. We got no fuckin' search and rescue. We got nothing. No one knows we're here. Hell, we don't even know why the fuck we're here!"

"Of course we do!" Mazer growled, abandoning his vocal restraint. "We knew all along why we were sent here. This mission has objectives—very clear objectives—and those objectives are gradually becoming our orders! And I do not expect you to have a continuing problem with that, Major." The Colonel's final word was a reminder to Russo of who was the boss.

"Objectives?" Russo shot back. "What kinda objectives are we talking about?"

The Colonel did not answer back. Instead he turned his attention back down to his equipment.

"They're not military objectives," Russo mumbled. "More like goddamn political objectives."

Mazer hoisted his gear onto his shoulder and shook his head in disappointment. "There's no difference anymore, John," he uttered walking away, leaving his disgruntled Major all to himself.

Russo stared at Mazer's back until he was out of sight. "Fuck you!" he snarled under his breath. He went back over to his rifle, picked it up and kicked his boot into the soft sand ground in frustration. He knew Mazer was right. He may have been recruited for Operation Inferno under the pretenses of "covert intelligence," but he knew from the start that McCabe was calling the shots. And that meant McCabe was answering directly to the President. Certainly

President Keane did not need a top secret ground team, especially a team of elite mercenaries, to simply gather intelligence data inside the Cambodian border. Small reconnaissance flights from Saigon would have done the trick. Although the specific objectives for this secret mission had not yet been disclosed, even to Colonel Mazer, Major Russo knew from the day he agreed to join the team that they would be precarious. But then again, by the summer of 1972, all of his country's so-called "objectives" in Vietnam seemed precarious to him.

What Major Russo did not know, what McCabe and the President did not yet know, was that Colonel Mazer had a few objectives of his own.

CHAPTER EIGHT

1992

Army for Peace Compound
Hanoi
August 12, Sunrise

In guesthouse number twelve, Dominic's eyes were wide open at 6:00am, partly from the jetlag and partly from anxiousness. It was Monday morning in Hanoi, and there was work to be done. Next to him, Julie slept soundlessly in his arms. Last night, he happily realized, was not a dream. He had held her naked body throughout the night. Being pressed up against each other for hours, their bodies were now comfortably entangled as one. Even Julie's smooth thin legs were entwined around him.

For the next ten minutes, Dominic delicately unraveled his body away from hers. Slowly, he slipped out from under the sheet and carefully off the mattress. Julie was obviously exhausted, for she did not move an inch the entire time. She remained completely motionless during the next twenty minutes while Dominic showered and dressed comfortably in a short-sleeve white shirt and khaki pants. There was no mirror in guesthouse twelve, so Dominic had to use his memory when brushing his wet hair back tight and neat. Usually he would be ready more quickly, but his body was a little sore from the night's festivities, and his attention was recurrently drawn to the sleeping beauty in his room.

Before he left, Dominic walked over to the bed and stared down at Julie. Her face and skin were even more beautiful in the natural morning light. He put his hand under her nose and felt the soft cool wind from her restful breathing.

Having seen his parents trapped in a miserable marriage, he had never been one to believe in love. This justified his unending quests for physical conquests. To him, love was "a trap" or "an illusion for the weak-minded" or his favorite definition of all, "a prescription for misery." It was also something he said existed only if you allowed it to. The key, according to Dominic, was to be mindful of avoiding it. You must be on guard. Be in control of your feelings at all times, or else you make yourself vulnerable. Love must be treated like any other highly-addictive, destructive drug—it was best to not even try it.

Abstinence was the most effective form of prevention. Love was way too dangerous to try. If he found himself thinking about love, he would abandon ship. If any of his girlfriends starting mentioning it, he would abandon ship. This was Dominic's strategy for years. He was too independent, too smart to succumb to such foolish vulnerabilities. And besides, women had always come too easy for him to consider falling in love. Much too easy. This, he felt, granted him not only the opportunity, but the obligation to screw everything he could.

That was, until last night.

In forming the long line of his physical conquests, sensitivity was perhaps Dominic's most cleverly employed nightly tool. He was an attentive listener. A compassionate, charming, entertaining speaker. Sympathetic. Empathetic. Combined with his appealing looks and keen awareness of even the slightest openings, Dominic was a devastatingly accurate bedroom magnetizer. His Oscar-caliber performances had won over some of the most distrusting ladies in New York City. Most fell head over heels for him. And come morning, he disappointed them.

Rarely would an encore performance be sought by Dominic, especially if he found himself wanting one. Therefore, his previous night's pageantry would always transform into an unsettled coldness at daybreak. It was all purposeful, of course. He wasn't a cold person by nature. So his morning strategy was not his favorite time but necessary nonetheless. Of course, he was always ready to defend his getaway and stay-away attitude: "I'm sorry if you feel I am being impolite, I just respect you and believe that you deserve my honesty." That, he felt, actually made him a better man than most.

Acting distant and detached when daylight came quashed any and all hope or expectations that may have carried over from the night. Strings needed to be cut. There was no need for discussion really, for he had already decided on his own that it was best for everyone. He had it down to a science. His logical formula had proven effective through years of testing. The hypothesis was twofold: Being sensitive in the evening brought him uncounted physical conquests. Being sensitive in the morning brought him unwanted aggravation.

Sure, he would often meet up the same women again, but only after it was clear as crystal that there were no ties, no expectations, no real future. As long as she accepted the deal, and he was not having strong feelings for her, well, he was more than happy to get together again. And again.

That was, until last night.

Now in guesthouse twelve, despite the brightness of morning, Dominic could not detach. In fact, it was the last thing he wanted. There was no coldness to manufacture. His heart was genuinely warm, and he could not and did not want to disguise it. His mind, always a reliable co-conspirator for his engineered detachments, was now enchanted by an inner woman. He sensed her intelligence, her character, her feelings. He didn't want to leave her. He wanted to stay with her all day and learn more about her, everything about her. Looking down at her peaceful, innocent radiance made him feel emotionally vulnerable. For the first time in his life, he felt like his many one-night stand partners probably had—hoping that the break of day did not signify the end of the affair.

Quietly Dominic crossed the room and stepped outside. The heavy morning air was a clear forewarning of the burning heat to come. Hundreds of insects buzzed and hummed among the wild plant life outside his bungalow. Dominic walked gently down the front steps and took a moment to scan the botany of colors. The choice was obvious. He bent down and picked a handful of the deepest purple flowers nature had to offer. Soundlessly, he returned bedside and laid them down on the pillow where his head once rested next to hers. The deal he was offering his overnight companion was quite different this time. He forgot about his independence, his philosophy. His stomach was excited and unnerved by the unusual emotions inside him. He could not avoid the foreign feeling of insecurity swirling inside him. He could not outthink his emotions. More surprisingly, he didn't want to. Gently, he kissed Julie on the forehead. As he turned away and walk back out the door into an unfamiliar world, an unknown destiny, he realized he was leaving his heart behind.

Visually, the city of Hanoi was an architectural museum. Hanoi's twisting blocks of yellow, two-storied colonial buildings retained—as was the intention of its plotters—the ambiance of a provincial French town in the 1920s. Dominic unfortunately did not get to see, much less appreciate, the colonial history around him. He was too busy weaving the motorbike he borrowed from the Colonel through the chaotic, dangerous city streets of Hanoi, a terrifying adventure for the new and inexperienced. No traffic lights, no lane lines, seemingly no rules whatsoever governed the packed passageways. Everyone was out for themselves—pedestrians, bicycles, motorbikes, cars, trucks, chickens, and cows—and no one, besides Dominic, seemed the least bit affected by the total transportation disorder. The continuous sounds of blowing horns and skidding tires rattled his nerves. And he thought New York City was a hectic town to navigate.

The refreshing breeze from the ride could not prevent beads of perspiration from accumulating on his unnerved face. Dominic was in the midst of the ride of his life. Everyone else was merely heading to work or school.

Finally, after fifteen minutes of turmoil and three near head-on collisions, Dominic arrived at his destination. Shell-shocked. In need of another shower.

Back at guesthouse twelve, Julie was wide awake, fully dressed, and rummaging through Dominic's luggage. With one eye on the door, she quickly emptied each of the compartments and sifted through all his belongings. When she was done with the bags, her attention turned to the closet...then to the drawers. She felt inside every shoe, sock, and pocket in his clothes, reading every piece of paper she came across. Once done, she was not visibly pleased with what she found—or did not find. Breathing heavily, she re-packed the mess that she had made and hurried out the front door.

The concrete building that matched the address Shay Krauze had given Dominic was in the government center located in the heart of Hanoi. Like most of the state buildings in Vietnam, it was painted bright yellow, garnished with the unmistakable red and yellow state seal of communism. It was also guarded by armed young men. After parking his motorbike, Dominic walked up to one of the guards and politely asked him if he spoke English.

The young guard just stared at him. "I only speak English," Dominic said pointing to himself. Still, only a cold stare was his response. He then tried slowing his speech, thinking as many foreigners do—that perhaps the speed, and not the language, was the reason why he was not being understood. "Does anyone speak E-n-g-l-i-s-h?"

No feedback. It was useless, he thought. The guard continued to stare him down like a prizefighter during instructions. Thankfully, his intimidating rifle was not in his arms. It was, however, in close enough proximity being draped right behind his shoulder. Realizing the guard's patience was wearing thin, Dominic looked around for assistance. Behind the guard, he saw three other guards eyeing the scene from a near distance. Their rifles were in their arms, not on their shoulders. Dominic realized he was in the middle of a wolf pack. An increasingly restless wolf pack.

His whole body began to sweat. *What a dumb mistake to just show up out of the blue,* he scolded himself. He should have tried to call first. Or maybe he should have asked the Colonel to help him out. There was no other choice but to try one final time to communicate with the guard. This time he used a different angle. With friendly raised eyebrows, he said slowly, "I am here to see General Kien."

The guard's piercing stare immediately evaporated. "Kien," he repeated.

"Yes! Yes! General Kien!" Dominic said enthusiastically.

At that, the guard left and went over to his fellow comrades. It was obvious from their body language and look-backs that they were discussing him. Dominic let out a sigh of relief when he saw the guards perch their guns back behind their shoulders. One of the guards then broke away from the pack and went inside the building. After the elapse of two more uncomfortable minutes, he returned, and the four soldiers again huddled.

Meanwhile Dominic gazed out into the busy government circle and pretended not to be nervous. His insecurity, however, was not comforted by what he saw. Out in the open government center, straight lines of countless living soldiers marched routinely around statues made in honor of countless dead ones. Elaborate red billboards and gold stars decorated the perimeter of the streets—none of which, he quickly realized, advertised a single product. Each one projected images and pictures of nationalism, pride, war, and soldiery. And all of them starred the revered founder of modern Vietnam, Ho Chi Minh painted around soldiers. To the rest of the world, he may have been dead for over two decades, but to the Vietnamese, "Uncle Ho," with his omnipresent smiling face and inspiring words was alive and everywhere.

Unknown to Dominic, the embalmed body of his country's former "public enemy number one" rested peacefully in an airtight tomb only a half a block away. Regardless, Dominic felt totally out of place standing in the heart of the communist center staring at propaganda. Like the sun's increasingly baking heat, the young capitalist could feel the looming aura of control all around him. Physically, the young American felt far away from the streets of Times Square. Philosophically, he felt even further.

A loud call from one of the guards snatched Dominic's attention. He looked over and saw the same four guards. One of them, the one he first spoke to, was waving him over. When he arrived at the group, two of the soldiers immediately grabbed him by each arm and shoved him up against the wall.

Although surprised by the suddenness, Dominic did not dare object to the unexpected pat down. He realized that, although their tactics were a bit harsh, they were understandable for security purposes.

The two guards then proceeded to lead him into the building and up three flights of concrete stairs. The building itself was open, airy, and, aside from a few more guards stationed on the floors, empty. There was no glass in the windows, only iron bars, which blocked out anyone crazy enough to intrude, while allowing a slight cross-ventilation breeze to pass through the hallways.

Once on the third and final floor of the building, Dominic followed the two guards into the corner office where an attractive secretary was sitting behind a desk. Her long, straight, deep black hair was parted down the center of her scalp. She was wearing a light-blue ai dai, a traditional silk Vietnamese dress. Dominic realized that the ai dai must have been designed by a man. For from top to bottom, it could not be more flattering to the female figure. The ai dai hugs a woman's entire body tightly—starting at her neck, downward snug around her bosom, skin-tight around her waist, draping the length of her legs to her ankles with a revealing slit back up to the thighs. It was a shame that the secretary wasn't also highlighting her smooth skin, high cheekbones, thin eyebrows, and catlike eyes with a warm smile. Instead, she veiled her lovely features behind a serious expression while she conversed with the guards.

While his hosts chatted in Vietnamese, Dominic gazed around the room without moving his head. The layout was simple, humble, almost unfinished. Off to the right of the secretary's desk were two empty chairs. Together with the secretary's small desk, they made up all the furniture in the room. Hanging on dreary gray walls above the two chairs was a colorful, poster-sized, framed picture of Ho Chi Minh. *The man is everywhere I turn*, Dominic thought. The rest of the room's four cinderblock walls were barren. Directly behind the secretary was a closed door.

After saying something to the two guards, the secretary picked up the black rotary phone and dialed. At the same moment, one of the guards turned around and looked at Dominic. He barked a one word order and pointed to one of the chairs. Dominic obediently walked over and sat down.

Conversation continued between the two guards for a couple of more minutes. Dominic was growing impatient. The humidity outside, growing thicker and stronger as the morning wore on, was also contributing to his frustration. What if he had been completely misunderstood?

"Is he here?" Dominic politely interrupted the two guards. "Is this General Kien's office?"

The two guards immediately looked down at him but offered no response. The secretary continued her very fast talking into the phone. "I am here to see General Kien," Dominic said again.

Still nothing. Not even a glance from either of them this time. Dominic used his forearm to wipe the annoying sweat off his face. "Dammit!" he said out loud while rising from his chair. "This can't be a General's office. They could be placing me under arrest for all I know."

The two guards immediately grabbed their pistols from their side holsters and pointed them at the middle of Dominic's head. "Whoooooooa!" Dominic exclaimed raising both his arms in surrender. "Easy boys!" He had never looked into the dark eyeball of a gun before. From his angle, the small barrels appeared larger than the tubes of the Lincoln Tunnel.

Suddenly, the secretary hung up the phone and said something to the two guards, who responded by slowly lowering their guns and placing them back in their holsters. The secretary looked over at Dominic for the first time. Like a principal staring at a student in detention, her expression was one of disappointment. "Please be patient," she said, shaking her head slowly.

Dominic was, at first, startled by hearing her speak in his native tongue, and then totally embarrassed by his unprofessional behavior. He slumped back into his chair, and humbly apologized: "I'm sorry. I didn't know you spoke English."

"Only a little," she replied. "I study at the University of Foreign Languages."

"You speak very well," Dominic complimented her, attempting to make up for his rudeness with flattery.

"Thank you," she said without smiling. She seemed to be concentrating on the proper pronunciation for her next sentence. "Mr. Huyen and Mr. Lang will be with you shortly."

"Thank you…thank you," he said sounding overly nice. A few more shifty minutes passed as Dominic, now silent, obedient, and patient, wondered who this Mr. Huyen and Mr. Lang might be. From the hallway, the rapid patter of footsteps began to resonate. *Here they come*, Dominic said to himself.

A brisk knock on the door and a well-dressed young whirlwind-of-a-man entered the office. Despite being almost out of breath and sweating from what must have been a full sprint across the city, he was brimming with nervous energy. His slender, kinetic body was crowned with fluffy, black hair that was unwillingly whisked off to one side, creating a wave high enough to surf. While bowing his head before the two guards, the sunglasses he was wearing fell off his face and onto the floor. Clumsily, he bent down and scooped them up, while he conversed with the secretary in Vietnamese at a speed faster than light travels.

Looking on, Dominic grinned. *Either today is this guy's first day on the job,* he said to himself, *or he's running for political office.* The latter was not likely, he realized, recalling the politics of the country.

At that moment, the young man turned around and bowed. "Hellooo," he announced. "It is very nice to meet you." His pronunciation, although exaggerated, was impressive.

"Oh, hello." Unwittingly, Dominic's slow and exaggerated speech parroted that of his new acquaintance. Holding his hand out in greeting, he stated, "My name is Dominic...Dominic Russo. It is very nice to meet you."

"My name is Quan."

The two men joined hands. Dominic grinned in amusement. Quan, unaccustomed to the Western method of greeting, held onto their shared grip and shook it up and down at a frenzied pace, saying, "I will be your interpreter for the meeting, Mr. Dominic."

Before Dominic responded, the door behind the secretary opened. On the inside, an older man smoking a cigarette stood stationary in the doorway. "Oh...ummm...okay," Dominic stated clumsily to Quan. They were still shaking hands, but Dominic's attention had been stolen by the man in the doorway.

Finally, Quan let go of Dominic's hand. "Mr. Huyen and Mr. Lang will see you now," he stated, extending his arm.

The swooping fins of an elaborate ceiling fan thinning and circulating the humid air was the first thing Dominic noticed stepping into the office. Indeed, it was a refreshing sight for his sweaty body. The layout of the room, he soon noticed, was also a surprising contrast to the modest office where he had waited with the secretary and two guards. In fact, the elaborateness before him was a contrast to the entire building. Off to the right, a luxurious mahogany wood couch, adorned with plush white pillows and two matching chairs, encircled a hand-carved coffee table. The timeless furniture rested on a majestic, hand-made Oriental rug. Dominic hesitated at the edge of the colorful carpet. He waited for Quan to walk up on it first, before he treaded its soft splendor.

At first impression, it seemed only the part in their hair—one had his on the right side, the other chose the left side—distinguished the two men inside the room. Even Father Time had treated them equally. Both had stopped growing at exactly five foot and three inches. And both carried slight pouches around their waists and similar gray dusting throughout their hair. Like Dominic, they were dressed casually, wearing light-colored short-sleeve shirts and slacks. The August weather in Hanoi simply would not permit more formal attire.

"This is Mr. Huyen and Mr. Lang," Quan explained to Dominic. "They are associates of General Kien."

The two men extended their hands and grinned at Dominic, peering at him the way a cat first looks at a canary in a cage when it is first brought into the house—polite and welcoming but ready to pounce at the first unguarded moment. Dominic looked at Quan, who was nodding his head and smiling unnaturally. Seeing that his own native translator was visibly nervous during the meeting's introductions made Dominic uneasy. He was confused. He needed to get the players straight. "Are you an associate of General Kien, also?" he asked Quan.

"Oh no, Mr. Dominic," Quan responded, "I am just an interpreter. Your interpreter."

Upon shaking both men's hands, Dominic was directed to sit down on the couch where a servant was pouring a setting of fragrant hot tea. *Just the refreshment I was hoping for in this boiling weather,* Dominic thought. Dominic accepted the offering and took a sip. It tasted like hot water. He then placed the cup and saucer back down gently on the table, looked at Quan and asked, "Where is General Kien?"

Quan raised his eyebrows and sat down right next to Dominic. "You must be patient, Mr. Dominic," he uttered in a low voice. "You must speak to Mr. Huyen and Mr. Lang first."

"Alright then," Dominic said under his breath. Sitting back on the couch, he spoke to Quan, "I'll go slow so you can translate." Quan nodded. Huyen and Lang settled more comfortably into the two chairs across the table. Dominic nodded at Quan and opened the conversation. "First, I want to thank you for seeing me this morning, gentlemen." His eyes shifted back and forth among the three men. Quan translated without a stutter. "I am here from New York representing Mr. Krauze. Perhaps you know of him. In any event, he has sent me here to Vietnam because we are interested in purchasing some gem products directly from General Kien." Quan's translation was smooth and immediate. Both men listened attentively and nodded their understanding.

Dominic was tempted to continue but he decided to stop right there and wait for feedback. Mr. Huyen bent over and slowly sipped his tea. After nodding at Quan, he then looked at Dominic and spoke first. Quan recited, "Mr. Huyen wants to you to prove to him that you work for Mr. Krauze."

Dominic's eyes frowned. He was taken off guard, not expecting such an abrupt demand. *Prove it?* he repeated in his head. By way of another taste of tea, Dominic bought himself a moment to think. *Why was he being asked to prove he works with Shay?* While he swallowed the warm sip, he concluded it was perhaps his youth that the two older men had difficulty reconciling with the business he was offering.

That being the case, he knew he needed to gain some respect...right now...before the conversation proceeded any further. Accordingly, he told his new acquaintances, "With all due respect to you two gentlemen...," Dominic nodded at Quan and waited for him to translate the phrase before proceeding. Once Quan was done, he looked back at Dominic with a concern. Dominic continued, "I am first going to require that you two prove to me that you are in fact associates of General Kien. And that you are in fact authorized to engage in negotiations on his behalf." Quan translated, albeit at a slower pace. Huyen and Lang were the ones who were now frowning. They began to mumble to one another in Vietnamese. Dominic confidently sat back in his chair. He may have been young, and nervous on the inside, but he projected the demeanor of a shrewd veteran when it came to business posturing.

Dominic knew well the game he was involved in. Some games are indeed international, universal. In effect, it was nothing more than two kindergarten kids claiming to each other during recess that "my Dad is stronger than your Dad." The stakes were different, but the mentality remained the same. Dominic crossed his legs while the two men continued to mumble. He started to enjoy the thrill of it all. His living was made by negotiating with friendly thieves in New York City. There he had learned long ago that when it comes to the gem business, respect must be established up front. You should never discuss precious stones without first gaining respect. In gem dealing, without respect you are only wasting your time.

Dominic also knew that you cannot gain respect in gem dealing simply by asking for it. If your reputation fails to precede you, though, you must command respect another way. A number of methods may be employed. Dominic was in the midst of employing the most effective one of all—stripping it away from the other side. Boldly, he interrupted Huyen and Lang's low-pitched discussion. "You must understand gentlemen...I was sent here by Mr. Krauze to speak with General Kien and General Kien only. I was not instructed to have any discussions with you two gentlemen...or anyone else for that matter."

Quan was visibly reluctant to translate. And when he did, the tone of his words sounded much gentler than Dominic's had been. After Quan finished, Huyen and Lang conversed for a few moments. Dominic sat forward and pushed even further. "I thank you for the tea gentlemen, but I'm a very busy man and I really don't have time to sit around and play any more games."

Quan translated the statement as nice as he possibly could. He was visibly nervous from the tension. Huyen and Lang showed no effect in their expressions. They continued to talk to each other, this time while staring at the young American. The situation was very uncomfortable to Dominic. He felt like a laboratory rat being studied by two scientists. After thirty seconds more, he realized the next move was his. His statements had brought him to a point of no return. He was left no other choice but to stand up and walk out.

He hesitated before he made his move. *Maybe I was too harsh,* he thought to himself. Perhaps he should have been more diplomatic. After all, he was the foreigner. Seconds ticked by. The time had come to back up his words. And risk blowing everything before anything began.

The instant he began to rise from the couch, Lang spoke out loud to Quan. Dominic sunk back down to a seated position and listened to Quan's translation: "Mr. Lang said that tomorrow you will be brought to the mines." Dominic nodded firmly. "There you will see the rubies and discuss business with General Kien himself. You will bring with you one bag containing one change of clothes. You will also take with you a camera so you can take some pictures of the rubies for Mr. Krauze."

Dominic grinned slightly. His hard line stance worked perfectly. He took a moment to recall the significance of what had just transpired. His two clever hosts had put him to the test. They sat back and waited to see if Dominic would have walked out on the meeting. The minute they saw him rise from the couch, they had the proof they sought.

Dominic was thankful to Huyen and Lang. Their actions had proved to him that the rules of business were universal, notwithstanding any flag, government, or political theory surrounding it. Philosophically, he no longer felt far away from Times Square. Krauze was exactly right. Business was business. Be it in Hanoi or New York City. Be it between Asians, Americans, or Martians.

Now that he had gained their respect, new questions arose. Lots of them. They swirled in Dominic's head, begging to be answered, preferably by Quan, rather than Huyen and Lang. "Tell them everything sounds fine," he responded politely to Quan, "and explain to me why I need a change of clothes without asking them if you can."

Quan responded, "You will need to spend one night there."

"Why?" Dominic asked. "Where are we going?"

"Two hundred and seventy kilometers west."

"I don't know kilometers. I'm American. Tell me in miles."

"I don't know miles, Mr. Dominic. I'm Vietnamese."

"Fine, how 'bout hours. Can you tell me how many hours away it is?"

"It takes eight hours to get to the mines."

"Alright then. What time do they want me to be here in the morning?"

"Oh no, Mr. Dominic. That won't be necessary. Mr. Huyen and Mr. Lang will pick you up at the place you are staying."

"Okay. Tell them I am staying at the Army for Peace compound."

"Oh, they know, Mr. Dominic. They already told me to tell you to be out at the front gate at nine o' clock am."

Dominic's eyebrows went in different vertical directions, but before he could ask anything further, Huyen and Lang rose from their seats and extended their arms. Quan jumped up and translated Huyen's words. "Mr. Huyen says that it was very nice to meet with you and that he will see you tomorrow morning."

Dominic had a million questions but bit his tongue. It was not the time to seem insecure or to appear flustered. "Thank you," he stated coolly. Huyen and Lang seemed to understand the expression. "Then I will see you both at nine sharp." Quan translated and then escorted Dominic to the two guards waiting in the front office. As the guards began to lead him out the door, he turned around to Quan and asked him. "Will you be coming with us tomorrow morning?"

Quan answered, "That has not yet been determined, Mr. Dominic."

CHAPTER NINE

1972

Ten miles southeast of Parrot's Beak
August 31, 1:55AM

Security assignment is a necessary task for a combat soldier. Back at the well-fortified bases, where there are a large number of troops, it is an often-welcomed responsibility. On security assignment, there is a chance to chat with the other soldiers assigned to your post about all the girlfriends you have in the States and intend to have, at least for a night, in Saigon. If your platoon happens to be deep enough within controlled territory, well-insulated from any threat of surprise, security watch can be a relaxing opportunity to smoke a couple hits of the native grass from a bamboo-carved, appropriately-named "Viet-bong."

Things are quite different when you are on watch alone, part of a small secret force isolated somewhere in a red-hot war zone. Things are very different when you are unofficially inside the border of a "neutral country" with your presence completely unknown even to your own army and allies.

There would be no relaxation, past or future girlfriend talk, or bong hits where Corporal Herman Mendez of Operation Inferno was on watch that night.

Corporal Mendez was the best marksman of the seven elite soldiers he was assigned to protect that night. He had signed up for the Marines over two years earlier at the age of eighteen and had already completed two tours of duty by the time he was recruited by Colonel Mazer for the Operation Inferno team.

He was a relatively quiet young man, seemingly reserved in his own world, but he was fearless. His physical and mental toughness had been put to the test long before he became a combat soldier for Uncle Sam. Without having demonstrated this, Herman Mendez would not have made it across the Pacific Ocean to the beaches of Da Nang. He had needed this toughness to survive his teenage years in the south side of Chicago, amidst the tornado of riots, gangs, and drugs of the early 1960s.

When Mendez did speak, it was never about family because he had none to speak of. His father was someone he never knew. He supposedly had a sister somewhere, but he never knew her either. His mother was killed by a street mugger when Mendez was seven years old. For the next several years, he was raised by a distant uncle who remained even more distant as a father, often leaving young Mendez with one of his girlfriends while he served time or went off on another drug binge. By the time child services became aware of the neglect, Mendez was not a child anymore. He was fifteen years of age—a senior citizen on the streets of Chicago. His whole life he had been a loner, really. Gangs and then platoons were the only family he ever had.

Mendez enlisted in the US Marines because he knew in any event he would have to become a killer to survive the unforgiving streets of the ghetto. The truth was he had already been a lifelong soldier by the time he joined the Marines. His survival training, though, was not simulated; it was real. Each new day was a battle for Mendez in his teenage years. The battlefield was the inner city. His outfit was a gang. Victory was had if he managed to survive…and stay out of prison.

To Mendez, the green jungles of Southeast Asia were not any different from the concrete, graffiti-painted jungles of the ghetto projects. If you substitute the buildings for mountains, well, then everything else felt the same to him. He was one of the many young Americans born into a war. It was not an official war as far as the United States Congress was concerned. But, then again, neither was Vietnam.

Mendez saw furious foxhole combat up at the Demilitarized Zone during his first tours of duty in Vietnam. During one legendary battle, he stayed in his hellish pit of mud alone, for two days, braving point-blank machine gun fire. Remarkably, he was calm enough to remain conservative with his ammunition, and deadly enough in accuracy to hold the line throughout the 40-plus hour ordeal. Eventually, his courageous heroics helped turn back the shell-pounding, strong-willed enemy onslaught.

Colonel Mazer had heard this and other stories about Mendez's fearless reputation from one of his fellow advisors. Two days after he agreed to lead Operation Inferno, the Colonel reached out to him. Mendez was immediately intrigued by the prospects of a so-called "secret mission" and agreed at once to enroll his expert marksmanship to the cause.

For the first seven days of the mission, everything had been running as the Colonel had hoped, smooth and uneventful. The team had mapped enemy supply routes in Cambodia and conducted covert surveillance on a hidden Vietcong port off the Gulf of Thailand. They took pictures, recorded journals, and kept logs. Oddly enough, they were even instructed to chart American armored vehicles crossing the border into Cambodia along an undocumented trail. Through it all, the Operation Inferno unit was indeed what it had trained to be—invisible and inaudible.

That night, at half past the midnight hour, it was all about to change.

In order to reach the coordinates within three days, the unit had to advance, steadfast and tactful, through the heart of highly-saturated Charlie territory. Pursuant to the Mazer's orders, they did not set up camp that night. They had not set camp for the past two nights due to their positioning within close proximity to a known enemy supply trail. Mendez's fellow soldiers, all six of them, were sleeping in their bags within fifteen feet of him. Their safety, the safety of the entire mission, was his sole responsibility that night.

It was raining heavily that evening. Combined with the new moon, this made visibility very poor. Mendez was not able to see beyond twenty feet, and, to complicate matters further, he could not hear anything above the storm. The steady pounding of rainfall reverberated in his ears as it pounded the hard shell of his steel helmet. Nonetheless, his exhausted platoon mates remained soundly asleep, entirely unaffected by Mother Nature's turmoil. Soldiers of war can sleep anywhere, even in the loud jungle during a thunderstorm. But never without holding onto their iron teddy bears—their loaded weapons.

Mendez, like any experienced combat soldier, utilized each one of his senses, and then some. Without his senses, he was all but lost. He needed to see, hear, smell and feel his habitat in order to survive. If just one perception became clouded, then a soldier of war's sense of impending danger is hindered, and he is unable to protect himself against the jungle's nightly predators. That night, the bitter elements of the Southeast Asian monsoon were depriving one of America's most durable warriors of his natural instincts. Corporal Mendez was, for the first time in his adult life, nervous—so nervous he was sweating in the cold rain from the adrenaline racing through his body.

Lightning blinked and thundered growled while as best he could Mendez feverishly surveyed the perimeter of men he was assigned to protect. Holding his trusted M-16 weapon upright across his chest, the young proven survivor stood stiffly with his back against a large tree. He was ready for any instant of danger though he knew, being a soldier of war, that the instant of danger was sometimes too late.

Out of the corner of his eye, during a flash of lightning, Mendez saw his worst nightmare. Charlie. *Shit!* he screamed silently inside himself. *Did he see me?*

Booooom! Boooooooom! The roar of thunder answered.

Mendez's body remained completely still. Only his eyeballs roamed. It wouldn't be long before lightning would again illuminate the jungle canopy. He affixed his line of vision through the darkness onto the estimated position of the advancing enemy. Within seconds, another flash of lightning beamed in the distance. Mendez caught another glimpse of Charlie. The situation worsened. This time he saw a diagonal line of four to five soldiers. Mendez's frantically analyzed the situation. He figured they must be a scout team approaching in a V-formation. By his estimation there would be fifteen to twenty soldiers to contend with…all combat ready!

Mendez knew not to shoot, at least not yet, since he remained undetected, and more than likely there were soldiers behind him. By the diagonal line of the soldiers in front of him, Mendez calculated that the Inferno team was situated directly in the belly of the V-formation and would therefore soon encounter Charlie from three sides.

Unfortunately, there was no way to silently alert the others. And to alert them without silence was suicidal. Enemy soldiers were too close. They'd all be dead before they knew what hit them. And he'd sacrifice his one advantage. The only advantage he had. Invisibility.

Boooom! Baaaaaaboooooooooom! Thunder exploded.

Mendez slumped down, using the tree behind him as support. He got into a seated position so that he could reach Major Russo, fast asleep on his stomach just off to his right. Extending his leg, Mendez firmly nudged Russo on the chin with his boot. Russo awoke and immediately began to rise, but Mendez quickly maneuvered his foot onto the Major's back and held him down to the ground. Russo looked up at Mendez's eyes. He knew by the force of Mendez's foot on his shoulder and the intensity on his face that something was up. Charlie was out and about.

In only a few short weeks, the Inferno platoon was formed and trained both mentally and physically to think synchronously and to react symphonically during surprise confrontation. A raise of the eyebrow, twitch of the nose, or point of the finger could speak a thousand words between them. Survival in a jungle of enemies required one mindset, one frequency of thought. And nerves of steel.

When Mendez glared down into Russo's eyes and moved his own eyeballs up once, the message to Russo was clear. Enemy was behind Mendez. Russo clicked off the safety of his AK-47 assault rifle. His nighttime Russian teddy bear was awake and eager to roar. He also detached a hand grenade from his belt. He was ready...a one-man wrecking crew awaiting the signal to blast.

Another distant bolt of lightning cut through the black jungle. Mendez caught another glimpse. Charlie was now only about twenty-five feet from the unit, which—thanks to the elements—remained undetected. The same elements that deprived Mendez's senses were now working as a blanket of cover for his men. The lifelong urban and jungle warrior stood firm, patient and planned. Major Russo anxiously awaited the move of his trusted subordinate.

Let's do it! Russo thought to himself. *What's he waiting for?*

Time was moving too slow for the impatient Major. Buckets of rain continued to pound the drenched, dark, jungle vegetation. Lightning had just passed and Mendez was waiting for Mother Nature's signal...thunder. It would drown out the sounds of his imminent attack. He was primed. The time was now.

Booooom!

The first rumble of thunder cracked and Mendez hurled a grenade to his left, unloading a 180-degree stream of bullets around the perimeter of his men.

Baboooooooooooom!

By the time the last crash of thunder echoed, Russo was tossing a grenade behind Mendez. Both went down to one knee, side by side, facing opposite directions pumping eight hundred rounds per minute into the jungle darkness. Streams of red, white, and yellow blitzed through the night at supersonic speeds. Walls of bullets cut down the jungle's thin branches like a chainsaw.

Five enemy soldiers had been eliminated during the first boom of thunder before the others realized they were under siege. The rest of the Inferno team awoke in a panic. The fury of firepower flying only a couple of feet over their heads was deafening. Mendez quickly held up his left hand in the shape of an L as he continued blasting. The signal was seen and understood by all: Enemy to the south and west!

The rest of the unit knew exactly what to do—fragment and spread out to the north. Remaining in their present position, one the enemy was now aware of, would allow the enemy the opportunity to take out the entire team with one direct hit of heavy weaponry.

As their leader, Colonel Mazer took the initiative and was the first to depart from the unit and head north. It was an extremely dangerous and totally unheard-of role for a colonel to assume. Mazer, however, was not a typical colonel. He had a reputation for demonstrating unbridled courage in the heat of a battle. The rest of the unit followed swiftly, moving in pairs. Like clockwork, they dispatched in intervals…every five seconds…in order to keep cover for one another. The last pair to retreat was Mendez and Russo. They had been firing furiously for over three minutes. Staying low and compact, they embarked under the rest of the unit's cover, eventually entrenching themselves two hundred feet northwest.

After few more deafening minutes of firing it was clear that the enemy had disengaged and retreated. "Hold it, boys!" Mazer blurted out. Relieved, Mendez finally let go of his smoking M-16. His hands were still shaking from the power of his pumping gun. He took off his helmet, tilted his head back, and opened his mouth to taste some of the last drops of rain. He had saved the team. Like the others, his heart was pounding hard against his ribcage. Defying death was always an exhilarating experience. And there was nothing quite like the rush of a sudden attack, if you survived it.

The rainwater that fell into his mouth tasted like leaves, but the cool jungle drink and shower was now a welcomed refresher to Mendez. After the sweat on his face was washed away, he gazed over at Major Russo. He was expecting a thumbs-up. What he saw was quite different. Russo was slumped down on the ground holding his shoulder.

Mendez rushed over to Russo's side. "Oh shit!" he exclaimed. "Are you alright, Major?"

Russo's face fought back the pain. "I think so," he replied, "I think they got me twice up here."

"Hang on Major. I'll get Doc," Mendez said and ran off.

Robert "Doc" Haynes was the Operation Inferno unit's "corpsman." Officially, he was called a medical specialist. Three years earlier he had enrolled his services to his country as an intern. During his two tours in Vietnam he worked as a surgical assistant but had also received high marks as a soldier. A year before, Doc had removed a bullet from Major Russo's thigh at a military hospital in Saigon, and, during his recovery, Russo and Doc had become good friends. Accordingly, when Mazer asked Russo if he knew of any good candidates to be the Operation Inferno team's medic, he immediately recommended Doc.

"Not again, Major," Doc said kneeling down. Quickly, he removed the pack on his back and opened it. Sliding his skilled hands into two rubber gloves, he said in warm his southern accent, "Ya know, I'm beginning to feel like I don't work for the government anymore, Major." Removing a shiny metal probe and a jar of alcohol, he added, "I feel like I've become your own personal physician."

Russo smiled. Doc was a likable character. His sense of humor was a great anesthesia for pain. After sterilizing the probe, Doc grabbed a thin flashlight and flicked it on. He turned back to Russo. "Let's take a look."

"Don't I owe you some money, Doc?" Russo stated, wincing in pain.

"No, sir," Doc responded. He was a master with his hands. Adroitly, he worked the wound with the probe while holding the flashlight in his other hand. His examination was delicate—as delicate as could be expected—but pain was not something a jungle surgeon could avoid. The only painkiller available was conversation. "Tell me Major, why do you ask me if you owed me money?"

"My Uncle Vinny."

At first, Doc did not respond. His attention was pinpointed upon his inspection of Russo's wounded shoulder. After a few moments, the odd statement sunk in. "Your Uncle Vinny?"

"That's right," Russo said blowing out the pain with a strong breath. "My Uncle Vinny used to tell me all the time that you should always owe your doctor money."

"Oh yeah? And why did he say that?"

"Cause that way he'll be much more interested in makin' you better."

Doc smiled. He had a million dollar smile. Had he not needed steady hands, he would have been laughing. "Is that right? Well, I guess that's good advice. How's your Uncle Vinny doin' with it?"

"Uncle Vinny's been dead a long time."

Doc ceased his survey and grabbed a white towel from his pack and a jar from his pack. "Sorry to hear that," he said.

"Oh, it's no problem," Russo said lightly.

Doc opened the jar and held the towel under Russo's bleeding abrasion. He wanted to keep the conversation moving in order to distract Russo from the coming pain of cleaning his wound with the stinging solution. "If you don't mind me asking, Major," he inquired, "how did Uncle Vinny pass away?"

Russo was snarling in discomfort as the peroxide stung his open flesh. His voice strained in answering, "He was killed."

Doc was finished cleaning. He grabbed some bandages and began to wrap the shoulder. "World War II or Korea?" he asked, assuming Uncle Vinny was also a fellow soldier.

"Neither—his doctor killed him."

"His doctor?!"

"That's right," Russo said dryly. "He said that my Uncle Vinny owed him too much money."

Doc burst out in laughter at Russo's joke. His deep, choppy laugh was funny just to hear. Thankfully, the wound was superficial. The shells had grazed the shoulder on an angle and luckily did not lodge itself inside the flesh. Stitches were not needed to close it back up. Doc's tight wrap would stop the bleeding.

By now the rest of the men had all reconvened around Major Russo. Symbolically timed, the rainstorm had passed over and the morning sun was rainbow-coloring the dripping moisture.

"Good work, Mendez," Colonel Mazer declared and then asked, "How many did we get?"

"Maybe five or six," Mendez responded.

"Out of how many?" asked Mazer.

"Probably fifteen," said Mendez. "Hard to say with the storm."

Actually, Charlie was not that fortunate. Only four out of eighteen men had survived Mendez and Russo's fierce onslaught.

"Scout maneuvers," injected Russo. "Most likely VC. Which means they're gonna soon know we're here so let's get cracking on some inventory."

There was little time and a lot of work to be done. The team, especially Mendez and Russo, had expended a lot of ammo, and without backup or incoming supplies, they could use all the bullets they could find. Quickly, exercising extreme caution, the team scoured the perimeter around them and searched for fallen enemies. They didn't need to be reminded that it may be only a matter of minutes before their retreating foes returned. In greater numbers. With more firepower.

Within a few minutes, however, the harsh, harrowing reality of the Operation Inferno mission manifested itself throughout the bloodstained floor of the Cambodian jungle. Although none of the soldiers said a word to Major Russo, Colonel Mazer, or for that matter, each other, each one of them knew. They knew now the identity of their fallen "enemies." The uniforms they wore and the weapons they bore told the story.

The soldiers that made up the Inferno team did not express any regrets. At least not out loud. None of them expected nor asked for their Colonel to voice justification for their actions. They were under orders and that was reason enough. To them, survival was all that mattered in an aftermath of bloodshed. Not principles. Certainly not explanations. Besides, it was not unusual for such tragedies to occur during times of war. And Operation Inferno was, after all, a top secret unit. Mendez surely could not have known that it was their "allies," a South Vietnamese dispatch platoon that had stumbled upon them.

With clear consciences, the seven members of Operation Inferno resumed their trek northward. It would not be long, though, before each of them, in their own way, realized the undeniable, continuing reality of their covert mission— even if Mendez had been aware of the identity the soldiers in advance, it still would not have made a difference.

CHAPTER TEN

1992

Army for Peace Compound

Hanoi

August 12, Noon

Having navigated his return through the streets of Hanoi alive and unscathed, Dominic had to wait. It took a couple of minutes for one of the pacing armed guards to unlock the front gate and let him back into the fortified AFP compound. Smiles, nods, and waves were exchanged as Dominic slowly rolled by on his motorbike. Words, of course, were useless.

The shaded journey through AFP's winding trails was quieter and safer than the streets of Hanoi but not faster. Without making a single wrong turn, it took Dominic almost ten minutes to make his way back to the site of guesthouse twelve.

Anticipation had been building steadily since the meeting. By the time he stopped his motorbike, his rushing blood pressure was flushing his olive skin face red. A quick turn of the key and the engine shut off. A swift kick of the stand and the motorbike was propped. His heart was pounding with worry. His stomach was spinning like a washing machine, tumbling like a dryer. As he made his way up the stairs and back inside his bungalow, he couldn't believe what was happening inside him. His body's organs were behaving like carnival rides, and he couldn't help it.

At the bedroom doorway he stopped to let out a long sigh of relief. There was a sign. A small gathering of yellow and red flowers had replaced Julie's sleeping body. Underneath them, the bed was made tightly, showing no indications of the entangled mess they had made of it. Even the clothes he had on last night were neatly folded and resting comfortably on the foot of the mattress. More important than that to Dominic, there was a note left behind on the pillow.

Dominic analyzed the scene. Julie didn't just get up and walk out. She didn't just forget the night and move on to another day. She put time, care into the room. What a wonderful sight. The inside of his whole body eased. His heart stopped its nervous pattering and settled back into a normal rhythm. The biological circus inside him was over. His tight mouth softened open to a half smile.

Before he opened the note, he placed it under his nose. His eager lungs filled again with her memorable scent. The rest of his body reacted to her aroma by tingling with desire. The sensual indulgence of last night came back to him. Despite the aches in his drained body, he could have her another dozen times over. It wasn't sexual desire that he felt burning inside him; he had felt that countless times before. This was altogether different. Last night took him beyond the realm of physical pleasure. It was more of a spiritual experience. In one fateful night his heart was removed from an ice-cold freezer and placed inside a warm oven. It was now ignited, burning with foreign feelings on foreign soil. Feelings he had never thought he would feel. Feelings he had never wanted to feel.

Julie captivated him. Mesmerized him. She escorted him to a higher, deeper, more intense state of being. In a way, he was fearful of it, yet he wanted to revisit it, become comfortable with it. And learn how to live in it.

Unfolded, the scripted note read:

> *Dear Dominic,*
> *Hope all goes well with your business ventures.*
> *Thinking fondly of you and wishing you luck,*
> *Julie*

Dominic plopped down on the bed, grinning with delight. He gazed up at the ceiling fan. The faint breeze and rapid spin of the fins hypnotized to his thoughts. His eyes hazed over as he traveled back into last night. Slowly, he went through the scene, recalling each moment, replaying every detail. The images were so vivid, so unforgettable, so easy to relive. Julie's soft voice moaning. Her thin, bare body squirming. The sweat dripping. The intensity. The passion. The unguarded emotion.

He began to worry again. What will he do tomorrow? How could he be sharp for business when all he could think about—when all he wanted to think about—was Julie? In one night, a woman, one single woman, had totally captured his soul. He struggled to recover his reason. *One night shouldn't affect a man that much,* he told himself. *One night can't change the world? Or can it?*

Dominic was fighting a losing battle. He had already surrendered to the cause last night when he opened his heart and poured out his feelings. Now it was too late. Any mental effort was futile. There was no way to reverse the process he had set firmly in motion. He couldn't take back what he already emotionally released. Even Dominic Russo, the logical, rational, strategic planner of his life, couldn't reason his way out of this one. His mind was rendered powerless. His heart had taken over. And once that happens, there is no way to outthink it. It's on its own course. A runaway train. Best not to fight it. Just strap in, enjoy the ride, and hope you don't crash. At least for a while.

Treading on such unfamiliar sentimental ground was frightening to him. He had always prided himself on exercising total control over his feelings. He was always so closed, so protectively mysterious. And now he found himself submissive to his emotions, all in the quick course of one night. Perhaps it wasn't fair, but it made sense. Sexually, the young handsome stallion had been a paramour his whole life. Emotionally, though, he was a fragile virgin. That is, until last night.

What about the future? he worried. *How could he leave here without her?* It was difficult enough to be apart from her for just one night and go to the mines. But after a few moments, his eyes blinked away from their daze. Reason made its return. Reality was restored. *He had to go to the mines,* he scolded himself. He had to make a deal. After all, that was the key to everything. Including a possible future with Julie.

Dominic ran his hands through his hair and took a moment to enjoy the refreshing breeze of the ceiling fan. He was proud of himself. The first meeting with Huyen and Lang, despite the mystery and the danger, had ended well. Very well. It was only posturing, really, but the streets of New York City taught him long ago that posturing is what business is all about.

The first step in Vietnam was behind him, and it was a success. He had earned the respect of his new associates, the most important victory of all.

The morning meeting also put to rest something else in his mind. Aligning with Krauze was indeed a smart move. Given the unfriendly reception and distrustful attitude he saw earlier, he realized he would not have gotten very far, if anywhere at all, had he decided to go it alone on this venture. Certainly he would not be in the position he was now in, namely, at the door of opportunity.

Krauze's power was greater than he had imagined. His name alone was the entrance key to a meeting with a key figure halfway across the planet. Thanks to the global reputation of New York City's holy villain, he, a young gem retailer, had himself a meeting scheduled with General Kien, "the Boss in Vietnam." Now that's influence!

Dominic tried to envision General Kien. He didn't expect him to be a physically intimidating man. He expected him to be older. Much older. Likely past his seventies. Evidently he was a well-guarded man, as access to him was clearly selective. The image that came to mind was one of a stubborn, self-assured, difficult to deal with disciplinarian. In other words, a typical military man. Just like Colonel Mazer. Just like his father.

In the gem business, speculation is preparation. With the stakes so high, Dominic forced himself to think of General Kien as a ruthless businessman. In his mind Dominic made the General a difficult, almost impossible man to deal with. Dominic felt negative expectations were the only way to properly plan for the worst in terms of negotiations. At this time, optimistic thinking would be imprudent, not to mention dangerous. Sure the chance to carve out a deal was there. But anxiousness was the last emotion Dominic wanted to convey to the General.

Dominic knew his work was far from over. Mentally, it was just beginning. And with Julie occupying his thoughts, the task to stay focused would be that much harder. *Have to remain sharp*, he warned himself, *and hopeful*. Sharp in his dealings with General Kien. Hopeful that the high stakes gamble he made on the terrace of the United Nations will ultimately pay off.

"Some night, huh…?" a familiar voice from behind asked.

Startled, Dominic jumped up from the mattress and spun around. Seeing the intruder, he shook his head and answered, "You scared the shit out of me, Colonel."

Colonel Mazer burst into a prolonged, almost mocking laugh while he removed the mirrored sunglasses from his face. "That's 'cause you're no soldier, kid. A soldier would have sensed my presence long before I made it into this room."

Dominic quickly stuffed Julie's note into his pants. He could not, much to his chagrin, do the same with the colorful flowers spread out on the bed. "Those are some pretty petals," the Colonel was more than happy to point out.

Dominic responded with a grunting nod that pretended not pay the comment much attention.

"You didn't get a chance to come over and meet the Senator last night," said the Colonel.

"Yeah well…if you've met one, you've met them all."

The Colonel chuckled. "That's for sure. Maybe tomorrow morning you can join us for a late breakfast up at the main house. We'll be eating at 9:30 sharp."

Dominic thanked the Colonel for the invitation but refrained from telling him there was no chance he'd make it. To a certain extent, he was disappointed he would be missing another opportunity to chat with the Senator. Had he not been struck by romantic lightning, he would have seized the opportunity to speak with him last night. After all, Senator Haynes, perhaps more than anyone else, would be determining whether or not the trade embargo will be lifted. Without the trade barrier, Dominic would be free to import gemstones directly to the United States. More money would be saved in shipping and tariffs, therefore more money could be made selling the stones.

"What did he say regarding the embargo?" Dominic asked, realizing he may not get a chance to ask the Senator himself.

"Not too much, really. He did mention that the Vietnamese authorities have been very cooperative about the whole POW issue. I don't see any reason at all why next week he won't be giving his recommendation to Congress to lift the trade embargo."

Dominic was glad to hear the news, though he didn't show it. It was great for business. "Is the POW issue still that much of a sticking point?" he inquired curiously.

"It's all political bullshit, kid. It's the politicians' way of continuing to criminalize the Vietnamese people. There's no merit to it. Like anything else back home in the good ol' USA—it's about votes." Dominic didn't say anything in response. He sensed the Colonel's thoughts were drifting into the past. "Do you know that when we fought here, any body that was not found was listed as 'Missing in Action'? Those were the orders. If the body's gone, then it's MIA. The goddamn bureaucrats back home figured that the less Americans killed the better it was for the newspapers. You know how it goes—the better the publicity for the war, the better the public's support. The better the public's support, the better the troops' morale. Brilliant thinking, eh?"

The Colonel's tone then soured. "But somebody in Washington forgot about a couple of minor problems. Like the families of those young men hanging on to false hope. And what to say after the damn war is over and we're supposed to swap all these prisoners who don't exist!"

Dominic remained silent.

The Colonel paused, but he wasn't finished venting. "Think about it, kid—when a plane was sent out, and it never came back, the crew was marked MIA. Never mind that it was probably blown out of the fuckin' sky. If no one saw a dead body, it didn't happen. It was all a bunch of bullshit. Still is. Do you know what happens to a body when it gets hit by a damn mortar rocket?"

Dominic didn't answer.

"It vaporizes, that's what happens. Nobody sees it. Especially during the midst of a fire-fight. It all happens in less than a blink of the eye. If there is anything left of the guy...it's nothing more than fuckin' fertilizer." Pointing at the flowers on the mattress, he added, "You know how many men who were listed as MIA whose blood and guts helped grow those damn flowers?"

Dominic interjected. "I read that out of almost sixty-thousand Americans killed here, there are only a couple thousand or so bodies still unaccounted for. That seems to be a low figure considering..."

"It's the lowest figure for any war in US history," the Colonel interjected. "Something like seventy-five thousand men are still unaccounted for from World War II, for crissakes. Eight thousand from Korea. I bet you don't know how many South Vietnamese bodies are still unaccounted for from the war?" It may have been thrown out there as a question, but the Colonel did not give Dominic a chance to guess. "Three hundred thousand. And that figure includes women and children."

Dominic was shocked. "I never knew that."

"Of course not. You're an American. Now you know how ridiculous it is for the Vietnamese to hear the Americans cry about their POWs! They have three hundred thousand of their own men, women, and children missing, and you don't hear them crying!"

"Well, hopefully, it all will end soon," said Dominic.

"I hope so, kid" the Colonel replied calmly. "There are a lot of children that need help in these parts. If there is political reconciliation between the US and Vietnam, then I'll be able to get a lot more funding for the AFP."

Suddenly, the Colonel's face and voice were no longer serious. "And you get to make yourself a million dollars in business deals," he said lightheartedly.

"Well, we'll see."

With that lead in, the Colonel switched topics. "So tell me, how was your first morning in Hanoi? The guards tell me you took a ride downtown."

"Yeah. And I'm happy to make it back alive."

The Colonel laughed. "I guess someone should have given you a quick

Southeast Asian traffic lesson."

"You mean a crash course?" Dominic said jokingly.

"That's right," the Colonel chuckled. "I've been here so long, it doesn't even faze me."

"It's amazing how everyone is so unfazed by the madness…including the animals."

The Colonel grinned. "Imagine if American personal injury lawyers were allowed in this country."

Dominic laughed at the thought. "This is ambulance-chasing heaven!"

Keeping his light-hearted tone of voice, the Colonel inquired, "So where did you go to this morning?"

Dominic didn't want to be revealing. "Just around the city a little."

The Colonel pried further. "Did you meet with anyone?"

Dominic grew uncomfortable and got up from the bed. "A couple people. No one special really."

"Was it productive?"

By now, Dominic was pretending to be concerned with unpacking the remaining clothes from his luggage. "Not really. I'm just getting a feel for things."

As usual, the Colonel was directing the flow of conversation. Dominic was annoyed. He knew exactly where the conversation was headed. He had been led down the same path a thousand times before by his father. This was the point where the Colonel was about to give his two cents worth of advice.

"Listen, kid," the Colonel spoke soberly. "I know you know what you're doin', and it's none of my business, really…but I want you to be careful."

"Of course," Dominic answered, folding his shirts. His apathetic voice expressed his sentiment. He did not want to hear any more lectures in his life, especially from another asshole.

The Colonel was not deterred by his young guest's apathy. "You're gonna find that things are different here, kid. It's not like the United States. This is the Third World. This is communism. A different history. A different culture. A different people."

"Thanks. It'll be fine," Dominic assured him. "I'm only looking into things. That's all."

The Colonel stepped closer to Dominic. "I know. But I also know that gems are illegal in Vietnam."

That statement caught Dominic's attention. He turned and looked at the Colonel, his face frowning slightly from surprise. "Illegal?" he repeated. No one had told him that. Not Krauze. Not Quan. Not Huyen or Lang.

"That's right," the Colonel answered seriously. "It's against the law to buy, sell, trade, or even dig for gems here."

Dominic, visibly bewildered, asked why.

"Well…from what I hear they supposedly got a shitload of rubies in the ground up in the northwest territory. Right now the whole industry has been banned because…well…I don't really know for sure…but I guess that the powers that be in Vietnam are afraid."

"Afraid? Of what?"

"Everything. They're probably not educated enough about the industry so they don't want to open up the market until they know exactly what they're doin'. You can't blame the Vietnamese people for being very cautious."

Impossible, Dominic thought to himself, *there must be some sort of mistake.* Just last year he had come across rubies from Vietnam at a gem dealer's convention in Atlantic City. "How long has the industry been outlawed?"

"Oh—buying and selling precious stones has always been illegal from what I've heard." After a slight pause, the Colonel elaborated, "The Vietnamese government is understandably wary about being taken advantage of when it comes to things like business and foreigners."

"But what about the mines? How do they stop people from taking…"

"The mines are under the control of the Vietnamese National Police," the Colonel interrupted. "They're the ones who make sure no one can get to the gems. They have a lot of troops up there. It's all, you know, exclusive military regions. No one, especially a foreigner, is permitted access to those areas. You and me couldn't buy our way into those places."

Dominic looked down and began to remove his shoes from his feet. He could not help but smirk. Something inside him desperately wanted to tell the Colonel how wrong he was—that by tomorrow afternoon he will be the first foreigner to gain access to the Vietnamese military region, where he will meeting with General Kien, the head of the Vietnamese National Police, to discuss buying rubies. However he resisted the temptation to voice his thoughts.

"Look, kid," the Colonel continued, "you may not know this—and you may not like this once you do—but I consider you like a son. And Marie, of course, is a daughter to me. So please, just keep in mind that it's a whole different world over here. There are shadows of corruption in everything. Believe me, I know. Now I don't tell anybody what they should or should not do when it comes to their business. That's your business. That's up to you. But what I am saying is that this can be mysterious place. A dangerous place. And if you're not careful it can swallow you up."

Dominic thanked the Colonel for the advice while he pulled off his socks.

The Colonel stepped closer to him and pulled out a small cellular phone from his pocket. "Take this and carry it around with you. If you feel like you may be in any kind of trouble, just call me."

Smiling, Dominic refused. "I should be fine. Thanks anyway."

"Take it," the Colonel urged. "Just in case of an emergency. You never know. My number is on the front. It can't hurt, right?"

Dominic didn't want to argue. "Alright, thanks."

The Colonel nodded. "Good." He then changed the conversation course: "Marie and Julie had to go to with one of my teams down to Hue to distribute some emergency vaccinations. You must have been gone before they left this morning."

"When will they be back?"

"Marie should be back sometime tomorrow," the Colonel said smirking. His answer was purposely incomplete.

Dominic could not resist. He had to ask. "What about Julie?"

The Colonel patted Dominic on the back and chuckled. "Don't worry, kid. She'll be back the day after tomorrow. She's really somethin' special, ain't she?"

Dominic nodded uncomfortably in response.

After checking his watch, the Colonel said, "Well, I got to get down to the river. We have a shipment of medical supplies coming in. Why don't you take a walk down and see the operation."

"Maybe later. Right now, I'm kind of tired. I'm gonna stay here and get some rest."

"I don't blame you. Jet lag is a bitch."

Dominic began to unbutton his shirt while the Colonel slid his sunglasses back on. Before he walked out, he had one more piece of advice for Dominic. "Do you know what the Vietnamese motto toward foreigners is?"

"No, I don't."

"It's very simple," the Colonel announced. "The Vietnamese people welcome all guests…who do not come as conquerors."

Dominic pulled off his white shirt. "That sounds a bit harsh for tourism."

"It may seem a bit harsh from an outsider's viewpoint. But for a country that in its history had to fight against the aggression of the Mongols, the Chinese, the French, the Japanese, and the Americans…I'd say it's a very polite slogan."

"If you put it that way—I guess you're right."

"Have a good nap," said the Colonel. With that, he swaggered out of the room and out the front door. Dominic followed behind and locked the front door. No more surprises, he told himself.

Back in the bedroom, he pulled off his pants and collapsed on the bed. He took in a deep breath and suddenly the lingering annoyance from the Colonel's visit totally disappeared. Julie's scent was on the pillow.

Tomorrow, he reminded himself, *I will be escorted to a place where even Colonel Asshole himself is not welcome.* The prospects for business now seemed brighter to him than ever.

CHAPTER ELEVEN

1972

Ten miles southeast of Parrot's Beak
Cambodia
September 1, 3:01PM

In the latter days of the summer, at the height of the day, the sun broils at its hottest temperature of the year, deadening the Cambodian forest with sizzling heat. For those furnace-like couple of hours, the jungle is the quietest and brightest it can be. And to an advancing pack of soldiers, that means it's the most dangerous time.

The shine of the overhead sun causes shadows to drop straight down, shrinking the both the range and angles of shade. With the wane of camouflaging shadows, visibility through the trees becomes clearer and deeper. Not coincidentally, during that same period of time, nature's orchestra takes a mid-afternoon break, as cover from the sweltering heat is wisely sought by all inhabitants. Insects stop their buzzing; birds cease their singing; and leaves quit moving from underneath the pathways of snakes and small mammals. The sound of a delicate tiptoe can now be heard from much further away. Combat soldiers in Southeast Asia refer to these couple hours of suspended action and noise as "graveyard time," and not because of the quietness.

At the height of the early September afternoon, more visible, audible, exposed, and vulnerable than they had ever dared, the Inferno team continued to stalk their way through the Cambodian jungle.

Hilliard walked point for the Inferno team because he was the best at it, a covert commanding officer's dream—fiercely disciplined, razor-sharp, and deadly as a cobra. Visually, he was misleading to his peers since he was so thin, short, and physically unimpressive but not to anyone who had heard of him or knew him. He had built his reputation as a "rat." In a place and time where rats were the most respected and most feared men of all.

For nearly three full tours of duty, Hilliard was a staff sergeant for the tunnel rat squad of the 1st Infantry Division. While thousands of men his age fled to the safe havens of Canada and Europe to avoid the draft, Hilliard's ongoing mission—one that he chose to do—was to strip to the waist and head face-first down into dark holes of the dank jungle soil into the forbidden world of the underground enemy, equipped only with a flashlight in his left hand, a pistol in his right, and a knife slip-tied around his right bicep. Legend held that, in an eye blink, he, a "tunnel rat," could drop his flashlight and draw his blade. Hilliard enjoyed disappearing underground to hunt for Charlie. Not in Charlie's backyard. In Charlie's bedroom and kitchen.

The tunnel rat did not take the larger, more powerful assault rifles. They were simply not maneuverable in the intensely constricted space. Grenades, too, stayed aboveground. This was useless weight in a two-foot circumference tube of dirt. Hilliard also chose to leave his flak jacket and helmet behind; he found them too bulky for this habitat. "Besides," he would add, "they're useless anyway…if they see me first, I'm a dead man." His black skin and shaved head served as his only armor.

Fear was something the slithery tunnel rat also left behind. The commanding officer of the 1st Infantry Division told Colonel Mazer over the phone, "the only thing I'm fearful of…is how fearless that boy is." If asked, most of his fellow soldiers would have stated, naturally off the record, that Sergeant Hilliard had often left his sanity behind. The others who knew him would say he had none to begin with.

Isaac Hilliard hailed from downtown Atlanta, and he preferred to forget it. War-torn Vietnam was a place better suited to his goals. All that Atlanta represented to him were empty memories of a father he had never known, a jailed mother, and the worst irrepressible nightmare of all.

As a child, he was raised transiently and impassively by the State of Georgia, but that was fine by him. He had no regrets about dropping out of school, never holding down a job, or dealing drugs to get by. He never asked for anything, never blamed anyone. And he held no grudges against society. He never really cared enough about himself to care about his own misfortunes.

In the course of his whole life, Isaac Hilliard only cared about one thing: his younger brother, Terry.

Although only four years older, he was a father figure to Terry, and Terry was a son to him. Big brother made sure his younger brother stayed in school, stayed out of trouble, and was well-behaved with his foster mother. Isaac protected him. Supported him. Did everything he could to make certain Terry didn't end up like his older brother, who used to sum himself up as "goin' nowhere with nuttin' goin' on." Terry heeded this advice, for he had the rare ability at a young age to learn from other people's mistakes without having to make them himself.

The Hilliard brothers loved sports and were both naturally gifted athletes. Terry's athletic body, though, was destined to take up a lot more space than his slim, sleek older brother. By the time Terry was thirteen years old, he was already taller and wider than Isaac, who was seventeen. His increasing size and skill earned Terry a starting position in his freshman year on both his high school's varsity basketball and baseball teams.

Isaac, of course, attended every game and cheered the loudest. He loved watching his younger brother perform, or as he would say, "do his thing." Those days, those moments, were indeed the best times of his life. It gave him something to be proud of, something special, something perfect. Terry was being scouted by colleges and bringing home good grades. "A shooting star," the back page of a local newspaper described him as. Scholarship offers rolled in. Clemson. University of Georgia. Florida State. Notre Dame. Auburn. They were all vying for Terry's athletic services. A free ride to the college of his choice was on the horizon. "After that," Isaac would boast, "maybe he'll turn pro. Or start a career in broadcasting. Or who knows…the sky's the limit."

The headlines forgot to remind Isaac that shooting stars live brilliant, fleeting lives.

Three weeks later the front page of the local press called it "a senseless act of violence" and "another case of being in the wrong place at the wrong time." Isaac knew better. The police called it "a random drive-by shooting." But the big brother knew that nothing was random in the streets of downtown Atlanta. The words "jealousy" and "rivalry" were kicked around for a while. These supposed motives were completely off-base. The instant he heard that his younger brother had been shot in broad daylight while standing in his high school parking lot, Isaac Hilliard knew exactly what it was. A message to him. His clientele had gotten too big.

Terry was young, good-looking, smart, and like his brother proudly bragged, "goin' somewhere." He had learned from his older brother's mistakes—and was now dead because of them. The irony stung Isaac like salt on an open wound. The pain was irrepressible. It was a wound too deep to ever heal.

The police, hounded by the press, found the two killers, but they were too late. Most local people were pleased. Law enforcement would have only brought what people from outside that neighborhood would call "justice." Isaac was able to do the only thing that he knew was called for. The only thing he had left to live for. Take revenge.

A week later, in the late hours of a fateful night, Isaac was only a squeeze away from shooting a bullet through the temple of his brain. Suddenly just before his finger compressed, he had a revelation which prompted him to put the gun down. Suicide, he realized, was not enough. Too easy. Too quick. Too cowardly. Talking out loud in the dark room he told the ghost of his murdered brother that he deserved much worse for what he had done. "Hell's too nice, my brother," he yelled.

That night, eighteen years old and full of hatred, Isaac Hilliard condemned himself to the only place on the planet evil enough to impose appropriate punishment for what he had done. Vietnam.

In the narrow dark confines of the enemy's tunnels, Sergeant Hilliard found and faced the war he wanted—one on one, hand to hand, face to face. Unlike those above him, Hilliard saw every one of his victims, and most of them saw him, if for only a split second. He killed men with bullets and knives, but anyone could do that in his opinion. Hilliard, however, was lethal with his hands and feet—in places too tight for most men to crawl through. Within seconds, Hilliard could snap another man's neck using his feet and legs, that is, without being able to even see what he was doing.

His predatory instincts and intuition for danger were second to none. Country did not matter to him. Politics did not matter to him. Life or death did not matter to him. Nothing mattered to him. Isaac Hilliard was America's craziest, deadliest close-quarter killer. Period. That's why Mazer recruited him. And that's why Mazer made him walk the point.

Like the rest of the team, Hilliard had over fifty pounds of gear strapped to his back, which appeared to double his weight, but he still managed to penetrate through the bush like a fleet-footed ballet dancer. Silently in stride, Hilliard's head rotated deliberately and continuously left to right. At the same time his keen eyeballs moved like pre-programmed monitors, scaling around the perimeter of the forest. Checking up the trees, down to the ground. Again. Around the perimeter of the forest. Up the trees, down to the ground.

Fearlessly and soundlessly, he led the Inferno team through miles and miles of Cambodia's dense undergrowth, marshes, swamps, and neck-high waterways.

During the long journey, the constant company of mosquitoes, slugs, leeches, various parasites, and fire ant bites were the least of the Inferno team's worries. Likewise, the unbearable heat, exhaustion, and perpetual threat of dehydration were of little concern. Their experiences had trained them to withstand, and even ignore, any unbearable, unimaginable elements. Besides, in Cambodia there were far more daunting possibilities for prowling soldiers to worry about. One was enemy soldiers. The other was friendly soldiers.

To Operation Inferno, enemies were everyone. North Vietnamese. Vietcong. South Vietnamese. American. Australian. Cambodian. They were also everywhere. Anywhere. High in the trees. Camouflaged in a bush. Even roaming underneath the soles of their boots. Lurking jungle gorillas. Seasoned experts in the art of guerilla warfare. Above ground, friends were the most dangerous. Any encounter with search-and-destroy American or South Vietnamese combat patrols would almost guarantee an overmatch of the Inferno team's man and firepower. If somehow the Inferno unit was successful in holding back an American platoon attack, then a soon-to-be napalm strike or air assault would be their reward.

Below the dirt, the possibilities were worse. For below the earth's surface lurked a less obvious danger. Danger from an underground world that only Hilliard was intimately accustomed to. The Inferno soldiers knew that under their boots stretched hundreds of miles of Viet Cong tunnels—a complex system of transportation, storage, housing, food and medical quarters that enabled the VC to launch swift and deadly guerilla attacks, and then virtually disappear into the thick air of the jungle. An entire civilization of moles— angry, deadly moles protecting their invaded territory— was burrowed below the jungle ground. And the Inferno team was treading on its roof. At any moment, VC could appear from under a bed of leaves, spring up from the inside of a tree stump, or surface from the bottom of a stream. Yet another reason why the experienced nose of Hilliard, the team's only tunnel rat, led the way.

But if anyone asked the Inferno soldiers: "What was the greatest fear of all?" without hesitation, their response would be "booby traps." The same was also said by every friend or foe, civilian or soldier, treading the jungles of Southeast Asia. The traps designed to kill, like trip-wired grenades or claymore mines, were actually easier for soldiers to come to grips with. Claymores were particularly lethal hardware and therefore the least frightening prospect to encounter. If one of those powerful hidden killers were tripped, then seven hundred bone-shattering, flesh-ripping, ball bearings would explode out at waist height. Instant death was almost a guarantee in the event of such a misstep. And instant death is never a bad way to go, especially in the minds of hard-core soldiers who think long and often about such things.

Quite another story altogether were the booby traps that were designed to maim. Those scared the hell out of everyone. What the VC leaders preached in their dark underground tunnels was certainly true: "A wounded enemy soldier was worth two dead." The thought of falling hopelessly into a pit of razor-sharp punji stakes, totally concealed by an undetectable mat of dirt and vegetation, was psychologically devastating to a trekking soldier. So was the prospect of having to pull the thick prongs of a bamboo whip out of the mangled torso of a fellow soldier. So was the possibility of stepping on a tied-up poisonous snake. One with venom strong enough to paralyze your entire nervous system with one bite. But too weak to kill you.

So was the constant fear of the once-steady earth suddenly caving in under your boot for a split second. Then, after that split second is over, a steel spike pierces clean through the middle of your foot. Perhaps a few moments after that, your worst nightmare would come true—seeing that the steel spike being pulled out of your foot was covered in human feces. Now you knew in a matter of seconds your viscous wound would be swelling up like a balloon, and gangrene would be setting in. Every soldier, of every rank, under every flag had heard a different story when it came to booby traps. Each more frightening than the last.

The Inferno team's situation was even worse to bear, for if they were maimed, a rescue helicopter could not be radioed to come whisk them away to the nearest base or military hospital for immediate treatment. Doc, with his small supply of first aid, his skilled hands, and his painkilling personality were all they had for treatment. These precarious circumstances were what made Doc's safety the paramount concern of the Inferno team. That's why he was designated to walk fifth in the line of seven soldiers. Fifth place was the safest. In that position, he would be removed from the dangerous front, two soldiers covered him from the vulnerable back, and more important than that, he stepped onto well-trodden footprints.

In the midst of the scorching, hazy, quiet height of the day, warfare raged uncontrollably in the Cambodian jungle. This warfare included the most dreaded, agonizing warfare of all. Psychological. Whether rockets were launched, bullets shot, or bombs dropped made no difference. With each one of Hilliard's careful, calculated steps, the tension mounted, the torment escalated. Hidden booby traps were everywhere. Some were deadly, some were not. The mere thought of them waged the fiercest, cruelest battles within the Inferno soldier's heads. Without warning, something, anything, can strike, bite, shoot, explode or stab. If lucky, the booby trap sprung, set off or stepped on, would be instantly lethal. If not, you would survive. Hobbled. Crippled. Maimed. Or mangled.

With each delicate footfall, those frightening thoughts haunted their minds. Nevertheless, the seven dedicated men of Operation Inferno trudged onward in a single-file. Silently. Cautiously. Courageously. Sweating through every pore. None of them relaxed, smoked, spoke, or took their index fingers off their triggers. For living their worst nightmare was only one step away…

CHAPTER TWELVE

1992

Its effort was valiant, but the air conditioner was no match for the sun's pounding rays. The absorbing black roof of the car was of little help. And when the slowly traversing car was once again halted by another herd of water buffalo passing across the roadway, Dominic had to again wipe the perspiration from his face. Quan was seated next to him in the back seat, more acclimated to the extremely stuffy conditions.

Dominic finally decided someone had to break the silence inside the vehicle—if for nothing else, to take his own mind off the oven-like heat. "How much further until we get there?" he asked Quan.

"About twenty kilometers," his reliable interpreter responded.

"Remember Quan, I'm American. Kilometers don't help me. Tell me how much time it will take."

"One hour."

Outside, the last of the near-ton water buffalo was led across the trail by a fifty-pound barefoot Vietnamese boy. Lang shifted back into gear and the car again continued its painstakingly slow transit through the pitted, muddy roadways. For a moment, Dominic's thoughts amused him. He realized the bizarre similarities between Vietnam's highlands and midtown Manhattan. In both locations, walking seemed to be the fastest mode of transportation. Even at a buffalo's pace.

Despite the temperature, the mood inside the car had been quite cold.

For the prior several hours, to Dominic's surprise, very little conversation had been exchanged among the parties. Up front, Huyen and Lang rarely spoke to one another, and not once did they speak to Dominic or Quan. When his two escorts did speak to each other, it was always brief. Only a few words were shared at a time.

Dominic had spent most of the bumpy, stop-and-go ride admiring the lush forestry and green rice fields of Vietnam's manicured countryside. The back-breaking tedious work of the Vietnamese peasant farmers, particularly the women and children, was truly remarkable to witness. For countless hours, they remained hunched over. Picking crops. Plowing fields. Redirecting waterways. The tools at their disposal, if any, were primitive. But their ingenuity and tireless effort was beyond compare anywhere in the world.

Inside his head, Dominic found himself daydreaming more about last night rather than the business ahead. Like a broken record, he continued to wonder if Julie felt the same as him. Was she was thinking about him? How they could be together? Would she think of coming back to the US with him? He asked himself these questions over and over. But could he even ask such a question…after just one night together? He was hopeful that everything would go well up at the mines. After all, he needed a deal. For if she stayed in Vietnam, a deal was his ticket back. It would give him the opportunity to return, again and again, to visit with her while he conducted business. Eventually he would convince her to come back to New York with him, or at least he hoped he could.

Dominic's trepidation made him shake his head in disbelief. He must have cut off the feelings of dozens of women in his life. Good women. Beautiful women. Women who desperately tried to communicate with him. Women who wanted to tap into his feelings. Women who sought to crack his emotional mystery and penetrate his mind. Women who needed more than sex. Women who wanted simply more of him.

One by one, he turned them all down eventually. Good girls and bad girls. He did not actively seek the obviously bad girls. Generally, they did not entice him. But a few were certainly enticing enough over the years. A few even left without a goodbye or leaving a phone number. Dominic was well-suited emotionally and well-equipped physically for women with short term objectives. Either way, he wasn't interested in feelings, his or theirs. How crazy it all seemed when he replayed it in his head. How impossible it was to fathom that less than two nights ago he poured a lifetime of trapped feelings into one woman. How many times did he say to himself how ridiculous it was for a woman to get so attached to him in just one night? And now he was the ridiculous one.

Moreover, how could he be so sure Julie was a "good" girl—the kind you bring home during the day—and not a "bad" girl—the kind you visit at her place only at night? Well, he thought she was one of the "good" ones. He felt so also. But could he trust his instincts anymore? He was vulnerable. Open and exposed, without any border fences. There was no emotional protection, no security, no cloud of mystery to hide behind. He wanted to talk to her. Hear her voice. He wanted to tell her how he felt—that his feelings were stronger now, more intense than they were that night. He wanted to know how she felt. A nervous smile spread across his moist face. He realized he was worried sick with love.

He saw now that all he wanted in his life was just this one woman to want to be with him. Just this one and that would be it. His luck with women couldn't run out now, *could it…with the only woman he ever really wanted?* The justice that would serve to all the shunned women in his past was too cruel for him to consider. He tried not to think about it, but his conscience was like a finger-pointing prosecutor. It kept reminding him of the things he had done, the crimes he had committed against other women's hearts. Would he have to face justice someday?

Internally, he took the stand in his own defense against his own conscience. *Time to address the charges directly, like a man.* Almost immediately, he accepted that he could not convincingly offer the ad hoc court in his head an affirmative defense to the charges—the accusations were simply too far beyond a reasonable doubt for even the most biased juror to deny. But he was not about to simply plead guilty as charged. He had to figure out at least a mitigating defense for his mental jury to consider. Before very long, he formulated one to go with—he was a bad partner, and it was less heartache all around to demonstrate that as soon as possible.

He acknowledged that he concurred with his sister's blunt assessment, he was indeed a "bad" guy when it came to relationships—more specifically, relationships that required mutual trust and commitment. What his defense did not acquit him of—what made him increasingly unnerved—was the more recent revelation in his mind—that "bad" guys like him should not prey on good women.

Dominic decided that his only hope for mercy was to accept responsibility and offer remorse. He was truly sorry for being rotten. *And wrong to lead so many on, no matter how briefly it lasted. Wrong to be unavailable. Wrong to remain closed off to no more than the moment.* He regretted manipulating and trampling on honest feelings. He understood that he had no right to do these things to such good women. He now saw the error of his ways, and he swore he would never do it again. For the rest of his life he would bear the guilt of his rotten "past" behavior. He concluded his silent summation by begging the court of his conscience for leniency: *Condemning me to a life sentence of guilt would be punishment enough for what I have done...right? Just don't take Julie away from me as a lesson.* To Dominic, that would be the cruelest and most unusual punishment.

Dominic shifted positions in the seat and wiped his brow; *enough of these insecure trials and tribulations.* There was too much money to be made to lose his focus now.

"Why don't Mr. Huyen and Lang talk to each other?" he asked Quan, distracting his mind from his own romantic insecurities. "They haven't spoken more than three words to each other for the past few hours?"

At first, Quan was visibly puzzled by the question. He looked at the two men in the front seat and then turned back to Dominic. "They are working," he said with a tone of obviousness.

Dominic felt almost foolish for even asking. "Ohhh...I see." He did not abandon the discourse, though. He was committed, albeit out of selfishness rather than interest, to fostering some sort of small talk conversation with Quan. "Do you like your job?" he asked.

"Yes, I like both my jobs," Quan answered.

"Both? Where else do you work?"

"I work at a hotel. Security."

Dominic was just as surprised as he was intrigued. Quan was such a nervous and frail man. Indeed it required a bold imagination to picture him in the role of security. A big gun would be necessary. And Quan did not seem like a gun carrier. "Really?" said Dominic. "When do you work there...on weekends?"

"Oh no, I go to work there at night."

"Two jobs a day. You must get tired. Do you sleep all weekend?"

Quan shook his head and smiled. "Oh no, Mr. Dominic. I work every weekend."

"What are your hours?"

"I work as an interpreter during the day and security all night."

Dominic raised his eyebrows. "Wow! When do you sleep?"

"I sleep one hour during lunch time break and two hours during nighttime break."

By now, Dominic was more than interested, he was fascinated. He had gained instant respect, even admiration, for his meek interpreter. "If you don't mind me asking…how much money do you make?"

Quan did the math in his head. "About fifty U.S. dollars per month."

Dominic defied his instincts, nodding his head instead of shaking it in utter disbelief. Verbally, he didn't respond. He felt too guilty to say anything, for he had more money than that in his pocket. How difficult it was for the American to comprehend someone working so long, and so hard, for so little.

"How much money do you make, Mr. Dominic?" Quan asked bluntly.

Dominic was a bit startled by Quan's first display of curiosity. He pretended to be distracted by the passing scenery while he pondered his answer. He was considering whether it would be best to lie and say he made less than he actually did—so as not to make Quan upset or depressed. He quickly realized honesty was the best approach. Quan had been honest in his answers, therefore deserved nothing less in return. "I own a jewelry store and my earnings are different every week," he stated while still looking out his window. "It depends on how good business is for that week. But on average, I would have to say it's… ummm… over one thousand dollars per week."

Quan's eyes lit up. He laughed out loud in amazement. Huyen turned his head around for a couple of seconds. Quan immediately stopped laughing, but the amazement remained firmly imprinted on his face. "Oh wow, Mr. Dominic," he said. "That is a lot of money. Do you have a wife and a big family?"

"No, I'm not married. I only have a sister. Both my parents passed away."

Quan's face blushed. "Oh, I am sorry…"

"No, it's fine," Dominic assured him. "Tell me about your family…are you married?"

Dominic could tell by Quan's expression that he liked being asked this question. "Yes," he said jubilantly. "My wife and daughter work with my mother in the rice fields." Suddenly, Quan's face and tone turned solemn. "I don't get to see them very much. They live far from Hanoi…so I see them only two nights every month. My father died many years ago during the Second War for Independence."

The ways of the universe are crazy, Dominic thought to himself. Had it been twenty years earlier in the very same place, he and Quan would have been under orders to shoot at one another—just like their fathers were—instead of becoming friends. It was inconceivable to think of Quan being his enemy. He was such a gentle, kind soul. "How old is your daughter?" Dominic asked.

Again Dominic noticed a proud sparkle in Quan's eyes. "She is six years old. Her name is Trinh. My wife and I are trying to save money so that she can go to a university some day, but it is very difficult."

Dominic offered a sympathetic smile and nod. "It must be very difficult."

In one brief discussion, Quan had grown much more comfortable around the first American he had ever met. So much so that he reached into his pocket and pulled out a faded, worn, black-and-white picture. "This is me, my daughter, and my wife," he proudly declared handing it to Dominic, "it's the only picture we have. I carry it everywhere I go."

Dominic felt honored by Quan's openness. He gazed at the picture and smiled. It was a genuine smile. His heart was truly warmed by the glowing happiness emanating from the dull image. In the picture, the three of them stood at the same height, all holding each other and beaming with bright smiles. Quan and his wife were squatting down on each side of their little girl, whose arms were around both her parents. Quan and his wife both had one arm around Trinh, and they were also holding hands in front of their little girl. Their heartfelt, interlocked, circular pose was truly moving. For a brief moment, Dominic couldn't help but imagine him and Julie entwined that way. He felt a longing, one which he had never felt before. For the first time in his life, Dominic yearned for a family of his own. "They're beautiful," he said, handing back the photo. "You're a very lucky man, Quan."

"Thank you," Quan said proudly.

"You know, Quan—I may be lucky to have the opportunity to make a lot of money, but I'd much rather be happy than successful."

Quan grinned at his new American friend. "If you are happy, Mr. Dominic, then you are successful!"

Dominic smirked at the wisdom of his new friend's words. At that moment, the slow car began to move noticeably slower, eventually coming to a complete halt. Immediately, Dominic looked out his side window. The stop was not for one of the typical reasons. He saw no line of cackling chickens or herds of water buffalo temporarily assuming their right of way. The reason for the standstill stood outside the front windshield—a closed, iron gate extending across the roadway. Over to the left, two soldiers dressed in olive fatigues with rifles strapped across their backs exited a wooden station house on the side of the road and approached the car. The friendly mood in the back seat disappeared. Frowning, Dominic turned to Quan and asked: "Where are we?"

"Military property," Quan responded quietly, without looking back at Dominic. His attention was now focused on the conversation between Lang and the guards. To his own frustration, Dominic did not know what was being said. He did not have to know the specifics, though, for it was clear from the soldiers' tones and expressions that the dialogue before him was not very cordial. The tension raised the temperature in the car even higher. Every twenty to thirty seconds Dominic now had to wipe the accumulation of sweat from his face. The guards, it seemed, were interrogating Huyen and Lang about him, the foreigner. They were angrily pointing at him in the back seat and speaking in very harsh tones. Dominic desperately wanted to ask Quan to translate. But Quan looked to be too consumed in the inquisition, not to mention just as nervous.

One of the guards, obviously not happy with the answers he was being given, stomped over to Dominic's side of the car, flung open his door, and snapped an order in Vietnamese into Dominic's face. Dominic waited for a translation from Quan. None came. Again the guard snapped a sharp order. This time, the wind and spit from the guard's mouth hit Dominic in the face. It was clear from the angry guard's body language that he wanted Dominic to get out of the car. Dominic didn't look over at Quan. Body language, he realized, was critical to the moment. He could not appear flustered or afraid. This was posturing of a completely different order. Cautiously yet firmly, Dominic placed his foot on the ground outside the car. Moisture from sweat was uncontrollably dripping off his hair.

Once he was fully standing, the guard pushed him to the side and proceeded to search inside the car. Everyone was silent as the guard probed underneath the seats. He ripped open all their small baggage and checked out all the contents. He found nothing of consequence. The other guard barked a one-word order. Lang immediately un-hatched the trunk from the front seat. The guard in the car jumped out, pushed Dominic aside again, and stomped to the back of the car. While he was scouring the trunk, Dominic tilted his head around and looked back in the car at Quan. Quan glanced back briefly but offered no message in his stiff expression. The guard slammed the trunk back down. He had come up empty-handed in his search.

He was not finished though. He stomped back over to Dominic and motioned for him to raise his arms. Again, Dominic obeyed. Despite his pattering heartbeat, he managed to keep a still face while the guard patted him down. He also did his best to hide his anxiety by tightening the muscles in his trembling legs while the guard slid his hands down them. Just like in an encounter with a vicious animal, it was crucial, Dominic knew, that the soldier did not feel nor sense an ounce of fear in him. The inspecting soldier made his way back up Dominic's stiff legs and felt a bulge in one of Dominic's front pockets. He reached inside the pocket and pulled out Dominic's camera. The guards face tightened with anger. A vein protruded across his high forehead. He was livid by the discovery. Holding the camera in Dominic's face, he started shouting. Huyen and Lang jumped in to explain and a heated exchange ensued. Suddenly the enraged guard grabbed his pistol and stuck it in Dominic's face. Dominic stared down the dark barrel. Fear was pumping through his veins. Quan jumped out of the car and became verbally involved in the argument. Dominic was amazed at the initiative and courage of his interpreter. Quan was desperately trying to appease the guards.

The situation, though, was not improving. The two guards were getting more angry. They were yelling louder and louder. The guard pushed his pistol into Dominic's cheek. Something had to be done. "Tell them it's for business," Dominic said out loud to Quan.

With his one statement, everyone, including the guards, stopped talking at once. The soldier pulled his gun back and stared directly into Dominic's eyes. Dominic stared back. "It's to take pictures of the stones," he stated firmly. Quan calmly offered the translation.

The other guard came around and both soldiers began to carefully examine the camera. Dominic looked slowly back and forth at both the guards. Purposely, his expression was not friendly. "I need that camera," he declared sternly. His exact words would not be understood, but he knew his point was nevertheless clear by his tone and expression.

The two soldiers were clearly surprised by Dominic's display of boldness. Dominic thought his demand may have passed over the fine line of boldness into craziness. Quan continued talking. After a couple of tense minutes, the guard handed the camera back to Dominic. No smiles were exchanged. Quan got back in the car and Dominic followed. One of the guards walked over to the iron gate and opened it.

Dominic exhaled with relief while the car rolled slowly passed the guards and into the military territory. He now realized the full significance of what he was about to do. He was, most likely, the first American the two young soldiers had ever seen in person. Who could blame them from being a little edgy about his presence? Even more momentous than that, he was almost certainly the only American to ever be let inside the gates of northern Vietnam's restricted military territory. As a guest.

Wiping his brow, Dominic gazed over at Quan, who was visibly relieved that the incident was over. Without Quan's calm persuasion, the angry guard might very well have pulled the trigger. Dominic was indebted to his brave translator. Questions filled his head about the incident, but he did not bother Quan with them. It was over now. And no explanation was necessary, really. The commotion, although tense, was once again, understandable. *If I were Vietnamese, I would be suspicious of a Yankee in these parts, too,* thought Dominic.

Quan turned and looked at Dominic, who smiled thankfully at his courageous interpreter. Quan smiled back in relief. Dominic could not resist breaking the ice. "Do you think I can take a picture of those guys?" he asked sarcastically.

Quan's smile disappeared entirely from his face. He did not get Dominic's joke. "Oh no—Mr. Dominic," he said gravely. Pointing at the front seat, he added, "You take pictures only when they tell you to."

CHAPTER THIRTEEN

1972

The silent advance of the Inferno team was systematically halted via an exchange of hand signals passed down from their point man. Once the line of soldiers behind him stopped moving, Sergeant Hilliard checked his compass and broke off from the pack without explanation. The team had reached another hilltop summit. And that meant it was time for another one of the tunnel rat's solos.

Gripping his M-16 with both hands, Hilliard was slow and careful when stepping over the tall rocky peak. Every step he took was slow and careful, but steps over the crests of small mountains were slower and more careful, for the possibility of being detected was at no time greater. Each one of the many crossings over Cambodia's endless rolling hills brought with it miles of a whole a new world ahead. Miles of possibilities. Miles of danger.

The rest of the tired team utilized their brief pit stop to sip from their canteens. At the front of the line, Colonel Mazer took the opportunity to check his watch and make a record in his log. His calculations were being pushed to their brink. He was expecting something soon, very soon. What it was, he didn't know for sure, but he had a good idea. And the very thought of it had him licking his chops in anticipation.

Out of the Colonel's visual range, at the very end of his elite line of soldiers, Major Russo checked his watch and compass. He, too, was expecting something. And after miles of consideration, he had formulated a good idea of what it was. But he was not licking his chops. He had a bad feeling about it. A very bad feeling.

True to character, none of the Inferno men dropped their guard while they waited for the return of their point man. Any body movements they made were stiff, calculated, and deliberate. Even taking a sip of water demanded delicacy of caution. Their soiled, camouflaged faces glistened with sweat in the late afternoon sun. Underneath their gear, their bodies were drenched. For three endless days, they had cut through the simmering heat and negotiated the dynamic jungle terrain. The feverish humidity made every step feel heavier, every exertion of energy that much harder. The still, dense air even had a haunting sound to it. A low-pitched symphony of insects buzzed relentlessly in their ears.

The Inferno team's belts were all two notches tighter than a week ago when they first began their mission. Collectively, they had sweated off a hundred pounds, mostly within the past three days. During the three days of silence each soldier had to constantly deter his mind from embarking on any thoughts of home, women, family, friends—all were pushed aside. Mental reflection dulls survival instincts, and the Inferno team needed the full attention of all its parts to survive. Certain thoughts were impossible to repress—those were the nightmarish flashes of possibilities. Booby trap possibilities.

Conditions the Inferno team faced would have driven a lesser-trained and lesser-committed soldier AWOL. It was most intense at the tops of hills for the forest was less dense along inclines and higher altitudes. Shade was scarce. Exposure was greater. The sun's rays were freer, thus more punishing. Knowing the Americans ruled the air was of no comfort; most of them did not know they were there. Except for two of them.

Aside from the one night encounter, Operation Inferno had—thanks to the tunnel rat's keen nose guiding and guarding each step of the way—remained out of sight, out of sound, and out of danger. Friends and enemies had effectively been avoided. Casualties were zero. Limbs were intact. Ammunition reserves were higher than expected. The intense, psychological jungle warfare of lurking unknown danger had been braved and weathered by each man. And no one had lost their mind...yet.

Alone, the tunnel rat did his thing—dancing his way down and around the mountain's steep descent. Never did he take one step or make one move in the jungle that he wasn't sure of. His constantly roving eyes played the role of radar by scanning the perimeter of the green valley for any signs. His nose acted as sonar by sniffing for the slightest scent of underground activity. His body jumped up, dove down, sprung up and spun around like an Olympic gymnast doing a gold medal floor routine. His steel-toed boots moved with grace and agility through the woods as if wings were tied to them. After over a hundred yards of undetectable advancement, Hilliard froze still behind a thick tree.

The ordinary eye would not have picked it up. A person with ordinary senses would have probably walked much closer to it before noticing it, for it was very well camouflaged at the bottom of the valley. Hilliard, though, sensed it from two hundred yards out. With one eyeball exposed from behind the tree, the tunnel rat zoomed in and studied the manmade structure for a few minutes. Slowly the details came into focus in his scope. He was able to make out the structure's concealed outline through the forest of trees. His sensitive nose also picked up some clues of human activity. Within a minute's time, he was finished spying. He had seen and smelled enough. The information was in and processed. The tunnel rat knew exactly who, and what, was up ahead.

So silent, so invisible was Hilliard in his traverse back up the hill that the rest of the team was caught by total surprise when he popped out from behind a rock. Using hand signals, the team's point man quickly relayed the message of his discovery to his anxious Colonel Mazer, who responded by signaling back to him. His orders instructed Hilliard to lead the team back southeast. The team needed to regroup and reorganize, that is, away from the discovered dangers in the jungle valley.

Now in the role of the team's caboose, Colonel Mazer backtracked through the jungle with intense eyes. The wheels of possibilities in his mind were spinning, making it difficult for him to keep his senses aware of any danger. The sweat on his face grew thicker from his self-serving thoughts. *This is it*, he proclaimed to himself. *We made it. Those sons of bitches probably thought we couldn't get here. But here we are.* The anxious young colonel was still unaware of what it was Hilliard had stumbled upon. But he knew by the coordinates that such "stumbling" was definitely no accident. This was exactly where they were sent to be. Where it was didn't matter. What it was didn't matter. What mattered was that the CIA planned it this way. And the President, who was probably sitting in air-conditioned comfort of the Oval Office, knew about it.

Right now, the Colonel imagined, he's probably schmoozing some short-skirted reporter, knowing in the back of his handsome head that Colonel Mazer was far away taking care of all his ugly business.

Using a relay of hand signals, Colonel Mazer sent a message to Hilliard to stop after he decided the team had been led far enough away from the discovery. However, the Colonel kept moving. He proceeded to pass each of his men. No eye contact was made with any of them. They all knew the routine. They expected their Colonel to desert them for a short while. He needed to be alone with his radio. When he returned, he would have their orders. Operation Inferno, after eight days in Southeast Asia and over fifty miles trudged, had reached their final destination. Somehow they all knew that their mission had only just begun.

Once far out of sight and earshot from the rest of his men, the physically tired, mentally zealous Colonel dropped his gear and picked up the receiver from his backpack. The time had finally come to radio Agent Phillips back in Saigon and inform him that the team had made it. "On schedule," were the first words Mazer said into the phone.

"Any troubles?" Phillips inquired.

Mazer figured that by this time Phillips knew more about their surprise late night encounter with a South Vietnamese scout platoon than he did. And his assumption was correct. The army's intelligence reports that had landed on Phillips' desk reported that a South Vietnamese platoon was ambushed by a small faction of Cambodian nationals. The minute he saw the report, Agent Phillips knew it was the Inferno unit. There was only one question that concerned him. "No trouble at all," the Colonel replied calmly.

Phillips had gotten the answer he was hoping for. He was able to infer from Mazer's words that the Inferno unit had not lost any men or limbs in the attack. "That's good," he responded.

Mazer smirked with pride into the receiver. They all must have been worried sick, he told himself. He imagined the relief President Keane and McCabe will feel when Agent Phillips tells them that there was no evidence of their presence leftover from the attack. They'll sleep better tonight, for sure, with their precious secret intact. The Inferno team that Mazer had recruited and trained successfully blasted away a small platoon—without suffering one casualty. That should bring another million-dollar smile to the President's face.

Agent Phillips moved on to present concerns. "Northwest of your present coordinates you will find…"

"Already scoped," Mazer injected.

"Good," Agent Phillips replied. His instructions for the team followed: "Watchdog the camp for the next two days. Get anything and everything you can on the command and the guards. There's been a lot of speculation regarding their activities, and we're looking for confirmation on a number of conflicting reports. At 1200 hours on the 4th, radio me for further instructions. No sooner. No later."

The instructions told Mazer the story. What Hilliard had spotted in the valley was what he had expected—an American POW camp. In Cambodia. "Over," he signed off, grinning from the accuracy of his predictions.

The Colonel made a quick return to his men and huddled them together in a tight circle. Verbal words were spoken for the first time in two days. He relayed orders using a low whisper: "Gentlemen, on the other side of this mountain is a prison camp. Over the course of the next two days, we are to get everything we can on it. I want to know how many prisoners they got and how many soldiers are watching them. I want to know every damn routine, shift, and schedule. When they eat. When they sleep. Even when they crap...and what color it is when it comes out, ya hear? I want you to also get me as much as you can on any outside communication, transports, and supply schedules."

Mazer paused to peer into the fiery eyes of his ardent men. They were eager to do their job, but they were also equally eager for information. Mazer realized the task he proposed demanded an explanation. He had to give his men something in terms of details. "What we have here boys," he told them, "is evidence of enemy collaboration. Do not concern yourselves with the nationalities of the guards or prisoners. It's all the same for us. Remember at any moment, anybody can show up here—so be on your toes. We'll use the same teams and the same shifts we used on the beach. And obviously we're still on red alert—so use your hand signals."

"What if someone's spotted?" Corporal Greene asked. Everyone, including Mazer, immediately looked at him. Perhaps he had just wanted to hear himself speak after having been silent for days. Then again, being the youngest, Greene always found it the most difficult to contain his curiosity.

"How can you be spotted if you're invisible?" Mazer growled back, obviously annoyed by the question. "I know one thing for sure—if somehow I fuck up and get caught—then I'm not about to compromise the rest of the team or this mission."

The fiery leader's profound challenge was clear. He asked from his team nothing less than what he was willing to give—his own life. Turning to Russo, the cunning Colonel stated fervently, "Major, after I get caught and take myself out, then you are to radio Saigon at the designated time and finish this damn job."

Colonel Mazer's impassioned statements underscored the kamikaze-like commitment that he expected from his men. After that, no other insecurities were voiced.

The Inferno team immediately went to work. They designated the rendezvous spot for their spying operations not far from where they were, on a highly-elevated well-concealed plateau about a mile from the southwest corner of the compound. One of the men dubbed the prisoner compound "Alcatraz" while they were setting up camp and the name stuck. The dense draping foliage around their base camp placed it out of visual range of any of Alcatraz's residents. There, well-insulated from detection, the Inferno men would take short power naps and feast from the Cambodian jungle menu of frogs and snakes in between their watchdog shifts. Naturally the team was used to being on red alert, wherein verbal communication was limited during observations and at the rendezvous site. Their set of hand signals would continue to be their primary form of communication. Weapons were carried at all times, but everyone on the team realized that if they were needed, then they had failed their mission. At least until further instruction.

CHAPTER FOURTEEN

1992

Once inside the military restricted territory, the scenery outside the car changed dramatically. In a matter of minutes, the countryside went from being one of the most intensely cultivated and overpopulated in all of Asia, to an untapped, uninhabited landscape. All in all, a remarkable transformation, both in nature and character.

Almost immediately, Dominic sensed the vibrant personality of Vietnam was lost inside the gates. Gone was the energy exhibited by all the bent over farmers tirelessly working the land in the unforgiving tropical sun. Only a few short minutes inside the restricted region, Dominic found himself missing the sight of determined little children barking directions at reluctant herds of water buffalo or scampering for their roaming chickens. Most of all, he missed their curious expressions, as if they were looking at an alien, when he drove by and observed them with his strange round-shaped eyes, likely the only round eyes they had ever seen in person.

Although alive with nature, the land before him was nevertheless dead in spirit. It was only a matter of time before Dominic would experience the distinct personality of this new Vietnamese habitat.

After climbing to the top of one of the rolling mountains, the exhausted car slowed down and rolled to a stop. "We take a break now, Mr. Dominic," Quan said. Huyen and Lang popped open their doors, stepped out of the front seat, and began to stretch.

Dominic didn't move. After coming this far, he wanted to continue going. "But aren't we almost there?" he asked.

Quan opened his door and stepped outside. Peeking his head back into the car, he answered, "Yes, we're almost there. We will be at the mines in approximately one-half hour. But this is a very interesting and very special place. It overlooks all of northern Vietnam. Please, come take a look and see."

Dominic reluctantly exited the car. Huyen and Lang walked over to a nearby well and hoisted up the bucket. The two unfriendly hosts seemed to have a change of heart. Dominic noticed that they were talking socially to one another while they shared a refreshing sip of well water.

The view from atop the mountain peak was indeed breathtaking. It offered a complete panorama of Vietnam's untamed northern countryside, where Mother Nature had been left alone to her devices and intentions. Rolling hills, swelled and softened by time, towered above fertile valleys patterned and nourished by the snaking Black, Mekong, and Red Rivers. Dominic and Quan took a few silent moments gazing out at the lush forestry, mirrored ponds, and flowing rivers. The fuzzy blue sky subdued the scenery like textured strokes of a painter's brush. The subtle elegance of the postcard-worthy view was quite a relief from the encounter with the guards in charge of guarding such peaceful land.

Refreshed from the beauty, Quan stated triumphantly to Dominic: "Over there to the West is Dien Bien Phu."

Dominic looked in the direction of Quan's pointing finger. The frown that came over his face was the result of thought rather than eye strain. He did not know what Quan was talking about. He didn't want to admit it either. "Ahhhh, yes...ummm Dian...banan...poo..." he stated, butchering the name.

"The site of the very famous battle," Quan said decisively.

Dominic was relieved. "Yes, of course...the famous battle."

"The very famous battle," Quan corrected.

Dominic glanced at Quan and noticed an unusual change of posture. His unassuming interpreter was now standing confidently, with his hands planted firmly on his slim hips, his chest projected out, and his chin pushed forward. Dominic had seen similar prideful stances before. Another one of those military things. His father use to project himself in the same arrogant fashion, and Colonel Mazer still did. They were military men, though. They wore their egos like clothes for all to see. Seeing Quan in the same stiff stance was a total surprise. A total change of character.

"That was our final victory in the First War for Independence against the French," Quan said in a voice that matched his firm footing.

Dominic was disappointed that he never heard of Dien Bien Phu, for it was obvious from Quan's statement and attitude that it was a celebrated event in Vietnamese history. Seeing Quan's pride was intoxicating. He had to know what it was that divulged Quan's arrogance.

"Why don't you explain to me what took place?"

A smile parted across Quan's firm chin. It was clear that he was glad to offer up a Vietnamese history lesson to his American visitor. "In 1954, Dien Bien Phu was a heavily-fortified remote village of over 13,000 French troops. At that time, it was considered impervious to attack. The French were very confident that Dien Bien Phu could never be taken from them. They even publicly dared my people to come and fight them.

But while they were teasing us, we were busy preparing. Over 200,000 Vietnamese men, women, and children carried supplies through 500 miles of terrain to our troops surrounding the village. There were no roads or cars. It was just like you see out there. We had to carry all rice, water, and ammunition by shoulder-pole or on bicycle. Some had to drag the big cannon guns through the jungle for over fifty miles."

"And they won the battle..." Dominic stated, trying to disguise it for a statement rather than a question.

"After fifty-six days of battle," Quan said boldly, "the French surrendered and Vietnam was independent from colonialism."

Dominic smiled along with Quan and looked out into the rough jungle terrain. "That is truly amazing," he said in awe.

Eventually both of their smiles faded. A lull came over the conversation. Under other circumstances, such an interlude would serve only as a natural prelude to the next topic. But this pause, this excruciating pause, was far from natural. Dominic knew, for the most part, the unfortunate history that followed. And he was not about to discuss his country's long and tumultuous involvement in Vietnam, especially with his new Vietnamese friend. Presumably, Quan did not want to mention it either, as he also purported to take in the scenery. Some things were better left unspoken. Even among friends.

Dominic strolled off to the east and finally found an icebreaker on the other side of the hill. Pointing down, he blurted out to Quan: "What is that?"

"Excuse me, Mr. Dominic?" Quan said awakened from his momentary daze.

"Down there," Dominic said still pointing, "that complex...those people."

Quan could not see what it was that Dominic was referring to from his vantage point—so he walked over and looked down. "Ahhhh…" he bellowed. "That is Penitentiaire."

At the foot of the mountain, a dozen men, wearing conical hats and connected by chains were tilling an open field. Beyond them, another two dozen or so men, shackled together, were being led by an armed soldier. The entire field was enclosed by a thick, black, wrought-iron gate. At the far end of the field was a concrete castle-like fortress.

"Is it a military base?" Dominic inquired.

"Nooo," said Quan. His tone invited more guesses.

"Then what is it? A prison?"

"That is correct."

"What kind of prison is it?"

Dominic did not see the puzzled look on Quan's face when he responded with, "A prison for prisoners."

Dominic grinned, realizing that his question was not phrased properly. At the same moment, Huyen and Lang returned from the well. They were visibly refreshed, even smiling for the first time. Quan immediately filled them in on the conversation.

Huyen looked at Dominic and began to speak. Quan translated: "Penitentiaire was built by the French in 1908. It was originally a penal colony that held our people who defied French control. During the Second World War, it was used as a military base and bombed by the Japanese imperialists. In 1952, it was rebuilt and restored back to its intended use."

After nearly seven hours of silence, Dominic was surprised to hear Huyen now acting like a friendly tour guide. Nevertheless, in lieu of the business negotiations ahead, Dominic was not about to forsake an opportunity to bond with his hosts.

"Ask him what life is like for the prisoners," Dominic directed Quan.

After hearing the translation, Huyen smiled and issued a brief response. The three men chuckled.

"What did he say?" Dominic asked impatiently.

"Mr. Huyen says very difficult," recited Quan.

Dominic grinned, but he was not satisfied with the response. He wanted to know specifics. "It looks like they're farming," he declared. "That's what I see most of the people in Vietnam doing anyway?"

Quan probably could have answered the question himself but he deferred it to Huyen and Lang by translating. This time, Lang spoke as Quan interpreted:

"Mr. Lang says that the men are punished because they are unable to be with their friends and members of their families. Part of their duties is to farm their own food. That is what you see them doing right now."

"What kind of crimes have they committed?" asked Dominic.

Quan did not translate. He answered the question himself. "Crimes against the Socialist Republic of Vietnam."

"Like murder and rape?" asked Dominic.

"Oh no, Mr. Dominic," Quan chided. "The government does not tolerate such things."

Dominic nodded slowly, assuming from Quan's answer that, in dealing with violent crimes, the Vietnamese government imposed swift death sentences over lengthy life sentences. "Well then," he said jokingly, "is it a prison for foreigners who buy gem stones?"

Quan began to answer, but he stopped, realizing—mostly from Dominic's sarcastic smirk—that he was joking. Instead, Quan translated the question to the other two men and the entire uncomfortable collection of men, including Dominic, laughed together for the first time. For the next few minutes, the three men conversed lightheartedly in Vietnamese while Dominic watched the prisoners work on the fields down below.

"Mr. Dominic," said Quan, "Mr. Huyen and Mr. Lang have just informed me that you may take some pictures of the famous Penitentiaire if you would like."

"Great, tell him I would love to…but are you sure it's okay?"

"Yes," Quan assured him. "You may take a few pictures—but only if you keep them for your own private collection."

Dominic looked over at Huyen and Lang who were nodding their assurance. The concession, Dominic concluded, was a gesture of good will from his business hosts. "Tell them thank you," Dominic said while he adjusted his camera. After shooting a few shots he turned back to Quan. "Will one of them take a picture of you and me together?" Quan translated Dominic's request and Lang reached out his arms for the camera. Dominic handed Lang the camera, showing him which button to press. Stepping back, he then placed his arm around his friend Quan and smiled.

"Hold it! Hold it!" Dominic said to Lang just before he pressed the button. The three men were puzzled by Dominic's abrupt words. "Please, Mr. Huyen," he said waving his other host over. "I would like for you get in the picture also." Quan translated Dominic's request, though the gesture had been clear by his body language. Without hesitation, Huyen walked over, and the three men smiled wholeheartedly for the picture. Dominic was pleased. In the heat of the moment, the coldness of his foreign hosts was temporarily melted by photogenic camaraderie.

CHAPTER FIFTEEN

1972

"Dem' barracks look like they were made for Gilligan," Greene, whispered into his partner JD's ear as they lay side-by-side in a marsh. Though their non-verbal vocabulary was extensive, the Inferno team's hand signals could not describe everything.

And military sign language, of course, could not effectively appease Greene's playful personality.

JD smiled without looking at his mischievous friend. His eyes remained focused on the structure before them, which, now that Greene mentioned it, did look like a hut on Gilligan's Island. Naturally, he had to return a comment back into Greene's ear: "You know it would sure be nice if we saw Mary Ann and Ginger walk out from there."

Greene couldn't resist. "Yeah," he whispered. "And don't forget Mrs. Howell…so you could have some fun, too." JD just shook his head and smiled. He was used to it by now. With Greene as a partner, he may have been safe from danger but not from ridicule.

During the surveillance of Alcatraz, Greene, JD and the rest of the Inferno team again remained true to its chartered purpose, unheard and unseen. Like spying ghosts they thoroughly scouted and observed Alcatraz, documenting every routine, practice and procedure without incident. None of the American guards or Vietnamese prisoners at Alcatraz had any idea that they were being watched so intimately.

Alcatraz had two separate and different structures on its grounds. The southern structure was a bamboo-tied, one-story barracks that consisted of three entrances leading into three separate sections. The northern section of the barracks was by far the smallest section. According to the data brought in by the team, the northern section room served as communication headquarters for the camp. A radio switchboard and one wooden chair were the only things in it. The middle section of the barracks contained a double line of bunks. The southern end was used for cooking and eating. It was the largest section of the three. It was also where most of the nine American guards hung out when they were not on duty.

Approximately one hundred feet northeast of the barracks stood the second structure, a heavily secured prisoner containment area. It was a fenced chamber fifteen feet wide on each of its four equal sides and eleven feet high. A fenced dome closed in the top of the structure, and a tight tangle of barbed wire on the walls and ceiling more than ensured containment. Dark nettings of leaves and jungle debris were spread out over the entire structure to camouflage it.

The American guards stationed at Alcatraz called the structure "the cage." But after two days of spying from the outlying woods, the Inferno men saw things differently. They found such connotation to be too nice. Cages were something animals were kept in at a zoo. The prisoners of Alcatraz were treated far worse than animals. Their home was a dark dungeon. Dug out in the center of the cage was a deep ditch where twenty-eight tightly-packed prisoners of war spent twenty-three hours of each day. Unlike zoo animals, the Alcatraz attractions were packed together in a muddy hole like human sardines. There was not even enough room for them all to lie down and rest at the same time. Sleep and rest had to be done in shifts. The luxuries of stretching out and relaxing all day like a caged polar bear, or pacing back and forth like a caged lion were impossible to indulge in with their crammed quarters. Once a day, at approximately an hour past noon, the prisoners were let up out of the dungeon for about an hour. "Rec time," the guards laughingly announced.

During "rec time", the weary prisoners were free to enjoy the open confines of barbed wire instead of a muddy hole. It also allowed them the opportunity to dump out their one bathroom bucket. Unfortunately, though, they could not dump it on the outside of the cage. The prisoners had no choice but to dispose of their waste in one of the corners of the cage. The suffocating odor caused by the accumulation of feces and urine filled every breath the prisoner's took. The jungle flies were grateful though. Hundreds of them continuously swarmed the small hill of waste in the cage. They, along with hundreds of mosquitoes, also feasted mercilessly on the frail bodies of the prisoners, who were far too weak to expend the energy needed to brush them away.

In all, there were nine American soldiers stationed at Camp Alcatraz. The cage was guarded by two soldiers twenty-four hours a day. Six of the nine soldiers rotated shifts every eight hours to cover the time. Aside from the occasional trip to the barracks, the guards on security detail never ventured far from their stations at the cage. The two soldiers on detail often stayed together, smoked cigarettes, and chatted. At their disposal was a detonation switch hooked up to dynamite lining the prison hole. If the enemy launched a rescue mission, it was guaranteed to end not only in failure, but disaster. With one touch, the filthy muddy hole could instantly be transformed into a bloody mass grave.

Oddly, or so it seemed in the eyes of the Inferno men, the overall mood of Alcatraz guards was casual and lax. This, of course, made it easier for the Inferno soldiers to play the role of ghosts. Rarely were the guards of Alcatraz seen scouting the forest with binoculars. Never once did they dispatch out into the woods to conduct a long-range perimeter scout of the compound. The men running Alcatraz seemed unusually assured considering their isolated position, not to mention totally unaware of the tense camouflaged ghost eyes watching over them.

Breakfast for the camp was at 0630 hours, lunch at 1200 hours and dinner was served at 1800 hours. At those times, all but two of the nine guards would be eating inside the southern end of the barracks, while the remaining pair was over by the cage on security detail. The Inferno men were most jealous of Alcatraz's meals. Beds and showers they could do without. The smell of stew, though, was difficult to bear. After eating their own meals, a couple of Alcatraz soldiers loaded a bucket full of food and dropped into the prisoners ditch. "Feeding time!" they would yell. Sometimes they just yelled without dropping down anything.

Once a day, at approximately 1800 hours, Alcatraz's head commander, Major Scott, radioed, presumably either Saigon or perhaps Phnom Penh, from the northern section of the barracks. Each time he recited a cryptic, single sentence update on the compound: "Major Scott reporting that the lion sleeps tonight. Over." As far as the unit surmised, he was the only person from the compound that made any outside contact whatsoever. Curiously, no radio small talk was exchanged and no in-depth reporting was conducted. Saigon, or wherever the camp's command post was, didn't respond back over the radio. The entire one-sided radio transmission lasted no more than ten seconds per day. It was unknown when and how the camp received its supplies. It was assumed that no mail was brought in. No girls either.

It was difficult for the Inferno soldiers to witness the inhumane sight of the twenty-eight Alcatraz prisoners, all virtually lifeless—dilapidated, filthy, and paper-thin. During one thunderstorm, one of the guards yelled down to the men: "Shower time, boys!" The prisoners did not respond to their occasional heckling captors and said little to each other. By the length of their facial hair and frailty, it was clear that each of them had been an inmate for at least a couple months. Mentally, their spirits were definitely beaten down, but not broken. Amazingly, despite the horrible living conditions, scarcity of food, and lack of energy, each prisoner still walked with the posture of a proud soldier when they were allowed up for their hour of "recreation."

After two full days, the watchdog phase of Operation Inferno was complete. Alcatraz's schedules and routines were witnessed and documented in the journals. No Inferno soldier was seen. None was heard. The ghost mission was accomplished. The information they needed was in.

At the team's rendezvous site, Colonel Mazer gave the hand signals to Major Russo. The two men would head deep into the jungle together. The time had come to radio Saigon and receive the team's final orders from an anxious Agent Phillips.

CHAPTER SIXTEEN

1992

Ruby Mines

Restricted Military Zone, Vietnam

August 13, 4:43PM

Light waves invisible to the human eye surrounded Dominic as they do everyone. To most, these insensible phenomena are of no profit. To a gem dealer, these waves are precisely the dimension where profit lies, for it is the business of his trade to pierce the realm of the unseen and behold its brilliant orchestra of colors. Colors that can only be witnessed therein.

Dominic and his entourage had arrived at the gem mines only about fifteen minutes prior, but business was already at hand. General Kien was not a procrastinating man. He obviously felt there was no need for him and Dominic to get to know each other on a personal level before negotiations. So as Dominic spread the random rough stones he himself scooped from the ground outside across the glass table in front of him, Huyen rose from his chair and shut off the lamps in the jungle hut. On cue, Lang switched on the ultraviolet light—the passageway to invisibility. After a few seconds of blinking in the darkness, the thin, long bulb fully ignited, filling the small room with an eerie, almost surreal, luminescence. The moment of truth had arrived. It was time to witness the fluorescence, or lack thereof, in the stones from Southeast Asia.

Scattered over the glass top table, the scarlet stones seemingly baked like cinders in the ultraviolet light. An inexperienced observer would no more dare reach out and grab them than they would burning coals in an oven. Dominic was quiet in concentration, calculating how much the fiery rocks before him would pay.

General Kien was the only person in the room not peering down at the glowing rocks. Huyen and Lang were fixated. However, no one was more impressed than the rookie in the room, Quan. The fascination in his inexperienced eyes could not be appreciated in the dim fuzziness. "Do you like, Mr. Dominic?" he asked demonstrating that he was an amateur when it came to business negotiations.

Dominic, of course, did not answer. Or look at Quan. Or even blink. The question was perhaps the worst one he wanted to be asked so he pretended he did not hear it. Besides, he was in another world, sifting through the red rock, meticulously scrutinizing every pebble with his expert eyes, up close and from afar.

Across the table, behind a thin cloud of pungent smoke flowing from the orange tip of his menthol cigarette, General Kien sat back in his chair, revealing no expression. His legs and arms were crossed in such a way that it would seem uncomfortable and unnatural if done by any other man, but General Kien had a noble grace to his posture. Physically, his diminutive stature, gray hair, and smooth skin were, at first encounter, adverse to his legendary reputation as a former General extraordinaire for the fierce fighting machine known as the North Vietnamese Army. But his proud manner and commanding way of words revealingly oozed the unquestionable power of his position. Perhaps Quan had best summed up the General when he told Dominic during the last few minutes of their long ride—"General Kien is a man of history, mystery, and myth."

Dominic asked Lang if there was a microscope available. Quan translated and Lang nodded. Huyen opened the small wooden cabinet next to his chair, pulled out an old Russian microscope and handed it to Dominic. It was probably a priceless antique, Dominic thought to himself, as he set it down gently on the glass table. The lamps in the hut were turned back on. Ultraviolet radiation exited. Incandescence returned.

Magnification, a gem dealer would proclaim, reveals the fingerprints of a stone. When viewed from under the lens, Dominic saw the crimson, intersecting, needle-like crystals embodied within the rubies. Such a kaleidoscope of silky fabric layers, he knew, were found only in the most precious of gems. He was pleasantly amazed, although visibly neutral, to see that the rubies before him rivaled those from Burma, which boasted the purest, most expensive red rocks in the world. After a couple of minutes he receded back into his chair, wearing a straight, unimpressed look on his handsome face. He had seen enough. Looking at General Kien with one eye slightly closed, he spoke his first words to him since he had said "Nice to meet you," as they entered.

"How much?" he asked. Quan translated. The General did not need a translation of the question.

As expected, the powerful communist businessman was a careful man of thought. His words, always patient and brief, came translated via Quan: "The General says that the price depends on quantity."

Dominic pointed out that price also depends upon the quality of cut.

Lang answered Quan's translation. "Mr. Lang says that our cutters, like our stones, are top quality."

Dominic nodded. He was only setting up his hosts. Having only a commission deal with Shay—and an undetermined one at that—he sought to the keep the business of buying as simple as possible. Therefore, he had no intentions of making a deal with the General for cut and polished stones. Cutting the stones in Vietnam would complicate matters by adding an extra step to the business. And more importantly, it would delay and therefore complicate his commission payments. It was better to buy raw, in bulk. Let Krauze use his own contacts in Thailand to cut. Rough rock was the quickest, simplest way to commissions. So rough rock is what he wanted. Tons of it. "That's good to know," he responded, "but I am only interested in buying rough rock…at least in the beginning."

"What is rough rock?" Quan asked before translating to the others.

"Exactly what's in front of us," Dominic explained. "Stone right out of the ground. We'll use our own people to cut the jewels from them. Tell them all they have to do is scoop it and send it."

Quan translated and General Kien, Huyen, and Lang talked among themselves for a short while. Dominic could not help but admire the General as he spoke to Huyen and Lang. He was impressed by the General's mannerisms, his understated and impressive character; the indescribable power manifested by his smooth presence. Even the way he handled a cigarette was aristocratic. With crossed arms, he would hold the cigarette out in front of him, never down by his side. Using his thumb and two fingers he would slowly, almost subconsciously, rotate it in his hand. The continuous revolution of the cigarette was symbolic of the patient and relentless thought process going on inside his head.

Never before had Dominic encountered such an assured and graceful businessman. He was fascinated by him. He liked to hear him speak, never mind that he could not understand a word. He wanted to see him move, listen to his opinions. But most of all, he wanted to learn about his experiences—because only a diverse sculptor of experience could have shaped such a distinguished man of character.

Quan translated, "Mr. Huyen would like to know the amount of rough stones Mr. Krauze will be buying?"

Dominic countered shrewdly by asking about the production capability of the operation.

After Quan translated, everyone turned to General Kien. "General Kien says," Quan interpreted, "they can mine one ton of rough stone every month. Production, of course, can also be increased to meet demands. "

Dominic looked around the collection of men in the small room. He knew that he needed to secure a "rock-bottom" low price in order to justify a liberal commission for himself. However, the rubies from Vietnam were of much better quality than he had expected, therefore he could not raise a credible "inferior-quality" argument when it came to setting a price. These gems were undeniably magnificent. And, more amazingly, the rest of the world did not yet know it.

Except for Quan, Dominic had to assume that the men in his company were well aware that a flawless ruby was extremely rare and could command higher prices than even diamonds of similar cut and weight. So in order to secure the best price possible, Dominic really had only one option: offer to buy everything. "Mr. Krauze will want to buy all of your production. Everything that you can dig up. Provided, of course, that the price is agreeable."

Quan hesitated a moment before translating. His face lit up. He was clearly impressed by the statement, and he was not a man who felt it necessary, or even possible, to ever hide his emotions.

Upon hearing the news, the General's chiseled face did not flinch. When he began to speak, Quan quickly removed a pencil and notepad from his shirt pocket. He wanted everything to be clear when it came to numbers so he wrote them down before translating. That way there would be no confusion or mistake on his part. After General Kien nodded approvingly, Quan slid the pad over to Dominic, stating, "Two thousand US dollars per pound. General Kien says that is the price."

"Too much," Dominic answered abruptly without even looking down at the pad. "Much too much." Actually, Dominic admitted to himself, the price was fair given the quality of the stones. "Listen Quan, tell the General that it's very simple. He knows that Mr. Krauze buys rubies from all over the world. If he wants Mr. Krauze to buy all of his production then he has to give him the best price in the world." Hearing the translation from Quan, the three men again conferred.

Dominic moved forward in his chair. Instead of playing ping-pong in negotiations, he decided to seize the moment. He knew the best way to seal a deal was to dangle cash, so he strategically interrupted their round table discussion: "Excuse me, Quan—let me save everyone a lot of time…" All three men stopped talking and looked at Quan, who began reciting Dominic's offer in Vietnamese. His tone, which was naturally unassuming in any language, at that moment seemed to mirror the conviction in Dominic's voice. "One thousand US dollars per pound. The first order will be for one million dollars. Half the money will be sent to me here tomorrow. The other half will be paid when the shipment arrives. If all goes well, we'll take everything you have. There will be no negotiating the price for the term of three years. And I want a guarantee that we will have no problems with the law about getting the stones across the border." His next statement was the most influential: "If the terms are acceptable I will cancel my trip to Sri Lanka and inform Mr. Krauze that we have found our new, long-term suppliers."

The three men listened intently to Quan's interpretation. Huyen and Lang did not mutter a word. There was, after all, nothing further for them to discuss. They both sat back in their respective chairs. Their ears, like everyone else's, were tuned in to General Kien. A bottom-line offer was on the table, one that only he could accept or reject.

General Kien was, of course, in no rush to speak. After disposing of one short cigarette, he stretched another long cigarette from the open pack on the table. Dominic studied the General's slow-motioned demeanor. The General's body, like his words, did not waste an action. His hands moved gracefully, almost as if they were trained to obey his commands. From his shirt pocket he pulled out a small glass bottle and removed the cap. Instantly, a sharp, unmistakable pungency of menthol filled the room. The General proceeded to slowly pour a line of the liquid menthol down the length of his cigarette. On cue, Huyen handed his boss an unlit match. It was clear from the routine that General Kien was a man who always lit his own cigarette. At that moment, he looked up at Dominic. His stare was not cold, nor was it scornful. It did, however, feel like an X-ray to Dominic, as if the General had the ability to see through everything. Into a person's mind. And through all bullshit. Keeping his penetrating eyes on Dominic, he ignited the match by striking it on the leg of his chair. The match burned for a couple of seconds, then he lit up. Two extended drags would be taken in and let out slowly before he spoke. But when he finally did, it was as smooth as the flavor of his cigarette.

CHAPTER SEVENTEEN

1972

Parrot's Beak
Cambodia
September 4, almost noon

The last half-mile stretch was the most difficult for Major Russo to keep quiet. He and Colonel Mazer had broken away from the others, trekking the total of about a mile north of the team base in order to conduct the radio call to Agent Phillips at 1200 hours. During the past two days of silence, the peculiar facts surrounding Alcatraz weighed heavily on Russo's mind. He knew his commanding officer had the same thoughts. First and foremost, it was situated in Cambodia, which made its establishment an illegal expansion of the unpopular war into a neutral country. It was also in the heart of Charlie territory, well over one hundred miles from a friendly base or major reinforcements. This made Alcatraz not only extremely vulnerable but also virtually defenseless to an enemy search-and-rescue or seek-and-destroy operation. Furthermore, it was a well-camouflaged position under a dense jungle canopy, thereby eliminating the possibility of effective strategic air cover from the U.S. air force in the event of a likely attack. Strategically speaking, there was only one way to put it—Alcatraz was just as much a secret as Operating Inferno was. Logic dictated that it was a suicidal camp. To an informed veteran soldier of Vietnam, such circumstances were too suspicious, too curious to ignore.

Colonel Mazer stopped walking and began to set up for the transmission. Before he dialed out, Russo broke the two days of silence. His voice was a whisper, but his tone was no less compelling. "Give me one logical reason for the establishment or survival of Alcatraz."

After a short pause, Mazer, clearly not as anxious to once again converse answered, "No."

Russo pressed him with the arguments: "It's not heavily-fortified. It's in the middle of remote, hostile, illegal territory. And it's made to house enemy POWs. We both know a goddamn wounded deer in a cage of hungry leopards has a better shot at survival than Alcatraz."

The Colonel nodded.

"So what the fuck is going on here?"

Mazer did not respond. Instead, he took a gulp of water from his canteen. He swallowed slowly and took his time before he looked up at his Major, who was waiting impatiently to hear something rational from his Colonel. "They're interacting with the enemy," he said bluntly.

"Nothing the team has brought in supports that," Russo retorted. "Nothing!"

"It's been two goddamn days, for crissakes."

"But it doesn't make sense even for two hours. You saw the conditions for those prisoners—they're treated worse than goddamn zoo animals. How would—how could the enemy allow its own prisoners to be treated that poorly? Don't tell me how it's all for the exchange of information. No fuckin' way."

"How do you know it's not all a big show?" Mazer questioned. "One big make-believe circus disguising the cooperation. You know damn well that the 'Cong would have a hundred volunteers willing to live in that cage like animals if it helped them win this war."

"Fine," Russo acknowledged, "maybe I can see it happening from the enemy's point of view…but what about ours? It makes no sense from our position."

"It makes even more sense," Mazer argued. "Like I said…treason is the only explanation for camp's survival. How else would it avoid certain detection and destruction?"

Russo was not willing to accept that explanation. "Okay. Say you're right. Let's assume it's treason. That explains its survival…but still doesn't explain its establishment. Since when did we have reservations about publicizing our captives before? Huh? Have you ever heard of a secret prison camp prior to seeing this?"

Mazer responded by shaking his head no.

"Of course not," Russo stressed. "You know better than me why we love to promote that stuff. It allows us to offset the enemy's POW bargaining chip at the negotiation table—you have fifty of our men, well, great. We have sixty of yours."

Mazer countered: "There are probably many fucked up reasons why Alcatraz was set up that you and I could never understand. Their lack of outside communication proves only that it is a closely guarded secret. Maybe the prisoners were unexpectedly stumbled upon and seized during one of the Army's "unofficial" incursions into Cambodia. Maybe they are gathering intelligence on the Cambodia nationals for something down the road. Maybe we are dealing with double agents. It could be totally rogue for all we know. The bottom line is we don't know. What we do know is that we got a bunch of shit bureaucrats sitting on their fat fuckin' asses trying to figure out what to do or say to appease the hippie protesters. In the interim, Major Scott probably cut some kind of deal with Charlie. That is probably what happened."

Russo took a moment to think. With his hands on his hips he asked Mazer, "And we're Washington's response?"

"No. We're the President's response." Mazer stated confidently while he picked up the portable phone and dialed.

Russo turned away disgusted. He unscrewed his canteen and poured some water over his head to cool his anger. The call to Agent Phillips lasted less than a minute. Mazer did not say more than one word multiple times into the receiver. He just listened intently, and responded with a "copy" a few times. It was all the more frustrating to Russo being unable to hear what Phillip's was saying on the other end of the line. But he had a pretty good idea what was being communicated.

"Let's move out," Mazer stated immediately after he hung-up.

"What's the deal?" Russo asked, as if he did not know.

Mazer didn't answer. He knew Russo knew what "the deal" was so he ignored him and gathered up the equipment and perched it on his back. Then he looked at Russo gave him the hand signal to move out.

Mazer headed forward. Russo stayed behind, fuming. He would have to wait to hear the final orders officially with the rest of the Inferno team. The middle finger was the only hand signal response that would properly convey his feelings, so he raised it defiantly to Mazer's back as he walked away. After the Colonel disappeared in the bush and was almost fifty yards away, Russo began to follow. But not before vowing to himself that it would be the last time he would ever follow Mazer.

CHAPTER EIGHTEEN

1992

Insects, bats, and other creatures of the night performed a discordant symphony of nocturnal music outside. Unusual howls and growls that would alarm even the bravest city slicker filled the air. Dominic was too uptight to pay any attention to the sounds of darkness outside his hut. He had other things bugging him.

Inside, the humming buzz of the lamp helped drown some of the jungle noises. After three frustrating disconnections, he waited for an operator who could understand English. Five minutes passed…ten…fifteen minutes ticked off his watch. He passed the time by watching his roommate, a black spider the size of his hand, leisurely crawl up the wall. Boris, as Dominic named him, would silently raise his long hairy legs, one at a time, and creep methodically and slowly up the bamboo uprights. His distorted shadow splashed over half the hut, making him seem more of a monster than he already was. All the while, Dominic felt Boris' eyes fixated on him. "Do not kill him," Quan had told Dominic earlier, before he retired to his own guest hut located further down the trail. "He is your friend for the night."

"That is my friend for the night?"

"Yes, he eats all the mosquitoes. And mosquitoes carry malaria."

Funny, Dominic was thinking while he waited on the phone, *we're supposedly friends—but neither of us trust the other enough to look the other way for more than a few seconds.*

"May I help you?" an operator finally asked in English.

"Yes, yes, yes!" Dominic declared. "Thank you. I'd like to make a call to the United States."

After dictating the phone number to operator, Dominic felt the temperature in his body increase while the line rang faintly on the other end of the receiver. He knew he had jumped the gun, symbolically and perhaps literally, by negotiating a deal—an exclusive, multi-million dollar deal—without Mr. Krauze's blessing. But this had purpose. It was part of the plan he had spontaneously hatched on the terrace at the United Nations while negotiating with New York's most notorious criminal baron.

"Yeeees," answered the deep, distant, distinct voice on the other end.

It was time to see if his gamble would work...

"Mr. Krauze, it's Dominic."

"Ahhh, Dominic." Shay's tired voice struggled to purr with melody. "Vaaat's doing?"

"I'm here at the mines with General Kien."

"How was your trip?"

"Long. Good, though. No problems."

"That's good. Sooo, how's their operation?"

"It's basic. They have the heavy machinery. The rest is a little primitive but it seems efficient enough. They only gave me a brief tour. Everybody's very secretive about things over here. The area is highly restricted. I think I am the first foreigner to visit here in a long time so I'm sure they don't want me to see too much unless we're actually doin' business."

"How much business are they doin'?"

"A bunch of trucks come in and out of here pretty regularly. And like you said, it's all run by the General Kien and the Vietnamese National Police. Every truck has "VNP" on its license plate. I don't know who they're selling to or where they are trucking it to but someone's buyin' a lot of rock from here."

"What about the product?"

"Top-quality," Dominic exclaimed. "I'm talking Burmese quality."

After a short pause, Shay stated, "Is that riiiiight?"

"That's right," Dominic assured him. "We are right in the heart of three river valleys. The Black, Red and Mekong River are all in this vicinity. It's very fertile ground. And untapped."

"Those minerals have been feeding the stones for thousands of years,"

Shay surmised.

"Definitely. These stones are outstanding. Way beyond what I expected."

"Mmmm…Can they cut?"

It was time for Dominic's first lie. "No, I saw some samples from their factory. Not good. We need to cut elsewhere until they learn what they're doin'."

Again, there was a short pause. "Weeeeellll, what kind of deal do you think we can make?" Shay asked.

"I'm not entirely sure yet," Dominic said delicately and falsely. "We have just been feeling each other out. They're not dummies when it comes to value. Like I said, they're definitely doin' business with somebody. And the whole operation is government-controlled. The trucks, the soldiers. It looks more like a military operation than a mining business."

"Are you sure they're selling only rubies?"

By now Dominic was holding the phone receiver and pacing back and forth in his hut. Boris' distrusting eyeballs kept pace with him, following his two-legged roommate's every step. "I don't know. But I'll find out. We've already had some preliminary talks. You know, just feeling each other out, really. They definitely want to do business with us, but they also know that with such high quality stones they'll be able to command premium rates. It looks to me like they can mine about one ton of rough stone every month. So, I think if we guarantee to eventually take all of it, you know, make an exclusive output deal, then I could maybe get us a price of about two thousand bucks per pound."

"Two thousand per pound!?" Shay repeated with concern.

Dominic was lying, but he knew that Krauze's surprise was a lie. In business negotiations of this kind, it was also expected. But Dominic had done his homework. He had made dozens of inquiries before he left for Vietnam. And the streets of New York City had whispered a different story into his ears. Mr. Krauze was paying more money for the lesser quality stones he was getting out of Thailand. "Look, I promise you this stuff is better than you think," Dominic continued. "One carat could be worth as much as ten thousand dollars on the retail market. It's that genuine. I say we offer to take one million dollars' worth to start. They'll have to agree. How could they not if we guarantee them that kind of volume?"

There was a long pause on the other end. Dominic's face moistened from nervousness. He sat back down at the edge of his chair and looked over at Boris, who by now had made his way onto the ceiling. Dominic feared that Shay was seeing right through the phone and reading right through his misleading plan. *I blew it*, he thought to himself, *I shouldn't have said a number.*

"Alright son, you got it," Shay pronounced, interrupting Dominic's building panic. "I'll take that deal. Provided, of course, that you can make it. But that number includes the broker fee. I repeat, it includes your fee. So if you want to earn a penny, you best carve out a better deal—'cause I'm not adding your commission on top of that price. Are we clear?"

Dominic smiled. He had expected Shay to play hardball and box him into a corner. His plan—to get Mr. Krauze to agree to worse terms than he had arranged—was working. The gamble he made on the terrace of the United Nations was indeed paying off. Mr. Krauze was willing to pay double what he had already done in the deal with General Kien, therefore his commission would amount to one thousand dollars per pound. Mr. Krauze was certainly not about to come to Vietnam to validate things. The old man hated leaving Brooklyn. Dominic would be the point person. He would serve as the liaison. The ambassador between the General Kien and Mr. Krauze. The liaison controls the communication, and, consequently, controls the deal.

After a strategic pause to insinuate his reluctance, Dominic finally declared: "All right then, wire half the money, five hundred thousand dollars, in my name to the State Bank of Vietnam in Hanoi. That's the government's bank. The account is already set up. General Kien said that he will make sure that the bank will keep everything under wraps. After I get the wire, I'll come back up here and oversee everything personally. I'll make sure everything goes off smoothly with the shipment. We'll pay them per shipment. This way no one can fuck with us."

Dominic's stomach was tingling with excitement. He was delighted. His life was completely changing before him. Unbridled thoughts of the future rocketed through his mind. He would have to stay in Vietnam for a few months, perhaps a year. He was looking forward to it. Big money was in Vietnam, Julie was in Vietnam. And he loved them both. Besides, he was well aware that the only way to insure his cut was to continue being the ringleader for the deals. The store would definitely have to wait, he told himself. Small potatoes. He was set to make five hundred thousand dollars in one shot in Vietnam. In just one shipment. In his wildest dreams, he could never earn that much in years back selling earrings to tourists. Mr. Krauze even told him that he had to work in his commission into the number. It was already done. Just like Mr. Krauze wanted. Not exactly in the order he wanted, but it all worked out in the end.

Dominic realized his life had never been better than at that very moment. All he had worked for these past years was a chance at the big time. And this was the big time. He had made himself a player in Vietnam. He had the most beautiful woman in the country. And he was soon to be rich.

"The money is on the way," Shay confirmed.

Dominic got up from his seat, clenched his fist and punched the air victoriously. Never before had he felt such power or exhibited such mastery. The euphoria rushed through him like a drug, and he was totally high on it. "Good," he said in formal voice, "I'll contact you tomorrow after I reach the bank to confirm receipt of the wire. At that time, you'll tell me where you want the stones to be sent for cutting and polishing. I'll handle all the shipping arrangements. I already ran some numbers. We can get into Bangkok for less than 15 percent."

After a deep breath he went on: "I'm telling you, Mr. Krauze, wait 'til you see these stones. They're gonna be a gold mine. I'll stay here as long as I have to. I'll watch every scoop. Don't you worry, I'll make sure of everything."

"That all sounds good son," Shay replied calmly, "but there is one thing you need to understand…"

"What's that?"

"You are personally guaranteeing this deal."

Dominic's eyebrows dropped. His exhilaration sobered. "What do you mean?"

"Very simple—you told me that is the best deal you can get for me, and I said okay. You told me to send five hundred thousand immediately, and I said okay." Krauze's melodic voice then plummeted to a deeper, threatening tone: "Now—if for some reason I don't receive what I am paying for or I find out you or that General were not one-hundred percent honest with me in the deal, then your store and everything in it is mine. You got that?"

Stunned, Dominic slumped spinelessly back into the chair. All of the built-up jubilation inside him collapsed to the pit of his stomach. He had already been dishonest in the deal. The plan, his gamble, now backfired on him.

"Guarantees?" Dominic uttered, trying to disguise his worry as confusion. "How can I make guarantees about General Kien? He's your guy."

"No!" Shay snapped. "You're there with him, aren't you? You're negotiating with him, not me! That means he's your guy, not mine! If you want him to be my guy then go get him and put him on the phone. I'll make the deal myself. But if you do that—then you are out completely, you get nothing…though, you would get to go back to your store and live happily ever after."

Dominic was cornered. *Of course Shay could make the deal himself,* he fumed, *now that I traveled thousands of miles, investigated the operation and verified the product!*

I almost got myself killed by more than one renegade soldier doing all the legwork for this fuckin' deal! There was no way Dominic was going to let Shay get away with using him to set things up and then cut him out. This, it was now clear to him, was Shay's plan all along.

Meanwhile, Shay's voice returned to its natural soothing tone: "Well—what do ya saaaay, Dominic. Are you willing to take the risk? Do you want to be a player in this high stakes game? Or do you want to play it safe and come home?" He was taunting his young broker. "It's your call—shall I wire the money or not?"

Dominic's mind furiously searched for answers. His face turned red as a ruby from the blood rushing through his veins. "Send it," he finally declared and hung up.

Leaning back in the chair, he reached up and put both hands on his sweat-soaked face. Peeking through his fingers, he saw that Boris was now directly above him on the ceiling. They stared at each other for a few minutes. "I have to figure out something, Boris…I don't know what…but I have to figure out something." His arachnid roommate stared back at him, offering no visual signs of sympathy.

Meanwhile, in a smoky dark hut two hundred yards from Dominic's, the eavesdropper removed his headphones and pulled the wire out from a telephone switchboard. For the next couple of minutes he finished transcribing information on the notepad. Behind him, General Kien was standing with one foot on the back of the eavesdropper's chair, savoring his menthol-flavored cigarette in his typical fashion—by inhaling deeply…holding it in…and then releasing the smoke gently out of the side of his mouth. After the eavesdropper was finished, the two men conversed in Vietnamese.

CHAPTER NINETEEN

1972

Parrot's Beak
Cambodia
September 4, 12:44PM

Colonel Mazer led the team away from the rendezvous site, deeper into the jungle. He needed to talk to his team. After about a half a mile he stopped and gathered in his men in a tight semi-circle in front of him. "Gentlemen, we have our orders," he commanded in a low voice. "I just received confirmation from Saigon that the officers of Alcatraz have been engaged in an ongoing conspiracy with the North Vietnamese. All I can tell you is that they have disclosed information to the enemy that has seriously compromised our positions in the South. We have been instructed to eliminate the camp... immediately."

"What about the men?" Russo asked from the far left, but he already knew that answer to his question.

Mazer responded to the question without looking at him. "They have all been designated for elimination. Prisoners and men." The Colonel then proceeded to gaze into the eyes of each member of the team, except for Russo, whom he knew was infuriated. He knew his orders would not be an easy pill to swallow, even for a team trained to swallow anything and not ask questions. "This is what we have been sent here for, gentlemen," Mazer continued. "You are about to embark on the most important mission of the entire war. Victory over the enemy is not good enough. That's not our objective here. Complete extermination is. No one can get away. No one can survive. No prisoners will be taken. And no one can have the opportunity to radio an alert of the raid. Our attack must be swift. Our attack must be lethal. There's no room for mistakes. Each second will count. Each of us needs to be one hundred percent successful in takin' out our targets or we don't go home. It's that simple."

The boys of Operation Inferno were primed. Mazer could see the fire burning in their eyes. Being mere watchdogs was making them nervous. They were warriors. Twentieth century gladiators needing a fight to feel safe. Eventually, someone would be detected if they stayed invisible. And when a combat soldier is nervous, his trigger finger gets very itchy. All their training and expertise was about to culminate in one, grand, bloody finale.

"Fuckin' traitors," JD growled with rage.

"Its rock and roll time," Greene uttered.

Mazer told them he was cut off from any communication with Agent Phillips, even in the event of an emergency, until after the mission was accomplished. The team was on its own. Anything short of complete success, and their own command—the very men who called upon their services—would categorically deny their existence. Seven of America's most lethal patriots were issued an ultimatum by their country and none of them flinched. They were prepared. It was official now. They were "unofficial" assassins.

"Mendez?" Mazer said.

"Sir," he retorted.

"Check out all the data we gathered, make sure everyone's numbers match up. I want you to review Alcatraz's routines and report to me and Major Russo in one hour. Doc will give you a hand but keep things low. I don't want those boys to hear our little party up here, understand?!"

"Aye, Colonel," he responded.

As Mendez began to walk away, Mazer stopped him by stating, "Don't forget to check those vehicle logs. I don't want to go in there if they have any kind of reinforcements on the way."

"Don't you worry, Colonel," Mendez stated confidently, "It will all be taken care of."

"Who's on lookout?" Mazer asked the remaining troops.

"I am," JD answered.

"Keep a close eye for the next few hours. From here on out, you're the only watchdog. All the unit's recon is done...so pay very close attention 'cause we're most vulnerable starting now. I want to know if anything unusual is going on down there."

JD nodded his head. "No problem," he said.

The Colonel addressed the others: "The rest of you refuel and relax. We'll set strategy in an hour. I want to get this thing done and get the fuck outta here by dawn."

The entire platoon dispersed except for Russo and Mazer.

Colonel Mazer brought his binoculars up to his eyes and peered down into valley toward Alcatraz. He knew his Major was fuming. He had been expecting another confrontation sooner or later. As usual, the rest of the unit was easy. They would never dare to question orders issued by their revered Colonel. They were trained attack dogs. Their job was to carry out orders, deadly orders. And they were the best boys in the business for this job.

But Major Russo was different from the other troops. Their relationship was different. They had a shared, tumultuous history. They had saved each other's lives on more than one occasion. Accordingly, Russo was the only man in the unit—the only inferior officer in the entire United States Army for that matter—who could defy the renowned Colonel Clifford Mazer. He did so, however, only far outside the presence of others.

"Attack?" he said in a harsh whisper, "Those are our fuckin' men, Cliff!"

"They're not our men, John," Mazer calmly replied, continuing his distant inspection, "They are enemy soldiers. And they have been targeted for elimination."

"Yeah!" Russo exclaimed into his Colonel's ear. "And they're being guarded by our fuckin' men."

The now irritated Colonel dropped his binoculars and quickly turned around and faced Russo. For a few tense moments he stared directly into the frowning eyes of his subordinate officer. Despite their differences in rank, the two men were physically equal in height and stature. Being unable to raise his voice, Mazer pressed nose-to-nose with Russo and said in a forceful whisper, "That's incorrect, Major. They're all enemy soldiers that have been targeted for elimination!"

"Do you realize what you're saying? Huh?! Do you realize what you're doing? You are asking me and the rest of the team to premeditate the murder of officers of the United States Army."

"They are no longer our soldiers. They have conspired with Charlie and therefore..."

"Dammit, Cliff!" Russo growled. The man inside, the man he had kept bottled up for so long, needed to vent his anger. He could not simply act like an obedient subordinate, like a killing machine without a conscience, anymore. "Will you listen to yourself? You sound like a programmed, goddamn bureaucrat! What is the rationale to all this? As long as we hide behind the flag during war then it's okay to murder our own guys? Is that it? That's fuckin' bullshit and you know it!"

Russo softened his tone offering a compromise, "Let's go in and arrest all of them instead of just carrying out summary executions. There's only a dozen or so, right? Let's bring 'em all in. If they're traitors, fine. We'll be able to prove it. Radio Phillips and tell him we'll secure the camp and the prisoners while…"

"What do you want from me, John!?" Mazer barked. "Huh? I'm a goddamn Colonel in the United States Army! And you want me to somehow start making distinctions between murder and war? Is that what you want from me? You want to start walking that fine line now? After all these years? For crissakes, look around. What have you, me, and everyone else been doing here for the last half a dozen years? They haven't even given us a goddamn declaration of war. You know what that means…don't you? It means that we're here fighting in fuckin' cold blood! I got news for you my friend, this ain't been no fuckin' war here. This never was a war for us. This has been coldblooded murder from day one. North Vietnamese, South Vietnamese, Vietcong, mother, daughter, baby—what's the fuckin' difference? We kill 'em all! Hell, all those fuckin' college protesters back home who don't like what we're doing over here…fuck 'em. We'll shoot and kill them, too!"

Russo kept quiet and stared intensely at Mazer with complete hostility. After a few moments, Mazer continued in a less harsh tone, "Who's kidding who, John? Did you ever take a few minutes to think about where we are? Did you ever think about where we've been? There are no casualties of war here in Southeast Asia. These ain't no enemies of ours here. Hell, this ain't even our war, John. This is somebody else's goddamn war. You can't get that through your thick head. If we were to pack up all our guns and bags and leave, ain't nobody from Vietnam is gonna follow us back to fight. If we simply all got up and left this place, this whole goddamn thing would be over for us. Therefore it's all been fuckin' murder for us!"

A solemn shadow cast over both men as they separated from their close distance. Russo put his hands on his hips and turned away. In many ways, his arguments with Mazer were nothing more than an ongoing struggle with his own conscience. Deep down he had known as well as Mazer that Operation Inferno would come to something like this. Something tragic. Something horrible. It was just that after six years in Vietnam—most of them away from his wife and two children—the man inside him found some sort of consolation in being a reluctant belligerent. Looking out across the mountain vista, he took in a deep breath of air and engaged in a rare moment of appreciation for the vivid greenery of Cambodia's rolling hills. He thought of home. His wife barely knew him. He barely knew his two kids. He barely knew himself. "What are we, Clifford?" he asked softly, exhaling the heavy air in his lungs.

"We're soldiers, John. We don't ask moral questions. We don't have a conscience. We just do. This mission is not my mission. It's not your mission. It's their mission. We're only the puppets. We're useless...lifeless...unless someone else is holding the strings."

Russo shook his head in disappointment. "Two mindless murder machines..."

"No, not mindless. If they say our men are spies, then they made that choice, not us. The truth is we don't know for sure. Not because we're mindless, but because we simply don't have enough information to make that determination."

"So we're hiding behind some kind of blind faith in the goddamn CIA for all this?"

"You keep torturing yourself trying to find some sort of noble purpose to all this bloodshed. I've got news for you pal, there ain't no more noble causes left in the world. It's all about power and money. We are part of the war machine. That's all."

"What if turns out that we're wrong?"

"I told you that we can't be wrong because..."

"I know," Russo interrupted, "because we are acting upon their determinations, not our own. But what if...what if they are lying and it's a setup not only for the camp but also for all of us? They could just as easily take us out after we take out the camp. No one knows we're here, so why would they take any chances and risk all of this coming out later on. Remember, we are doing the President's dirty laundry here. You know that better than me. You also know that's a very dangerous responsibility because once we're done here, and the President's underwear is nice and white again, me, you and the rest of the boys are still gonna know where all of his old stains came from."

"You don't think that I have thought of that possibility from the beginning?" Mazer exclaimed. Pointing to himself, he then added, "You think I trust those motherfuckers anymore than I trust the damn 'Cong? C'mon John, you know me better than that. Why do you think I wouldn't take any of their agency boys with me on this one? Not one. I made goddamn sure of that. I chose every person in this unit and that was for a reason...so this entire team would be my boys, our boys, not theirs. This way, if they fuck around with us, then they're the ones who'll get fucked! Trust me—I've got it all worked out."

CHAPTER TWENTY

1992

Ruby Mines

Restricted Military Zone, Vietnam

August 14, 3:00AM

Repeated attacks of shaking chills, severe headaches, high fever, and profuse sweating set in. The symptoms can last for several hours. The lucky ones get them only every three days, the less lucky every two or less. It spreads in the dark of night via the soundless wings of sixty different species of mosquitoes throughout the poorest climates on the planet—tropical, sub-tropical, and even temperate regions of the world—to millions of people each year. A seemingly harmless bite that does not even wake you up from your sleep, left untreated, may end in death.

In Vietnam, a mosquito net is called, appropriately, a "life saver" when draped around a bed at night. Its fine delicate netting protects its inhabitants within from malaria, one of the oldest diseases known to man. That night, however, the mosquito net in Dominic's hut would be life-saving for different reasons.

"Goddammit!" Dominic barked out loud.

The bathroom of his jungle hut did not have a light. Electricity was cut off every night at midnight. It was three o' clock in the morning, and he had not slept a minute. Everything, it seemed, was unraveling. The "toilet bowl" his body squatted above was nothing more than a small hole in the bathroom floor. And what should have been a traditionally routine bathroom visit had become another flirt with disaster.

Typically, from the front, aim does not present itself to be a waste removal problem to human males. Targeting outputs from behind—particularly loose, liquid, uncontrollable ones—were, as Dominic had been discovering all night, an altogether different story. To complicate matters, his stomach, unnerved from the earlier phone conversation with Mr. Krauze and unaccustomed to the local food, was playing cruel tricks on him. Too bad his downtrodden mood prevented him from appreciating the self-deprecating—or, more accurately, "self-defecating"—humor of his recently completed struggle for bathroom accuracy.

Convinced that his body had nothing left to expel, Dominic finally buttoned his pants and turned on the "sink"—a drooling hose on the floor that also doubled as the shower. He covered half the spout with his thumb in order to increase the water pressure across the floor. He couldn't tell if it was actually working, because it was too dark. Better, he felt, not to get a good look at the mess. The weight of the world was on his mind as he sprayed the soiled bathroom floor.

While the water washed across the floor and down into the hole, Dominic's mind began to cleanse itself from the stress. Mr. Krauze was not the problem, he eventually concluded. All he had to do was call him tomorrow night and simply tell him he had just ironed out a deal for a thousand bucks per pound. *He will never know that I had secured that price before I spoke with him the first time. Besides, he'll be too impressed to even think I was dishonest.* At that price, he was confident Mr. Krauze would offer him a generous commission. *At least ten percent,* he figured. *That's fifty grand on the first shipment alone!*

It was now more important than ever to make certain the shipments go off without incident. General Kien and his men had to be kept honest. The poundage of the shipment must always equal exactly what is paid for. There could be no mistakes. Dominic would make sure of it. He had no other choice. After all, it was his store, his livelihood, perhaps even his life, that Mr. Krauze was using as insurance for their honesty.

Dominic turned off the rubber hose and wiped his face on the towel. He was beginning to feel better, both physically and mentally. His somersaulting stomach settled. Things will be easier, he assured himself, with all parties, including him, being completely honest with the deals. They'll be plenty of money to go around.

Gazing back into the bedroom, he admired the faint rays of moonlight seeping between the bamboo seams of his hut. Encircling his bed, the meshed lacework of his mosquito net filtered the moon's rays into finer, hairline streams, creating a chamber of glowing moonbeams that dissected the thick night air. He noticed Boris' moon shadow was increasing his size as he crawled silently across the wall. Nevertheless, it was a peaceful sight for his easing mind. But it was all about to change.

Out of the corner of his eye, Dominic saw the door to his hut slowly opening. Silently, without warning, two shadows stepped inside. Dominic stepped back and froze while they quietly passed the bathroom and stopped at the foot of the bed. Defying his racing adrenaline, Dominic slowly reached down, grabbed his shoes, and slipped them on his wet feet. One of the shadows extended his arm out toward the bed.

Pop! Pop!

Two shots, muzzled by a silencer, were fired from the shadow's gun into the mattress. The mosquito net shrouding the bed, Dominic realized, had combined with Boris' moon shadow to obstruct the intruders' deadly sight. There was still a chance. They didn't realize that no one was in the bed. As one of the assassins grabbed the thin netting encircling the bed and ripped it down to confirm the hit, Dominic tiptoed behind them and darted out the door, where the speed of his sprint quickly matched the rush of adrenaline through his body. He was fifty yards deep into the darkness, the unknown, strange darkness, before his intruders realized their target was off and running.

For a while, Dominic paid no attention to the commotion of voices and engines behind him. His only concerns were to keep his fists pumping, his legs driving, and his nose and mouth inhaling the dense air. But as the sound of a speeding vehicle behind him grew louder, he realized that survival demanded a better plan. As far as options went, though, he had none. He didn't know where he was, nor where the trail he was on would lead him. Perhaps to greater danger. Less likely to safety. He was alone. Unarmed. Surrounded by enemies. The rumbling noises behind him increased. His killers were gaining. He had to get off the trail and out of sight.

His first leap through the tall grass that lined the trail was successful. He did not, as he feared, hit a tree, land in a lake, or twist an ankle. Instead, he had landed squarely on his two feet where the night around him was suddenly darker. Another line of plants, taller than he, stood in front of him. This time he stepped through it. Again, another line of plants appeared. It was a harvest field. A farm of some kind. Not rice, he concluded. He had seen thousands of rice fields in Vietnam. The stalks were too high, the ground too dry, for it to be rice. Although his vision and mobility were now severely limited, he nevertheless felt much safer concealed in the high crops. A rumbling vehicle on the trail passed by him while he swiftly continued to slice his way through the walls of vegetation. His assumption was accurate; for the moment he was safe in the woods, but he was far from being out of them.

CHAPTER TWENTY-ONE

1972

Parrot's Beak

Cambodia

September 4, 4:49PM

The intelligence gathered by the Operation Inferno unit was thoroughly analyzed by Colonel Mazer and Major Russo in plotting the surprise attack on Alcatraz. When it came to small-scale offensive strikes, they were one of the best tandems in the world. The strike itself, although much smaller in scale to many of their previous collaborations, was nevertheless the most difficult to coordinate given its unique objectives. Unlike all other military offensives, mere defeat of the enemy would not be sufficient for the final phase of Operation Inferno. "We need to design an invisible ambush with a one-hundred percent kill ratio. And it needs to be over before anyone realized it has begun," Mazer reminded Russo during preparations.

Mazer scheduled the attack to be launched at exactly 1900 hours. The early evening time was chosen by Mazer despite Russo's urging to commence it during the late night hours. Mazer, however, was adamant about not initiating the attack under the cover of darkness. This way, he felt, in the unlikely event that one of the targets gets away, the team would not be handicapped by the night in its pursuit. "The dimness of dusk will be more than adequate camouflage for us," he told to Russo during their tactical discussions, "so it will likely be more unexpected at that time and, more importantly, it will allow us to get a visual on any dogs that stray."

1900 was the compound's most relaxed awake hour; hence, it was most vulnerable for a daylight strike. During that hour, most of the soldiers, aside from the pair on cage detail, usually played cards together in the southern section of the barracks. And target consolidation was essential to the success of the mission in lieu of the unit's limited resources of both artillery and men. "If you want it early evening," Russo advised his Colonel, "then I agree. We gotta go off at 1900."

Mazer wanted the men to strike using guns rather than more powerful grenades. Russo believed that imposing such restraints created more risk for the team, but eventually he agreed with Mazer that it was a greater priority to preserve heavy weaponry in case they had any more "chance encounters" in the future—a likely prospect in both their opinions.

"How long 'til they come get us?" Russo asked referring to the unit's evacuation.

"I'm gonna make 'em come right away. As soon as everything is done."

Russo unnecessarily reminded Mazer, "Cause after this strike, you know we're gonna have some company inside an hour. One way or the other, there's a good chance that it's gonna be boys from Mississippi flying American iron eagles." His statement reflected his strong opinion. "The chopper better be here and gone before then."

The Colonel agreed. He knew the team would only have so long before it had to contend with its own countrymen. He also knew that there was a distinct possibility that the team would encounter nearby Vietnamese or Cambodian units. "I know it," he told Russo. "That's another reason why we just can't level the place, John. We don't know what kind of communication hookup is in there. If it's a sophisticated system, and it has a standby or monitor mode or something like that, then Saigon or Hanoi will know about the attack right away…as soon as it blows. If we do this thing right, there's a chance that no one will know anything has happened until 0900 tomorrow morning. By that time we'll be long fuckin' gone."

Mazer divided the men into two teams of three. One team would be assigned the prisoners and the two cage guards while the other team would be assigned to take out the soldiers in the southern end of the barracks. Mazer would remain back at the rendezvous site on the hill to oversee the attack.

At 1700 hours, Mazer called the team together for its briefing on the attack. By then, they were all anxious to get the mission over with. They were growing uneasy with watching and waiting. Sooner or later, someone was going to be detected. And if that happened, the Inferno unit would immediately lose whatever advantage it had gained from their spying.

"Major Russo, Mendez, and JD will take the cage," Colonel Mazer commanded in low voice. "Mendez, you have the north guard and JD, you take the southern one. Get in real close, gentlemen. Smell their breath first and use one bullet per target. Remember, I need confirmation of kills, so don't clear until you got 'em, ya hear? Major Russo will serve as cover at an easterly point twenty yards from you both. Not that you'll need it, right gentlemen?"

"No, sir!" Mendez and JD chimed.

"What if they're together?" Mendez asked referring to the two guards. His point was well founded. He didn't want anyone from the Inferno team to be hit in a friendly crossfire.

"Good point, Mendez," the Colonel said. "If they're together, then you take 'em both out. Don't forget 1900 on the nose is takeoff. After you get confirmation on the guards, take out the prisoners. If you want, you can use grenades for that, but not for anythin' else, unless absolutely necessary! And remember gentlemen, this probably won't be our last fight outta here. It may be hellfire getting out once we're done, so stay razor sharp. I want you two done and heading back to me inside of ten minutes. Is that clear?"

"Yes, sir!" they both responded.

"Good! Now—Doc, Greene, Hilliard—you gentlemen got the barracks. First Greene, I want your approach to be from the north. You got the north and middle entrances. Hit 'em both quickly. There shouldn't be anyone in there but make sure. If you see any whites from eyeballs, smoke 'em. I don't care if it's a damn rat sniffing around on the floor."

Greene nodded.

"Second, Doc, I want you positioned about fifteen yards back in case anyone scrambles. Make sure you keep Hilliard in visual range. He may need support." Doc looked at Hilliard and gave a slow assuring nod.

"And finally, Hilliard," the Colonel stated. "You're the point man of this attack. You got the southern end. Kick in blasting 'cause that's where they'll be. Burrow in real close now. Close enough for a visual. See what's goin' on in there. That way you can hand signal Doc if you need 'em. If you want, just tell me now, and I'll put Doc with you right from the start."

"That won't be necessary," the tunnel rat assured his Colonel. Then, turning to Doc, he said, "If I need you, I'll let you know."

"Give me a signal either way," Doc requested.

"Fine," continued Mazer. "Give him a signal either way. Remember we don't have any time to fuck around. Make sure your watches are synchronized because I want both teams blastin' at exactly the same nanosecond. Get confirmations and get your asses back here. We don't know when others will arrive, and I don't want to be caught with our fuckin' drawers down. It should only take thirty seconds of blasting. That's all. Hilliard, grab some weaponry in there if you can but make it quick. I don't want you sitting down to taste the goddamn soup..."

"I don't like soup," Hilliard said.

"If something goes wrong, give me the hand signal, and I'll smoke the place," Mazer said. His role would be the unit's scout. He would watch the strike unfold through his binoculars from a perched, masked position on the hill. The Blooper would be in his arms, ready to correct any mishaps.

Major Russo didn't like some of the arrangements. He felt that Mazer should cover the barracks team, and Doc should stay back. This way, in case anyone got hit at least Doc would be able to attend to them. If Doc went down, then the rest of the unit might suffer. Why risk losing the unit's most valuable man?

Mazer was not persuaded by his Major's reasoning. He believed that although Doc was indeed valuable, the scout position was nevertheless the most crucial role in the strike. The scout may have to make the delicate decision as to whether or not to take out the entire barracks. That decision, the Colonel and Major both knew, could mean risking Inferno team casualties. Although an accomplished soldier, that decision was not one Mazer was about to defer to Doc.

"Any questions, gentlemen?" Mazer asked the men.

No response.

"Good. Now listen—everything comes down to this. The beginning of the end of this whole fuckin' war is in our hands. This is why I called upon you gentlemen. Remember, I had my choice of any soldiers in the whole goddamn military for this mission, and I personally chose each of you."

Mazer deliberately paused and looked into the fiery eyeballs of each of his six choices, a masterful leader in the midst of a final curtain call to arms. "This is what we trained for," he continued, "seven men thinking as one. With one purpose. Seven men of destiny. You've already made me proud. Now go down there and make yourself heroes."

CHAPTER TWENTY-TWO

1992

Restricted Military Zone, Vietnam

August 14, 3:28AM

The cell phone must have rung a dozen times. Still, Dominic was not about to hang it up before someone answered. Finally, after a few more rings, the other end finally picked up. "Colonel?" he whispered anxiously, "It's Dominic."

"Dominic?!" the groggy voice on the other end of the receiver answered. "It's almost four in the morning. What's the matter?"

"They tried to kill me," Dominic blurted.

"What? Who?" The Colonel's voice cracked with surprise.

"Two men came into my hut and shot at my bed. I was in the bathroom at the time. That's the only reason why I was able to get away."

"Those sons of bitches!" Mazer mumbled and then added, "I told you that I didn't like those people you're involved in! Where are you now?"

"I'm in some military territory northwest of Hanoi. They brought me to meet with a General Kien and see some of the gemstones."

"Dammit! You must be in the restricted regions. Are you in some kind of house?"

"No, I took off. Right now I'm standing in the middle of some farm. Some tall-grass field."

"By your room?"

"No. About a couple miles away. I ran quite a bit."

"In what direction?"

"I don't know."

"When you left the hut, did you run left or right."

"I ran right."

"OK. Don't go anywhere. Stay right where you are and stay calm. It may be the only safe place. I'll get someone there as soon as I can."

"Hurry Colonel! Daylight is a couple hours away," Dominic pointed out nervously.

"I know it, kid—but you are over four hours from here! What I need to do is call some Vietnamese government officials and let them know where you are. You just sit tight and don't worry. Help will be on the way soon, I promise."

"Okay. Thanks, Colonel. And just one more thing. Please don't say anything to Marie or Julie. I don't want to worry them."

"Of course not."

Dominic closed the phone and put it back in his pocket.

In the darkness of his bedroom, the Colonel hung up the telephone, turned on the lamp next to his bed and then immediately snapped the receiver up again. He mumbled to himself while his fingers spun the rotary and dialed out. After three rings, someone picked up the other end but did not speak. The Colonel did. "He's hiding in the southern crop," he growled into the receiver. "Two miles from his room. Get on it immediately. Call me back as soon as you get confirmation...And don't fuck up this time!"

Dominic covered his face with both hands. Tears welled in his eyes. He quickly wiped away them before they fell onto his cheeks and shook his head in defiance of pity. He was pacing. *Stop feeling sorry for yourself,* he mumbled. *They weren't successful. You're still alive, aren't you?* He realized that General Kien and the others had set him up. The reasons why, he did not know. For now, it didn't matter. The important thing to him was that the Colonel now knows it. The Vietnamese government was about to know it. And best of all, Shay Krauze would soon find out. Those thoughts calmed his nerves, eventually enough so that he sat down. From behind, a gentle hand patted him on the shoulder. Despite the frailty of touch, Dominic stiffened in fear. He could not bear to turn around. If lucky, he was captured. If not, he was dead.

"Don't shoot," Dominic pleaded, demonstrating his surrender by raising his hands.

"Mr. Dominic?" the familiar voice asked.

Dominic spun around and leaped up. "Quan?"

"Yes, it's me," he said innocently and asked, "What has happened?"

Dominic eyes locked on Quan's hands. He saw no weapon. He then surveyed the vicinity to see if Quan had brought company. There was no one around. The two men were alone. Nevertheless, Dominic backed away from his once-trusted translator, slowly, without saying anything further.

"Mr. Dominic," Quan asked him, "are you okay?"

Dominic continued his inching backwards. His fists clenched. He was ready to swing and run away.

Quan started walking toward Dominic. "Mr. Dominic please...don't leave, you'll never make it."

This time Dominic responded, "You son of a bitch! You set me up!"

"No, Mr. Dominic. You are wrong! I did not betray you. I am not a part of any of this. I told you, I am only a translator."

"Yeah, sure," Dominic barked, "You had no idea."

"That is correct," retorted Quan, "Please believe me."

Dominic spread his arms, "How can I believe anything you are saying? For all I know you were sent in here to kill me."

"Kill you?" Quan was shocked. "Oh no, never, Mr. Dominic."

"This whole damn compound is after me," said Dominic. "They were supposed to be friends, business partners, whatever! And it turns out they want me dead."

"Believe me, Mr. Dominic, please. I don't know what's going on, but I do know that neither of us is safe."

"Great, now you're telling me they're after you too...and I'm supposed to believe you!"

"You have to believe me, Mr. Dominic." Quan shook his head. "I am only a translator, not a soldier. I didn't know about any murder. And now I am a witness to this whole thing. Murderers don't like witnesses, Mr. Dominic."

"Why should I believe you?"

"Because we are friends, Mr. Dominic."

"Fine. If you say you're my friend, then leave me alone. Let me go my own way and you go yours."

Quan continued shaking his head. "I can't let you do that."

"You can't let me do that?" repeated Dominic. "You have no choice. I'm leaving!"

"You'll never make it without me. There is too much commotion about you. I heard it from my guesthouse. There are many people after you. That is why I left my hut. I saw you run off and came to look for you."

"I'll take my chances on my own."

With that, Dominic turned and began walking away. Quan followed him.

"You'll never make it out of military territory," Quan pleaded. "You must listen to me or there is no chance."

Dominic kept walking. For all he knew, Quan had been lying to him all along. "Leave me alone."

Quan reached out and grabbed Dominic's shoulders. His frail hands gripped with unusually strong resolve. "Mr. Dominic, please!" he implored. "You don't know where you are going. You don't know the language. You don't know the terrain. Let me help you!"

Dominic looked into Quan's eyes. They appeared as innocent and gentle as they had always been. But in Vietnam, Dominic had learned that appearances can be deceiving.

"I am the only chance you have for survival, Mr. Dominic, please believe me," Quan said, releasing his hold and dropping his arms. "If you attempt to get away without my help, you are certain to get caught."

Dominic searched his feelings, but despite his best efforts, he could not find a trace of trust. The bond he had forged with Quan had all but vanished in a cloud of betrayal. However, his reason beckoned that he had no choice. He was a stranger, not only in a strange place, but in a hostile one. By the time the Colonel informs the proper authorities to coordinate and send up some kind of rescue team, it'll be at least several hours. By then, he would surely be dead. Indeed, there may be only a slim chance of survival with Quan, but there was no chance without him. He reached out and felt around Quan's thin waist. No bulges. He frisked Quan's pockets and legs. Nothing. "Where to?" he asked.

Quan gave a quick nod. "This way," he said excitedly. "We must get a moto'bike."

Dominic followed Quan through the thick foliage. They did not speak a word to each other. Every so often they would stop and hide as spotlights from passing trucks flickered through the field they were crossing. Finally, after about twenty minutes, they came to a wooden structure that was elevated a foot off the ground.

"What is it?" Dominic whispered to Quan.

"Security checkpoint," Quan replied. "There should be two moto'bikes parked around front. We need to get to them."

"How?" asked Dominic.

"Quickly," Quan responded. If not for the seriousness of the moment,

Dominic would have thought Quan was being sarcastic. "Follow me," Quan added, "we will only have a couple of seconds to start the bikes and speed off before they start shooting."

"Are you sure that will be enough time?" Dominic asked nervously.

"No," Quan answered. His candidness was not soothing to Dominic.

Cautiously, he led Dominic around to the side of the security house. From the knock of footsteps and the sound of conversation, it seemed as though there were two men inside the one room structure. Quan held up his palm to Dominic—an indication for him to stay—as he got down to the ground and crawled underneath the wooden structure. With Quan gone, Dominic's conscience began to torment him. He is alerting the guards, he thought. He set me up. He works for them.

Before he could quiet his suspicions, however, Quan suddenly reappeared. His face and clothes were dirty from his prowl. "We will have to make a run for it, Mr. Dominic," he whispered, "There are two of them. Both are armed, and they are on alert for a foreigner."

Some plan, Dominic thought but did not say. Steal a motorbike out from under the nose of two armed soldiers who are on alert looking for me!

Quan pulled Dominic down to his knees. "We will get as close as possible," he instructed. "At the last second, we will have to run for it. I'll take the furthest one and lead the getaway."

The two men crawled soundlessly to the front corner of the structure and peeked around. The motorbikes were a mere thirty feet away. Dominic noticed the cigarette smoke seeping out the front doorway. Without a door, he fretted, the soldiers would be able to shoot at them from the inside. Quan noticed Dominic's concerned expression and promptly brought a finger up to his lips to stop him from sharing the obvious fact that the odds were stacked against them. His attention was clearly on the dialogue exchanging inside. After the elapse of about a minute, Quan raised three fingers. Dominic's heart began pounding harder. The countdown was on. Screw the odds. It was time to act. Dominic focused his stare upon his waiting motorbike. Inside his head, he furiously went through the starting motions. Turn the key, squeeze the clutch, kick down, shift and vrooooom! Quan pulled down one of his fingers. Two remained upright.

There was no turning back now…and no room for mistakes. Quan dropped another finger to his fist. One more to go.

The final finger took an eternity to fall—but as soon as it did, Quan was off in a flash with Dominic right behind him. They both leaped and mounted their motorbikes.

Key, clutch, kick, vrooom! Dominic was ready to fly in a flash. Quan, however, could not get his bike started. The scramble of the startled guards could be heard behind them. Quan kicked down, again and again, but his motorbike simply would not turn over. Dominic's suspicion screamed: *It's a trap! Quan set you up! Get the hell outta here!* His motorbike was in gear. Both his heart and the engine were racing at equal speeds. The spinning back wheel was held back only by his firm clench of the brake. Behind, the two guards were shouting with shotguns in hand. Quan's motor still would not turn over. He looked at Quan's face. Quan yelled out to him: "Go!"

Dominic surged with strength as he reached over and grabbed Quan by the shirt. "C'mon!" he yelled and yanked him off of the stubborn bike, pulling him onto the back of his. One of the guards got off a shot that hit Quan's abandoned motorbike as it fell to the ground. Dust fogged the air. Dominic let go of the brake. Like a rocket, they sped off into the darkness.

CHAPTER TWENTY-THREE

1972

As the shades of the twilight sky settled in, Operation Inferno unit's most fearsome and prolific prowler, Sergeant Hilliard, emerged from the dense jungle vegetation on his hands and knees inching his way toward the barracks of Alcatraz. His body was covered in mud, his face disguised by camouflage cream. With two minutes remaining until the attack, he had plenty of time to position himself in close range for the strike, exactly as his Colonel had instructed him. Acutely aware of his surroundings, he began maneuvering in cat-quick advances, staying low and soundless in his approach to the southern section of the barracks. He was well in his zone. The killing zone.

Inside the southern section of the barracks, an unlucky seven of Hilliard's fellow American soldiers were engrossed in their customary after-dinner card game, completely unaware of their silently approaching compatriot. The air was filled with the hypnotizing guitar and howling lyrics of "Gimme Shelter" by the Rolling Stones, which blared monophonically from their small radio, making the silent caution of their impending predator seemingly unnecessary.

With a minute and a half left, Major Russo and JD broke away from Mendez in the jungle by the cage. The three of them were set to reunite shortly after the strike. As soon as they left, Mendez immediately noticed the southern guard assigned to the cage began walking in the direction of his northern associate, but he was not alarmed by the target's sudden movement. It appeared casual... unsuspecting. Most likely, the American guard was heading over to his partner for another friendly cigarette gathering, a scene he had witnessed numerous times over the last couple of days in his role of watchdog. No problem, though. All systems were still a "go." If the two guards stayed together, Mendez, the unit's best shot, would simply take them both out. Perhaps with one bullet.

Back outside Alcatraz's barracks, Hilliard checked his watch again. The tunnel rat's back was now against the wall of the barracks, with forty-five seconds until the strike. Gazing through one of the slits in the porous wall, he counted seven soldiers inside the smoky room. The unit's calculations had been exact. Six were sitting at the wooden bench playing a game of poker using cigarettes for currency. The metal bowls that had housed the night's stew were piled at the other end of the wooden table. Their cups of warm beer remained in front of them, still a long way off from being discarded. Another soldier, a handsome boy who looked no older than seventeen, was standing above the cooking pot scooping himself another serving of the tasteless dinner.

Rage built up inside of Hilliard as he peered inside and witnessed the disgraceful leisure of his country's traitors. He could barely contain his boiling anger. *These men ain't gettin' back home*, he fumed in his head. *They're mine now...all mine...and they gonna die right here in the jungle.* Hilliard was increasingly infuriated by the good time being had inside—the drinking, the music, the smoking, the hot meal. The rhythm of the Keith Richard's guitar acted as an opiate, leading Hilliard into a deeper state of rage. He felt like a packed cannon of anger on the brink of eruption, blaming the traitors before him for everything miserable in his life. There was no mission anymore. He forgot about Doc, lying in the near bush awaiting a signal like they had agreed. The pending strike was now a personal vendetta for Hilliard—a culmination of all his repressed anger. In his racing mind, he saw the group of soldiers before him as the rival drug dealers from Atlanta, who murdered his brother, Terry.

Hilliard's sweaty palms gripped his impatient M-16. Again, he checked his watch. Twelve seconds remained. He would count off the remaining ticks in his head. Ten...nine...eight...a few drops of sweat ran down his camouflaged painted face as adrenaline rushed through him. Six...five...four...he gripped his teeth and snarled, it was payback time. Three...two...one...takeoff!

At that instant, Hilliard spun around, kicked the door down and leaped into the room, landing on both feet with his intimidating weapon aimed forward. Shocked, the once-relaxed soldiers looked at Hilliard and froze with fear. No one said a word. Hilliard's face said it all. His smile quivered with desire. His nostrils locked wide open. His ravenous eyes didn't blink. His stiff head bopped slightly up and down to the beat of the blaring music. The sound of gunfire was heard in the distance. The ambush had begun as planned. That is, except for Hilliard's role. The most important man in this attack did not fire. He hesitated for the first time in his life.

Sergeant Hilliard's patience was not the result of novel regret or remorse. He had no second thoughts. His hesitation was the product of his revenge. His fury had put him over the edge. Rather than performing his deadly duties swiftly, like the skilled, instant killer he was, he was relishing the impeding rush of violence, engrossed in a freeze-frame of power and ecstasy. Without turning his head, one-by-one, he peered into the eyes of every single soldier that he sentenced to death. He savored the moment. He did not say a word, but he was communicating his message to them clearly. For he wanted each one of them to know who their punisher was, and, more specifically, that their grim reaper was not just a "round-eye", he was one of them!

Major Scott, Alcatraz's commanding officer and warden, seized upon the delay of his apparent assassin and reached for the pistol at his waist. Before he was able to squeeze the trigger once, Hilliard exterminated everyone in the room with a blast of bullets.

Outside by the prison, Mendez, JD, and Russo assembled at the gate to the cage. Five feet away the two guards laid dead, their bodies entangled on the ground. They had been together smoking cigarettes and talking about going home when Mendez took them out. Two bullets each, three seconds total. Unlike Hilliard's victims, they never knew what hit them.

"Get the key," Mendez directed JD.

JD went over to the dead guards, reached into one of their pockets, and pulled out a key. He then went over to the barbed wired gate of the cage and unlocked it. Russo remained outside the cage, safeguarding the area, while JD and Mendez stepped inside slowly. The smell of human excrement was unbearable.

Down in the ditch, twenty-eight exhilarated prisoners were anxiously awaiting their liberation. Visions of family filled their minds as soon as they heard the attack above them. They were going home. Finally.

Mendez and JD stood back, out of the prisoner's visual range. They did not want to see, nor be seen, by the men in the ditch. Together they each detached pins from their respective grenades. Their sluggish pace evidenced their reluctance. They did not look up or at each other. Even trained attack dogs knew that this was cold-blooded. This was not justice. This was mass murder.

Dispirited, Russo neglected his guard and stood with his head down outside the cage gazing at the two fallen Americans. The cigarettes they had just lit up were still burning on the ground next to them. *How did it come to this?* he asked himself. He recalled all the scenes of bloodshed and death he had experienced over the course of the last six years. Men had died in his arms. Babies had died from his guns. All the dead faces he had seen flashed through his mind like a sped up movie. He thought about all the lies he had made to himself, the conscious ignorance, that brought him to this—the ordered murder of his own men and the soon-to-be execution of unarmed, captured prisoners. He was ashamed for not having the guts to stand up to the truth. He was ashamed of being a soldier. He no longer knew who the enemy was. The past six years was a blur of violence. At that moment, Major John Russo was no longer a soldier of war. His war was over. And his soul was the casualty.

Mendez and JD tossed their grenades up into the air over the ditch. At the same time a tear fell from Major Russo's eye for the first time since childhood. He walked away from the inevitable blast, deep in thought about his kids, his wife. Down in the hole, the eager prisoners all watched the flight of the falling explosives, their moment of emancipation instantly transformed into a moment of execution. They were not free. They were not going home. They would not be reunited with their families. They were going to die in a ditch.

At the instant of the grenade's impact, a stream of bullets from the jungle bush hit Mendez and JD. Both men cried out in agony as their bodies were driven into the fencing behind them. The barbed wire viscously tore into the skin on their backs. Their dying bodies collapsed forward and fell into the smoking prisoner's ditch, converting it now into a mass grave of both Vietnamese and American soldiers.

Russo's instincts took over. Immediately, he ran back over and dove to the ground behind the entangled bodies of the deceased guards. With his AK-47 lodged on top of their bloody bodies, he fired a short round back into the trees. It was a drawing shot, intended to lure a response that would reveal the position of the attackers. None came. He shot again. No response.

"Dammit!" he said aloud, "It's a fuckin set-up! I told him we were being set up! Those sons of bitches!"

Another short round fired from the other side of the barracks. Cautiously, Russo began to make his way over, hoping that Mazer was alive and had seen the ambush through his binoculars in spite of the darkening sky.

CHAPTER TWENTY-FOUR

1992

Restricted Military Zone, Vietnam

August 14, 3:35AM

A continuous cloud of dust kicked up behind Dominic and Quan's racing motorbike. "Stay left, Mr. Dominic!" Quan yelled into Dominic's ear. His hair, like Dominic's, was pinned back by the headwind.

The pitted, rocky trail was not designed for speed by any vehicle. And Dominic's vision was limited. Severely limited. Without goggles to protect from wind and insects, his squinted eyes streamed a path of tears to the back of his head. Fortunately, he managed to notice a large pothole up ahead. Unfortunately, it was too late to maneuver around it. So he yelled out to Quan, "Hold on!" and accelerated. Quan squeezed his arms around Dominic's waist tighter. They went airborne over the hole. Quan almost fell off the back when the front tire hit the ground first.

Regaining control, Dominic leaned back from his aero-dynamic crouch and shouted to Quan, "Are you alright?"

"Yes! Yes! Continue!"

"See if they're gaining!"

Checking behind them, Quan saw the shine of headlights lighting up their wake of dust. A truck was quickly gaining. "Yes, Mr. Dominic!" he yelled back. "They are gaining! They are definitely gaining!"

"Lemme try to lose them!" Dominic suggested. "We can outmaneuver them with some turns!"

"No!" Quan retorted firmly. "We must keep moving north! They'll be a lot more soldiers after us very soon!"

"Where are we heading?"

"To the water!"

Dominic grimaced with doubt. "Water?"

"Yes! It is the only way out!"

"What about a boat!"

"I think there will be one for us!"

"You think?!" said Dominic rolling his teary eyes.

Quan was unable to see the doubting look on Dominic's face. Bluntly, he replied: "Yes!"

The dark, ragged trail finally straightened out for a long stretch. With no turns to navigate, the rumble of the truck increased, overpowering the sound of their speeding bike. Up ahead, Dominic noticed a small light expanding in circumference like an inflating lit balloon. "Someone's approaching from the front!" he shouted out to Quan. "What do we do now?"

Quan squinted his eyes tightly in the blowing wind. "Keep going!" he encouraged Dominic. "The way to the river is up ahead!"

"Yeah, but so is that!" he yelled pointing ahead. "We're heading right at another motorcycle!"

On the open straightway, the truck behind them was now gaining soundly. Quan looked back, then forward. "Just keep going, Mr. Dominic! Keep going!"

Before Dominic responded a gunshot was fired from the truck, landing only a few inches from their spinning back tire. Quan turned his head. His eyes squinted from the blind of headlights. The shadows of the men inside were familiar. "It is Huyen and Lang!" Quan yelled into Dominic's ear.

"Those fucking bastards!" Dominic cursed.

"Yes! Those fucking bastards!" Quan repeated. Out of the passenger side window, Huyen again took aim with a sawed-off shotgun. Quan turned his head around and braced himself. "Duck!" he screamed as another shot was fired. There was a loud clang. The bullet had ricocheted off the motorcycle's exhaust pipe.

"Are you okay?" Dominic called out.

"Yes! Now go!"

Dominic had a sinking feeling about the oncoming motorcycle. Even if they could somehow make it to the turn off, only the truck would be lost because it would be unable to follow them into a narrow trail, but the bike up ahead would still be right on their tail.

Another gunshot from behind struck the handlebars, right next to Dominic's grip. Immediately, he let go of his grasp and shook his hand in the air to make sure it was not hit. "Where's the turnoff, dammit?" he screamed at Quan.

"About two kilometers!" Quan yelled back.

"Quan…!" Dominic answered.

"I know, I know, Mr. Dominic. You're American! Soon!" Then pointing ahead Quan explained, "It's up there, right past that big rock on the left!"

Dominic squinted and saw the large boulder. By his estimation, they were doomed. The motorcycle ahead was coming on too fast. It would reach them before they reached the rock, that is, if Huyen and Lang failed to shoot them or run them over first. Again a shot rang out, whizzing right pass Dominic and Quan's ears and hitting the radiator of the truck. This one, Dominic realized, came from the front!

"This is it Quan! We're goners now!"

"Keep going, Mr. Dominic! Only a few more seconds!"

As the truck closed in, Dominic felt the warmth of its blaring headlights on the back of his arms. The front motorcycle assassin was closing in head on, and he was already past the rock marking the turnoff!

Another gunshot blasted from the front. Dominic and Quan instinctively ducked down. The truck's windshield shattered. The warm bright headlights of the truck turned away from them. At a blink of the eye, the night behind them grew dark again. Then a loud explosion erupted, lighting up the sky. With Dominic and Quan ducking, certain of their impending death, the motorcycle in front of them flew passed them on their left. Dominic slowed up to make the turn off. Both he and Quan glanced back and saw the truck engulfed in flames on the side of the road.

The bullet, Dominic speculated, must have hit Lang. And the motorcycle assassin must have overrun them in the confusion. He shifted gears and accelerated into the darker, denser, jungle bush. There was no time to bask in the miracle just bestowed on them.

The tired engine of their motorcycle purred as Dominic weaved through the mud and rock of the jungle as fast as he could in the rough terrain. Both he and Quan kept looking behind, but the motorcycle assassin had not pursued. He had mistakenly killed Huyen and Lang instead of Dominic and Quan. They both knew he would be back any second to correct that mistake.

"The bank of the river should be coming up," said Quan. His voice was subdued by their recent death-defying encounter.

Dominic was not as relieved as his fellow passenger. A river, he felt, was a dead end. "What river?"

"Song Bo," said Quan. "The English translation is Black River."

"And that will lead us out of here?"

"Yes. It will lead us back to Hanoi. And away from this territory of soldiers."

Dominic was still pessimistic. "And you're telling me there will be a boat waiting for us?"

Quan did not need to answer the question, for at that instant, the trail opened up on the bank of a calm reservoir where three wooden fishing boats were anchored away from the shoreline. Dominic stopped the motorbike. Immediately, Quan called out to one of the fishermen who was in the process of pulling up cages from the water. Dominic turned off the motorcycle as the two men spoke across the water in Vietnamese. After a couple of minutes, a half of a smile cut across Dominic's cheeks. The fisherman had turned his boat's engine and was heading to shore where he and Quan were standing.

The boat slowed down, eventually stopping about five feet from the water's edge. A barefoot woman and a young child came out from the deck below and stared blankly at Dominic. He smiled wholeheartedly back at them and waved. Quan was still conversing with the fisherman when Dominic interrupted: "Thank them for me, Quan. This is very nice of them to help us."

Quan looked at his American friend with a dry expression and asked: "How much money do you have on you?"

Dominic's warm expression was lost in the cold realization. He began to search both his shirt and pants pockets. From one of his back pockets, he pulled out a fifty-dollar bill. "All I have is a fifty dollar bill," he said discreetly to Quan, hiding it from the curious fishermen's family.

Quan said a few words to the fisherman in Vietnamese, and then turned to Dominic: "OK, give it to him."

"Give it to him?" Dominic echoed. "The whole thing?"

"Yes," Quan urged, "the whole thing."

"But…"Dominic said reluctantly handing the money over to Quan, "didn't you tell me that fifty dollars equals an entire month's salary. Plus, it's all the money we've got."

Undeterred, Quan took the money from Dominic, handed it over to the fisherman. He hoisted the motorbike onto the back of the boat, held out his arm and invited Dominic to get on the boat first. "That's capitalism, right, Mr. Dominic? Supply and demand. You should know that."

Dominic shook his head as he stepped up into the unsteady boat. Quan followed, and the boat started its slow descent downstream. Dominic was still disappointed, staring at Quan while they walked to the front end of the boat and sat down. "You obviously didn't learn how to negotiate from me when you translated the deal I made with General Kien," he stated sarcastically.

"Oh no. You are very wrong, Mr. Dominic. I negotiated a good deal for us."

"You call spending all our money a good deal. This guy probably doesn't make fifty US dollars in a month."

"You are correct. He probably makes about twenty, maybe even ten. That is why I made the deal for only forty."

"Forty? Okay. fine then. Where's my change?!"

"Right there," said Quan pointing to a small barrel of half-dead fish.

Dominic shook his head and both men shared an easing laugh.

After a couple of minutes, Dominic noted that the motorcycle assassin had not pursued them through another boat. Relieved, Dominic asked: "Do these people live on this thing?"

"Yes, they are boat people. The young boy has probably never stepped his foot on land."

"That's amazing!"

Quan explained: "They need to be on the boat at all times because they need to fish at all times. That is how they survive. When you are a fisherman, you must fish constantly because sometimes fish do not want to get caught."

"I see," Dominic said. "Where are we heading?"

"Hoa Binh. It is a small port a few hours down the river. There we will get off the boat. We should be safe. It is far from military territory. From there, we'll drive the moto'bike. We should be back to Hanoi by nightfall."

Dominic nodded, and turned his thoughts inward as he peered out from the gliding boat. By now, the approaching sunrise had grayed the dark sky, and the morning dew sparkled on the lush forestry lining the water. The fading image of the saving moon valiantly hovered in the still air above, while the blooming sails of distant fan boats cast an early shadow on the water's surface. Morning was drawing near. Until a half hour ago, it was a morning that

Dominic thought he would never see.

Dominic was too consumed in thought to appreciate the majesty of the impending morning. There were many things he needed to decide. What would he tell Marie and Julie? How would they react? Certainly, he told himself, both of them must leave Vietnam. But his conscience begged to differ. Would his sister really abandon her work with the children of Southeast Asia? Would Julie? They had to leave, he would insist; they were in too much danger here. He would get them out on the first plane.

The battling thoughts in his mind fought it out for only a few more minutes until the weariness overcame him. Leaning against one another, both he and Quan, complete strangers a few days before, fell asleep.

After twenty minutes of peace a loud baaaaang rang out and echoed in Dominic's ear. Disorientated, Dominic awoke and fell to the floor of the boat. Quan landed on top of him. The fisherman and his wife were screaming in Vietnamese. "What the hell is going on, Quan?" Dominic yelled. Before there was an answer another shot was fired. This one landed in the water. "What's happening?" Dominic repeated, nudging Quan. No response. The fisherman accelerated the boat's engine to maximum speed. Dominic peeked over the boat's side. Full daylight had arrived. On the river's embankment, he saw smoke disperse from the barrel of a rifle. Another soldier. Another assassin. "Quan!" Dominic ordered.

Still no response. Quan laid motionless. Turning down, Dominic saw a pool of blood had stained the wood deck of the boat. His hands were also covered in red. It was spilling out of Quan's head. "Oh no!" he shouted, grabbing the head of his fallen friend. Blood was everywhere. Another shot rang out. Dominic hugged Quan's head tightly. "Quan! Oh God, no! Please no! Please Quan!"

There would be no response. Quan had been hit by the first bullet. He never awoke from his sleep. "Nooooooo!" Dominic cried out. The echo of his shrieking voice resonated for miles. His friend, his only friend, was dead in his arms. The gunshots stopped, but the damage had already been done. Clutching the body of the man to whom he owed his life, Dominic wept. The tears from his eyes fell off of his face and landed in the pool of Quan's blood.

After a few minutes, the fisherman's wife, barefoot, wearing a conical hat covering most of her face, emerged from the deck below carrying a bucket of wet towels. She stepped to the front of the boat, knelt down and took Quan's body away from Dominic's bosom. She was mumbling in Vietnamese, the same few sentences over and over again. It was a prayer of some kind, or so it seemed. Dominic watched with watery eyes as the woman gently wrapped Quan's head in white towels. She then tilted her head back, looked up at Dominic, and said something to him. He tried to figure out what she was saying, but he could not. Hearing her speak in a foreign language made him sadder. He missed his translator. Undeterred, the woman kept repeating her statement. Finally she began to drag Quan's body to the side of the boat by herself. Dominic realized she was going to cast the body into the river. "No!" he said out loud. It was his first reaction. But then he realized she was probably doing it out of respect, in accordance with her customs. Like Quan had told him, they were boat people, and this was probably part of their tradition.

Dominic said he was sorry as he helped her lean Quan's body over the side of the boat. She grabbed Dominic's hand and pressed it against Quan's chest while she recited what seemed to be another prayer. She then let go of Quan and nodded at him to do the same. But before he did, he reached into Quan's front pocket and pulled out the faded black and white photograph of his family and placed it in his own pocket. The ritual was over. It was time to cast the body of the man to whom he owed his life into the waters. Dominic let go. His tears fell into the Black River as he leaned over the boat and watched Quan's body float away. The best friend he ever had.

The fisherman's wife dipped the bucket with the remaining towels in the river, knelt down, and began to mop up the blood from the deck. Dominic attempted to help her, but she shook her head and gently pushed him away. He slumped back down into the boat. He was devastated, blaming himself for Quan's death. If not for his own greed, he realized, he would never have come to Vietnam. And Quan would have never been involved in this mess. *I took him from his family. I took his life.* And now his wife and daughter have no one to take care of them! Staring emptily down the calm river, tears of anger began to fill his eyes, replacing the sorrowful ones.

Through his blurred vision, Dominic saw the young boy approaching him. He wiped the water from his eyes to gain focus. The small boy was now standing in front of him holding a steaming cup of tea. He could not have been older than seven. His hair was unkempt, his shorts ripped. His bare feet were almost totally black from dirt. But his heart was too big to be contained in his miniature chest. He held out the wooden cup to Dominic, who reached out with a thankful smile, took the cup, and sipped.

The boat began to slow down. The engine was then turned off completely. Dominic looked around. They had come to a port, where the chaotic boat traffic rivaled that of the adjacent streets. Fish was being sold. Fruits were being picked up. People were being dropped off. Civilization, Southeast Asian river-style, had returned.

"Hoa Binh?" Dominic asked the mother. She nodded as the boat drifted next to a wooden dock that extended into the river. Dominic gave the cup back to the boy. "Thank you," he said, bowing to mother and son, "for everything."

Lifting the motorbike off of the boat, Dominic noticed two soldiers standing among the crowd at the end of the dock. Immediately, he spun back around to hide his foreign-looking face. They must be looking for him, a foreigner, coming off a boat. The fisherman walked over to him and said something to his wife in Vietnamese.

"I'm sorry," said Dominic. He tried to explain: "There are people trying to kill me."

The fisherman and his wife frowned trying to understand. Their young boy wore an expression of curiosity. Dominic feared the confused family would soon cause a scene to get him off the boat. And then he would be killed. The fisherman and his wife continued conversing as Dominic's mind scrambled for a plan. He had none. And to make matters worse, the patience of his hosts appeared to be wearing thin. After a few tense moments, the fisherman grabbed the motorbike, hoisted it in the air and lay it back down on the deck of the boat. Dominic wanted to say "No!" but he stopped himself. He could not afford an ounce of attention. He kept his eyes on the soldiers. Their attention, thankfully, was in another direction.

"What are you doing?" Dominic asked the fisherman politely. "I need that."

The man responded by pointing him off of the boat. Dominic took a moment and thought about the situation. Unfortunately, he had no choice but to do as instructed. He nodded to his host and placed one foot on the dock. Suddenly, a hand grabbed his arm and turned him around. The wife of the fisherman pulled him back into the boat. With a confused face, Dominic asked her, "What is it?"

She removed her conical hat and placed it on his head. She pulled it down so that it covered over half of his face. Dominic tilted his fully-disguised head back and grinned at her. She smiled back at him while she adjusted the tie under his chin. The fisherman then extended his hand. It had the fifty dollar bill in it. "Oh no," said Dominic. "No way. That money is yours."

The fisherman shook his head and pointed at the motorbike. Dominic realized their plan. "Ohhh...I see," he said to them. "You're keeping the bike because they'll be looking for it—so I get to keep the fifty bucks." With that, Dominic reached out and the fisherman handed him back the money. Dominic thanked them all once again.

At the other side of the busy dock, Dominic spotted two empty fishing buckets. Stepping off of the boat, he immediately went over and picked them up. With one in each hand, he turned back around, raised his head and looked at the fisherman's wife drifting away in the boat. She nodded, smiling at him. The little boy waved goodbye. Head down, Dominic turned and walked among the hustle and bustle of the dock to the shore looking like a true Vietnamese fisherman.

CHAPTER TWENTY-FIVE

1972

Parrot's Beak

Cambodia

September 4, 7:16PM

He took in a deeply satisfying breath and shut his eyes. The smell from his fresh kill tingled his sensitive nose. Inside the southern end of Alcatraz's barracks "Gimme Shelter" continued to play from the small radio and Hilliard, the mass executioner, stood victoriously over his fallen prey. He turned the volume of the music even louder. His head bopped to the hypnotic beat as he gazed around at the seven former Alcatraz soldiers, now the listless, blood-spotted bodies sprawled out across the table and floor. Their metal-filled corpses were now enjoying the same song they were listening to moments before.

Hilliard pulled off his helmet and dropped it on the floor. He hated helmets. He slid his shoulders out from the X-belt of extra ammo draped across his body and let it drop to the ground. In one swift motion he ripped off his velcro-fastened flak jacket and let it fall to the ground also. He hated combat gear. It offered too much protection. Too much restriction for such a maniacal, agile killer.

Sergeant Hilliard's dark sweat-glistening upper body was now naked. That's the way he liked it. Free and exposed. The tunnel rat was back in his uniform of choice. In his hand, he kept a firm hold on his M-16. His smooth bare chest gasped for air. Nerves underneath the painted skin on his face twitched uncontrollably with the music. He was grinning with delight. He was in his zone, howling along with Mick Jagger: "It's just a shot away…it's just a shot away."

Inside his heart, he didn't feel like a war hero. He never did. Never wanted to either. Heroes don't feel malice. And his malice was insatiable. He wanted more. More blood. More death. More punishment. He needed more aggression… more revenge. His pre-possessing anger made his once razor-sharp senses immune to the shots of unknown origin being fired outside the barracks. He was unconcerned with the mission, indifferent to the danger outside. He was on his own mission—his own psychological course of destruction.

The power of killing was like a drug—a highly-addictive, mind-altering narcotic. He had begun experimenting with it while burrowing in the underground tunnels, the dosages gradually increasing with every kill. And now he was overdosing on it. The drug of death was flowing through his veins. Reality warped into one violent purpose. There was no turning back. The need for more blood overtook him. Everyone in the room was dead. But the deadly rodent wanted more. He had to have more. He was high on death.

He reached down and picked up another M-16 off the floor. It had belonged to the formerly good-looking seventeen-year-old soldier who was now lying face down on the floor in a small pool of his own blood. Gripping an M-16 firmly in each hand, the rat fired both. He let out a long scream of vengeance while hundreds of rounds of metal were pumped into the already dead American corpses. None of the lifeless bodies flinched. They were dead. He kept killing them.

After about ten seconds of overkill, Hilliard raised his roaring weapons and violently cut up the room. Debris from the bullets clouded the room in a dust cloud. When the borrowed gun in his left hand finally ran out of ammo, Hilliard threw it down to the ground and ceased firing. His face and chest were dripping with sweat. His frenzy had left him almost completely out of breath and trembling with violent delight.

In no hurry to return to the unit's rendezvous, the possessed warrior slowly wiped the sweat from his dripping brow and stepped over to the stove in the back of the room. His face was quivering—a sign of his continued vehemence. He reached out and grabbed the long wooden spoon set in the near-empty pot of lumpy stew. Stirring it a couple of times around, he scooped up a sampling. He was smiling. It was an involuntary, evil smile. As Mick Jagger sung the lines, Hilliard raised the spoon to his mouth. His hand and arm were quaking from firing all those rounds. Eyes closed, he savored the taste of the lukewarm unintended leftovers.

While swallowing, he opened his eyes and saw a familiar figure in the doorway. Instantly, his pupils diluted from shock. Not fearful shock—for to Hilliard, the sight before him was a welcomed surprise. Finally, Isaac Hilliard, America's bravest tunnel rat, had found the ending he was looking for. He was exterminated before the stew reached his stomach.

———

Before Major Russo made it to the barracks to check on the commotion, the Southern end exploded into a wall of flames. The powerful impact of the blast propelled him off his feet and down into the damp ground. His face was cut, his fatigues muddied from the unorthodox landing. The burst of flames had blinded him temporarily. On his knees he held his hand over his eyes, awaiting the return of his vision. Curling fire and smoke mushroomed above the leveled barracks and filtered through the trees into the night sky. Wiping his eyes, Russo thought to himself, *Hilliard, too!*

CHAPTER TWENTY-SIX

1992

The full moon hovered low in the cloudless night sky like a softly glowing light bulb. Its low-watt image glistened on the calm waters of West Lake in peaceful contrast to the events Dominic had experienced during the past couple of days in Vietnam. The time was a couple hours past midnight, and Dominic had finally made it back home to the Army For Peace compound—physically exhausted, emotionally devastated. But alive.

"Thanks for everything, Colonel," he said at the door of his guesthouse.

"You sure you're all right sleeping here?" asked the Colonel. "Ya know, you can come and stay at the main house with me. I have a real nice guest bedroom there. It has a queen bed, nice bathroom, and everything."

The nice bathroom was tempting. "No—thank you again. I'm fine here, really."

"Well, I put on extra security at the gates, so there's nothin' to worry about. There ain't no way in here undetected." The Colonel then reached under his belt and handed Dominic a pouch holding a military knife. "But take this and put it under your pillow," he urged his guest. "It'll make you feel better."

Dominic accepted the gesture, saying: "Thanks. I'm really only concerned about Marie." It disappointed him that he had made back to the compound after the midnight hour. Marie had already been sleeping in her guesthouse.

The Colonel and Dominic agreed to wait until the morning before they told her anything.

"Don't worry, kid," the Colonel assured him, "I have my best guards on patrol. They'll be scouting the area like owls all night. If there is so much as a mouse running around here, then my guards will know about it."

"What did you tell Marie and Julie?"

"I did what you asked me to do and told them nothing. They don't know you're back. They don't even know that I spoke to you. Julie's been down in Da Nang the whole time. I haven't even spoken to her at all. She should be back here sometime early in the morning." The Colonel then placed his hand on Dominic's shoulder, saying: "I think it's best that we let Marie sleep and wait for morning. That way both she and Julie will be here and you can explain everything to them together."

"You're right. Let her get a good night's rest."

"Listen—you need to get some rest yourself. Come tomorrow I'm gonna have this General Kien brought to justice. You can go to the bank with that."

Dominic shook his head in dejection. "He's probably untouchable, Colonel. He's a war hero."

"Fuck 'em," the Colonel barked. "I don't care if he's a damn war hero! No one's untouchable. I got the authorities working on it as we speak. And tomorrow I'll be speaking with Senator Haynes. He'll demand that this General Kien be brought in or else he'll march right into the US Congress next week and tell the whole fucking world at the Senate hearings what happened to you here." Pointing at Dominic, he then added, "Don't forget kid, with the embargo about to come down, Vietnam can't afford a setback like this. We will have the full cooperation of the Vietnamese government officials. You can count on that."

In the midst of the turmoil, Dominic had not considered the impact of a political crisis. "Maybe you're right," he said.

"Damn right I'm right. Now go get some shut-eye."

Dominic shut the door to the guesthouse, locked it, headed directly into the bedroom and collapsed on the mattress. For twenty-four hours he had been on the run. His body was exhausted. Unfortunately, it wasn't long before he realized that his mind was not ready to rest. With his eyes wide open, he laid on his back in the dark room.

He knew his problems were not over. There was one that still needed to be attended to. A very big one at that—Shay Krauze's money. It was imperative for him to get to the State Bank of Hanoi first thing in the morning before

General Kien or any of his men did. What a fool, he thought to himself, to have Krauze send the half million dollars to the place where General Kien had told him. It was clear to him now that all along General Kien had no intentions of doing business with him or Krauze. *His plan was to get me to make Krauze wire the money… kill me…then take the cash.* Dominic may have been lucky enough to slip through General Kien's fingers—but he knew that if Shay's half a million dollars disappears there would be a worse wrath to contend with back home.

And Shay Krauze's wrath was one he would not be able to avoid on a motorbike.

Other faces and places of the past few days swarmed inside his head. Julie—he wished she was there with him again. Back in the same bed. Totally naked. Totally vulnerable. He felt he had come to know her so well in such short time. He adored her. It was pleasing to know that Marie was also fond of her. His sister was the only woman in his life he treated well. Before Julie. They both were healers in a world filled with sickness. They both were helpers in a world of poverty and suffering. He would take care of them both now. Forever.

Huyen and Lang. Mysterious. Cunning. And now, deservedly so, dead. He felt a sense of justice that they had been eliminated by one of their co-conspirators. Their sinister smiles can burn in hell forever.

General Kien. So enchanting and charismatic. But in the end a fool to his own greed nonetheless. His attempt to cross Krauze may still make him a rich man in Vietnam. But if he succeeds, he best be a quick spender, for revenge is guaranteed.

Quan. His translator. His protector. His friend. The only true friend he ever really had. He owed him his life. He took out the picture and thought of his loving wife and daughter. Because of me, they will never see each other again. Tears again filled his eyes from the guilt. He did not deserve him.

After tossing and turning from these stressful thoughts, Dominic abandoned any hope of sleep and decided to take a walk. Grabbing a flashlight and the Colonel's knife, he walked out of his bungalow into the musty night air.

Unlike Dominic, the rest of Hanoi was asleep. The vision of Vietnam's founding modern leaders was alive and well in the dead streets of the city. As planned, the 10:00pm curfew had made Hanoi the quietest and safest capitol city in the world at night. It worked so well that come 10:00pm, Hanoi resembled more of a ghost town than a capitol city. None of the familiar sounds from the daytime hustle and bustle—horns, trucks, motorbikes, animals, and people— could be heard or seen. A roaming mouse's paradise.

To Dominic, the unnerving silence that night was a loud reminder of the police state he was in. Control—unwritten, underhanded, understood control—indeed permeated the air all around him. But crime statistics notwithstanding, Dominic felt securer slipping the pouch holding the knife under his belt. Once outside, the twisting maze of trails in the compound were all the more complicated to decipher without the help of daylight. Aside from the glow of the moon's rays, there were no other guiding lights. For a moment he considered visiting his sister, if for nothing else just to see her safe. While switching on the flashlight, his reason prevailed; he quickly dismissed the thought. He would see Marie in the morning. There was no need to risk waking her up and worrying her sooner rather than later.

Heading nowhere in particular, Dominic chose a trail to the left of his guesthouse and began to walk. His pace was brisk, especially for an early morning stroll. He kept thinking, reflecting, as his eyes fixated on the shine of the flashlight. Consumed by the colliding thoughts in his head, no matter how fast he stepped, he could not stop his thoughts. As his paced quickened, the impressions—past, present and future— ran through his head.

After ten minutes, an eerie yet heartwarming realization from the past came upon him. Absorbed, he slowed his pace, allowing the budding realization to swell inside him. Soon he was breathing heavily…then very heavily—a product more of mental rather than physical exertion. Finally he stopped walking altogether, for the realization had borne unto a revelation.

Vietnam, he envisioned, was his destiny. A spiritual crossroads. The same way it was to his father before him. They had come by way of different circumstances, at different times, for different reasons, but as it turned out, the fate that awaited them halfway around the world was strikingly similar. They both encountered greed, betrayal, and death here. It was a test of their will and survival. And, like his father, he would not be the same person after his experiences in Vietnam.

In effect, though not in title, the son realized he'd become a soldier of war, just like his father before him. This ironic thought enveloped Dominic with a feeling of exuberance. Now he too could relate to the same kind of world— evil and violent—that had so mercilessly condemned his father. The challenge, as Dominic envisioned, was for him to not allow his experience in Vietnam to sentence him to a life of cynicism and misery. His destiny, he pledged to himself, would not follow suit. *I'll take Julie home with me*, he decided out loud, speaking to his father's ghost for the first time since his death. *I'll take her and Marie home tomorrow, and I'll move on happily from this damn place! Because of this place!*

This achievement, he now believed, would not only be an exorcism for him but also a postmortem enlightenment for his angry old man.

Unfortunately, John Russo's ghost could not speak back to his son. If somehow he could, he would have warned him that the war, his war, was far from over…

———————

A prism of twinkling light beams filtered through the dark woods; Dominic's inceptive spiritual reflection ceasing at once. Instantaneously, his attention, as well as his perception, turned sensory—the brightening lights through the dense trees coupled with the increasing engine hum of an approaching vehicle. Instinctively, Dominic shut off his flashlight and stepped into the dense bush that lined the trail. Because his eyes were not yet adjusted to the darkness, he clumsily made his way behind a fat tree, approximately five feet off the trail. His first thought as he glanced back at the trail was that perhaps he was being too paranoid. After all, he was safe. As safe as these circumstances permitted, deep inside the secure AFP compound, closed for the evening, like Hanoi. The rumble of the oncoming vehicle grew increasingly louder. Dominic crouched down behind the tree, trying to see with only one eye. The sluggish vibrations indicated to him that it must be a truck. As it rumbled by him, Dominic's eyes widened in fear. He was horrified, for he had seen that same truck before up at the gem mines. He knew it unmistakably by the license plate. How could he forget it: VNP.

Oh shit! he yelled to himself, *Those sons of bitches!* And most disturbing of all to him, how the hell did they get in here? He was standing right there when the Colonel demanded extra security at the front gate. *How could I have been so stupid?* he raged silently. *I should have never come back here. General Kien knew exactly where I would be!* Realizing he had brought danger upon Marie and the Colonel, he grabbed the sides of his hair in his fists and squeezed. *Oh God, what have I done?* he cried out to himself.

Like a bolt of lightning, a hidden, distant voice from the back of his mind erased his desperate thoughts. Regrets, he now knew, would have to wait. His assassins were back and he had to act now! He did not have the training, but as an involuntary soldier of war he would have to learn now in the battle.

His first concern was Marie. He could not go to her, he realized. At least not right away. *That would only place her in more direct danger.* His only chance was to get back to the main house and alert the Colonel. He looked around frantically and determined that this dense, unknown forest would take too long to navigate. He had no choice. He would have to abandon cover and use the trail.

Without hesitation, he made his way back to the clearing—but this time he stayed on its outer edge, close to the trees. This way, at the first sign of danger, he could simply slip back into the darker cover. Behind him was the plodding rumble of the truck. He traded the flashlight in his hand with the knife from his waist. He looked up into the sky. He had only the moon's faint glow to light his way from here on.

After only a half-dozen steps, the mirrored blade from the knife in his hand reflected a sharp beam of light into his eyes. He looked ahead and was immediately blinded by a flash of lights coming around the turn. *Uh oh!* he thought. The noise from the first truck had disguised the sound of the oncoming vehicle. Now he was caught helplessly in the flood of headlights. Without looking, he leaped back into the dense bush, falling unintentionally directly to his knees. The unplanned hard landing scratched his face, cut his arms, and hurt his knees. But he felt no pain. His surging adrenaline prevented him from feeling it. Sluggishly, the truck rolled nearer. Frozen in the night shadows, Dominic questioned himself. *They saw me…had to have…right?*

There was no way to be sure so he remained still, poised upright on all fours, behind a thick log. He realized running was impossible in the dark, dense woods. It would only give the assassins an audible target to shoot at. Safer to be hidden in the black underbrush. Aside from his pounding heart and racing adrenaline, the exterior of his body was altogether motionless.

The truck slowed down right in front of him, so close, he could reach out and touch the tires. Squeezing his knife, he silently and delicately wiped each side of the blade clean on his pants. By now, his heart was knocking as loud as the truck's diesel engine. The noxious smog of hot exhaust was blowing directly into his face, filling his nose and lungs with poisonous fumes. Desperately, he fought back a cough. Unable to stand it any longer, Dominic was compelled to take action. He would stab one of the tires and make a run for it.

Dominic raised the knife in the shadows. Before he thrust forward, the truck shifted gears. The worn, muddy tires slowly rolled passed him kicking dirt up into his face. Caustic fumes cleared from the air. Once again, temporary relief was granted. He knew, however, that he was running out of lives.

Springing to his feet he peered at the truck's license plate. It read VNP. *Another one?* Nothing was making sense anymore. *Why would they come to kill me in two, loud, sluggish trucks?*

By now, suspicion was overcoming his fear. Steadily, he was becoming more angry than afraid. His curious mind filled with questions, and he became more concerned with finding some answers than he was with his own safety. Abandoning reason, he daringly grabbed the flashlight at his side, flicked it on, and flashed its thin beam at the back of the fading truck. The weak line of light fought gallantly through the clouded trail of dust from the truck's wake, managing to reach its destination. Dominic saw that the open bed at the back of the truck was fully loaded with wooden crates. With that, his plans changed. He would now follow his stalkers.

But he was under no illusions. His plan was a crazy proposition. But it was also an emancipating choice for he felt clueless, helpless any other way. General Kien wanted him dead, and it was obvious now he would stop at nothing to achieve that goal.

Watching the path of the truck's headlights carefully, he noticed that the trail ahead began to horseshoe around him. This time he decided to cut through the darkness of the trees—the preferred road of choice for a soldier of war. Although he knew he was following danger, he felt better being the hunter instead of the prey.

Aggressive swings of his razor-sharp knife enabled him to clear much of the dense vegetation from his path, allowing him to keep up with the sluggish route of the truck. Once he saw the headlights stop, he ceased his clamorous swinging and squatted down. The engine of the truck shut off. Delicately he inched closer and closer toward the action. Voices immediately replaced the sound of the truck's engine. Vietnamese voices.

The truck had parked on the bank of the Red River where the trail itself had ended. Camouflaged by the trees around him, Dominic observed the scene before him. In all, about a dozen local workers began unloading the crates from the truck by hand and lining them up on the river's beach. A man dressed in a military uniform held a clipboard and checked inside each of the crates as they were set down. After all the crates were unloaded on the beach, the men then split into pairs and spread out all the way down a long, narrow, wooden dock.

The assembly line commenced. Two men carried one crate to the next pair of workers, those workers then carried the crate to the next station. Eventually, it traveled by hand quickly down the dock where it was loaded onto a flat barge afloat in the river. At the foot of the dock, the military man with the clipboard was barking orders to the workers. It was clear from his tone and hand signals that he wanted the workers to move faster and faster. The crates were obviously full. And heavy, for it was a struggle for two men to lug each one.

To Dominic's left, about twenty-five feet in front of him, the remaining crates were lined up in a row. He felt a compelling desire to know what was inside them. He needed to see what was inside them, but this was a very risky proposition. Only five or six crates remained, and the assembly-line routine was very efficient—taking less than one minute in between stations. Dominic tried to calculate how he could possibly get to the crates undetected, open one up, and look inside in such a short window of time. To do that, he realized, he needed to make some kind of diversion. Something that would disrupt the efficient flow of crates.

As the men came back and led away yet another crate, Dominic's stomach churned. He was running out of time. There was no way to disrupt the men without bringing their attention to himself. He knew he had to get a glimpse… just one glimpse. Before another thought entered his head, he moved. Without a plan.

Keeping low in the soft, sandy ground, Dominic adroitly made his way closer to the dwindling line of crates. He watched the nearest workers. There were now only three crates remaining in the line when Dominic emerged from the trees and quickly crouched behind them—making sure first that the closest workers were turned the other way lugging a crate. Suddenly, there was a loud thump on the other side of the crates. Dominic's heart rate increased to maximum speed as he peeked slightly over one of the boxes. *Oh no! They're heading back already?*

The two workers closest to him had dropped the last crate. It was broken wide open in the sand. The man with the clipboard, who Dominic now saw was belted with a pistol on his side, was screaming at them. From his position, Dominic was unable to see the contents but now that was the least of his concerns. The two workers were only a few feet away and moving closer to him. Already they were too close to make a run for it—so he had no choice but to take his chances on remaining undetected behind one of the last three wooden crates.

But which one? At first, he hunched down behind the middle crate because he knew it would be too difficult for the men to grab it next. After a couple of seconds, Dominic realized the crates were too narrow to fully disguise his body; he needed to be behind two of them at once for complete cover. The choice now was left or right. The workers closed in. Precious seconds ticked by as Dominic looked left. Then right. Left again. Right again. *Which direction?* As the workers reached down, Dominic shifted over to his left. His upper lip was trembling. He sat with his back pinned to the crates and reached for the knife at his side. In a few short seconds, he realized he may have to plunge it into another man's chest to save his own life. Although he heard Vietnamese,

Dominic could tell that the two workers were counting off a lift: "Moi...hai...ba!"

Dominic unintentionally clamped his eyes shut and held his breath as the two men jerked a crate off the ground. Dominic's heart pounded against his sweaty shirt. His grip on his knife tightened. After a couple of seconds, he opened his eyes and let out a sigh of relief. The men had chosen the right crate, literally and figuratively. But his relief would be short-lived.

As he peeked around the crate again, Dominic saw the two workers had picked up the pace to make up for their drop. Or perhaps, given their supervisor's mood and gun, to save their own lives. This time he realized they would be back in no time. *Damn!* There was no choice but to flee back into the dark woods without seeing anything. Before escaping, Dominic turned around and looked carefully at the crates. They were covered with dust. Quickly wiping his hand across the side of one he saw they were marked "UN Medical Supplies."

His detective work was over. Further inspection was suicide. Frustrated at having more questions rather than answers, Dominic squeezed his knife and plunged it deep into the wooden crate. The powerful blade went in clean to the handle. Removing the blade, Dominic swiftly crawled back into the dark sanctuary of the jungle and headed rapidly toward the Colonel's main house. The two workers did not notice him.

———————

Meanwhile, two other "workers" crept through the woods to guesthouse number twelve. Their clothes and weapons were black. Like Boris the spider, they silently approached the back door of the bungalow and picked the lock. Once inside, their pistols were drawn. Silencers locked in. This time there would be no doubt. They were ordered to confirm the kill before they moved on to the next one. They would not make the same mistake twice.

———————

While walking up the back steps to the main house, Dominic was startled by the sound of the Colonel's angry voice calling out, "No!"

Knife in hand, Dominic froze for a moment, and slowly he tiptoed the rest of the way, positioning himself on the back porch directly next to the open window—perfect position to listen in.

"Goddammit—nothing has changed!" the undeniable voice snapped. No response. "Everything is proceeding as planned!" Again the Colonel's voice. Again no response. No one else was in the room. He was on the phone. After a long pause, Dominic heard the Colonel answer calmly, "That's right. The shipment is going out now and the news will hit by the morning. Figure around 9:00pm your time, just in time for the late night news." With that, he heard the phone being hung up and then the loud sound of the Colonel's boots hitting the wood floor. He was walking toward the door to the back porch.

"Shit!" Dominic said under his breath. The last thing he needed was to get caught eavesdropping on Colonel Mazer's phone conversations. With his adrenaline racing again, he grabbed the deck fence, leaping over it in one swift motion, pulling his entire body back underneath the raised porch while in the air.

Dominic bit his tongue to silently weather the pain from sliding on the unforgiving gravel under the porch. The Colonel opened the back door and stepped out on it. His boots were now right over Dominic's head. The smell of cigar filled the air. Dominic didn't move. He held his breath. Not even his eyelids were blinking. His mind, however, was racing: Did the Colonel hear his jump? Could he see him through the wooden deck? *Maybe…hopefully…his battlefield senses had dulled with age.*

After almost of minute of tension, the questions in Dominic's mind were answered. He heard the Colonel's boots stepping down the steps, passed by right in front of him, and heading down one of the trails. Dominic remained motionless for the next minute while he watched the Colonel's unmistakable strut disappear down the trail. After the Colonel's dark image melted into the blackness, Dominic began breathing again; he had successfully eluded detection from an accomplished detector.

Dominic didn't like what he had heard. *What fucking plan? What fucking news?* Nothing was adding up anymore. With the Colonel gone, he decided to do some investigating in the house. Pulling himself out from underneath the porch, he hurried up the steps and slipped into the Colonel's house. Once inside, he paused. The house was dark, except for a distant light down the hallway. To the right was the room where the Colonel had been on the phone. Dominic grabbed the doorknob. It was locked. *Damn!* Quickly, he reached in his pants, pulled out his wallet and fumbled through it. He found what he was looking for—an old credit card. Not just any old credit card, his trusty "Brooklyn key." The same plastic card that allowed him to sneak back into his house after his late-night teenage trysts so many years ago. His lightly sleeping father never once caught him. Or maybe he just never mentioned it. Dominic slipped the plastic card through the door seam. *Bingo!* With one swipe the long-expired card unlocked the door.

Dominic entered the room. Closed the door. Locked it. It was completely dark. The smell of cigar smoke wafted around the room. He instinctively felt around for a light switch, but then caught himself. *Bad idea.* The open window would reveal the rays of light and either hasten the Colonel's unsought return or alert any roaming security guards. Neither was desirable. Even the beam from his flashlight could be seen from afar. Temporarily out of ideas, he began to inch his way forward in the smoky darkness and crrrrrrash! His foot knocked a small lamp off a table. His body froze. Every nerve inside him jumped. Even if no one heard him now, his break-in would not go unnoticed.

With his eyes better adjusted to the room's dark shadows, he noticed the silhouettes of file cabinets and a desk in front of him. He sighed with frustration. Without light, he realized, being there was not only risky, but useless. Turning to his right, he examined the open window and noticed it was garnished by long velvet curtains that were tied on each side. It was the only window in the room. Dominic tiptoed over to it, gazing outside and down the trail. No sight of the Colonel. No guards. Quickly, he cut the decorative fasteners with his knife and pulled the curtains together to completely conceal the window. Like an eclipse, the room darkened further to absolute pitch black, effectively blocking out the full moon's light. No one could see a light in the room now. Sweat dripped from his chin while he inched his way around the blackness. Finally, his foot bumped into the desk. Reaching out, he felt the shade of another desk lamp. He flicked it on.

He adjusted the curtains, better securing them tight around the window, not allowing a glimpse of light to escape. He hurried back to the desk. On the desktop, various papers and folders were spread out. He sifted through them. They were records for medical supplies, shipping documents. Nothing of importance. Opening the top desk drawer he saw a calendar, some pens, a notepad. *Nothing still!* Looking down he noticed one of the drawers was locked. Using his sturdy knife, he stabbed into the wooden drawer and twisted the blade. Again and again, he stabbed the drawer and twisted the blade. After several plunges, the wood was totally chipped away around the lock and battered drawer broke open. His hands were shaking. He knew time was passing, and he moved at a frenzied pace. Breaking and entering was one thing, burglary another.

Inside the drawer, Dominic saw a small handgun and a light green folder that had "RUSSO" boldly typed across the front. Dominic took the gun out and placed it on the desk. He opened the folder. Three black and white pictures fell out onto the desk.

Impossible. That's not possible. How did they get here? They were his pictures.

Taken with his camera. By him. A couple days ago. Dominic's face turned pale white as looked at the photographs he took of the prison—the Penitentiaire—while inside the military zone. In the back of his head, he heard the echo of Quan's voice telling him, "Mr. Huyen and Mr. Lang have just informed me that you may take some pictures of the famous Penitentiaire…"

The photographs were taken from too far away to make out any faces—but close enough to see numerous men in chains working on the fields. The armed soldiers watching the prisoners were also in view. The camera had automatically dated each picture: 8/13/92.

Dominic's legs weakened in fear. *Why? How? Who?* He had to put both hands on the desk in order to remain standing. He couldn't digest his thoughts. He couldn't rationalize what he was seeing before him. "What the fuck is going on here?" he mumbled to himself. Why were his pictures developed? And why were they now in the Colonel's desk in a locked drawer? He recalled that he had left his camera in his hut up at the mines when his deadly intruders started this nightmare. When the two assassins came in, he just ran out. He took nothing with him.

Behind the pictures Dominic saw one sheet of white paper. The typing on top read: PRESS RELEASE 8/15/92:

Dominic paused for a moment realizing this was today's date. And today was only a few hours old. The text itself read:

```
    Two young Americans, Dominic Russo,
24, and his sister, Marie Russo, 25,
were brutally murdered in Hanoi earlier
today. Evidence strongly suggests that
Dominic Russo was about to release three
photographs taken by him of an apparent
POW camp he encountered seemingly by
chance while traveling the countryside
of Vietnam on August 13, 1992.
    Retired Colonel Clifford Mazer, world-
renowned humanitarian and head of the
Army for Peace, found the photographs
along with a smashed camera in Dominic
Russo's bungalow. He immediately turned
over all evidence to the custody of
Senator Robert Haynes, who is visiting
```

Vietnam to investigate Hanoi's POW
efforts.

Colonel Mazer was too distressed to
comment on the tragic slayings. Both
victims were his very close friends.
Marie Russo was a social worker for the
Army for Peace, and Dominic Russo was a
visiting guest.

Senator Haynes is scheduled to speak
at the Senate Hearings next week on the
issue of the US-Vietnam trade embargo.
He has cut his goodwill trip short and
is scheduled to leave Hanoi today.
He released a statement about an hour
ago saying, 'As far as I am concerned,
these horrific crimes were apparently
perpetrated in a cover-up attempt by
the Government of Vietnam. This blatant
and appalling act of terrorism will set
back the issue of the trade embargo and
political reconciliation indefinitely.'
No word yet on the reaction of President
McCabe and the White House concerning
these shocking events.
###

Dominic's classically handsome face, cut and dirty, was gnarled in anger. He read the text again. And again. His body temperature, once burning with fright, now frosted over, cold as ice. Fear overwhelmed his feelings. Horror roiled in his veins. Everything in his mind was replaced by a frigid flow of rage. *It was all a setup...some kind of conspiracy...with me and Marie as patsies!*

Before he could act, Dominic was distracted by the approaching sounds of footsteps. In an instant, he swiped the gun off the desktop, turned off the lamp and knelt behind the desk. He clenched the pistol, the first gun he ever held, and pointed it straight at the door across the completely black room. The steps grew louder as they ascended the stairs. They were unmistakable. His head was full of questions, but for the moment, answers would have to wait. As soon as that door opened, he was going to shoot. To kill.

The porch door creaked open. There was a jingle of keys right outside of the room. Dominic tightened his grip on the pistol and swallowed. *This is it!* he screamed in his head, psyching himself up enough to squeeze the trigger.

The door to the room slowly swung open. Dominic saw the silhouette of a man in the doorway. Smoke was rising from his head. There was no doubt in in Dominic's mind. The last image that entered his head as he pulled the trigger was of Marie—hoping that she was alive.

Click.

Nothing.

Click.

Again nothing. The gun was not loaded. The lights went on. There was the Colonel, standing in the doorway with a smirk on his face. And a gun in his hand. For a few tense seconds, he peered, callously and vengefully, into Dominic's eyes. "Son of a bitch," he mumbled, raising his weapon.

Before he could aim, Dominic reacted. In a flash, Dominic dropped the gun, grabbed the knife, and darted for the curtain-covered window. There was no time to make sure the unseen window was open far enough for his whole body to fit through. He had to take his chances. He ran directly at the closed curtains and leaped into them, through them, ducking low and tight while in the air.

Bang! Bang! Two shots rang out from the Colonel's pistol, and Dominic crash-landed on the porch with the screen under his feet. He managed to avoid both the glass and the Colonel's bullets. As the back door flung open, Dominic hurdled over the fence and dashed down the trail into the darkness. The Colonel fired into the night to no avail. "Goddammit!" he snarled stomping back inside.

Dominic sprinted into the darkness toward his sister's bungalow using the flashlight to guide him. "Please!" he said aloud. "Please no! Not Marie!"

A dark shadow had already made its way through the woods, entering Marie's guesthouse with a master key. Silently and slowly the shadow edged down the hall into her bedroom. Unlike her father, Marie Russo was a heavy sleeper. She never knew that an intruder was in her room...

After a few minutes of full sprint, Dominic arrived at his sister's guesthouse, hurdling over the front steps in one leap, and kicking down her front door. His knife was drawn. Adrenaline pumped through his body, fueling him with both strength and anger. "Marie!" he yelled in the entranceway. No response. "You son of a bitch…no!" he shouted, opening the bedroom door. When he turned on the light switch, tears filled his eyes.

She was not in her bed. The sheets were on the floor. *There must have been some sort of struggle.* He checked the floor. No blood. He checked the adjacent bathroom. Nothing.

Dominic gathered his thoughts. *At best, she was kidnapped. At worst, already dead.* One thing was certain to him—company would be arriving shortly. His mind struggled with what to do next. It wasn't long before he realized his only chance was to get out of AFP's compound to alert someone…anyone. *But how?* Patrols were everywhere. Enemies were everywhere. An image then flashed in his head—*the Colonel's boat.* It was his only chance for escape. He needed to get to West Lake.

CHAPTER TWENTY-SEVEN

1972

Parrot's Beak

Cambodia

September 4, 7:39PM

The twilight shadows of the Cambodian jungle faded to darkness. Occasional lightning blinked and thunder growled. But despite all the usual preludes, rain did not fall. Flames of fire crackled the remaining wood and flesh from the destroyed remnants of Alcatraz's barracks. No more gunshots were heard. No more explosions.

Major Russo, covered in mud and blood, had survived the ambush. But for him, it was not over. He dropped his AK-47 rifle. It was caked with too much mud for him to trust it anymore. Instead, he drew his favorite weapon, a Colt .45 semiautomatic pistol. He knew that no greater stopping power could be held in one hand. He surveyed the area around the destruction, coming upon an unexpected sight.

In the distance, Russo noticed a familiar soldier. Stepping a couple of feet closer, he recognized the man's face behind the thick layer of camo' cream. It was Doc, standing legs apart and pointing his M-16 at someone directly in front of him. The other soldier's back was turned. Russo was unable to make out who it was. Could be anybody, he thought to himself—an Alcatraz guard, Charlie, or someone from another scout platoon. The seasoned Major approached cautiously, staying low as he closed in on the scene. From twenty yards out, he was able to positively identify the other man without seeing his face. It was his Colonel.

Something was not right, but Russo still chose not to reveal himself. His battle instincts were on alert. His pistol up and ready. He closed in further.

The standoff remained fixed, almost frozen, as Russo approached. Neither man was saying anything to the other. Even when Russo was almost next to both men, neither of them looked over at him. Their attention was locked on each other. Russo looked into Doc's eyes. The friendly sparkle he had come to expect was replaced by an insidious, trembling glare.

"Drop it, Doc!" Russo barked.

"No way, you son of a bitch!" Doc yelled. His voice was cracking. His usual calm demeanor was overrun with horror. "If you're gonna kill me, then I'm takin' him with me!"

"Nobody's gonna kill anyone, Doc," Russo stated trying to calm him down. "Now just drop the gun and relax, for crissakes!"

Colonel Mazer stood there and didn't utter a word. He was peering sternly into Doc's tearful eyes.

Russo looked behind Doc's shoulders for a moment. He saw Corporal Greene's body face down in the mud next to the burning remnants of the blown-up barracks. Multiple gunshot wounds branded the young warrior's back. In less than two months, he would have turned nineteen. Nevermore would he joke with his buddy JD or appreciate the ocean's beauty at sunrise or hold his baby girl.

Four of the Inferno team's seven soldiers were gone. Among the assumptions swirling in Russo's head was that Doc had flipped out and turned on the team. It would not have been the first time a soldier in Southeast Asia had done this.

"It's over, Doc," Russo barked, pointing his powerful Colt at Doc's head. "Just drop it!"

But Doc was too far gone to be calmed. "Fuck you! Fuck you! Fuck you!" he shouted. "You fuckin' bastards!"

Russo realized he might have to squeeze the trigger and kill his friend, the same man who had removed two embedded bullets from his own body so recently. It was the last thing he wanted to do, but it seemed as if he had no choice. Doc was maddening to a point of no return.

"Did anyone put you up to this?!" Russo asked him. Doc didn't answer. He was no longer listening to his Major. He retreated into his own world, mumbling to himself as he repeatedly shook his head and wept. Russo watched carefully. Doc's body was slowly weakening. First, his shoulders slumped...

then his spine hunched...and finally, the tight clench of his machine gun eased.

Russo remained poised through these tense moments. Although physically yielding, Doc was still armed and extremely unstable. Mazer stood silently, emotionless, with his hands on his hips as he watched the emotional breakdown of one of his men.

"Why?" Doc cried out. "Whhhhhhy?"

After a distant rumble of thunder, the leader of the Operation Inferno unit finally said: "Cause it had to be done."

Russo spun his head and looked into Mazer's eyes for the first time since he arrived. "What had to be done?" he immediately interjected.

"This," Mazer asserted. "It was ordered."

Horrified, Russo immediately shifted the aim of his pistol to the head of his Colonel. His grimace marked his contempt. Doc, now completely listless, dropped his weapon to the ground and fell to a seated position.

Russo shortened the distant of his gun to Mazer's face. "What the fuck are you sayin'?"

Shaking his head, Mazer replied: "Now come on, John. Don't be so goddamn shocked, will ya? You knew it had to end like this. You knew it when we first got into this thing."

Russo shook his head. He was disgusted. He vented his fervor by smacking Mazer on the side of his face with his pistol-held fist. "Fuck you!" he yelled. "You sick, twisted demon! You set up and murdered your own men! Your own boys!"

Mazer didn't go down from the harsh blow. He absorbed the pain without expression. He did not even use his hands to wipe the line of blood from the fresh wound on his cheek. He just stood there, staring coldly into the eyes of his long-time comrade. "You set yourself up," he stated calmly. "You made yourself blind. You made yourself naïve. You're to blame. Not me. Not the CIA. Not the White House. Not this damn war. Nothing and nobody is to blame but yourself."

Russo gripped his pistol tighter.

"Go ahead, do it," the Colonel continued unfazed. "You think it'll make you a hero? Is that what you think, huh? A hero of what, John? Your country?" With that, the Colonel let out a choppy laugh. "Your country set this whole fuckin' thing up. You think by killin' me anything will change? You won't be a hero—you'll be a fuckin' martyr 'cause I'm your only ticket outta here. Face it, boy. You're nothin but a goddamn pawn, Major Russo. We all are."

"You're the fucking pawn!" Russo yelled. "You let them do this. Not me!

And I got news for you, Cliff—I'd rather die here than let you get away with it!"

Mazer shook his head and laughed in disappointment. "You still don't get it, do you? You think I could have prevented this whole thing but you're dead wrong about that. Don't you realize that if it wasn't me, then it would be someone else? Say I turned them down for this mission. You know what would have happened then? Someone else would have done this fucked mission, and you and I would be sent on another enemy goose chase—you know, the ones where they would tell me behind closed doors that it's acceptable for me to lose up to one hundred of my men in the offensive. Acceptable to lose one hundred men! What makes that any fucking different than this?" he shouted.

"I'll tell you the difference. You don't shoot your own boys in their goddamn backs! That's the fucking difference!"

"Yeah. You're right. I just lead them into battle as sacrificial lambs, knowing that there is no grand scheme to win this damn war. Knowing we're here fighting in vain 'cause we don't have the balls to do what it takes to win this thing, yet we got too much fucking pride to pack our bags and get the fuck outta here and stop all the worthless slaughter. You and the goddamn bureaucrats consider those to be acceptable killings!"

"This is not the only alternative!"

"John, there are no alternatives. It's all the same damn thing. Nothing will ever change. Our country is not even a democracy, yet we are here trying to make this country one. Where is the democracy with the CIA running around dictating foreign policy behind closed doors? Without any accountability. The men who control this whole damn charade operate without restraint or responsibility, John. They just use us for anything they want. If we don't cooperate then we become sacrificial lambs ourselves. There are no alternatives."

"So instead we sacrifice our souls?"

Mazer exploded like never before. "My soul was sacrificed when my mother was raped and killed in a POW camp! My soul was sacrificed when the same goddamn CIA did nothing when they came and murdered my old man! Don't you talk to me about no fuckin' sacrifices!"

Russo paused and reflected for a moment. Mazer had never before spoken of such things. "So that's the reason for all this. Your whole life's been a lie. And these premeditated murders will never bring you revenge for your parents. It just turned you into the same sadistic mentality that betrayed and murdered them. You're everything they were opposed to!"

"You think you're supposed to be alive right now!" Mazer screamed. "I was ordered to take you out, too! The only reason why you're here is because

I let you live! They expect you to be dead like the others. I risked everything sparing you! I allowed you to live! I wanted you to live!"

"So I'm supposed to thank you for sparing me? I should be grateful to you for allowing me to live? Live as what? Huh? A government pawn of murder?"

Mazer shook his head and his voice was lighter. "That's where you're wrong, John." Mazer paused. "We ain't pawns no more. This mission changes everything."

Russo was bewildered. "How's that?"

"We're free now," Mazer stated emphatically. "This mission gives us freedom. And not just freedom. Power. We got the power now, John. The power to do what we want. Whatever we want."

"You're deranged. They own us."

"No, we own those motherfuckers now. They can't touch us. They can't use us. And they will never fuck with us again. They wanted every one of us dead, but we can change that now, right now, because now we're in control. This is what I've been waiting for years. We can decide the game to play now 'cause we hold all the cards."

"Fuck you," said Russo. "What makes you think you haven't been set up to die with the rest of us? The President and McCabe probably plan on leaving you here to rot in the jungle. Either that, or they're gonna send somebody in here just to put a bullet in your head. Or drop a bomb on your isolated ass!"

"I've taken care of everything," Mazer assured his longtime counterpart. "All that's left to do is radio Phillips and explain to him that it would be a great mistake for the country if something should happen to us. You see, I have taken measures that guarantee our survival. Tapes have been made. Pictures have been taken. Letters have been written. Hell, I've used their own million-dollar surveillance equipment against them. McCabe, Phillips, the CIA fucks, and the goddamn President himself. Blood is on all of their hands from this thing! And I have already made arrangements for all the information to be sent out to the press—unless, of course, I am able to return home quickly and safely. Then, and only then, will I be able to stop the presses and keep the whole world from hearing about the order—issued by the President of the United States and carried out by the CIA—to exterminate unarmed, captured prisoners of war as well as our own soldiers!"

Mazer continued in a more solemn tone: "We are now the keepers of the greatest secret in American history, John. We could bring down the President, McCabe, and the whole goddamn CIA with all the evidence I've gathered. Do you know what that makes us? Huh? It makes us the most powerful men in the country. Untouchable! We can write our own ticket. We'll be rich. Those bastards will pay for this for the rest of their lives." The Colonel finished his triumphant speech with, "We'll make them pay us for everything they've done!"

Bang!

Colonel Mazer grabbed the side of his stomach and collapsed to the ground. Stunned, both he and Russo spun their heads to Doc. There he was, a stark contrast to the shaking mess he was moments before—on his feet, shoulders square, spine straight, wearing an altogether composed expression. The pointed pistol he was holding was still smoking from the gunshot.

"What the fuck are you doin'?" Mazer yelled at Doc, wincing in pain, holding both his hands on his bleeding side. "You stupid son of a bitch! Haven't you heard anything I said? You can't make it without me! They won't even send a chopper to come get you!"

"Oh, I heard you, Colonel Mazer, sir," Doc answered calmly. "I heard you loud and clear. But you see my problem is this—unfortunately you didn't plan to spare me or bring me back home with you and Major Russo. In fact, I recall that about ten minutes ago you were trying to kill me, just like you killed the others."

He took a deep, calm breath before continuing, "But unfortunately for you Colonel, you underestimated me. You thought you could save my ass for last because it would be easiest. Well, as we all can see, that turned out to be a big mistake, now didn't it? I caught your ass before it had a chance to take me out and finish the job." Doc paused, a side smirk on his face blossomed to a full smile. "I guess you trained me better than you thought, Colonel Mazer."

"Fine! Fine!" Mazer exclaimed. "None of that makes a difference anymore. Things have obviously changed, and there is no reason why we can't all go back!"

"Now, now Colonel, sir. Things may have changed for you and Major Russo, but things have not changed one bit for me. I'm sorry if you find it insulting, Clifford," said Doc, as a smirk eased across his face when he said his first name, "but I just cannot now—all of a sudden—accept the word of a man who tried to shoot me in the back."

"You have no fuckin' choice," Mazer spat out. He was losing blood, but not his angry energy. "I'm the only chance you got!"

"You may be," Doc acknowledged, "but I still don't trust a snake. You see, I look at it this way: I serve no purpose here, therefore there's no reason to stop you from taking me out. Now in order to insure my safety and a ride home, I just became the only choice you got!"

The wounded Colonel didn't say anything. He had no response to make. He knew it was a wise move by Doc, and nothing could be done to change it now. He needed Doc's medical help. Or he would die.

"You know I could have killed you, Clifford," Doc continued, "but I liked all that untouchable shit you talked about. I want to be a powerful "Secretkeeper" like yourself and Major Russo. That's why I shot you in the abdomen. Without proper medical attention you'll probably die in…ummm… let me think." Doc paused for a moment to appear deep in thought. "Yeah. I'd say probably within the next half hour or so. On the other hand, as long as I'm around to remove the bullet and clean that nasty wound every couple of hours, well, in that case—in my medical opinion—I am confident that infection won't set in and you should eventually be just fine."

CHAPTER TWENTY-EIGHT

1992

Dominic dove down hard to his hands and knees at the edge of the forest. His lungs struggled for a few moments to recapture lost breath. His clothes were torn and wet with mud. Many scratches lined his face and body, each one a temporary tattoo of his speedy traverse through the dark thorny jungle. The knife gripped firmly in his right fist had served him well cutting through the often thick bush. He had made it to West Lake. Alive and in one piece.

Peering out from a crouched position, he surveyed the perimeter of the U-shaped beach. It was deserted. No workers, no trucks, no more action seen or heard. The clear full moon twinkled on the surface of the silent calm waters. The peaceful imagery before him did not calm the worry inside his head. Escape, survival, Marie, and Julie dominated his frantic thoughts.

Off to the distant left he noticed a boat, the Colonel's boat, anchored out on the still waters. From his angle it was difficult to approximate how far away it was. Probably at least two hundred yards offshore—too far to make a swim for it. Scanning further left, he noticed a faint, sandy, shadowy image of an overturned rowboat on the beach. That's it! His ticket off the compound.

Before he planted his first step toward the rowboat, a calm voice from behind changed his plans: "You're no soldier, son."

Dominic dropped his head down between his shoulders. He was in no rush to turn around. He knew who it was.

"I must compliment you on your survival tactics up at the mines," the calm voice said. "You did a helluva job slipping away and finding your way back to Hanoi, but you didn't think you could get away from me, now did you?"

Dominic slowly rotated his head around. The dark outline of Colonel Mazer's rigid face was standing over him. In his hand by his waist, Dominic saw an unmistakable shadow of a pistol.

"Where's Marie and Julie?!" Dominic demanded.

"Drop that knife, boy!" the Colonel ordered back. The twinkling blade in Dominic's right fist was the only thing the Colonel could see under the dark canopy of trees.

Dominic ignored the demand and repeated his growl, "Where are they?"

The Colonel moved the gun closer to Dominic's face. Dominic recognized it. It was the same gun that had failed him back at the mansion. Looking down at his weapon the Colonel pointed out, "Now don't be fooled. This here gun works just fine…when it's filled with bullets."

Dominic stood up. Staring at the Colonel's shadow with malevolent eyes, he tossed the knife a few feet away onto the adjacent beach. When it landed, the sharp blade cut through the sand and disappeared in the soft ground. With a firm shove the Colonel pushed Dominic out of the dark forest onto the moonlit beach.

In the full moonlight, the two men could now see each other's faces. Dominic stood straight up, his eyes fixed upon the Colonel's. He was without fear. His own life meant nothing to him right now. His only concern was for the two people in the world he cared about. The only two people he loved. "Where are they?" he grumbled again.

The Colonel released his tightly gathered eyebrows. His glaring eyes softened with delight. A smile tilted awkwardly above his chin. "Oh, don't worry, son" he said assuredly, "you're going to be with them real soon."

"You son of a bitch," Dominic snarled, "you're gonna burn in hell."

"You know," the Colonel said, basking in the moment, "that temper of yours reminds me of your old man."

The Colonel's statement suddenly triggered Dominic's recollection. His life might be about to expire, but he was thinking clearly. Very clearly. His thoughts focused on the Colonel's indomitable ego—how he felt compelled to always project an attitude of toughness to the world. You could see it in his walk, hear it in his talk. One on one, in a crowd of people, it was always there, always the same.

Dominic knew all about proud, cocky, invincible men. Men who were prisoners of their own images. After all, he had years of experience in dealing with the Colonel's right hand man. And those years had taught him that a strong attitude can be a weakness. A weakness Dominic was experienced in exploiting.

Dominic stared deeply at the Colonel. The Colonel's stoic stance, the shadowed stature of his body, was all too familiar to him. Suddenly the Colonel's grinning face began to blur. Dominic watched intently as another more familiar face crystallized in its place. The face of his father came into focus. And he was not at all happy to see his son; John Russo's expression was cold and confrontational. Dominic had seen that angry look in his eyes a hundred times before. And now that he saw it again, he realized exactly what to do. The late Major John Russo would never back down from a physical challenge...especially from a civilian boy.

"What's the matter, Colonel?" Dominic said in teasing tone, "You too old for hand-to-hand combat anymore? You have to use a gun now?"

The Colonel's delighted face came back into view. Immediately, his moment-of-glory smile recoiled half an inch.

"What's wrong, old man?" Dominic taunted as he inched the front of his foot into the sand, "You're not scared of a civilian boy, now are you?"

The Colonel's forehead wrinkled. His eyebrows cinched together. His lips clamped and straightened into a thin hard line. Seeing the Colonel's face reacting to his words, Dominic continued pestering, "Well then, go ahead. Pull the trigger. You're washed up anyway, old man. You're finished. Your whole plan is ruined."

The Colonel didn't respond. Dominic pressed, "You're supposed to be a legendary warrior? Bullshit! You're scared of a fuckin' civilian boy."

The Colonel remained silent. It was obvious to Dominic what was going on in his head. His mind must be screaming at him to ignore his foolish pride and finish the job. His pride, however, was likely assuring him that the job would be done, but first there was a challenge to meet. And his pride never backed down before.

Dominic sensed the Colonel's bind. He knew a warrior's pride was too strong to be overruled by reason. "Go ahead," he mocked, inching his front foot down into the soft sand a bit more, "squeeze the trigger, old man. Prove once again that you're nothing but a coward."

The Colonel did not respond with words. His deep, penetrating stare told the story though. There was a good chance, Dominic realized, the Colonel's ego was more inflated, more stubborn, than his father's used to be. After all, during their glory days, the Colonel was his father's boss. He was more revered, more renowned, and higher up in the military command pecking order.

"C'mon! Pull the fucking trigger! Get it over with already. You're too scared to fight so what are you waiting for? You're no Colonel. You're a phony, full of shit, cowardly old man."

Dominic's words were working. The Colonel's internal rage became transparent. No one spoke to him in that tone and manner…not in the last twenty years at least. Slightly lowering his extended arm, the Colonel finally responded. His voice came out in a harsh whisper. "You better watch your mouth, boy."

With his toes dug into the ground, Dominic resumed the mockery. "If you want, Clifford, I'll give you a chance to call a bunch of your men down…so when you start to get your ass beat, you can have them take me out."

The Colonel's arm lowered some more. Another couple of inches and the gun would be out of direct range.

Dominic had one last verbal bomb to drop: "Come to think of it, you always had other people do your dirty work, didn't you, Clifford? During the war, you hid behind my father. He was the real soldier. He did all your dirty work, while you took the credit and kissed all the brass ass you could find."

This statement of Dominic's put the Colonel over the edge. His gun was now pointed straight down. He was ready to tear Dominic apart with his bare hands.

But Dominic didn't allow the enraged veteran that chance. With one fast kick of his buried foot, he blinded the Colonel's eyes with a spray of stinging coarse sand. Ducking his head down like a battering ram, Dominic launched into the Colonel's legs at full steam. Temporarily sightless, the Colonel managed to raise his gun and fire off a shot. The aimless bullet sailed above Dominic's crouched, onrushing body.

Before the Colonel squeezed off a second shot, Dominic's head smashed violently into the Colonel's kneecap. The gun flew out of the Colonel's hand from the impact of the tackle. Both men fell down hard on the soft beach.

Immediately, Dominic popped off the ground and straddled the Colonel's body. His knees pinned the Colonel's arms back helplessly to the ground. Furiously, Dominic drilled his fists into the Colonel's hard face. With one shot, the Colonel's nose burst open with blood. Another shot shattered his front teeth. Another cracked his jaw. Two more caved in his cheekbones. Again and again, Dominic unleashed his revenge with swings of his pounding fists, yelling

"You son of a bitch!"

Suddenly the Colonel slammed his knee up into Dominic's exposed groin. Just like that—with one vicious crippling blow—the onslaught was over. Dominic collapsed off the Colonel and immediately doubled over in pain. The wind in his lungs emptied. He was breathless, gasping violently for air, completely short-circuited.

With a few moments of relief the Colonel was able to get up to his hands and knees. His right knee was shattered, his nose and jaw were broken, his eyes were swollen half shut, and the rest of his face was battered—but there was no disputing the old warrior was still tough as nails. He had absorbed an ugly beating, but he still had something left. Blood dripped off his face onto the sand. He searched for his lost weapon with his hands, crawling and sifting through the sand, as he could hardly see through the slits in his puffy eyes. Dominic was next to him, curled in a ball, writhing in agony.

Eventually the Colonel felt something hard in the soft beach. He raised it up from the ground. It was not his pistol. It was the knife. His knife. The one he lent to Dominic for the night. A toothless, crooked smile cut across his broken jaw. He liked killing with a knife better anyway. It was more personal. More intimate. More enjoyable.

Rejuvenated, the Colonel managed to stand up and limp his way over to his young guest, who remained incapacitated by pain. The Colonel's imposing shadow cast over Dominic's curled body.

Dominic looked up and saw the Colonel's bloody face, blazing eyes, and evil smile. He desperately wanted to swing his arms or kick his legs, but he was still paralyzed. His aching body simply would not respond to his commands.

With both hands, the Colonel gripped the knife and raised it over Dominic. With only one leg to support him, his body was unsteady. The wobbly, shining blade was pointed straight down. Dominic shut his eyes. He knew it was over.

Baaaang! A gunshot rang out in the calm night behind the Colonel.

Dominic opened his eyes and looked up at the Colonel. His fingers slowly opened. The knife dropped out of his hands. The falling blade whistled through the still air and disappeared in the sand only inches from Dominic's neck. Blood seeped out of the Colonel's mouth. He slumped down to his knees.

Baaaang! A louder gunshot fired from behind the Colonel. The shooter was closing in.

The Colonel crumbled face down onto Dominic. The second bullet had severed his lower spine. The old soldier was dead. Shot in the back. He would never know who his killer was.

Dominic's crippling pain finally was beginning to ease. His body was regaining some of its lost strength, enough at least to push the Colonel's heavy lifeless body off him. Sucking in a deep breath, Dominic fought his way up to his hands and knees. The pain in his groin was still numbing. So numbing he still couldn't raise his head and look up. With his head slumped down, he took in and let out several deep breaths. Finally, mustering every ounce of energy, he slowly made it up onto his feet and saw the dark outline of his savior.

When the shooter plodded forward into the faint glow of moonlight, his dark silhouette came into focus. Dominic could not believe his eyes.

"Ahhhh, Dominic."

He recognized the melody of the voice, but the man's appearance did not fit. The shooter's plump chin and cheeks were fully exposed and baby smooth. His hair was slicked back with gel. There were no dangling Shirley Temple curls on each side of his face. No thick-lensed glasses. No protruding eyeballs or visible nose hairs. A yellow polo shirt, red shorts, and brown sandals replaced the expected black suit and white shirt. Dominic's nose caught wind of a fresh splash of aftershave—even the smell of this man was pleasant.

Holding a pistol at his side, Dominic's savior looked down at the Colonel's dead body and shook his head slowly. Baffled, Dominic stared at the man standing before him. The voice was unmistakable, but could it actually be him? Could he really be here in Vietnam? And how could he look like this?

"Mr.... Krauze?" Dominic said tentatively.

"Ya know, it ain't easy being ugly sometimes," the man said without looking up. "It takes a long time to put on a beard...attach the curls...dress in all those hot clothes." He shook his clean-shaven face once and continued, "and wearing those thick glasses. Oh, you don't know the headaches they give me."

Dominic was dumbfounded. His body began to tingle in awe of the criminal ingenuity, the criminal identity, in front of his eyes. It *was* him. It was really Shay Krauze! He may have lived and prayed among his fellow Hasids, but only he and God knew how many other identities he assumed to carry out his business.

Dominic was speechless. Shay Krauze had no true identity. *He was nobody. He was anybody. Who could ever trace him? Who could ever keep up with him?* It was so innovative, so wickedly clever, that it was frightening to fathom.

Shay didn't look at Dominic. He just kept talking as if he was in his own world. "Ya know what else I don't like? I don't like travelling. For me, New Jersey is too long of a ride. Plus you got the traffic...you got the tunnels. And how about during rush hour? Yeeesh…now that's *meshugganah*. What headaches I get whenever I have to go there." Still peering down at the Colonel, the masquerading crime lord shrugged his shoulders. "So can you imagine how angry it makes me to have to come all the way here?"

Dominic was too confused by Shay's appearance to respond. But his eyes didn't blink once; they were fixed on the gun in Shay's right hand.

"But," Shay continued, "these are the sacrifices one must make."

Dominic cut in with a firm statement. "I'll get your money back first thing this morning."

"Ahhhh yes, I almost forgot…the money," said Shay. "Ya know, five hundred grand does not garner the same respect as it used to."

"Over here ,it's like five hundred million," Dominic pointed out. "That's why General Kien and Colonel Mazer set us up."

"Dominic, Dominic—you mean General Kien and Colonel Mazer fucked up," Shay clarified.

Dominic frowned curiously and asked, "What do you mean?"

Shay looked into his eyes for the first time. A cold expression froze across his smooth round jovial face. Dominic noticed the gun in his hand still pointed down, but his index finger hadn't moved off the trigger.

Despite the tense moment, Dominic stared back into Shay's eyes. He began to fill in pieces to a new puzzle, a different puzzle, far deeper and far more sinister than the one he had previously pieced together.

"You were a team?" Dominic said in a low voice.

Shay turned his hand up and pointed the pistol at Dominic. "You should know by now, Dominic, that I don't have any teammates. I have business to do. There are those who further my business interests and those who get in the way."

Dominic reflected on Shay's words. So it was he who was tricked on the terrace of the UN. He had been used from the start. A puppet, a pawn, a patsy. And he now was a dead man.

"There were never any gems, were there?"

"Oh sure there are. There are plenty of gems. I can assure you that what you saw were not phonies. We've been doing business for years, the General and me. We'll be doing business long after you're gone, too. You know—a little opium here, some jewels there."

The mention of drugs made Dominic think back to the mines, to the dark field of tall crops he jumped into during his escape. "The General farms the drugs," Dominic realized in a low voice.

"Oriental poppy to be precise," Shay clarified, "and from that you get your opium, which gives you your heroin."

Dominic remembered the trucks, the crates, and the scene on the beach where he saw the men in an assembly line loading the boat. It was all coming together. It was all making sense. "You used the UN to fund the whole thing, didn't you?" he said. "The UN sent the Colonel medical supplies, and he sent you back the heroin on the same ship. In the same crates."

Shay's face beamed with pride. "Now isn't that humanitarian of them? I must tell you, Dominic, that your shrewdness has impressed me. Just like with that little deal you put together with the General. I admit—you had me fooled back at our last meeting. You purposely never set the numbers with me so you could carve out a real hefty commission for yourself. Here I thought you made a crucial mistake because of your inexperience, but I was the one who was mistaken. You set yourself up to earn a hundred percent commission! Now that was sharp. Very sharp." Shay nodded his head to emphasize his point and continued. "By the way, I did wire the half a million dollars you requested. That's right—it's sitting in the same bank that you told me…earning interest as we speak. Ironically, it was the payment for you and your sister's murder." Tears welled in Dominic's eyes. Shay told him, "I must say, it was much easier on the conscience when I realized you were trying to rob me."

Dominic wiped his hands across his face in disbelief. It was all too impossible, too horrible to digest. He asked himself what he did to deserve this kind of life. And death.

Shay continued with the details: "The plan was that as soon as you called me from the mines, I knew you were a dead man, so I wired the money. Unfortunately, things got messed up. It's my fault really. I should have known better than to pay some foreigners to kill you."

"Why did you?" Dominic snapped at him. "Why didn't you just have your guys take me out back home and leave my sister out of it?"

"Well, originally we planned to use only Marie. But when the Colonel found out that you were coming to visit her, we figured using both of you would be much better for the publicity. It was a wonderful plan on paper, really. But unfortunately General Kien and the Colonel let you get away. It's quite amazing when think about it…here I had two legendary soldiers—war heroes to their respective countries—and they couldn't even whack two kids. So I had to come all the way over here to correct their mistakes."

Dominic looked down at the Colonel's dead corpse and offered up a smile to his would-be assassin. "Everything is fucked up now, though. Your business is over. You just killed your point man. And you're still a fat ugly bastard."

"I'm disappointed in you, Dominic. You should know by now that I never kill to end business. I only kill to expand business. That's a lesson you should have surmised from your mother and your father's untimely demise."

When he heard this, Dominic's rage boiled his blood. Shay took another step closer to him and pointed the pistol an inch from his face. "That's right. Your insufferable old man refused to shut his mouth. You would think he would have gotten the message after your mother was rammed off the road. And now, how ironic—I get to reunite the family."

Dominic didn't shut his eyes. He stared directly down the small barrel of the pistol. He was going to watch the bullet shoot out. He was determined to die without fear.

"Drop it, Shay!" an approaching voice behind Dominic shouted.

Shay looked behind Dominic and smiled. "Ahhhh. You're just in time."

"I said drop it!" the stern voice demanded.

"This is peeeerfect," Shay assured the shadowy figure. "Better than we planned. All we have to do is change the press release to include the Colonel."

Dominic turned around. He saw Senator Robert Haynes emerging out of the shadows of the dark forest, dressed in a dapper suit, holding a small gun. As Shay pushed his gun up against Dominic's nose, the Senator stopped next to Dominic. His gun was pointed at Shay's face.

"It's over!" the Senator barked, "Now drop it, I said!"

"What are you talkin' about?" Shay barked back. "You'll take over the operation here yourself!"

The Senator cocked his gun and put it next to Shay's watermelon-sized head. "This is the last time I'm telling you—put it down!" he ordered.

Shay shook his head in disappointment. He took a few steps back and began to slowly lower his weapon, saying, "Alright, take it easy..." Dominic glanced at the moonlit lake behind Shay and saw the reflection of his wide back on the surface of the still waters. He noticed that as Shay was lowering the gun in one hand, his other hand was reaching for another pistol secured behind him at his belt. There was no time to yell to the Senator. Reacting instinctively, in one swift motion, Dominic reached down to the sand, grabbed the Colonel's knife and whipped it at Shay.

The lessons on throwing a knife properly that John Russo taught his teenage son paid off at that moment. The spinning blade hummed through the air and disappeared with a piercing thump into Shay's thick chest. Both guns fell out of his big hands. Shay grabbed the knife and tried to pull it out.

But he couldn't. Blood from the wound spouted like a fountain. The Senator fired his gun at Shay. More blood spread over his yellow shirt. His heavy body fell backwards, hitting the sand, which seemed to shake from the impact.

Shay Krauze was dead—his eyes wide open with a shocked look on his face.

Dominic leapt to pick up both of Shay's guns off the ground.

"I'm sorry, son. I'm so sorry," the Senator said placing his hand on Dominic's back.

Dominic spun around, gripping both guns tightly. His hands and clothes were splattered with his and Shay's blood. Confusion ran through his mind. *What were Shay and the Senator referring to? How did they even know each other?* He was certain of only two things—he was not safe and no one could be trusted—especially the democratically-elected official standing right in front of him.

It was impossible for Dominic to reconcile what had just happened one minute before. A high profile United States Senator had just fired a gun at American's most powerful and undetectable underworld figure to save his life. For the past week the international press and, more intently, the eyes of two countries were fixated upon the Senator's every move throughout his mission of good will to Vietnam. Now, in the middle of this night, only Dominic's bewildered stare fixated on the Senator's movements.

The Senator stared back at Dominic only for a moment, then turned around and threw his own pistol as far as he could toward the lake. Both he and Dominic watched it fly through the air and splash into the water.

Dominic's head was filled with unanswered questions about the Senator's confrontation with Shay. The Senator didn't turn around to face Dominic. He couldn't. His shame prevented him from answering Dominic's expected questions while looking at him in the face.

"How did you know Mr. Krauze?" Dominic asked.

The Senator's tall body was visibly deflated; his once proud political posture slumping from shame. "We were business associates," the Senator replied.

"He's a murderer," Dominic reminded him.

"I know, son," he replied. "…so am I…so am I."

Dominic did not have to ask another question. The Senator began his confession in a low voice: "Back in '72, your father, Colonel Mazer, and I were sent here on a secret mission. They called it Operation Inferno." Staring blankly into the lake, the Senator recalled these vivid memories as he spoke. "We were dropped into Cambodia and ordered to stake out one of our own POW camps. After a couple of days they told us that the men guarding the camp were acting as spies for the enemy. We were ordered to wipe it off the face of the earth. And to eliminate everyone with it—enemy prisoners, our own boys in uniform." The Senator took in and let out a deep breath. "So we did."

Dominic thought about his old man. He was no doubt a fearsome soldier. He was also a tortured soul and an angry man. But Dominic knew his father was a man of honor, not a premeditated executioner. "No. I don't believe you," he said. "Not my father."

The Senator's voice raised a level. "It was all a lie, son. The President of the United States of America lied to your father. He lied to me. Our men were no spies. We were set up and betrayed by our very own Commander-in-Chief. We were supposed to be massacred after our mission was accomplished. We were not supposed to survive. We were not supposed come back home." He paused again, shaking his head in disgust a few times.

Dominic took a moment to recall who the President at the time was. He was too young to have a personal opinion about the man, but history had heralded President Keane as the man who ended the Vietnam War. He was regarded as someone who brought peace to the divided country. No President was capable of such a horrific crime against his own country, certainly not Keane.

"But Keane ended the war?" Dominic stated confusedly.

The Senator continued, "Originally, they kept the prison camp very isolated and vulnerable to enemy attack. They hoped that the North Vietnamese, Cambodians, or whoever else was wandering the jungle would eventually wipe it out. They knew our young boys guarding it had no chance in the event of an attack, so they rigged the prisoners' holding cell with dynamite. As soon as an attack came, the guards were instructed to blow the whole place to the moon. It was the perfect war crime. There would be no evidence. Our boys were guaranteed to be slaughtered. The prisoners were guaranteed to be vaporized." With that, the Senator paused again.

Dominic asked him in a stern voice, "But why would he...?"

"The camp housed the political leaders of the Vietcong," the Senator quickly answered before Dominic finished the question. "The CIA had kidnapped them in a series of classified missions. These guys weren't soldiers; they were civilians, so they were put in a prison where no reporters could find out about them. At first, I'm sure the Agency wanted to just extract information from them. But things changed after Keane realized he needed to end the war to win re-election. The country, his own advisors, and his own party were turning against him and the war in droves. He knew we couldn't win a war under those circumstances. Our allies knew it. Our enemies certainly knew it. So he had one choice—bring the troops home without a victory. He called it "peace with honor." But behind the scenes he determined it was too risky to set the South's most prominent communist leaders free. He figured that without strong leadership, it would take at least five years before the Vietcong could effectively reorganize and start fighting again. By that time it would be someone else's problem. Keane would be out of the White House and on his Kentucky horse ranch by then. He would ride off into history as the President who brought peace. So before he signed the accord, he sent us in to eliminate the future threats to his presidency and his legacy."

"Including American soldiers," said Dominic.

"Yes, including Americans!" the Senator declared, still not turning around. "The President didn't want to take any chances. Colonel Mazer was the man ordered to eliminate our entire team. Me, your father, everyone! The plan was to get the Colonel to kill us first. Then they were going to smoke him dead from the sky." The Senator continued, "But the Colonel had a different agenda. He was prepared for the set-up…boy, was he prepared."

"What happened when you came back?"

"Well, we were untouchable." Suddenly, the Senator's tone of voice changed. He sounded more familiar, as though he was making one of his speeches. "A seat in the Senate, millions of dollars from the UN, a license to deal drugs, total immunity—we had it all because we were keepers of the biggest secret in American history! The crime of the century—ordered by the President of the United States, plotted by the CIA."

After a deep breath, the Senator's out-of-public voice returned. "I'm so sorry, but Julie didn't have a chance."

Dominic's face tightened. "What are you talking about?"

"The Colonel knew she was with the Agency. They always had agents watching him."

Dominic asked, "She was an agent?"

"For twenty years, they've been keeping tabs on us," the Senator said. "They couldn't do anything except watch, of course. We called ourselves the Secretkeepers. The information we had on them would shut down the whole Agency if it ever got out. They knew if they exposed us, or killed us, then the information we had would automatically be released to the public."

Dominic couldn't believe what he was hearing. Even Julie had lied to him. But she was too frail, too beautiful to be a secret government agent! Besides, her feelings could not have been faked. They were too innocent, too genuine. How could she possibly reveal so much honest emotion to him if she was only acting as a spy?

Dominic looked at the Senator's shadowy back. "You must be mistaken about Julie!"

The Senator turned his head to the side yet stopped short of looking squarely at Dominic. "Who do you think saved you up at the mines?"

Dominic frowned while he digested the Senator's words.

"Someone took out Huyen and Lang, right?" he asked Dominic. "And I can assure you that it wasn't me or one of our guys."

Dominic was astonished. The scene on the dark trail up at the mines flashed through his head. The oncoming motorcycle. It was no accident. The driver wasn't shooting at him and Quan. Julie was the driver, and she was shooting at Huyen and Lang. Julie had saved his life!

"Where is she?" Dominic demanded.

The Senator hesitated before responding. The guilt was hard to bear. "I don't know, son. I don't know if she made it back alive. All I know is that General Kien's men were after her. I'm sorry to say the odds were not on her side."

Dominic had to blink away the tears welling in his eyes. He could not even think about losing her. He had one final question for the Senator. "What about my father?"

The Senator cleared his throat and rubbed his face before speaking again. "Your father and I go back a long way son. He was the toughest damn soldier I've ever seen." Pausing to stop his voice from cracking, he added, "But he was also a good man. And because he was a good man, the Inferno mission really messed him up. He never forgave himself—even though he was just a pawn of our government.

From the minute we boarded the chopper to head home your old man wanted nothing to do with the Colonel's big plans. Your father never cashed in. He could have been rich and powerful. Hell, with his battle record, your father could have been the damn President if he wanted to. But he didn't want any of it. Instead, he opened a small jewelry store in New York City and just minded his own business…for years."

The Senator did not wait for Dominic to ask about him.

"I was a different story," he confessed. "I cashed in."

Suddenly his voice perked up, as if he was talking out loud to his own conscience. "Hell, they set us up and then they tried to kill us. So why shouldn't we have blackmailed those sons of bitches?" The Senator curbed his anger by looking out over the lake. A thin lining of clouds had made its way in front of the moon. For a few moments, all that was heard was the lapping of the calm water on the beach.

He continued in a voice matching the tranquil setting. "But everything got so fucked up. Our greed, my greed, it just got bigger and bigger. When the Colonel and Krauze started running heroin out of here, the money really started pouring in. For years it was a perfect arrangement. But then Krauze started to have some problems with the Colonel…some shipments were coming in short…the product was cut. It may not seem like much in the grand scheme of things, but in the drug business a shipment cut one percent could mean the difference of a million dollars.

Krauze, of course, immediately found out that it wasn't General Kien who was selling us short. That meant there was only one other suspect. Krauze made his inquiries and found that the Colonel was supplying some dealers out of Hong Kong. That's when he approached me and told me how the Colonel was robbing us—how he was operating other businesses…separate businesses…ones that I wasn't getting a piece of."

The Senator shrugged as Dominic's mind reeled with all the information. "So right then and there we decided to make a change. I made sure all the precious secrets about Operation Inferno would not go public until after the Colonel's murder, so Krauze made arrangements to take him out along with you and Marie. We had it all planned out perfectly. I was going to step in and take over the operation. Of course publicly it was perfect, too. My speech is already written out and memorized."

Closing his eyes and switching to his television voice, the Senator recited his lines: "Fellow Americans, the morning before his senseless murder, Colonel Mazer and I had breakfast at his home in Hanoi. During the conversation he said to me, 'Senator, the cause of peace must endure. Children are starving. People are dying. These are worldwide battles we must never stop fighting. That is the war we must win.' In the wake of this unimaginable tragedy, those words have become a call to duty for me. Tonight I am announcing that to further the cause for peace in the world and to continue the wonderful work that the great Colonel had so selflessly devoted his life to, I am stepping down from the US Senate to take over as head of the AFP in Vietnam. Thank you."

The Senator opened his eyes and turned his head to look at Dominic before he continued more solemnly. "We had it planned perfectly. I would be the last of the Secretkeepers. And there were only two things in the whole world that could stop the Secretkeepers' drug trade. One of them, your Dad, was gone. For years we let him be, and he let us be. We just watched each other. Unfortunately, when Krauze got word he started talking to some guy in the CIA about our drug dealings, we had no choice. First, your mom was run off the road…then, when he still didn't stop, well, you know the rest…"

Tears rolled down the Senator's cheeks. Ignoring them, he continued explaining, "The second thing that could stop us…"

"Was reconciliation between Vietnam and the United States," Dominic realized out loud.

Senator Haynes nodded. "That's right. We were immune from the powers of the government. But we still had to worry about the public finding out. That's why the US trade embargo against Vietnam is perfect cover for our operation. No American tourists. No publicity. No press. It all added up to no worries!"

Dominic raised his gun and pointed it at the middle of the Senator's back. Being a combat veteran, the Senator sensed what was coming without looking. "You didn't have to use my sister as your pawn!" said Dominic.

The Senator again nodded his head and said, "I was supposed to go into the Senate hearings tomorrow and tell the world how the government of Vietnam murdered you and your sister."

Dominic straightened his arm and was set to pull the trigger when the Senator added, "But I couldn't do it."

Dominic hesitated. The Senator explained. "Seeing the Vietnamese people here during this trip brought back very painful memories. It made me realize…" Dominic could not see the tears streaming steadily down the Senator's face. "There was too much suffering, too much horror, too many deaths for such a poor country…it was time to heal."

"Excellent speech, Senator," Dominic said to the tarnished politician, "but it won't bring back my mother, my father, my sister, or Julie! And it certainly won't save you!"

Senator Haynes raised his hands and lowered his head in anticipation of his execution. "Your sister's fine," he said in a low voice. "She's in my guesthouse. I used a harmless chemical to knock her out. I didn't have much time before the Colonel's men arrived to kill her. She'll need another few hours of sleep before she'll wake up, but I promise you, she'll be fine."

The one-time military doctor then put his hands on his head and stated, "Now go ahead, son—do what you need to do."

CHAPTER TWENTY-NINE

1992

Hanoi

August 15, 10:10AM

Fast streams of cyclists weaved between makeshift wooden food stands as dauntless pedestrians crossed the untamed streets. The sounds of zooming engines, honking horns, and clucking passenger hens on the back of motorbikes created the morning's music. Another Saturday morning in Hanoi, and the populace, like any other morning, was briskly on the move.

"How do you get used to this?" Dominic howled from the back of the motorbike, tightly clenching on to Marie's waist. Grinning boldly, Marie fearlessly accelerated the scooter and headed towards a tight space between a large diesel truck and plodding water buffalo. She knew her brother's eyes would be shut.

"Get used to what?" she yelled, squeezing through cleanly.

Dominic opened his eyes. "Never mind!" he exclaimed.

Rounding another sharp corner and passing a rickshaw filled with live chickens, Marie pulled over and stopped in front of the State Bank of Hanoi. For the fourth time she asked her brother, "Now will you please tell me why we're here?"

Jumping off the back, Dominic told her, "Just wait here, will ya? I have something I need to do."

"You better hurry. Your flight leaves in an hour." Jokingly, she added, "And I don't want to have to rush to get you there."

Climbing up the front stairs three at a time, Dominic disappeared through the front doors of the bank. Marie removed her helmet and grinned. She loved her brother dearly and was certainly going to miss him. He was the only family she had left.

But Vietnam was her home now. And after the tragic events of the past few days, she felt needed in this country more than ever. Despite Dominic's repeated pleas for her to return with him to New York City, she could not go. How could she abandon the children of Southeast Asia in the face of her own adversity when they face adversity every day of their lives?

That she would have some tough days ahead of her was undeniable. It was going to be extremely difficult, if not impossible, to secure funding for her charitable efforts in light of the recent scandal. But she had to try. She had to do more than try. She had to do everything in her power to help the children. They were her life, and she wouldn't trade this for all the money or safety in the world.

"Let's go!" she yelled to Dominic as he exited the door.

At the bottom of the steps, he asked her once again, "Are you sure about this?"

"Dom, I told you a hundred times that I'm sure. Now c'mon, don't worry about me. I'll be fine!"

Smirking at his sister's typical stubbornness, he reached into his shirt pocket and pulled out two folded checks. He handed one over to her saying, "All right then, just hold this for me for one minute." Walking toward the mailbox on the corner, he shouted back to her without turning around, "Now, don't look at it! I'll be right back!"

Dominic knew his sister was too nosey to be trusted. Without looking, he knew exactly what she was doing while he made his way to the mailbox.

"What the fuck is this?" she yelled on cue.

Dominic held back his grin, pretending not to hear. At the mailbox, he placed the other check, along with a letter and Quan's family photo, in an envelope addressed to Quan's wife. The letter was written to Quan's daughter, Trinh. It described how her father's heroism had saved his life and changed the course of history for his country. He also added that he hoped to visit with her on his next trip. He also enclosed all the information regarding the college fund "her father had made sure he set up for her in the State Bank of Hanoi before he passed away." Last, Dominic included a deposit slip for fifty thousand dollars. In his last sentence, he assured her more would be on its way.

Dominic dropped the letter down the mailbox chute and headed back toward his open-mouthed sister.

"It's a donation," he said nonchalantly.

"Donation?"

"Yeah…you know…for your new charity."

For a moment, Marie was speechless, not just from the gesture but from confusion. "But this check is for four hundred and fifty thousand dollars!" she said incredulously, "How? How did you…"

"Before I left New York, Shay Krauze asked me if you needed anything," he said dryly. "Now move over. I want to drive!"

CHAPTER THIRTY

1992

The August heat in Washington DC almost matched the heat of the moment. Inside the Oval Office, President Peter McCabe and his three closest advisors had been engaged in crisis-control talks throughout the night. All of the spin doctors were steadfast in purpose. They had come up with a number of ways of how to handle the matter at hand.

"He has no credibility, Mr. President," one of the advisors stated. "We have loads of dirty laundry on him."

Looking out the window at the White House lawn, the well-groomed President didn't say anything. He had said surprisingly little all night. With his arms crossed and standing tall, he admired the shiny clear drops of dew on the morning grass.

The morning sun cast an extended shadow of his long body across the Presidential Seal carpet in the middle of the room. Twenty years it had taken him. Twenty years to get the American public to finally trust him enough to elect him their leader. And re-election was in the bank. That is, until now.

Running his long fingers through his neatly combed hair, he remembered back to a time when someone else's re-election was in jeopardy. The cycle of history, he thought, can be so ironic sometimes.

The President's thoughts fast-forwarded to the present day. He was proud of the job he had done as Commander-in-Chief. Damn proud. His popularity polls showed overwhelmingly that the public felt the same way. Things were sure to be different by the end of the day though.

"It's ancient history," another loyal advisor called out to him. "There are no witnesses, records…nothing. He has no proof, Mr. President. All he's got is his own word, which we all know will be worth absolutely nothing by the time we get through with him."

Another advisor chimed in, "That's right. If no else saw it, it simply cannot be corroborated."

The President turned around and looked solemnly at his loyal roundtable of thinkers. They were anxiously awaiting his response, but his mind was clearly elsewhere as he gazed into each of their eyes. He had known all three of them for over thirty years. They had served him well, through two failed bids for the party's nomination and then, finally, during the successful campaign for the White House. Through it all, they had been fiercely loyal. Protecting. And patriotic.

He remembered the days when he wore their shoes, when his hair was a lot longer, fuller, and darker. He knew exactly how they felt. He used to feel the same way. He knew how badly they, even more than he himself, wanted to weather the storm and win the upcoming election. He could hear the echo of those same rallying cries from twenty years ago. Protect the presidency, no matter what the cost or casualty. Do whatever it takes. Just get the job done.

So much has changed since the days when those phrases defined his philosophy and guided his decisions. So much has come and gone since then. But unfortunately, ironically, so much was the same.

"Gentlemen," he finally said to them. His voice was natural, without pride or pretext. "All night I've listened to your opinions. And you're all correct in your viewpoints. Yes, I have no doubt we can overcome this. I have total confidence that we'll be able to put together a surefire strategy to deny, cover up, recreate, erase, or do whatever it takes to avoid this looming crisis. I know we can do that." The most powerful man in the free world paused for a moment, and then added, "But that should never again be the reason why we do things."

Not far away on the steps of the Capitol Building, the international press was gathered, sensing the typical calm before the storm. When the black limousine pulled up and parked, mayhem erupted. Hundreds of reporters, television cameras, and photographers converged on the shiny car. The door popped open and two burly men wearing black suits and mirrored sunglasses stepped out of the front seat and began brusquely trying to clear some space.

The door to the back seat opened up and man of the hour Senator Robert "Doc" Haynes stepped out, dressed neatly as always, in a black pinstriped suit and a yellow paisley tie.

A blitz of questions was hurled at the Senator as he was escorted up the stairs. He did his best to give the cameras his trademark political smile, but the typically outspoken Senator kept quiet. One of his husky attorneys shouted, "The rumors and speculation will all be put to rest today." he shouted. "The Senator has nothing to say at this moment."

Just before the Senator reached the final step, one particularly loud reporter shouted, "What are you going to say today at the hearing, Senator Haynes?" The Senator turned around at the top step, and the chaos immediately quieted. Again the same reporter asked, this time in normal voice, "What will you be telling the Senate Committee today?"

After a long pause, the Senator replied briefly: "A secret."

CHAPTER THIRTY-ONE

1992

Gemco Jewelry Store

Canal Street, New York City

September 17, 4:44PM

The hustle and bustle didn't feel the same to Dominic. The thrill of the sell was gone. The rush of the deal forgotten. Old intentions, former motivations were both replaced by new feelings, a new agenda, a new life. His heart, having been both opened and broken in the span of a week, now led the way; his rational mind, having been demoted to second in command, followed along now, happy to help out in any way possible.

At last open for business since his return from Vietnam, by the middle of the afternoon Gemco was jam-packed with shoppers. A few weeks ago Dominic would have been the most excited gem dealer in New York City to have a crowd like that. But those few weeks were an eternity in passing. Today, the familiar vibrancy and colorful salesmanship of Gemco's suave proprietor was nowhere to be found. Today was this budding young star's final curtain call; and it was nothing like the old act. "What you see is what you get" was his new, and final, motto. No haggling. No sales talk. No handsome persuasion or professional charm. If you didn't like the price, fine, have a nice day.

Outside the packed store, the thick lingering summer air was slowly being pushed out by the clearer, easterly Great Lakes breeze. As always, Canal Street was energized. But that afternoon it was even more enlivened, perhaps from the changing season, perhaps also from the stir of Gemco's one day only final sale. The word was out. It had spread like wildfire through the five boroughs. Fine jewelry was on sale at fire sale prices. Get some while you still can.

Hundreds of eager customers had already passed through Gemco's front door with cash in hand, only to exit happily with jewelry created with precious metals and stones. Naturally, fellow dealers were the first and friendliest among those clamoring for a piece of the action. But Dominic chose not to sell off to other colleagues. The hungry wolves were shut out. Had he had decided to sell to them, he would've liquidated his entire collection in less than an hour without even opening the front doors. Instead, Dominic wanted the public to benefit from the bargains. "One item per customer," the sign on the front door read, and Dominic meant it. He wanted it that way. He didn't really know why, he just did.

The wolves, of course, did not go quietly. They attempted a variety of tactics aimed at getting their paws on pieces from Gemco's fine collection. Pursuant to protocol, shame of being exposed was no deterrence—all in a day's work for a conniving gem dealer.

Some of the wolves tried sending in family members to do the buying for them. One of the more desperate ones sent in his seven-year-old daughter in to buy a five hundred dollar bracelet. Others tried more subtle tricks like wearing disguises and changing their voices. Dominic, as usual, was on to them; for the most part he saw through their cunning schemes and foiled their attempts. There is something about a customer buying a piece of jewelry that is so genuine, so impossible to imitate, that it was easy for Dominic to pick out the gem-dealing wolves.

"How much for the bracelet?" a deep voice in the tight crowd asked.

"Half off what the price tag says," Dominic said out loud for all to hear. "Everything today is half off the amount on the price tag."

Down at the other end, another young male with neatly cut blonde hair held out four hundred dollars over the counter. "Hey buddy," he called out, "I'll take these diamond earrings."

Dominic hurried over. He took a moment to stare into the customer's eyes. Assured of authenticity, he then accepted the cash. "Came in from Long Island," the smiling customer said to Dominic, "heard you were having the sale of the century, and I came right over. I need to get back in good graces with my wife."

Dominic smiled back handing him the jewels in their case and wrappings. "These ought to do it."

"Closing up shop?" Dominic heard a female voice from the crowd ask.

"Yes, ma'am, I am," he answered without looking up. His head was turned down towards his earrings display. Three short hours ago, thirty-five pairs of earrings filled the tiny display boxes. Now, only three pairs remained.

"Why?" the same woman asked, surveying what little remained available for purchase.

Dominic glanced up at the curious customer. She was barely visible. A pair of wide black sunglasses covered the top half of her face. Atop her head sat a tight blue baseball cap branded with the Yankees snow-white intersecting NY logo, pulled down her forehead so low that it shadowed most of her face. Halfway down her back her straight black hair was gathered into one long ponytail. "I'm moving," Dominic answered.

"To another location?"

Dominic grinned and shook his head slightly. "No, not to another location…I guess you can say I'm just moving on."

The woman smiled, wished him good luck, and turned away from the forward-pushing crowd. A slight breeze from her movement tickled Dominic's ever-attentive nose. The scent hit him like a bolt of lightning.

Dominic placed both hands on the top of the glass counter and held his breath. The impatient crowd continued hurling questions at him, but his ears were tuned out. All of a sudden he was unconcerned with business, oblivious to the commotion. He couldn't hear anything, couldn't see anyone. He focused acutely on the scent he had just smelled. That scent. That one glorious scent. That was it. He could smell it in a room filled with a thousand fresh cut flowers.

The crowd in front of him grew puzzled. Customers stopped calling out to him and began whispering among themselves. "He must be in some sort of trance," one old lady observed. "I think he's sick," her husband surmised. A young boy asked Dominic if he felt all right, but Dominic didn't respond. He didn't even look at the concerned child. He was in another world. His body was tingling. His knees weak.

Dominic blinked back to reality and frantically scanned the crowd. His eyes and reason doubted what his nose told him. He had to see her face…her body…but the packed room prevented him from getting a good look.

Dominic quickly locked all four of the glass jewelry containers, leaped over the last one and gave chase. Rudely, uncharacteristically, he pushed his way through two dozen of his waiting patrons. It was slow moving. When he saw the front door swing open, he stopped and stood up on the tips of his toes. He saw the back of a blue baseball cap exiting the store. Pushing forward again, Dominic thought back to her appearance. *Damn!* He didn't get a good look. He remembered a baseball cap, sunglasses, black ponytail and baggy clothes. They told a different story. But his nose told him no lies.

Before he could reach out and grab the front door, an old man cut in front of him announcing, "I want to buy the rest of your necklaces."

Immediately five other customers circled in and badgered him with questions, comments and offers. Dominic was trapped. Glancing outside the storefront window he saw her back disappear from sight.

"I'll be right back," he said out loud. "I promise. There's something I must do first."

The old man in front of him was disappointed. "What about my offer?" he asked.

"One item per customer," Dominic stated pushing his way through. "Pick out the one you like best. I'll be right back."

The crowd of anxious customers stared at each other in disbelief as they saw Dominic leave the store, abandoning, at least for the moment, his entire precious inventory. They had money to spend. Lots of money was clearly burning in their hands. And there was no one to give it to. "What the hell kinda place is this?" an angry patron called out.

Another young woman responded, "Give him a break, he probably just needs some fresh air." Running against a cool breeze, Dominic searched Canal Street; she couldn't be far, he thought frantically. Halfway down the block, he stopped running. There she was, across the street, walking briskly. Her black ponytail bounced up and down against her back.

Without looking, he darted across the congested street. Brakes screeched. Horns blew. Cabbies cursed. Middle fingers pointed out of trucks. Dominic kept moving, indifferent to the road rage directed at him.

"Julie! Julie!" he yelled as soon as he stepped on the sidewalk. Twenty yards ahead, the girl in the baseball cap and oversized blue jeans stopped walking. Slowly she turned around. Her sunglasses hid her eyes. Dominic rushed over.

Face to face, they stared at each other. Neither said a word. On each side of them uninterested pedestrians streamed by, but their scene, their immediate world, was frozen still.

Dominic was breathing heavily, too confused, too afraid to do anything, except stare. He was worried that he was dreaming. He was worried that she was nothing more than an illusion, a mere hallucination of his heart. He wanted to say something, but, afraid that the wrong word, the wrong action might ruin the moment. He couldn't speak. He just stared at her.

When Dominic saw a tear emerge from underneath her black sunglasses, he reached out and gently pulled the dark shades off her light face. His heart pounded. She made no motion to stop him.

Those eyes. Those sparkling, crystal-blue, beautifully sad eyes. How wonderful to see them looking back at him. Dominic reached out with his arms and embraced her. His nose instinctively pulled in an exaggerated breath. His heart warmed. His eyes watered over. "I thought you were dead," he whispered.

"I know," she said in a soft voice. They squeezed each other tightly. For the next few moments they didn't whisper a word, but only communicated their feelings through a passionate embrace.

She pulled away from his arms and wiped her eyes. "There are some things I must tell you," she said.

Dominic already knew some of the story. "I know why you were in Vietnam," he told her. "I also know you saved my life."

The statement sparked the memories. In her mind's eye, she recalled the furious scene on the dirt trail up at the mines. How difficult it was to get off a shot, let alone an accurate shot, while her motorcycle raced down that dark bumpy trail. Thank goodness that bullet, that one miraculous bullet, found its mark inside the truck, an inch above and a split second from disaster.

"My mission was to only observe," she said. "Not to get involved. I was not supposed to fall for you. But I did..." Dominic's whole body tingled.

She continued, "But when I realized you were in danger, I knew I had to follow you. I abandoned my mission. I had to do whatever I could to protect you."

Dominic's heart burned with emotion. "Why didn't you come back?"

She hesitated before speaking—thinking to herself that she had never told anyone what she was about to say to him. She took a deep breath and said, "I don't remember my father. A month before my fifth birthday he was listed MIA. I was very young, but for some reason I knew he was not going to come home. The night of my thirteenth birthday, my mother came into my room and read me a letter. It had been sent to her years earlier, but it was addressed to me. The letter was beautiful. It said how my father, Corporal Gerald Greene, was a great American. How he devoted his life to end a horrible war. How I should be proud to be his daughter. It went on praising his heroics. It was signed by Colonel Clifford Mazer. I still have it. I read it once a year, every year, on my birthday."

"Operation Inferno," Dominic mused.

"When I got older," she continued, "I started searching for answers about my father's disappearance. All I found were closed doors and dead ends. I was told there were no records. Nobody knew anything about what division he was in or what mission he was on. After a while it became clear to me that my father had disappeared long before he got to Southeast Asia.

I wrote to Colonel Mazer a dozen times. But he never wrote back. Finally, when I was twenty years old, I managed to reach him by phone. He told me that he lost hundreds of soldiers during the war and didn't remember my father. I told him he had to remember. I said his letter about my father was too special for him to have forgotten. He said that I needed to bury my father and move on. The instant he hung up I realized I needed to get on the inside, deep inside, so I could get some answers."

"The CIA," said Dominic.

Nodding, she said, "I made the right friends and moved up quickly in the ranks. Eventually I learned about the Secretkeepers file and put in a request to be assigned to the case. It was just a monitoring case but when the Agency found out that the UN was going to donate another ten million dollars to the Colonel, I got the undercover assignment."

"But all you could do was watch?"

"That's right. Once in a while we were able to covertly disrupt a drug supply, but we had to be very careful. Mazer was not to be touched. I eventually found out the reasons why when I read a highly classified statement from your father that I was not supposed to see. From then on, it was torture for me. Here I was next to the very man who murdered my father, and I couldn't do a thing about it. No one could. From that moment on, I felt worse than when I knew nothing."

A large tear spilled out of one of her eyes. "But when I met you," she said, "things changed for me…"

Dominic wiped away the tear from her face with his hand.

She blinked away the next tear before it spilled over and continued, "I began to see something in my life that I never saw before—a future. I never thought it could happen—certainly not that fast and not under those circumstances. For the first time in my life I wanted something other than—something more than, my father's honor. You made me look ahead, Dominic Russo. You made me want us."

"What about the Agency?"

"It's a life sentence. You sacrifice your own freedom to protect freedom. Your life becomes a complicated web of different identities and secrets. To help bring down Mazer, I was willing to make my life a mystery. But there is no future with a mystery."

Dominic's eyes softened. "So you had to kill yourself off to be free?"

Nodding and offering Dominic her hand, she said in a Russian-accented voice over the noise of the hustling crowd, "Hi, my name is Katrina…"

Dominic grinned, took the "foreign" lady's hand, and bowed in courtly homage. This time a handshake spoke a thousand words.

ACKNOWLEDGEMENTS

SPECIAL THANKS to:

The people of Vietnam and Cambodia for their warmth, education, and inspiration.

Lynn Eder for her editing, enrichment, and keeping me focused. I enjoyed working with you.

Carlos M. Flores for his fearless service in uniform and all his fellow soldiers and veterans.

Michael Jabbour for his cover design, layout, formatting and technical wizardry.

Sarah Jabbour, in gratitude, for all her sacrifices to causes so important to me.

Jeannie Kang for her original artwork.

Lily J. Noonan for the book updates.

Mr. and Mrs. Chung Hwang for their artistic contributions.

My students—they have taught me so much.

My friends, clients, family and colleagues, who have supported me and my causes over the years.

My sister, Kathy, for being who she is to her brother and the rest of the world.

My departed parents, Michael and Barbara, eternally.

www.ingramcontent.com/pod-product-compliance
Lightning Source LLC
Chambersburg PA
CBHW051241250626
47155CB00009B/3117